MW01673624

DOG ISLAND

ANN M.
ANDRASHIE

DOG ISLAND

Spring Harbor Publishing~an independent clean read publisherorg.

ISBN: 978-1-7370479-1-9 (ebook)
ISBN: 978-1-73704790-0-2 (paperback)

123456789

SONG CREDITS

"Bridge over Troubled Waters": Written by Paul Simon, performed by Paul Simon and Art Garfunkel, January 1970 on Columbia Records.

"Me and Julio Down by the Schoolyard," written by Paul Simon, performed by Paul Simon and Art Garfunkel, released 1970, Columbia Records.

"Hello Darlin'": Conway Twitty, 1970.

"Kiss an Angel Good Morning": Written by Ben Peters and recorded by Charley Pride, 1971.

"Running Bear": Written by J. P. Richardson (aka The Big Bopper) recorded by Johnny Preston, 1959.

"Morning Has Broken": Written by Eleanor Farjeon, 1931, as a Christian hymn but most known to be recorded by Cat Stevens, 1971.

"The Happiest Girl in the Whole USA": written and recorded by Donna Fargo, 1972.

"You Ain't Woman Enough to Take My Man": Written and recorded Loretta Lynn, 1966.

PROLOGUE

The foremost question put to me is, where did the idea for Dog Island come from?

It wasn't until the loss of my dog Milo did I fully come to understand just how much of a Heavenly gift our pets are. He was sent to me, if you will, to help care-take for my elderly mother who was suffering from dementia. Little as he was, Milo never failed her, nor me, with late-night warnings that mother was stirring about the house, or was finding the end of the driveway during the day. Our protector, counselor and constant companion he was. Mom, who was not an avid animal lover, had many one-sided conversations with, "that boy" as she referred to him.

After the loss of my mother, I decided to get for Mr. Milo (now a young man indeed) a little girlfriend: Pixie. A whole 4.13 pounds of pure sass. And we loved her. That same year the three of us ended up with yet another, "Gift"—a stinky, smelly hound girl named Scarlet, whom my daughter decided to rescue from a local animal shelter that could no longer keep her. With my children raised and gone and the loss of mom and my father a few years earlier, the three of them were therapeutic in helping me deal with such loss. But then the unthinkable occurred. One night, Milo and Scarlet had gone.

I woke early to search for them, and as I stood in the yard with the morning sun beginning to rise, I saw something in the neighbor's huge tree, something I had never seen before and have not since. A flock of crows, at least a hundred, flew from the branches. Silent at first. Following them, their caws and cries grew as if encouraging me.

I went with them to the little strip of woods behind the house. They sat in their limbs, and I looked down and picked up a wing. Odd, I know. One whole crow's wing and nothing more.

Embracing a Native American belief, I knew, deep down, Milo was gone. Those crows had faithfully carried their message from The Other World to this one. On that late September afternoon, we found Mr. Milo's little white fur body laying five miles away, up on the highway, across the bridge.

A close friend of mine affirmed my grief by giving me a framed picture of my Milo with a copy of the poem, The Rainbow Bridge. I hadn't known of such a place, until that time, and it took a while before I could look at such a wonderful gift. But I did, and afterwards, I took Pixie and Scarlet to the place I could no longer walk, the place the four of us had been to so many times as a family: Pine Hill.

It was in its meadows that I walked with my grief. It was there that I found that place called Dog Island. After enough time had passed, and I could see beyond my tears, I sat down to write what you are now holding in your hands. It's okay to cry and feel grief when we lose our little friends. How we love them so, and they love us. We can never let go of that, can we? Nor should we.

I hope for you, Dear Reader, that you will find peace in your sorrows, understanding in your tears and laughter when it comes to light.

God's Sweet Blessings to you and your own little Angels,

Ann M. Andrashie

To Mr. Milo and Pixie, Scarlet and Dakota:

Still missing you all and always will.

Meet me at The Bridge

Love ~~

Momma

APOSTLE ISLANDS ~ BAYFIELD
WISCONSIN

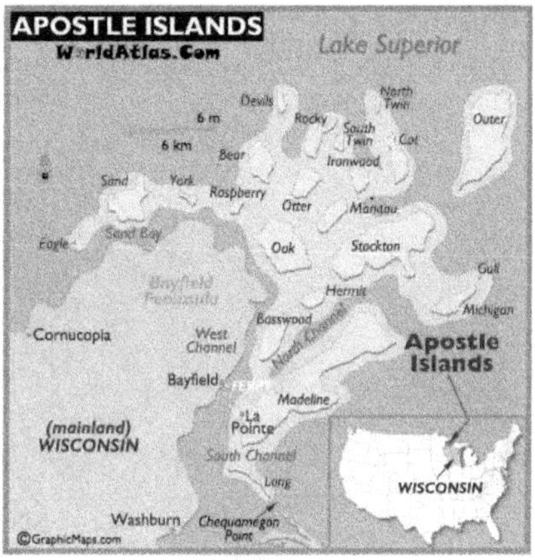

CHAPTER ONE

It was difficult for Mosie Bitmen (AKA Katherine Rose) to pay attention to Sister Vern Mary rather than Judy Larson and Theresa Mavis, the two most popular girls in the entire seventh grade. After all, Judy did have the longest red hair in all of Saint Anne school, probably in all Barrington, quite possibly the entire state of Illinois.

So when Judy gave those tresses of hers a toss, Mosie had to look; she couldn't help it. It was captivating the way those locks glimmered and sparkled like strawberry soda with a splash of ginger ale mixed in for good measure—unlike hers, tar black and straight, cropped to her ears and cut "pixie style," as her ma, Willowdean, called it. *Definitely not fit for a true Indian Princess like me*, Mosie thought, as she sank in her seat watching Judy hold a note up for Theresa Mavis to see.

Theresa Mavis . . . everyone knew Theresa was destined to grow up to be a Montgomery Ward catalog model like her mother. After all, she was too pretty to look at, especially with all that hair springing about that *perfect* face of hers like dainty lemon twists.

Mosie took one last glance at Judy while Sister Vern Mary grabbed a hunk of chalk and turned to the blackboard; that's when she saw Judy passing Tommy Peterson the note with the secret code pencil sketched on its front: an Indian with two feathers drawn on its head, and an overly large, O mouth. For Mosie it meant misery.

"Paper and pencils please," Sister said, writing in those big fluffy letters of hers: *History Test Review Questions.*

Mosie opened her desk, stuck her head inside, and stared at the pile of Puff Facial tissues booger-glued together, the ones Tommy snuck in her desk before class. Suppressing a snicker, Tommy took Judy's note. *Bet he's grown ten more of those damn brown spots on that ugly face of his since the beginning of the year,* Mosie thought, glaring at him and his freckles through the cracks in her desk.

"Number two," Sister said scraping chalk across the blackboard writing: *Name the first ten presidents.*

Mosie stabbed Tommy's snot-rags with the tip of her pencil, and slid them up and out of her desk dropping them to the floor. She kicked them in the aisle and fumbled with her binders pretending to find the right one. That was a trick of procrastination she learned two years ago in fourth grade, 1970: the year Sister Vern Mary came to Saint Anne's school; the year Judy and Theresa noticed Mosie's skin being a tinge or two darker than everyone else's (except for Sister, who being black was at least fifty times darker); the year Judy and Theresa discovered contempt and decided to fashion a select group of fancy fair-skinned girls Mosie dubbed *The Perfects.*

"Question number four. . . ."

Tommy leaned back in his seat and handed the folded piece of paper to Theresa. Mosie's stomach pinched. The part she dreaded most was about to happen: Theresa reading the note. Squinting at Mosie, she held the paper in the air for everyone to read.

It said: *Who am I?*

Theresa mimicked Judy and poked her fingers behind her head like Indian feathers. "Yi-yi-yi-yi. Yi-yi-yi-yi," they mouthed in unison, slapping their hands against their lips like Indians in old Western movies. Then came the giggles.

"What is so funny?" Sister said, spinning toward the stifled snorts and snickers filling the classroom. Judy and Theresa (and Tommy) blinked at her innocently. It fell silent except for Sister's black skirt rustling toward Mosie.

"Are we having a problem, Katherine?" she asked, sneaking Mosie an understanding wink.

"No, Sister," Mosie said with eyes that watered with tears as she looked up at the face that was darker than her own.

"Well, something's funny," Sister said as she turned to Theresa and Judy (then Tommy). "I would like to know what it is. And until I do, we will sit quietly with our hands folded on our desks."

Sister glanced at the clock hanging on the wall and scurried to her own desk. She opened a drawer and pulled out a book. "I have more time than you do," she said glimpsing at Judy and Theresa (and Tommy).

Judy swooped a handful of hair over her mouth, let the strawberry plume fall. She stuck out her tongue. The young nun didn't bother to look up but merely smiled and opened her book.

11:50 a.m. Recess. Mosie sat on the curb at the end of the playground and ignored the constant chatter and occasional overly-excited screams from the younger students. Her best friend in the world (and only friend) Candy Nelson, sat next to her, extra mayo seeping from the sides of her bologna and cheese sandwich.

"The Perfects," Candy said, ignoring a glob of white mayonnaise splattering in her lap. "They get away with everything because they are oh so *perfect*." She reached her chubby hand into the family-sized bag of Jay's potato chips and chucked a handful into her mouth. "Here, want some? They're ruffled. I like the ruffled ones."

"No, no thank you," Mosie said, picking at her tuna fish sandwich.

Candy pointed her pudgy nose beyond the bobbing heads of students meandering aimlessly in their designated playground areas. "Look at them girls sitting on that blanket on the convent lawn with Judy Lard-Ass and Theresa May-Piss.

"Sitting and eating their *perfect* lunches from *perfect* lunch boxes anywhere they want because they're *so perfect*. They don't do nothing except sit and talk about boys; afraid they might get a grass stain or a wrinkle in their *perfect* dresses. I can't believe Lard-Ass and May-Piss get away with teasing you like they do."

Candy plowed her porky fingers back into the bag, she shoved another handful of chips into her mouth. "They're so mean," she said, bits of chips spraying from her lips. "Them and that clique of theirs. If they really are so *perfect*, they'd know you're an Indian Princess and wouldn't pick on you."

"Thanks Candy," Mosie said, "but I sure don't feel much like a Princess. Not right now anyway."

Pulling the crust from her sandwich, Mosie watched Judy stand up and brush crumbs from her paisley skirt. Theresa reached up and ran her hand over the backside of Judy's' skirt. Judy cinched the silk sash around her thin waist and sat down.

Candy got up and put her butt in front of Mosie. "Oh dear," she said, jiggling her round rump under her plain, blue jumper. "I think I pooped myself. Would you be a dear and wipe my, '*Judy?*'"

Mosie laughed watching Candy's hips wiggle. "Thanks," she said. "Thanks, for being my friend."

Candy sat and put her hand on Mosie's. Mosie didn't care if Candy's hand was sweaty and had salty chip grit on it. "Friends forever," Mosie said.

"Forever," Candy repeated as she sank her teeth into her sandwich and pocketed it in her cheeks. "Uh-oh, look what's coming."

Judy and Theresa were strutting toward them across the playground as if they were one of the gangs in "West Side Story." The other *Perfects* trailed behind.

"Come on," Mosie said, watching them get closer. "Let's go in."

"In?" Candy said, her light-green eyes popping open wide. "We can't go in; the hall monitors won't let us."

"Sure they will, after I tell them you ate too many Jay's again. Remember what happened the last time, when your blood-sugar dropped and you ate a whole bag to get it back up and you got sick and puked all over the front steps, and everyone had to use the back doors until the janitor could clean it up?"

Candy snorted a chuckle. "Oh yeah," she said as she pulled herself off the curb and picked up her lunch boxes. "That sure was a mess, huh?"

Holding hands, they headed toward the school.

"Oh-oh, they're getting closer," Candy sniveled.

Judy and *The Perfects* zigzagged to the right, then the left, blocking their path.

"Aw, look," Judy she said, putting her hands on her hips.

"They're in love."

"Naw-uh," Candy snotted back.

"Oh, I think you are," Theresa jumped in. "Don't you girls think so?"

"Stop it," Candy whimpered, burying her face in her hands.

"Just stop it!"

"Gads, what a bawl-baby." Judy said turning to the girls. "Isn't she a bawl-baby?"

"Shut-up," Candy screamed. "Shut-up, shut-up, shut-up!"

Theresa patted her flat, model sized stomach. "If you ask me, she's more like a *blubber*-baby; or maybe a, *blubber-ball.*" The group cackled, squealing with delight.

"Blubber-ball, blubber-ball, Candy 'Jell-O-son' is a big fat blubber-ball," they chimed together.

"Shut-up, shut-up!" Candy yelped.

Mosie's face blazed with fury as she watched Candy run through the group of second graders and up the steps to the school. She turned to Judy, then Theresa, and her heart beat like a band of tom-toms gone mad. That's when Judy stopped laughing, and so did the others.

Carrying the storm brewing inside her, Mosie's legs marched forward. *One little, two little, three little Indians,* she counted in her head remembering how back in the second grade, Tommy Peterson repeated the rhyme over and over to her, the day he slipped a nasty old toad in her galoshes and made her scream.

She didn't see Sister Vern Mary (nor Principal Mother Prudence) as they stepped out on the steps to toll the bell that called them into school. Nor did she notice the students turning to watch her. "*Perfects, just perfect*!"

Sister Vern Mary's shout for her to, "Stop raising your fists and turn away," came too late. Mosie already took aim. Her knuckles hitting something hard seemed to echo cross the schoolyard. Mother Prudence ran to Judy's side, her long black habit flapping like a sail of mercy.

"You're all nothing but a band of *perfects*!" Mosie raved on, waving her fists in the air. "*Perfect* hair, *perfect* teeth, *perfect* skin. Everything's *'purrr*-fect.' "

She didn't hear the screams coming from Theresa or the other girls as she chased them around the schoolyard like a brood of chattering chickens being captured for slaughter. Not until Sister Vern Mary caught her and gave her a good shake. That's when she stopped and saw Mother Prudence holding her habit to Judy's nose whisking her off the playground.

"Go, Mosie go, go-go-go!" Candy was yelling from the very top of the school steps, her chubby arms flapping victoriously in the air. Mother marched past her and through the doors as she led Judy and her nose inside.

Falling against Sister Vern Mary's chest, Mosie couldn't tell where the nun's habit began and her coffee-colored skin started. "I understand, Katherine," she said, the layers of thick, scratchy material making her voice sound a hundred miles away. "How *well* I understand, but it's over now."

For the hundredth time that year, Mosie stared at the nameplate on the door: *Principal Mother Prudence.* And for her hundredth time, Sister Vern Mary, took a deep breath and opened it.

With hands tucked tensely inside her long, black sleeves, Mother Prudence turned from the large window overlooking the now vacant playground. Mosie knew what she was about to say. She looked down at the cold gray floor and started counting its little flecks of pink. And she was right. Peering down her nose, Mother said, "Katherine Rose Bitmen, a month of rosary, three times a day on your knees. And not while lying in bed like last month!"

CHAPTER TWO

I'll be just as wrinkly as, 'Ole' Prune Bags' by the time I get done with all that praying," Mosie said to herself as she pedaled home on her bike. Halfway down Wool Street, she spotted her neighbor Mr. Bennington in his flower garden, pruning his "Award Winning Roses." Her pa, John, said, "The real prize Mr. Bennington earns puttering with them is the time he's able to spend away from Mrs. Bennington."

Coasting into the driveway, Mosie jumped off her bright yellow ten-speed Schwinn Super Sport, the one Pa gave her for being so smart (though Willowdean, her ma, had said no). *It's not right giving gifts for something a person is born with,* Ma said. *It's like giving Mosie a present because she inherited your Bitmen navy blue eyes, and not my Blackbird-Sweetwater black.*

Standing in front of the fancy metal gate to the backyard, she gave her fingers an extraordinary ride up and down the impressive swirling silver *B* like she, and Candy did to their Barbie's just a short hundred years ago.

"Hi Mr. Bennington," she called across the driveway. Counting, "one, two, three . . . One stick up and two loops down," she waited for him to poke his head out from the rose bushes. "One, two, three . . . One stick up and two loops down."

"Afternoon," he said peering through clumps of pink. Mr. Bennington never called Mosie anything when it was only them standing around. She figured he didn't know whether he should call her Katherine or Mosie, like most people did, unless when Mrs. Bennington was there. Then it was Katherine (definitely Katherine.)

He grinned at her and looked up into what Mrs. Bennington referred to as their parlor, (though it was just an ordinary living room made up real fancy). Mrs. Bennington pulled the white lacy curtains to the side and looked out. Mr. Bennington stopped smiling and went back to his roses.

Mosie waved. "Hi Mrs. Bennington."

The set of girdled breasts stepped away from the window, and the curtains fell back in place. Mosie wondered if her pa was right about Mrs. Bennington being so stuffy and crabby. He said it was because she "spent most of her life in a corset that was too tight for a woman her size."

Pulling the pin from the gate, she skipped to the back porch squaring her eyes at Willowdean's Dream Catcher hanging from the ceiling.

It wasn't the beads and feathers or blue agate wove in the web of willow reed and sinew she disliked, but what stuck inside them hidden from the naked eye.

"It came with me from The Great Lake," Willowdean had explained. "Dream Catchers protect us from bad dreams and bad Spirits. They get trapped in the webs. Only good dreams and good Spirits can find their way through."

That was one of the best parts of being twelve years old going on thirteen—having just enough time left to listen to stories and believing in them (especially if you're an Indian Princess, or at least thinking you are).

Willowdean was good at telling them, maybe even better than Sister Vern Mary with her fantastic storybooks, the ones the school librarian, Miss Quincy, ordered special for Sister Vern Mary; the ones filled with pictures of emerald-green forests, and bright-yellow fungus brackets bonded to tree trunks. The ones fairies bathe in after dining on colorful toadstools.

Except Willowdean didn't call her stories enchanted, or magical fairytales, or even made-up myths like Sister did. *Traditions*, that's what she called them, *Traditions*. Legends that passed from one generation to the next each held a special meaning and purpose.

Mosie's brother Val said their ma believed in such things like dream catchers and traditions on account of her being an Anishinaabe raised on the Red Cliff and Bad River Indian Reservation up North near Bayfield, Wisconsin. And Mosie believed him, especially since he turned eighteen and seemed to know just about everything, like their pa claimed.

"It's 1972 man, but sometimes for them it's still the 1940s. It's part of the generation gap, man," Val explained.

Mosie didn't know much about generation gaps, Indian reservations, or even protests, like Val did. He said she didn't have to, not yet anyway. Nevertheless, she did like her ma's stories and how she used them to teach right from wrong. "It's how we've taught our children and each other from the beginning of creation," she said (unlike John, who believed yelling and using the belt occasionally couldn't hurt.)

Mosie made the sign of the cross as she pulled the feathers dangling from the dream-catcher. "You better work this time," she said, hoping a good crossing with an extra feather jiggle might cause those bad spirits to let go and escape to

Judy Larson's house, maybe even Theresa Mavis' or, better yet, Tommy-Pissermans.

But it didn't. All it did was sway with Willowdean's, "Yes, Sister," and "I am sorry too, Sister," seeping through the kitchen door.

Through its window, she watched Willowdean anxiously twist the telephone cord around her fingers, rubbing her pregnant belly. Mosie looked back at the web made of sinew and Spirits and gave it a glare.

She opened the door, acted as if nothing had happened, and headed for the platter of still warm butterscotch Toll House cookies sitting on the counter. Grabbing one, she listened to the one-sided conversation.

"Yes," Willowdean was saying. "I hope you will be talking with the other girl's parents also. Yes, yes we will. Thank you for calling."

Mosie bit her Toll House and focused on the dots on Willowdean's maternity dress, counting only the red circles, not the white.

"Guess that was Sister Prudence, huh?" she said.

Willowdean crossed her arms.

"Ma, Judy Lard-Ass started it, her and Theresa May-Piss. All I did was stick up for me and Candy like you're always telling me to." "Breaking someone's nose is not what I meant, and you know it," Willowdean said as she sat across from her at the kitchen table. She handed Mosie a glass of milk. "And what have I told you about using that type of language?"

"I love dogs," Mosie blurted, hoping Willowdean might pity her for not having one and forget about the fight. Willowdean cleared her throat.

"Yes, yes you do," she said and smoothed the dots lying across her lap with her permanently tanned hands.

"I'm going to have one someday, maybe two, or even three. Maybe, even a *whole litter* of them." Mosie dunked a cookie in her milk and bit it.

"That's a subject for another time. Right now, we're talking about what happened between you and Judy."

"Well, I still like dogs," Mosie said, trying one last time. It didn't work. "Ma, you know Judy's jealous of me because I'm an Indian Princess, and she's not, and that's why we fight."

"Mosie, we've been through this too many times already," Willowdean said getting up heading for the sink. "You know I am not an Indian Princess and neither are you. You have to stop thinking that." She picked up the green bottle of Palmolive dish washing liquid and gave it a good squeeze.

"Well, Val said you are, and he don't lie."

"Val says that just to be nice," Willowdean said. "He says it just like how your father sometimes calls you Pocahontas. It doesn't mean you're *really* Pocahontas, now does it?"

"No-oo, I guess not," Mosie said watching the bubbles rising in the sink.

"Well there, you see? To be a Princess of any kind you have to be a child of a royal family, and my family was not royal, not by any means."

Mosie took another bite of her cookie. She knew living on the reservation meant her ma didn't have much money growing up (even if she was an Indian Princess). However, she did have her Granny Blackbird, and according to Willowdean, *there wasn't a price tag big enough to pin on her chest.*

That much Mosie did know on account of her sneaking about the house listening to stories she wasn't supposed to hear. Like how Willowdean wasn't able to get an education like many of her people living on the reservations back then. And how Indians sent into the cities to work were even poorer.

"You're smart, Ma," Mosie said, while fidgeting in her chair and stretching her toes toward a loose butterscotch chip on the floor. "Way smarter than Candy's ma, and as smart as Sister Vern Mary, too, I bet. And you're pretty too, even prettier than Theresa Mavis's ma, even if you are sort of plumpy even when you don't have a baby inside your stomach, and she's a Montgomery Ward catalog model . . . pages 89, 122, 138 *and* 227. It's only her foot wearing some sexy nylons on that last one, but you can still tell its Mrs. Mavis because the ankle is so skinny. I know it's true because Theresa brought the catalog to school and made Sister Vern Mary show it the whole class, and Sister don't ever lie."

Willowdean smiled and started to wash the dishes. "That's very nice of you, Katherine, thank you."

Mosie smiled back nice and big. She saw Willowdean was forgetting about Judy and her broken nose and Sister Prudence calling. "You're welcome," she said this time counting the white dots on Willowdean's dress instead of the red ones. *Three, four, five, six . . .*

"Ma, what do you think your and Pa's baby will be, a boy or girl? What do you think you'll name it if it is a boy? And what if it's a girl? You won't name her Mildred or anything like that, would you? Geez that would be awful if you did." *Eleven, twelve . . .*

"Mildred? Now why would you think . . . ?"

Thirteen, fourteen . . . "Do you think it'll like me? I sure hope Pa doesn't tug his pants at it when it cries; I heard babies cry a lot."

Willowdean chuckled. "No, your father would never tug his pants at a baby."

"Do you think it'll have Pa's Nordic blue eyes like me? What about its hair? Geez Ma, I sure hope it don't look like me and Val." *Eighteen, nineteen . . .*

Willowdean saw her daughter's shame, a shame that should have died a long time ago on the reservations. Gently, she touched her cheek, sugar brown as her own. "Katherine, do you know why you are called 'Mosie?'" she asked, standing straight and tall, her eyes shimmering with pride.

Keeping her eyes on Willowdean's swollen feet Mosie shook her head. "No, not really."

"Well, maybe it's time I tell you, Willowdean said. "Your father chose your Christian name, Katherine Rose, after his mother. He wanted to call you Rose, but Val insisted on calling you Mosie instead of Rosie. That's how your father's people name their children. Our people, the Anishnaabeg, The First Nation, also have a tradition in naming our children. It's through a Dream Quest. And like all Ojibwa mothers, I did not name you. It was my Nokomis, my grandmother, who named you. She is the one who gave us your real name."

Like warm caramel, the words rolled off Willowdean's lips. "Naanoondaagoziwag-manidoo-nandaagosiwag aazhoogaam. That is your true name, in the way that it holds your Spirit within it. It means 'Thunder across the Water.'"

Mosie scrunched her face. "Thunder across the Water?"

"Yes, Thunder across the Water," Willowdean said, her lips splintering into a smile.

"Ma, how could your granny name me if she were, well, you know, dead? Did she come to you like . . . like a ghost?"

Willowdean shook her head. "No, not like a ghost but in a dream. Nokomis Blackbird came to me in the Dream Quest. That's when the Spirit World touches ours, in dreams. Like all good ancestors, my Nokomis was faithful. One night after you were born, she showed me, The Great Lake. In the distance, far across its mighty waters was a storm with much thunder. One day you will understand the meaning of this, and so will I."

"Oh," Mosie said knitting her eyebrows. "Thunder across the Water. I do like that. Ma, is Mary Worth one of our people?"

Willowdean's face pinched into a question mark. "Mary Worth? No, no I don't recall a Mary Worth."

Jumping from her chair, Mosie patted Willowdean's stomach. "Thanks Ma. You know I don't care what the baby is. I'll love it no matter what."

"Yes, I believe you will, won't you? But Mosie, nevertheless, practice being proud of who you are so you may teach your little brother or sister to do the same."

"It'd be a lot easier if I were an Indian Princess," Mosie said as she pulled away from Willowdean's belly and gentle hands. "Ma, are you going to tell Pa what happened?"

"No, no I am not."

Mosie breathed a sigh of relief.

"*You* are," Willowdean said.

CHAPTER THREE

Mosie knew if Val's Simon and Garfunkel's, "Bridge Over Troubled Waters" *did* exist (like they were singing about on her hi-fi) she would be sitting on that bridge instead of her bed.

She could hear John at the kitchen table just like she did every night at 6 p.m. And she could smell him, too. The dry-bitter smell of his Tareyton cigarettes floated down the hall and came with the usual complaints of his workers while Willowdean finished making supper.

"I can't trust those yo-yo's alone for one minute," he was grumbling again. "They're ruining my business. Today a fellow walked in wanting to order cabinets for a big housing project, and that fathead Skids goes and tells the guy we're back-logged. *Back*logged for the love of Pete! A big order like that! What kind of idiot says something like that?" Taking a drink of his after work Hamm's beer, John got quiet. Very quiet.

He cleared his throat and started talking again. Mosie could tell the way he said, "Val," meant there was bigger trouble than Judy Larson's broken nose and, "real dumbbells like Skids."

Creeping down the hall she hid round the corner (like she wasn't supposed to on account of her spying problem).

John, watching Willowdean spoon gobs of mashed potatoes into the big yellow spuds bowl ran his fingers through his wavy blond hair. He stared at the spots on Willowdean's dress and lit another cigarette.

"Police," he said taking a gulp of his beer.

Mosie's ears froze to the words. Willowdean's shoulders tightened.

"I got another call from the police department. Val and those hoodlum friends of his were arrested in Chicago again last night protesting. Protesting! Willow, I can't take any more."

Falling forward in his chair he stared at the floor trying to find his guts. "Willow, I sold the cabinet shop today. We're moving to Bayfield. We have till the last week of May."

Willowdean gasped jabbing her serving spoon into the firm mound of white potatoes. "You *what*?"

John took another slug of beer. "Sold . . . the shop."

Mosie jetted from the corner holding her head, light as a helium balloon. "I'm going to freak!" she said running in a circle. "I . . . I'm going to freak out!"

Willowdean grabbed her kitchen chair and sank in it, shaking her head.

"Mosie, stop that," John ordered putting his hands on Willowdean's.

"I . . . I can't, I'm going to freak, I am . . . I am freaking, I'm freaking out right now . . . Ah geez!"

"What did you say?" Willowdean asked.

"I said I'm freaking out. . . ."

"No, not you, your father. What did you say?"

"Listen Willow, I'm just as shocked as you are. When I woke up this morning, I had no intention of selling the shop, not today anyway."

Willowdean pulled her hands from his. “I don’t understand, John. Why? How could you without even discussing this with me?”

“Knock it off,” he ordered, turning to Mosie. She sat next to him, catching her breath.

“Willow, after I got that call from the police department, I looked around the shop with all those idiots in there and thought, ‘What the hell am I doing here?’

“My son’s in the slammer, *again,* and I have a cabinet shop employed with nothing but numbskulls. My daughter is constantly in trouble in school because kids pick on her. The Benningtons have managed to drive me insane for the last eighteen years, and now we have another kid on the way. Willow, I was going nuts.

“Then out of the blue, some guy walks in off the street, tall fellow with long white hair. Not one of those damn hippie idiots toting flowers around like some jackass, but a decent man, a hardworking-man with hands rough and worn as mine.” John grabbed another smoke. Coughing, he looked at Mosie, her eyes wide as her gaping mouth. “Sit back on that chair.”

She waited for him to light his cigarette. “Go on, Pa,” she said.

“Well, this man see, says he's been living up in Bayfield since the beginning of time, as he put it, and wants to go somewhere quiet. *Quiet.*” John laughed. “Can you imagine someone from Bayfield saying something like that?

“He claims the tourist industry is starting to boom up there, and city folks are nabbing up what property they can. The next thing I know, he’s hauling out his wallet and starts showing me pictures of him at a boat factory up there. Says he owns it but hasn't been in operation for some years and that he's looking to sell it to someone who can use it.

"Well, we got to talking and I told him about the cabin we got up there and one thing led to the next. So I called Pete Rosemont and had him come down to the shop."

"Pete Rosemont?" Willowdean asked.

"Yeah, you remember that big shot who wanted to buy me out a couple of years ago? Well, I gave him a call to see if he was still interested, so he came down and signed the papers."

"John," Willowdean gasped. "You can't just buy a business not knowing if it's legitimate. What if this man is a con artist, what if . . ."

John took a puff from his smoke and chuckled. "Willie-Willie Willie, what, you think you married an idiot?

"I called Max Porter at Barrington Reality and had him check it all out before I did anything. Turns out the guy's a hundred percent on the up-and-up. Porter said if it were him, he'd jump at the chance."

"Well, I don't know what to say," Willowdean said narrowing her eyes. "What about, well, *you* know." Tugging the ends of her long black hair, she glanced at Mosie.

John nodded. "Don't worry about that," he said taking her hand giving it a squeeze. "I checked *that* out, too. And we'll talk about that later, without 'ears' here. Besides, 'Bitmen's Fish N' Boats' sorta has a nice ring to it, don't you think?"

Willowdean plucked at the dots on her dress. "I don't know John." I just don't know."

"Honey listen, if Val takes an interest in this new business, he might snap out of this bullshit of his and stick around. He might even find a good woman up there to settle him down.

Seems to me some of the best women are found in Bayfield." Raising his eyebrows, he grinned sheepishly at Willowdean.

"Good try Mr. B," she said tucking in her lips trying not to smile. "But you're not going to smooth talk me, not this time so stop."

"But Willow-Deanie, I don't know what you're talking about. I was just making a statement, that's all." He turned to Mosie and winked. "Did you know your mother's smooth and dark like the maple syrup that drew me to her?"

Mosie giggled at the blush on Willowdean's face.

"Don't encourage your father," Willowdean said biting her lip.

"Go on Pa, tell it," Mosie said even though she heard the story 50,000 times before (at least).

Lifting his empty beer bottle he gave it a jiggle. "It is a doozy," he said watching Willowdean get him another beer.

"Well let's see, it was 1955.

"My parents had just bought the cabin up north in Bayfield, Wisconsin, and it was the first time me and my brother Andy ever left Illinois. We were pretty excited. Me being a young man of sixteen and Andy eighteen.

"We'd only been there a few days when my mother and father sent me and your uncle Andy to get some of that fresh maple syrup us Illinois tourists buy up like gold. Turned out we had to buy it at your grandmother's novelty stand down by the lake." John took a swig from his beer and a puff on his cigarette.

"Anyway, we were looking over the other stuff your grandmother had for sale when we heard a group of young girls coming up behind us. They were giggling and carrying on like girls do at that age, so I didn't pay any attention to them. But your uncle Andy sure did. He started poking me in the ribs, telling me I'd better turn around quick before I'd miss a sight I'd never regret.

"Well, after paying for my candy, I turned around, and there she was, coming out of Lake Superior, glistening in the sunlight just like the brown maple sugar candy inside my bag. I swear she was the most beautiful creature God ever created. I thought maybe she was one of those freshwater mermaids my dad told us boys about. Well, the closer that mermaid got to me and your uncle, the harder my heart started pounding. I still got the shirt with my heart bumps in it to prove it if you want to see it."

"Pa," Mosie said, giggling as John got out of his chair pretending to go get the shirt. He chuckled and sat back down.

"By the time that girl got to us, I did the damnedest thing. I went and swallowed my own tongue and started choking on it. Andy knew he had to do something and quick, so he pulled out that pen and notepad he was in the habit of carrying around and wrote something down on it and handed it to my mermaid girl. He wouldn't tell me what it said. But the next morning bright and early, he insisted we go down to the lake and look for some of that driftwood that our mother liked so well, the fresh stuff that comes in during the night."

John stopped to prick a pork chop from the platter. He put it on his plate, then one on Mosie's.

"Then what happened Pa?" she asked. Willowdean looked at him and smiled.

"Well, there I was, walking down the beach minding my own business, picking up a piece of wood here, a piece of wood there, when I happened to look up. And there she was, my mermaid girl. I think she said, 'Hi John, I'm Willowdean Blackbird.' Now I'm not sure if that's what she really said because angels have a language all their own, you know. But that's what your mother tells me she said any way.

"She said, when I looked up at her, it was my stunning blue eyes that captured her wild side." He gave them a flutter. "It must be true because your ma is still here after eighteen years, and she ain't given me one bit of grief."

"Tell another one, Pa," Mosie said, not sure what parts she should believe, and what parts she shouldn't.

"No, now that's enough you two," Willowdean said.

"Okay, how about this one. Your mother weighed only fiftyseven and a half pounds the day she walked down that aisle to marry me."

"Oh John," Willowdean tsked, "I did not!"

"It's true. Your mother's wedding dress was a minus size seven." Mosie glanced at Willowdean's inflated waist and hips.

"I don't think *that's* true," she said.

"Well, it is. Matter of fact, after we said our vows and sealed them with a kiss, we headed back up that aisle as Mr. and Mrs. John Anthony Bitmen. That was one of the happiest days of my life." Looking thoughtfully at his Hamm's, John sighed.

"But what I can't figure out is how in the world your mother managed to get twice that size by the time we got to the door."

"John Anthony Bitmen, you're terrible." Willowdean said trying not to laugh.

"Well now, it's not so bad," John said. "At least, I know I'm not sleeping alone."

Mosie looked at Willowdean's arms. "Ma, are there Indians in Bayfield?"

"Yes, yes there are."

"It's a different world up there," John added. "People are more friendly, not so afraid of their neighbors or the fellow walking down the street. They live at their own pace it seems."

He looked at Mosie chewing her pork chop. Then came the promise, the one Willowdean knew he would regret for the rest of his life.

"I suppose the best part about moving to Bayfield," he said trying to hide his grin, "is you getting a dog."

Mosie swallowed fast and hard. "A dog, a *real* dog? You mean that, Pa?"

"Yep you can finally have that dog you've been whining about since the day you were born. And with a little fixing up, the cabin will make a fine place to live."

A dog, a real live, honest-to-goodness dog . . . Mosie's mind glowed as John went on about concerns over new cabinets and fireplaces and how they wouldn't have to hear the Bennington's complain any more (at least not hundreds, possibly thousands of miles away).

"How far is Bayfield?" Mosie asked. "What about Candy, what about—" Her voice was lost to the thunder rolling up the driveway. It was Val's van. John locked his eyes on Willowdean.

"I don't want either of you mentioning any of this to him," he warned getting up from the table. "I'll tell Val in my own way, in my own time."

Tugging the back of his pants up, he headed for the door. Mosie followed.

"Stay in here," Willowdean said grabbing her arm.

Pulling herself onto the sink, Mosie looked out the window and watched Val climb out from the rusted pea-green van.

Unlike John, regular sized with a scrappiness carrying him tall, Val was tall, carrying his browniness with an internal strength dressed in his peaceful ways.

Standing on the black-top driveway Val's filthy sandaled feet peeked out from the strings hanging from the hems of his bellbottomed jeans. The long, shiny black braid he left with the night before was now a knotted and twisted ponytail.

Mosie watched him take off his sunglasses as he reached to shake John's hand. John refused.

"Pa's mad, isn't he?" she asked

"No, no he isn't. He's disappointed. There's a difference."

"Ma, you know that song Val likes so much, that one about a bridge over rushing water and how when we get in trouble or sad or lonely, we need some place safe like that bridge?"

Willowdean thought a moment. "Oh, you mean, 'Bridge Over

Troubled Water.' Yes, yes I do."

"Well, maybe that cabin in Bayfield is Pa's bridge over his troubled waters, and yours might be a real garden and mine is a real dog. But what about Val? What's his bridge?"

Val got back into his van. John gave his pants several tugs.

"I don't know," Willowdean whispered watching her son drive off. "I don't know."

CHAPTER FOUR

Church isn't so bad if a person gets to sit next to their best friend and then afterward stop off at the Lincoln Street Liquor Store for chocolate bars and Slim Jims. However, when that doesn't happen, Mass can seem like a day in Purgatory.

The problem was, Candy had left for her uncle Louie's house before Mosie could tell her about the move. So when Willowdean asked, "How was Mass?" Mosie wanted to say it sucked but couldn't since she had just eaten Jesus (who she knew didn't taste nearly as good as Willowdean's Sunday chicken baking inside the kitchen oven).

"Pa's crabby," she said sitting next to him at the kitchen table. She took off the white lacy doily pinned on top of her head. "He wouldn't even stop at the liquor store."

John grabbed his Tareytons and Hamm's then loosened his tie. "You don't need a damn candy bar and Slim Jim every time you go to Mass," he said sucking in his lower lip.

Willowdean glanced at him and turned up the volume on the radio.

"Now that's real music," he said taking a swig of beer, tapping his fingers on the kitchen table to the beat of the polka.

"*Wally Gatche, Wally Gatche*," Mosie mocked. "It's the Wally Gatche *Polka Party*."

"Don't annoy your father," Willowdean said scrunching her eyes at her. "He's had a hard week."

"Not as hard as some people," he said taking a puff of his smoke. He coughed and watched Val saunter into the kitchen and canter next to Willowdean. "How's my favorite girl?" he asked kissing her cheek. He shot a wink at Mosie and poured himself a cup of coffee.

"Hey Moe, how's it hangin'?"

She shifted her eyes at John. "One," she chirped, watching John give Val a glower.

Leaning forward in his chair, John pointed his finger at her. "Don't start that damn counting bullshit, or you'll be sorry," he said, agitation seeping from his eyes.

"Well, do we have to listen to polkas?" Mosie asked.

"Well, we're not listening to that crap you and your knot-head brother here calls music."

Val yawned. "Man, that was a trip," he said plunking in the chair between John and Mosie.

"Two," Mosie said under her breath fiddling with her doily. "Two glares."

"Look," John said, "I already told you, and I'm not saying it again: Don't!"

Mosie watched the white smoke from his cigarette roll from his nostrils and rested her chin on the palm of her hand. The thuds of his calloused fingers drumming the tabletop kept rhythm with the *omppa-pa's* floating through the kitchen.

Val slurped his coffee. "Man, those Chicago cops don't know anything about the right to a peaceful protest," he said, his voice rough. "We have rights, man."

John stopped drumming. He stared at Val, his eyes nearly disappearing with strain.

Mosie turned away. "Three," she said quickly covering her mouth.

"Damn it, Willow," John barked as he rubbed the back of his neck. "This is a damn nuthouse.

"Mosie, go help your mother. And you Val, the only rights you have *my man*, is showing respect long enough to stop embarrassing me and your mother. Can you handle that, *my man*?"

"We weren't doing anything wrong, Pa. Those cops started it," Val said looking up from his coffee. "We told them we were cool, but they just wanted to bust some heads, man. So when they came at us with those billy clubs of theirs, we sat down. We told them, 'Man, we don't want no trouble, we just want to exercise our rights like all Americans.' They said filth like us don't have any rights. That's when they started beatin' on us. *Man*!"

John moaned shaking his head. "God help me," he said as he slipped his beer to his mouth.

"This country's in trouble, Pa, and we need to fix it," Val said with all the seriousness in the world. "If we don't speak out who will, the establishment? It's crooked as Nixon himself. And look at our environment man, Corporate America is destroying us."

John snorted. "What do you know about our government?

You're still wet behind the ears for the love of god. Besides, what has your country done to you or any of those long-haired hippies you call friends? If you don't like it here, then go live in Russia, and then you'll have something to cry about."

Val ran his fingers through his long black hair. "You just don't get it, man. We love our country as much as you do, that's why we don't want to see it lost to people like Nixon."

"Son, have I got a news flash for you and those friends of yours," John leaned in close. He belched. "I'll let you in on a little secret that might save all of you a lot of wasted time.

"See son, this country was always governed under people like Nixon, and people like you and me aren't going to change that no matter how much you and those fools try. So stop."

Mosie pulled herself up on the sink and looked out the window. "It's the Benningtons," she said.

"Mrs. Bennington is biting her fingernail, the one with the big fancy diamonds on it. And her hair, it's even bluer than last week, and it's piled up even higher . . . I'd say it's at least five feet high. And she's wearing one of her fancy Sunday dresses and Mr. Bennington, well, I can't see him. Mrs. Bennington's blocking him. She just picked up the newspaper, and now she's—"

Willowdean pulled her down. "Here," she said as she shoved a fresh beer in her hands. "Take this to your father." She patted the wrinkles from her apron and waited for Mrs. Bennington's knock at the door.

Just as Willowdean opened it, John flipped the cap off his bottle. Instantly, Mrs. Bennington handed Willowdean the extra fat roll of the Sunday edition of the Chicago Tribune.

"Here dear, in case someone trips on it," she tried to stretch her neck past Willowdean's shoulder taking in as much of the kitchen (and the '*Bitemens*') as possible. "I hope we're not intruding." Val grinned giving her the peace sign.

John slapped him in the stomach. "Knock it off you imbecile," he snapped before Val had a chance to call out his notorious, *Peace out, man!*

"Four and one," Mosie giggled. "Four and one. Four glares and one slap."

John took a fast slug of beer.

"Oh dear," Mrs. Bennington raised her eyebrows and backed out onto the porch.

Willowdean tugged the newspaper from her hands. "Thank you, Mrs. Bennington. Is there anything else?"

"Well there is one little thing . . ."

Mosie slid from her chair and cowered near the crack of the open door. She watched Mr. Bennington pretend to tie his shoes like he did every time he was with Mrs. Bennington (even though his laces never needed it). She figured it was his way of hiding from Mrs. Bennington, the same way she, herself hid in her desk from Judy and Theresa (and Tommy). Mr. Bennington peered at her, the skin around his gray eyes wrinkling red with embarrassment.

"May I please have a word with you outside?" Mrs. Bennington asked using that tone of voice John claimed was a high fluting put-on. "I hate to ask this, but . . . are Valerie and his friends going to be home next weekend? My daughter and son-in-law will be in for a visit from the city, and as you know, Willowdean, they do have two young children."

Mosie, mocking Mrs. Bennington, held up two fingers emphasizing, *two*. Mr. Bennington laughed a bit too loud.

"Royal, will you *please* stand up straight while we address Mrs. *Bitemen*?"

Mosie pushed her eye closer into the crack of the door and saw him rolling his eyes. He stood up, slouched, and waited for Mrs. Bennington who was eagerly nibbling the tip of her long, salon-styled fingernail. Her diamond rings fired flashes of rainbow colors that jumped up and down on Willowdean's Sunday dinner stained apron.

"It's Bitmen, not Bitemen," Willowdean corrected loud enough for Mosie to hear.

"As a matter of fact, we were planning on holding a corn and pig roast for Val and all his friends. You and your little darlings are more than welcome to join us."

Mrs. Bennington's congenial expression of hope drooped with disappointment.

"As a matter of fact," Willowdean went on in *her* own best elegant voice, "John left explicit instructions with the butcher that the pig is to be almost oinking when I prepare it. Its meat is so much more succulent when it's that fresh, don't you agree?"

Mr. Bennington bent down with a snorting laugh and pretended to rub a dull patch from his shoes. Mosie smiled at him. He smiled back.

"Oh dear," Mrs. Bennington said with a sniff. "I will certainly have to let you know. Come Royal," she said as she turned away. "I do believe we're expected at the Worthington's for bridge, and we really must get dressed."

"Well, at least I asked," Willowdean wiped her hands on her apron and watched Mrs. Bennington scuttle home, Mr. Bennington at her heels.

The Bennington's didn't bother Mosie, especially Mr. Bennington. She even felt sorry for him, especially when John accused him of wearing too much Brylcreem and liking women's underwear, but "not in a good way," as he put it.

"Royal might be able to buy anything he wants with all that money of his, including woman's undergarments for himself, but he sure can't buy a backbone," John said more than once.

Mosie sat in her chair, rested her chin on her hands, and watched him drink his Hamm's. She thought how glad she was her ma knew how to handle special situations like the Benningtons, especially after seeing John do it a few Christmases ago.

It was one of the few times of the year Willowdean would go to the back of her closet and pull out the big willow-reed trunk her granddaddy Sweetwater made her. The one with the special birchbark drawings on its lid. No one knew what was inside it except for the special tablecloth (the one that got Mrs. Bennington in trouble that one year with John).

Every Christmas Willowdean deftly pulled out what she called her *Spirit Seed Cloth*. "When my Granny Blackbird was a little girl, she and her granny made this," she'd explain, gently unfolding the tablecloth in her lap. "They're made from real seeds called Manidoominens." Thoughtfully, she'd run her fingers across the tiny seeds that formed little red and orange flowers with green and yellow leaves.

"They were sewn on with needles made of small bones and thread from horse hair, see? Back then they didn't have sewing needles and thread as we do now. I mean, they had needles and thread elsewhere but not on the reservation where my Nokomis Blackbird grew up.

"Even if they did have sewing needles and thread, I'm sure my Nokomis and her Nokomis wouldn't have used them, not to make this anyway. No, this is a very special Spirit Cloth. It was made for the day my Granny would marry."

One year Mosie asked Willowdean if she and her mother had made one together. That was the year she found out her momma didn't have a mom, or a daddy. Just her Granny Blackbird and her grandfather Sweetwater.

"When I was just a girl, my momma passed on," Willowdean explained. "Afterward my daddy ran off leaving me with Granny Blackbird. She was living on the Bad River Reservation and raised me there until Grandfather died.

"She was so poor she and I had to move to the Red Cliff to be by my grandfather Sweetwater. My fathers' father. "That's why I use my mother's last name, Blackbird, instead of my nindede's, my father's, Sweetwater."

And that's why the tablecloth was extra special to Willowdean and why that Christmas when Mrs. Bennington spotted it spread across the dining room table and ran her fingers across it *(just for a quick touch)* John decided it was time Mrs. Bennington learned what having true manners really meant. After that, Willowdean had another story to add to her tablecloth. The story of how John '*Bitemen*' slapped Mrs. Bennington's fingers for touching something they oughtn't.

Mosie looked up at Val. He had that faraway stare John claimed came from hanging around, "all those damn hippies," and smoking something other than Tareyton cigarettes. *Pot, weed, smoke*, Val called it. John said, "Anyone who smokes that shit is a true bird-brain."

Mosie wanted to tell Val they were moving to Bayfield, and how John said he was going to get her a dog and him a good woman. However, she knew better and put her thoughts on something else, something like Willowdean's medicine book.

That, Willowdean never offered to show to anyone and kept it tucked inside her willow-reed trunk on top of the Spirit Seed Cloth. And John had one heck of a story regarding that book, probably the *biggest* story he ever told.

"Hey Pa," Mosie picked up her head from the table. "Tell the story about Ma's book, please?"

"Man, that would be a real trip hearing it again," Val said tipping back in his chair.

John unrolled the Tribune. "Naw," he said. "Too tired."

"Ah, come on Pa, pleeese?" Mosie said twisting in her seat.

"Say's here, Nixon enjoyed his trip to Moscow." Val and Mosie stared at him. Blue smoke swirling around his head.

"For crying out loud," he huffed putting down the newspaper. "All right.

"The moment your mother and I got married, we left Bayfield behind and headed 450 miles south to this very house, right here in Barrington, Illinois. That was in 1954."

"The year Val was born," Mosie cheered.

John rolled his eyes. "God forbid. Anyway, we were just coming out of Hurley, Wisconsin, some sixty miles out when out of nowhere, your mother's granny stood smack-dab in the middle of Highway 51, dressed in her Ojibwa clothing.

"We were so happy to see one another, neither your mother nor I noticed Granny giving your mother a book made of birch bark. Then, just as fast as Granny materialized, Granny disappeared. We were so stunned it wasn't until we hit Minocqua and stopped for gas that we saw the book. We opened it and boy, were we shocked. Inside, drawn by Granny herself, were her Midewiwin' teachings. Now what's really strange about the whole thing is this: Granny had died a year before we got married."

"Wild, man," Val laughed. "*Wild*!"

"Uh Pa," Mosie chuckled nervously, "that can't be true, can it?" John smiled and went back to his newspaper.

"Ma, is that true?"

Willowdean didn't say yes, and she didn't say no. She just gave a look that said, *maybe your father is telling the truth.*

"You kids have never gotten sick and never gone to the doctor, have you?" John moved his elbows for Willowdean to clear away his ashtray and empty bottles of beer. "Mosie, get up and help your mother set the table, and Val, if you're planning to eat here tonight instead of Cook County Jail, you're washing the dishes and cleaning the kitchen afterward. Your choice, take it or leave it. Nothing's free in this world, so get used to it."

John got awfully serious waiting for Willowdean to take her seat across from him. She glowed, looking over her little family. John crossing himself started grace. They all followed, even Val.

"Bless us O' Lord, for these are gifts for which we are about to receive from thy bounty, through Christ our Lord, Amen," they said in unison, crossing themselves once more, even Willowdean.

Mosie didn't count the puckers in John's brow as he looked over his little tribe. Not this time.

"Everything looks really good, Ma," Val said, as he handed her the first choice of the golden baked chicken.

"Why thank you, Val," she took the best piece placing it on his plate. She knew John was about to keep his word, and so did Mosie. They sat quietly.

"What's wrong with everybody?" Val asked as he heaped a load of mashed potatoes on his plate. "Somebody died?"

John pushed his food to the side. "Val, we have to talk," he said. Val chomped down on his chicken leg. "Sounds serious."

"Well yes, Valerie, it is."

Val stopped chewing. '*Valerie.*' The name stung him. The only time John called him "Valerie" was when something terrible occurred, like when Uncle Andy died.

Val braced himself and swallowed what was in his mouth then dabbed his lips with his napkin. “Yes, Father, what is it?” he said looking square into John’s navy blue eyes.

Mosie held her breath.

“Son I sold the shop. We’re moving to Bayfield.”

Val held his stare then turned away. “When?” he asked, taking a drink of his Coca-Cola.

“One month, the last week of May.”

Nobody said a word. Not even Mosie.

CHAPTER FIVE

Like every Sunday night, Mosie was sitting on "The - Adventures of Mutual of Omaha's Wild Kingdom" flutter on the TV screen. Val sat next to her and stared at the pack of wild dingoes chasing down a lone cougar cub.

"They never get away, do they?" she asked.

"Some do if they're smart enough and fast enough," Val said as he glanced at John.

John gave him a sharp look.

"Can't they just eat some plants and be happy?" Mosie asked. "Where is the cougar baby's parents anyway? Why don't they do something to protect their kid? Why don't the cameramen do something, why can't—"

"That's enough," John leaned back in his recliner.

Val poked her in the ribs. "Hey Moe," he whispered as he plucked strands of her short black of hair. "After your bath, I'll show you how to style your hair-like Twiggy. It's short enough. It will be far-out, man, I promise. Besides, Ma and the old man want to talk to me about, *the move*."

"Watch who you're calling, 'old man,'" John shoved a smoke between his lips. Flipping open his silver Zippo lighter, he pressed its flame to his cigarette. "I can still beat your ass." He snapped the lid over the tiny flame.

Val leaned next to Mosie and said, "Watch this. Hawk-ears," he barely uttered.

"Damn right," John stretched through the haze of Tareyton smoke surrounding him.

"Val," Mosie pulled him to her and cupped her mouth to his ear so John couldn't hear. "I don't want to move, but Pa promised me a dog."

"Yeah well, he promised me a woman. Like I don't have enough of them already."

"But there's more," Mosie whispered through her cupped hands. "This morning, before church, I overheard them talking about some people in Bayfield named Lenny and Corrine." Val bit his lip. Hard.

"When they saw me peeking around the corner, Pa got so mad. Ma looked really nervous. Are they some of Ma's family?"

Val narrowed his eyes at John. "Lenny and Corrine, huh?"

"Yes. Lenny and Corrine."

"Hey Moe, tell ya what. Why don't you go take your bath? I think it's time me and the old man have that talk."

"Yeah," John echoed back keeping his eyes on the dingoes. "Go take your bath. And tell your mother I want to see her."

"Why do I have to go? Why can't I be in on the meeting?"

"It doesn't concern you, that's why," John said. "Now go take your bath and get ready for school tomorrow."

"For crying out loud," Mosie got up from the sofa heading to the kitchen. "Even though I live here, nothing ever concerns me. Well, I'll tell you one thing, when I get my dog, no one's going to tell me what I can and cannot do with it. That's *my* promise."

Through the backdoor of the kitchen, Mosie spotted ma looking at the clouds hanging in the early evening sky. She walked outside and stood next to her.

"See those long wispy clouds?" Willowdean asked, putting her hand on Mosie's shoulder. "They're dictating reports from the next world to this one. I call them Heaven's Whispers."

Mosie squinted at the ribbons of orange and red. She could smell the sweet scent of Mr. Bennington's roses.

"They're telling Mother Earth to have a nice warm day tomorrow, but in three days they must rain on her. Well, it is a little dry." Willowdean chuckled and turned her eyes to the top of the pine tree growing in the Bennington's back yard. In it a crow was flapping its wings. It settled into a roost as if waiting to listen to Willowdean.

"Katherine, there's something I want to tell you. It's been on my mind from when your father promised you a dog."

"Big one Ma, I'm going to get me a big one."

Willowdean sighed. "Mosie, remember how I taught you The Great Spirit gives us one another to help us teach lessons to each other and to also help one another through those lessons—and how even a brief, seemingly unimportant smile has a purpose? Well, in the same way, animals also have a reason for living; to help with lessons only *they* can teach. That is why both people and animals are gifts to us and each other."

Willowdean paused and pointed to a lonely cloud shaped like one of the dingoes on TV.

"No matter where we live we can see Animal Spirits, if we look for them. They're in the clouds coming and going from the life bridges nestled secretly somewhere in the Apostle Islands, the ones out in Lake Superior.

"And when the right time comes, Animal Spirit sends us just the right one. To some he sends cats from Cat Island, birds from Gull Island and so forth. But somewhere out on the Great Lake is a special island called Dog Island."

Willowdean searched the sky as if looking for something from long ago. The dingo cloud grew larger and broke off into little puffs of fluff. The crow cawed.

"When the animal's lessons have been learned, the animal's time comes to an end and returns to Animal Spirit. He takes them back to their islands from where they came.

"Katherine," Willowdean said as she took Mosie's tender young face in her hands, "when an animal—a pet—dies, it brings one of the hardest lessons of all, and my daughter isn't ready for that."

Mosie looked down at the grass. "Well, Pa promised I could have one, and I'll take real good care of it, you'll see. I promise."

"I'm afraid that is one promise your father is going to wish he never kept."

"Ah Ma, you worry too much," Mosie said as her thoughts turned ginger brown along with the clouds. She put her arm around Willowdean's waist. It went halfway then stopped. She tried not to repeat the rhyme Judy and Theresa used for Willowdean. *Fatty-fatty two-by-four, couldn't fit through the bathroom door, so Mrs. 'Bite-me' did it on the floor then licked it up and did some more.*

"You know what Ma? I think Mr. Mavis should have a dog."

"Mr. Mavis? Why would you think something like that?"

"Well, if he had a dog, he'd be warm at night and wouldn't have to turn on the light."

"I'm not sure what you mean."

"Well, I bet he has to turn the light on at night to find Mrs. Mavis because she's so skinny, don't you? I bet she couldn't keep a tadpole warm if she had to, let alone Mr. Mavis. With a dog, he could sleep through the whole night all nice and warm, don't you think?"

"Katherine, what made you say such a thing?"

"Oh nothing. Pa wants you in the house. He says it's time for *the meeting*. You know, the one that only adults are allowed to attend. Ma, you won't regret letting me get a dog. I promise. I really do, you'll see."

They turned from the sky and the clouds (and the crow) and headed to the house.

The skip down the hall brought Mosie to the bathroom. Opening the door, she grabbed a towel and quickly covered the mirror avoiding her reflection. Thoughts of Granny Blackbird showing up occasionally was giving her the heebie jeebies. "That's all fine and well if she wants to visit Ma now and again but I sure don't want to see her," she said as turned on the tub faucet.

She looked over her shoulder while making sure the towel was still tucked tight. She started thinking about Candy and her dead Aunt Margaret, who Candy claimed started showing up a few days after she had died.

Ghosts like using mirrors, Candy explained. *Just like Mary Worth. Except her, you have to call on yourself.*

Recalling Candy's instructions, Mosie shuddered: *It's best to use a lit candle, but this will do,* she had said as she took John's flashlight, turned it on, and held it under her chin. *Now, stand in front of the mirror and I'll turn out all the lights. Bathroom mirrors work best.*

Mosie whistled and sauntered back to the mirror. She re-tucked the edges of the towel then cracked the door open a bit and looked down the hallway. She was alone.

Put the candle up to your face like this . . . turn around three times and say . . . Mosie struggled not to repeat the words Candy had said. It didn't work. The hair prickled up on her arms.

I believe in Mary Worth—I believe in Mary Worth—I believe in Mary Worth. Now look in the mirror. Mosie couldn't help it, she just couldn't. Glancing at the towel she could still see Candy holding John's flashlight under her chin, as dark, sinister shadows materialized on her chubby face. *You'll see her in your face!* Candy had shrieked. *She's all rotty and decayed cause she's been dead for so long! Sometimes she even drags those long rotty fingernails of hers right across your face till you bleed, or she might even gouge out your eyes so she can use them herself!*

Plus sometimes if you're wearing nylons, she'll make them melt right on your legs! You can ask Judy Lard-Ass if it's true. Her cousin, Cindy, who lives in Palatine, has the burn scars to prove it, you know!

"Ah, hog-wash," Mosie cracked the door open just a bit more.

They use mirrors, the foot of your bed, and of course, you can always find them under your bed too. It just depends on them and what they like best.

"Agh, it ain't true!" Mosie insisted and grabbed the plastic pitcher Willowdean kept inside the bathtub.

She filled it, rinsed the tub, and pushed down the silver plug. Again, she looked at the mirror and checked the door.

After running her hand under the water to make sure it wasn't too hot (or too cold), she slid into the bathtub.

"Hmm, a name for a dog, my very own dog," she hummed and lay back to stare at the curtain rod.

I hope them buggers don't use shower rods to attach to, she thought, corking her nose. She slipped under the water keeping her eyes open, "Just in case.

"Stinkers, Tippers, Tide, Joope, Princess, Heidi, maybe Buddy or even Bruno," she said to push away thoughts of Willowdean's granny, and Candy's dead Aunt Margaret (and of course, Mary Worth). Tonight she had something more frightening to think of:

How to tell Candy she was moving.

CHAPTER SIX

Mosie sat at the kitchen table, stirring her Monday morning oatmeal. She put a few globs on her toast and ate it like a sandwich just like Candy taught her. Leaning over, she watched Willowdean add another item to the moving list.

"I don't see anything for a dog written on there," she said.

Willowdean pulled away. "No, no you don't. That's something your father will have to think about. Now sit back before you get that mess on here."

"Hey Ma, when Candy starts crying when I tell her we're moving—which I'm pretty sure she's going to do—and when Judy Lard, I mean Larson, and Theresa Mavis start teasing her, what if I can't help myself and wallop her again, and what if Mother Prudence—"

"If you think that's going to happen, then wait until after school to tell her. Now please, just eat."

"I can't Ma; I can't just sit there all day and not say anything, geez, I'd burst or do something even worse, like *freak out* and have to go to the office again. I'm just saying, if that were to happen what do you think Pa would do? I'm already grounded for a week for popping Lard, sorry, Judy." She put another scoop of oatmeal on her toast.

"I just wish Candy had been home this weekend instead of going to her Uncle Louie's because of her Aunt Margret dying.

That was a month ago already. Why do they have to go spend more time with him anyway, geez! Why can't he come to their house?"

Willowdean rubbed her temples. "Go brush your teeth, it's almost time to leave."

"But Ma, I didn't even get a chance to eat. Not that I'm hungry or anything knowing I'll get into trouble today somehow, one way or another. Hey, how come adults get to make all the decisions? Why don't they ever get into trouble? Why don't they get grounded? Why does—"

"Katherine stop it and go, you're going to be late. And please tell your brother to get up."

She tapped on Val's door, but did not dare to look inside. He didn't wear anything but his skin when he slept. Nobody knew that, not until Candy found out that night she showed Mosie how to play Mary Worth. When Candy had opened Val's door and screamed, Mosie thought for sure that old witch was reflecting herself in Vals full-length mirror.

"You up?" she pushed the door open just enough to plant her lips in its crack.

"I'm cool," Val answered.

"Ma said you have to get up."

Val was always cold in the mornings. Mosie wanted to tell him if he wore pajamas like everyone else, then maybe he would be warm. "Hey Val, what do you think I should do when Candy starts crying when I tell her we're moving? I mean, if Judy Lard-Ass catches her crying and starts teasing her again, and I end up clobbering her again . . . how do I get Old Prune Bag to call Pa instead of Ma?"

"Man," Val mumbled from under his sheets, "why'd you want that old nun calling Pa for instead of Ma?"

"Because," Mosie said, "if I have to tell him like I did last time, he's going to ground me till moving day for sure, but if Prunes calls him, by the time he gets home maybe he'll of half-forgotten about it and won't be so mad."

"Cool," Val said again and pulled himself out of bed.

"Hey Val," Mosie said, "maybe Pa should tell you this and not me, but if you wore PJs to bed you wouldn't be so cold when you get up in the morning."

Val laughed. "When you going to tell Candy?"

"Soon as I get to school."

"What time is it?"

"School? You know, 8:45, like always. See, you are getting birdbrained from smoking that stuff like Pa said."

"No, man," Val laughed. "I mean, what time is it now?"

"Almost eight, but Ma said I have to leave; she thinks I'm going to be late, geez!"

"You go ahead. I don't think Judy's going to be giving you any trouble today."

Mosie scrunched her face. "Well, okay," she said.

Like every school day since first grade, Candy was sitting on the waist-high brick planter under the big silver cross. Next to it, spelled out in large, silver-steel letters (all capitals) was *SAINT ANNE.*

Candy hopped down from the brick wall and snuck behind Mosie as she coasted to the bike rack and then parked her bike inside it. She put her hands over her eyes. "Guess who?" she yelled.

Mosie turned and shushed her. "I have to tell you something," she said looking over her shoulders. "And it isn't so good; it's bad, *awfully* bad, and I don't want anyone to hear us when I tell you."

Candy's eyebrows pinched together. "Wow, you look sad, Mose. No one died like my Aunt Margret, did they?"

"No, but maybe that would be better than what I'm going to tell you." They headed to the secluded stairwell leading into the school basement, and sat on the third step from the bottom like they always did when they didn't want anyone hearing them talk. Taking Candy's hands, Mosie swung them back and forth.

"Candy," she began, her voice shaking. "Val and his hippie friends and the Benningtons are driving Pa crazy, and he doesn't want to raise another kid here in the city." Candy fidgeted while Mosie paused to force the lump in her throat to stop growing.

"Boy Mose, this has to be bad. I haven't seen you this upset since the army tried drafting Val by mistake for the Viet Nam war, and you thought he was going to go fight the Viet Cong."

Mosie looked down at her shoes. She wanted to rub them like Mr. Bennington did his. "It's worse than that. It's worse than anything a person is ever going to have to tell you in all your life, a thousand times worse, besides when someone tells you that your parents are going to die."

"Well I don't want to hear it then." Candy put her hands over her ears. She started humming.

"You have to hear it Candy, and I'm the one that has to tell you."

"What? I can't hear you," she said and hummed even louder.

Mosie grabbed Candy's hands and pulled them from her ears. "I said: if someone else tells you, you're going to be twice as mad so just listen. And try not to cry too loud, okay? I don't want to have to break anything else on Lard-Ass or May-Piss or any of the other *Perfects.*

"Okay," Candy said, her voice cracking.

"Well see, Pa, well, he went and sold the shop and bought another one so we have to move." "Where, Buffalo Grove?" Candy asked.

"No. Up north." Mosie said.

"Lake Zurich?"

"No." Mosie swallowed back her tears forcing the words. "More up north, *way* up-north. Bayfield . . . Bayfield Wisconsin."

"Bayfield? Where your ma is from?"

"Yes, I'm afraid so. The last week of May we're moving to Wisconsin, northern Wisconsin, hundreds and hundreds, maybe even *thousands* of miles away!"

Candy started blubbering, quietly at first. But the more Mosie talked, the louder Candy got, till finally she was erupted into a full fledged frenzy.

"No, no you can't, you-you-you just can't, it's not fair!" she screamed.

Her sobs floated up the stairs past Judy's ears, lighting up her nasty-green eyes. "Come on girls," she said, "I hear Blubber-Ball, let's go."

Theresa led the way hot on the trail of Candy's howls. Peeking around the corner, she nodded to Judy. "Right there," she whispered pointing to the brick wall.

Judy held up her finger. "One—two—three . . ." With a squeal and a hiss she jumped from the corner. "Aw look, they're breaking up! Oooo, kissy-kissy," she said as she bent forward with puckered lips. "Is it going to be a *Long Lonely Summer*?"

Mosie squared her eyes at her. "I'm not afraid of you, Lard-Ass."

Judy backed away stepping on Theresa's foot as Mosie made her way up the stairs.

"And Judy isn't afraid of *you*!" Theresa said, shoving Judy at her. "Gee girls, better look for a playground monitor; I think the Little Indian Princess is going to try to scalp Judy again."

One of the Perfects checked the front of the school and pointed down Chestnut Street. "Hey, look," she flipped open her purse, pulled out a hairbrush and ran it through her profuse curls.

Turning from Judy and Mosie the others swooned.

"Do you hear that?" Mosie tapped Candy's shoulder with the tip of her shoe. Pulling her hands from her face, Candy smiled. Val, in his van along with Paul Simon (and "Julio") playing in the eighttrack was on their way to do a little schoolyard visiting.

Val stepped out of the van and peered at the girls from behind the rims of his rose-colored, Byrd's sunglasses. A smile spread across his face as Judy began fainting. Theresa caught her. Val grinned and ran his rich, dark eyes over them. "Hey man, any of you lovely little chicks seen my sis?" he said snapping his gum.

"Val!" Mosie yelled running to him.

"Hey *cool chick*." He held up a brown paper lunch bag. "You forgot this."

"No, no I didn't. I have my lunch box in my knapsack."

Val shoved the bag in her hand.

"Ohhh, I get it," she said, "Thanks, Val."

"Yeah, thanks," Candy said, tippy-toeing herself up to his cheek and giving him a kiss.

The Perfects squealed.

As she barged through the front doors with her black habit flapping in the wind, Mother Prudence yelled, "Valerie!" She looked down the steps at Judy and the girls. She was too late; their eyes had already gone googly. Sister Vern Mary stood behind her.

"Turn that unholy music down, and if you are through here you must leave these premises," she ordered, tucking her hands inside the cuffs of her sleeves.

"Orders from the Vatican, I suppose," Val said. "Go on Moe, it's cool."

He headed for his van and his dark eyes followed Sister Vern Mary's shapely form. She blushed at his grin of approval.

"That is *enough,* Valerie," Mother Prudence ordered. She muttered something to Sister Vern Mary and went into the school.

"I better go. Old Prune Bag is probably on her way right now to call the Pope to have me exiled from heaven," he said. He winked at Sister Vern Mary as she watched him get into his van.

Turning up his eight-track, he held up his two-finger peace sign and waited. Sister poked her own two fingers out from her sleeve. They smiled, and Mother Prudence watched from her office window as Val and Paul Simon drove away singing:

"*And I'm on my way; I don't know where I'm going, I'm on my way I'm taking my time . . . Good-bye to Rosie the queen of Corona . . . See you, me and Mosie, down by the schoolyard.*"

CHAPTER SEVEN

Willowdean's voice bounced off the walls, "Yes. . . . that will be nice," she was saying. "Yes, we will talk when you get here." She clopped the phone back in its cradle. Creeping from the doorway Mosie asked, "Who was that?"

"Mrs. Nelson. We thought it would be nice if you and Candy could spend the weekend together."

Mosie looked at the calendar on the wall. The days had sped by faster than she expected. "Yeah," she said, "the last weekend we might ever be together for the rest of our lives." She figured Uncle Louie had put dead Aunt Margaret to rest so she and Candy could spend more time together before the big move (now only three days away.)

Willowdean pulled open the curtain above the sink and looked across the driveway. Except for the soft puffs of pastel blossoms, the Benningtons' rose garden was empty. So was the parlor window.

"I know it's hard leaving a friend like Candy," she said. "And I know you don't believe this, but you will make other friends."

"No, no I won't," Mosie kicked one of the boxes of canned foods with her new Keds (red, her favorite color). "Who'll want to hang around with me? Look at me. I'm a . . ." Instead of saying *Indian,* she flopped down in her kitchen chair and bit the tip of her tongue.

Willowdean sat with her and patted her hand. “You have to trust me; there are others in this world like Candy who do not see the color of a person’s skin but what’s inside. And that’s what really counts.”

“Yeah, that’s what Sister says too.” Mosie rested her chin on her fist and tapped her foot against the table leg. “And I look beyond Candy’s, well, her chubbiness. I didn’t even notice it, not until *The Perfects* teased her about it. But even then it didn’t bother me. I mean, it’s not *her* fault she has low blood sugar and has to eat more than others.”

Willowdean nodded. “That’s what real friends do. They overlook each other’s faults. We all have them, don’t we?”

“That’s one thing I’ll always remember about your ma,” Mosie said to Candy as they watched Mrs. Nelson plunk three full bags of groceries from the A&P on the counter. “It’s how good she is at picking out snacks.”

“And I helped,” Candy proudly added.

“But I’m keeping the Green Stamps,” Mrs. Nelson teased.

Pulling a tray of little sandwiches out of the refrigerator, Willowdean chuckled. “That’s fine. There is no A & P in Bayfield.”

As Mosie sat between Mrs. Nelson and Candy, it was hard for her to tell whether Candy looked more like her Mrs. Nelson or more like her pa, Mr. Nelson.

“Here sweetheart,” Mrs. Nelson said as she slid an extra gooey butterscotch Toll House onto Candy’s plate, reminding her to eat a little additional nourishment. "You need a little extra so your blood sugar doesn't drop. It's so hard for us girls with low blood sugar to keep our weight off." Mrs. Nelson sighed and slipped a couple extra Toll House's next to her own pile of sandwiches and chips.

I bet she could keep two *Mr. Nelsons warm at night*, Mosie thought, wondering if Mrs. Nelson felt her skin-roll squishing into the sides of the wedding rings on her finger. *But what if she rolls over on him by accident, and smothers him; how will they get those rings off her finger, in case she marries someone else? I bet she'll have to keep them on forever, even when they bury her.*

"Willowdean," Mrs. Nelson curled her nubby, little sausage fingers around her fourth cup of coffee. Her eyes bubbled up. "I don't know what I and Candy are going to do without you two. Thanks for being my friend, Willow." Her chin was bouncing so hard, Mosie thought her bottom lip might fall off.

Willowdean put her hand on Mrs. Nelson's. She didn't care if it was rough and dry and had a bit of red scaling coursing across the knuckles.

"Friends forever," she said.

"Forever," Mrs. Nelson repeated and sucked in her pout long enough for them both to sink their teeth into their sandwiches.

"Come on Candy," Mosie watched Mrs. Nelson bury her eyes against her fist and tried to swallow her sandwich on top of her sob. "We have to discuss our plans for when we visit each other."

Grabbing her knapsack, Candy followed Mosie down the hall and tossed it and herself on Mosie's bed. She leaned back on her elbows and read the thick black writing labeling the boxes lining the wall. "Mosie," she sniffled. "I bet you have them all counted too, don't you?"

"Twenty-six!"

"Did you pick a name out for your dog yet?"

"No, not yet. Boy, Candy, I wonder if naming a baby is this hard."

"I bet it is, maybe even harder," Candy shoved a pillow up her shirt and rubbed her belly like Willowdean. "Hey, why would anyone name their baby Horace or Milton or . . ."

Mosie giggled. "Oscar. Come here, baby Oscar," she said, pretending to call a child to her knee.

"Oh look, isn't baby Horace just beautiful?" Candy said.

"Well, my baby Matilda is cuter than your little Norbert," Mosie laughed.

Candy stopped. Their moms' laughter floated down the hall. She looked back at the boxes. "I can't believe you're actually moving, Mose. Who am I going to mess around with? Who am I going to ride bikes with? Who's going to, well, you know, protect me from Lard-Ass and *The Perfects*, and Tommy Pisser-men?"

Mosie shifted closer to her. "I can't believe it either," she sniveled back. "I'm scared, too, Candy. I don't think I'll ever have another friend, ever, that's good as you."

Candy grabbed her and started bawling. Mosie patted her head. "Mose, do you think when we're old like our moms, do you think we'll be sitting together, drinking coffee and eating little sandwiches while our kids play together?"

"That's a lot of years from now, Candy. We'll just have to make it happen, that's all."

Mosie flopped onto her back and shoved a pillow under her head. "I bet they'll play Barbies and Mary Worth. And will probably ride bikes together and stick up for each other and . . ."

"Eat Frito Corn Chips for breakfast when no one's looking?" Candy pulled a huge bag of Fritos out from her duffle bag. "I was sort of saving these for tomorrow morning, but . . ." Ripping the bag open with her teeth, she let Mosie take the first handful.

The girls stared at the dates written on the notebooks Willowdean had given them: *Sunday, May 27, 1972.*

"There," Mosie said, drawing a giant smiley face next to the title on Candy's *Future Plans Notebook* (identical to hers). "Finished. Now your turn," she handed Candy the marker.

"Okay, how about this." Candy scrawled a huge heart with two eyes and a grin inside it. "Now yours is done," she said giving it back to Mosie. "And look, no feathers."

A knock on the front door echoed through the house. Their eyes locked.

"Oh-oh," Candy said, starting to cry.

"Maybe it's the Benningtons," Mosie said softly, as they listened to the chatter filling the house. "It is Sunday, and the Benningtons always bring Ma the Tribune on Sundays."

Candy shut her eyes so tight her face was blotching pink. "Yeah, that's who it is. It's the Benningtons," Candy insisted, rocking back and forth, tears rolling down her cheeks. "It *has* to be the Benningtons."

Mrs. Nelson stuck her head in the doorway, bearing a grim smile. Mosie's eyes welled up.

"*No*," Candy said. "I think I'm going to throw up!"

"No, no you just have a bellyache from eating too many Fig Newtons for breakfast is all," Mosie said, trying to sound brave.

"Oh Mosie!" Candy howled.

"Oh Candy!" Mosie wailed back.

"I'm sorry," said Mrs. Nelson, stepping into the room. "But it's time to go."

For the last time, on that last Sunday in May of 1972, Mosie Bitmen and Candy Nelson walked hand in hand from the bedroom at 130 Wool Street and down the hallway to the front door.

Standing on top of the steps was Willowdean holding a birchbark basket in front of her. Inside were three little boxes wrapped in white tissues. Bending down, she looked Candy in the eyes.

"A long time ago," she said, "I made something for you, for all of you. I have kept them until they were needed."

Candy swallowed a tear-swollen hiccup as Willowdean placed one of the boxes in her hand.

"Thank you for being a good friend to Katherine Rose. You have taught her a lot."

"And this is for you, my friend," she said turning to Mrs. Nelson handing her a box. Then to Mosie she said, "Naanoondaagoziwag-manidoo-nandaagosiwag aazhoogaam, this is yours for your new journey."

Tearing off the paper they opened the boxes and stared at the small, beaded deerskin purses inside.

"They are medicine bags," Willowdean explained, "but not the kind you find with a doctor." Pulling hers from inside her blouse she held it up for them to see. Candy ran her chubby fingers through the soft, brown fringes dangling from its bottom while Willowdean explained.

"As you go through life, you must put those things that make you strong inside them, even if they seem hurtful at the time, and you want to forget them. Keep that medicine and what it taught you, all the days of your life for when you need it, like our good-byes. I know that doesn't make much sense now, but I promise you, one day it will."

Mrs. Nelson's bottom lip started trembling again as she studied the bright little beaded purse, the one that looked most like Willowdean's.

"One day you can share your medicine with others when they need it," Willowdean said, placing Candy's around her neck. She held it up to her puffy red eyes. "See how the tiny seeds form a blackbird? Well, I'm a Blackbird by name, and that makes Mosie one also. Sweetwater is my other name, my father's name. The blue seeds represent both my name, and the Great Lake where we will be living. See the Blackbird flying over the Great Lake?" Candy nodded. "The tiny rose floating down the middle represents Mosie, because her middle name is Rose."

Candy stared at the little purse, let it dangle from her neck, and then threw her arms around Willowdean. "Oh Mrs. Bitmen," she sobbed, "don't go, please don't go. *Please* don't take Mosie away."

Willowdean softly tapped Candy's budding chest."We will never leave you, not in here," she said.

Candy turned to Mosie and put her finger to her cheek catching her tears. Placing them in her medicine bag, she stepped forward and left the last words and waves of farewell for her mother and Willowdean.

CHAPTER EIGHT

Mosie raced out the front door and stood between Willowdean and Mrs. Bennington. As she tied her red Keds she read the huge red letters splashed across the yellow moving van, her stomach prickled with panic: *Mayflower.* Val's van was nowhere in sight.

"We're leaving with or without him," John growled, tugged his pants nearly over his head, and made his way past the green *Dutch Flier* painted on the side of the *Mayflower.* He swung open its back doors.

Nervously, Willowdean scratched her arm and concentrated on the crow sitting on top of the Benningtons' pine tree. Mrs. Bennington stood next to her and kept yammering on about what good neighbors the *Bitemens* had been over the years."Bitmen, Mrs. Bennington, not Bitemen," Mosie corrected.

Mr. Bennington winked at her, and went back to wiping the few strands of wet, early-morning grass from his canvas shoes.

"Of course, yes, *Bitmen,*" Mrs. Bennington repeated, making her way to John. She stuffed the top half of her body inside the van and said, "My goodness, this is enormous." She turned away, eagerly walked up the plank, and slithered inside. "I never realized you people had so much stuff."

"Too bad you didn't bring an inventory list with you," John hissed shoving an end-table to the side. "You coulda had it printed in the Tribune, or better yet, you coulda shared it with everyone yourself. Bet you would of loved that."

"What, what did you say, John?" Mrs. Bennington asked, eying up Willowdean's black walnut dining room set.

"Nothing, Mrs. Bennington, you just go ahead and enjoy yourself in there," John smirked, lifting his foot to her backside as he headed down the ramp.

Mr. Bennington snickered, pretending not to see John.

He stopped half way down the plank and turned to the rumble of Val's van chugging its way home down Wool Street; his cuss words rattling out his mouth so fast he didn't have time to move his lips.

With cobra-like instincts, Mrs. Bennington sprang from the Mayflower. "My goodness, John," she said pulling a scented handkerchief from the folds of her bosom, giving it a sniff. "That is not how we talk in the presence of a lady!"

John's eyes turned to fire. Mrs. Bennington took a few steps backwards.

"You *better* run," Mosie said tugging the sleeve on Mrs. Bennington's sweater. "I've only seen Pa this mad three times. Believe me, you don't want to see it either."

Hoping to reach Val before John, Mosie hid behind Mrs. Bennington's fanny and gave it a shove to get it started.

Willowdean grabbed Mosie's arm and whisked her into the house. "Stay in here," she said as she headed outside.

Through the living room windows, Mosie watched the collection of longhairs and love beads pour from Val's van. She couldn't see her pa, but she could hear him.

"Son, don't . . . please," he was saying.

Then came the words, the ones she thought her father would never say. The very ones he insisted no man should ever dare utter.

"Begging you . . . I'm . . . I'm begging you, please . . ."

One by one, the group climbed back into the van, including Val.

"Valerie, no—" Mosie heard herself yelling as she raced out the door. This time Willowdean couldn't stop her.

Looking up at Val inside the van, she choked out, "Don't go, please Val, don't go."

He slid his sunglasses on and started the van. He looked at John. John spat on the ground.

"You can protest all you want in Bayfield," Mosie sobbed. "And . . . and. . . . and . . ."

Val kissed his two fingers and placed them on Willowdean's hand. Willowdean grasped them and held them tenderly to her cheek. "There once was a time when your hands fit perfectly inside mine," she said while folding and unfolding her fingers around his. "When you were a little boy learning to walk, you would curl your fingers around mine. Wherever I wanted to go, you would follow." Closing her eyes, she let the memories fill her heart. "It goes quickly, you know."

Val leaned from his window and kissed her. "I love you, Mother," he said, and tenderly stroked her hair. "Tell the old man, no, tell my Father, it took a lot of guts to do what he did. Tell him that I say *thank you.*"

Willowdean pushed down her tears, reached into her pocket, and pulled out a set of keys. "I put your things in our room," she placed them in his hand. "It's bigger."

Mosie moaned. "Ma, no. How, how can you do this?"

"Because it's time," Willowdean wiped their tears with her apron. "Because its time."

Val's smile burned with love. "You'll be okay, both of you, I promise. Ma, you raise that baby good, and Moe, you go get that dog of yours, and I'll catch *you* on the flip side."

In a moment too fast, a moment too soon, Val was gone.

And the crow cawed.

CHAPTER NINE

John couldn't take the driving anymore (or the crying). He figured between Willowdean and Mosie, they had shed 350 miles worth of tears (enough to get them to Tomahawk, Wisconsin). He looked at his wristwatch. "Nine o'clock," he said as they pulled into the hotel parking lot. "It isn't fancy, but it's a place to stay for the night."

Mosie read the billboard painted with a young naked Indian child on it carrying a suitcase. "Alamo Plaza," she said, staring at the kids tanned behind.

"Looks a little like our own little Pocahontas did a few years back," John chuckled. Willowdean pinched his arm.

"Maybe I should just go get us registered," he said, rubbing away the sting.

Mosie snuggled against Willowdean. "I'm scared," she said. "Ma, why do they have that painted on their sign?"

"A marketing idea, I suppose," Willowdean said with a yawn and held her close. "You know, Tomahawks and Indians? There's nothing to be frightened about. We're fine, just fine. And Bayfield's a very nice little town. You'll see."

"I bet Val would protest that, the sign I mean, not the move, he already did that."

"Yes, I suppose he would," Willowdean kissed the top of Mosie's head. "Look, here's your father now."

"Thanks Ma," Mosie whispered, "thanks for letting Val stay at home until he decides to come with us."

Willowdean sighed. "I just hope he can get along with the Benningtons."

Tapping on the window, John proudly held up a key. "Half rate!" he beamed and helped Willowdean out of the Mayflower.

"I'm going to bring in what we need for the night, and then we'll go and get some supper. I heard there's a nice sit-down restaurant in town. Pine, Pine Loft, Pine Stump, Pine, something. I don't know"

The room was small. A bathroom and two beds (one big, one single), and a television that sat on a dresser, its blackness stared at Willowdean and Mosie. The smell of bleachy Comet and Lemon Pledge had long left the room, leaving a mustiness of mildew and old perspiration clinging to the heavy brown drapes and wooly carpeting under their feet. Mosie fell backward on the single sized bed next to the window. She didn't bounce.

"It's just for the night," John said from the doorway.

"Geez, I hope that damn cabin isn't *this* small."

"Mosie!" Willowdean snapped.

"Well, Pa talks like that all time."

Yes, yes he does, but *you* don't."

John waited for Willowdean and Mosie to fall asleep before going outside. He locked the door behind himself, shoved the key in his pocket, and looked up at the white star-specks scattered in the blackness above him. “This is the best damn thing I ever did,” he said as he pulled out a fresh pack of Tareytons. “That city’s a damn prison.”

Looking down at his worn shoes he wondered when he last bothered to buy a new pair. “Val just got some last week.” He looked back at the stars. “I wanted him to see life beyond the city. I wanted him to experience . . . ah-hell,” he cussed as he whipped his cigarette onto the pavement. “Damn kid is still wet behind the ears.” He headed for the small bar across the street and waited for the clock to tick its way to midnight.

Mosie watched his shadow pass the red neon light that blinked behind the window curtain next to her bed and heard him drop the hotel key. He bent over with a slurry curse, picked it up, and then unlocked the door. He staggered across the room and slipped into bed next to Willowdean.

“Stars,” he mumbled. “Hundreds and hundreds. Thousands and thousands . . .” He was drunk, and Mosie knew it.

He didn’t say much more that night or the next morning as they headed up Highway 51 north. Only a wince now and then, and a rub of the forehead (mainly when Mosie or Willowdean whined).

Mosie wanted to tell him he smelled like Val sometimes did when he came home late, but she didn’t. Instead, she slid down between him and Willowdean and politely asked, “Ma, how much further is it?”

“Oh, a good six hours at least,” Willowdean answered, as she blew her nose in an unused napkin.

Mosie sighed and peered over the hood of the Mayflower to watch yet another car pass them.

“Why do they make different colored license plates?” she asked, trying to think of something other than the odor seeping from John (and thoughts of Val staying behind, *and* the fact she and Candy probably would not spend another summer together.)

"Who picks what states get what colors? Why did they make Wisconsin's yellow? Do prisoners really make them? How did all these trees get here? Did someone plant them? Do we have more than one tree at our new house? Am I still going to be able to ride my bike to school? Is there a public swimming pool at the park? Do they have a park? Man, there sure are a lot of trees. Ma, did your family buy all these trees and plant them here. Ma? And why do they call a tree store a nursery?"

John rubbed his eyes. "Mosie, *please* that's enough!"

"Ma, can we change seats?"

Carefully, she climbed over Willowdean making triple sure not to touch her big belly. Willowdean slid next to John and held the napkin to her nose. "Why don't you roll your window down and see if you can spot deer in the woods?" she said. "You might even see a bear. That would be interesting, now wouldn't it?"

Dazed with too many thoughts and too many miles of travel, Mosie rested her chin on the windowsill and let the clean northern air clear her head. She began noticing the land starting to change.

The flat southern Wisconsin pastures were beginning to roll with pine and hardwood trees—the very ones John and Willowdean talked

Dog Island about for so many years, the very ones still covering Willowdean's Wisconsin from so long ago.

The roadside with its wide shoulders of gray gravel, was narrowing and turning brownish red. Finally, no pastures were seen. Only green thick tree branches reaching out as if their very survival depended on touching one another. They were now entering Northern Wisconsin, the outer edge of Iron County. Next stop: Hurley, Wisconsin.

And along that narrow northern roadside, Mosie was able to claim a count of zero bears, one dead bloated deer, and too many thoughts of Granny Blackbird.

CHAPTER TEN

"I don't want to see no ghosts," Mosie spewed as she hid her eyes from the shadows path between the blur of tree. John yanked the cigarette from his mouth, What are you," he scoffed, "some kind of nut?"

"John," Willowdean scolded, "can't you see your daughter's afraid?"

"Afraid, afraid of what? Look at her for Pete's sake. She looks like a silly five-year old. Scared of ghosts. It's stupid! She's twelve, not five. I thought you talked to her about that Mary Worth garbage."

"Oh yeah?" Mosie said pulling her face from her hands. "Well, you know what's stupid? Getting drunk because we had to leave Val behind, *that's* stupid; and at least I'm not stinkin' up this stupid old moving van, and at least—"

John sucked in his lower lip. "Watch who you're calling stupid, little girl; I'm your father, and not some candy-assed kid!" "That's enough, you two," Willowdean barked.

"Well he started it, Ma. Why does he get to call me stupid, and I can't call him it back? It isn't fair."

"*Me?* You're the one who started it, not me," John grumbled.

"Am not," Mosie said.

"Are too."

"Am not!"

"Stop, both of you. And stop this truck right now," Willowdean ordered, pointing her finger at a barrage of brown rock lining the sides of the highway. "And don't argue."

"Oh, for crying out loud," John rubbed the back of his neck. "We're never going to get there at this rate. 'Stop here, John; stop there, John; slow down John, I hear glass tinkling. John-John-John . . ." He pulled off the highway, opened his door, and jumped out. The sound of his work boots crunching across the burnt-brown gravel stopped. He flagged his hand at Mosie.

"Come on," he said. "Your mother wants us out."

"Pa, no. You're being mean and besides, I know this is where Granny Blackbird was standing when you saw her, isn't it?"

Willowdean raised her eyebrows at John. "Yes, yes it is," she answered. "That's why I wanted to stop here. To show our respect for her and for you to see there isn't anything to be afraid of."

Mosie folded her arms and clamped her eyes shut. "One, two, three—Nope, I'm not getting out. Four, five, six—"

"Oh, for the love of . . ." John groaned and propped himself against the van. "What the hell are you counting now?"

"Crickets, the crickets clicking in the ditch. Six, seven, eight—"

"Okay look, maybe I shouldn't have called you stupid. Maybe I should have called you, I don't know, 'scaredy-cat,' instead. Now will you *please* get down here?"

"Nine, ten—well, you shouldn't yell at someone because they're scared, you know. And you shouldn't drink because *you're* scared, either, geez. *That's* really stupid."

“Yeah-yeah. We all do stupid things, now will you *please* get down here?”

“Well, I don’t know. Fifteen, sixteen, seventeen. . . ” John pinched his eyes with his fingers. “Willow!”
“Listen to your father,” she said.

Taking John’s hand, Mosie slid out the van and stood next to him. She tried not looking inside the dark woods. Willowdean scooted across the seat and took John’s hand to help her down. He gave her a cigarette. “Thank you,” she said and kissed his cheek. She headed for the middle of the highway, raised her arms to the pure, clean sky, and said a prayer that came as easy to her, as John’s came to him:

“Oh Great Spirit, whose voice I hear in the winds, and whose breath gives life to everyone, hear me,” she began in her native tongue:

"I come to you as one of your many children. I am weak, I am small. I need your wisdom and your strength. Let me walk in your beauty and make my eyes ever behold the red and purple sunsets.

"Make my hands respect the things you have made and make my ears sharp so I may hear your voice. Make me wise, so that I may understand what you have taught my people and the lessons you have hidden in each leaf and each rock.

"I ask for wisdom and strength, not to be superior to my brothers, but to be able to fight my greatest enemy, myself.

"Make me ever ready to come before you with clean hands and a straight eye, so as life fades away as a fading sunset, my spirit may come to you without shame.”

"What's she's saying?" Mosie whispered, her eyes large as the tires on the Mayflower. "It sounds like witchcraft."

"Your mother doesn't know anything about that stuff. That's a prayer her granny taught her."

"Pa, was her granny a witch?" Mosie asked as she kicked chunks of gravel with the tip of her tennis shoe.

"She was a Midewikwe, what your mother's people call a medicine woman."

"Oh. Pa, did she have any brothers or sisters?"

The tiny wrinkles around John's eyes tightened. He made the sign of the cross while Willowdean sprinkled cigarette tobacco on the highway. "Saint Gertrude, protect the old woman from the flickering flames of purgatory," he said, crossing himself again. Willowdean turned and smiled.

"Pa, why does Ma put tobacco on dead things all the time?"

"It's a blessing of sorts, the way her granny taught her to show God respect for giving us that person or animal. That's what your mother told me, anyway."

"How do we do that? I mean Catholics, how do we show God respect and gratitude?"

John took a puff from his cigarette and squeezed out a look of puzzlement. "By being good Catholics."

"Oh," Mosie flipped pebbles over with her foot. "Will Ma put tobacco on you when you die?"

"Yeah, I suppose she will."

"What if I die, or Val; do you think she would then? Would she go and put ashes on me?" John didn't answer.

"Pa, why are the rocks and dirt here reddish-brown?"

"Iron, lots of iron. At one time, these parts had some of the best iron ore mines in the country. That's why they named this, Iron County," he watched Willowdean crossing the road. She stood next to him. They stared at the tobacco on the highway. "I miss her too," John said while kissing her on the forehead.

Mosie climbed up into the Mayflower and looked back at the black splat on the road where granny once stood. *I can't wait to tell Candy about this,* she thought. *It sure looks like witchcraft to me.*

Playfully, John winked at Willowdean and turned over the engine. "Pasty Joe's, here we come," he said, tooting the horn. "Pasty Joe's or bust!"

"Pasty Joe's?" Mosie asked.

"Yep, Pasty Joe's," John repeated as he pulled out onto the highway. "It's in Ironwood. Ironwood, Michigan, an old mining town just under the overhead bridge in Hurley. They have the best pastys around, been in business since 1946! That's twenty-six years, twenty-six years selling nothing but pastys, and they're still in business. Probably will be, even into the next century. I haven't had one since I took Val deer hunting that year up in Bayfield."

"Yeah," Mosie said, "but what the heck's a pasty?"

"A meat and potato pie, with or without onions, with or without rutabagas. You eat them with ketchup, without ketchup, with gravy, without gravy, or just plain. The miners ate them. They'd stick them next to the light on their helmets to keep them warm 'til they had a chance to eat . . ." he went on, as they sailed down Highway 51.

There wasn't much to look at except more trees, a dead porcupine and a few lonely houses.

CHAPTER ELEVEN

Mosie's head bounced softly against John's arm while she slept. Willowdean watched the late afternoon clouds changing from dollops of whipped cream into early evening smears of orange chiffon. Her thoughts rolled back to the years she spent living with her Grandfather Sweetwater and Granny Blackbird; eight more miles and they would be passing through the Bad River Indian Reservation in Odanah, Wisconsin-once her home.

"Hello darling, nice to see you . . . it's been a long-time . . ."

John twanged with Conway Twitty on the radio. He turned himself (and Conway) down.

"You okay, Willow?"

"I will be," she answered, stifling a sob.

John dug in his pocket. "Look at those beautiful black eyes of yours," he said, handing her his handkerchief. "Honey, what's wrong?"

"Oh, just foolishness, I guess. Taking a song like that to heart. I didn't realize how much time has passed since I've been gone." She stared at the clouds growing dim with the sky and sniffled again. "I can't help wondering if Grandfather forgave me for leaving."

John looked down at Mosie's head that was gently bobbing on his arm. "Is she still sleeping?" he asked. "Or is she playing possum?" "She's asleep," Willowdean said as she studied Mosie's eyelids.

"Good," John said. "Look Willow, it was different back then, not like nowadays. We made the best decision we knew at that time. You know Lenny would never have kept his mouth shut. If he would had, maybe we could have stayed." He took a drag from his smoke and glanced down at Mosie.

"It's too bad Lenny and Corrine didn't leave town sooner. Two peas in a pod, those two."

Willowdean blew her nose. "It's funny isn't it, how one night can change so many lives, even in families."

"How much did she hear us talking, you know, that Sunday? Did Val say anything to you?"

"No, no he didn't. But he did ask me to thank you. He said it took a lot of guts to do what you did. He *does* love you, John."

John sat back and tossed his cigarette out the window. He turned up the radio.

"John, I know he meant it. I'm just afraid if Mosie finds out why we left Bayfield in the first place we'll end up losing her. She's already ashamed."

"Ashamed? Ashamed of what?"

"Of me, John, of her heritage. Did you know she rarely will go into a store with me? When Mother Prudence would call, I knew what the fights were about even if Mother Prudence didn't, or at least pretended she didn't."

"Ah come on now Willow, all kids go through that teasing crap. Hell, I was embarrassed of my old man and old lady, too. Until I figured out I was too old to care what other people thought." The fine thin lines around John's mouth crinkled into a smile. "Matter of fact, I was thirty-seven years old when I figured that one out."

"Oh John," Willowdean said. "You *are* thirty-seven." John chuckled.

"This is a different type of shame," Willowdean said. "I just hope we don't lose her like we did Val."

"You didn't lose him, Willie," John turned on the headlights. "He just needs time to think things through, that's all. He'll come around." Grabbing Willowdean's hand, he gave it a tender squeeze. "You're a good mother, and you did a good job raising him. But now, he has to do the rest of his growing on his own, like we did, that's all."

Willowdean peered down at Mosie.

"Ah shit, don't you worry about her Willow," John laughed. "That kid's got spunk. Had it the moment she was born, screaming her head off like she did. I swear just being born pissed her off right from the start. And her questions! How many questions can a kid ask in one day?"

"In a day?" Willowdean laughed. "Try an hour!"

John patted her knee. "Feel better now?"

"Yes, yes I do," she sighed. "Except I am a little nervous coming back. Are you sure Lenny and Corrine are gone?"

John pointed to an open strip of woods. "Say, we're almost to Ashland. Look."

Through the moonlight, Willowdean caught glimpses of dark, inky water; its thickness swelling the bank ran along the highway. With it came memories of the Great Lake. Watching it push itself back into the blackness from whence it came, Willowdean whispered . . . "Hello Gichigami; it's been eighteen years since I've seen you."

Eighteen more miles they'd be home.

"Home," Willowdean said, watching house lights twinkle on the hills of Bayfield in the distance. Gently, she nudged Mosie. "We're home."

Mosie sat up blinking at the night. Her questions coming so fast she barely took a breath. "This is Bayfield? This is where we're going to live? It's so small! Where's our house? Can I feed the deer when they come into the yard? Is that Lake Superior? *It's huge!* Can we swim in it? Can we go see it right now? Can I bring my dog there?"

"Settle down," John chuckled and shook his head. "We can't fly you know. We live about two more miles on the other side of town, down on Highway 13."

Mosie watched the muted glow of Bayfield's streetlights and flickering television sets turn into tiny specks. Then, within a blink, all the golden dots were gone. No headlights, no red tail lights from other cars passing inside a darkness she had never seen before.

John slowed down. "Is this it?" he asked.

"Yes, yes, this is it," Willowdean answered anxiously as she leaned forward and grabbed the dash.

With an exaggerated grunt, John turned the steering wheel to the right and navigated up the dirt driveway. Mosie clung to the dashboard and closed her eyes. It was there in the darkness of the North Woods, and its unquenchable quiet that the Mayflower stopped.

Mosie swallowed. The blood rushed through her and crackled in her ears.

"Well, the yard light still works," John said. "See, that's our yard light. Without it, we wouldn't be able to see our hands in front of us."

Mosie looked down at her fingers and wiggled them. Pa was right. "Are there bears here?" she asked.

"Bears? Why sure, of course. There's bear and deer and just about anything else you can think of. The hunting's good on our land, that's one reason I kept it, so Val and I can . . ."

Willowdean stifled a sob. So did Mosie. She wanted to tell John they should go back to their real home, back to Val and Candy and Mr. and Mrs. Bennington and their roses. But she didn't. She kept her eyes on John and watched him open the door of the Mayflower.

"Well Mrs. Bitmen," he reached his hand up to Willowdean, "what do you say I carry you over that threshold *one* more time?"

"Well, *Mr.* Bitmen, I suppose it *is* the proper thing to do after all." She tucked away her tears and took John's hand to let him guide her onto the soft, damp ground.

"Just one moment, my dear," he reached back up to the van.

"This time I have *two* beautiful young ladies to attend to."

He lifted Mosie out of the truck, tenderly took both their hands, and led them to the front door of the house. Opening it, he flipped on the lights. Willowdean gasped.

CHAPTER TWELVE

MONDAY, JUNE 5, 1972

Dear Candy,

How are you? How is your mom? Fine I hope. I am good.

Ma and I have been busy putting everything away. Some of her good china got broke when we went to Pasty Joe's in Ironwood Michigan. They sure do have a lot of potholes there in Ironwood. Pa said it's because of the frost in the winter. He said they have to heat the graveyards in the winter otherwise the frost will push the caskets out of the ground. This way it keeps them from popping up especially in the spring. He's is very busy with his new boat business and has been working long hours.

Our new house is a log home, not a cabin like I said it was. Pa said people like the Benningtons' would give their firstborn to have a house like this. I don't think I would. He surprised Ma and had most of the inside redone before we got here. She said it does not look anything like it did before.

It is bigger than our old house. The kitchen is nice and has what Ma calls a snack bar instead of just a plain old counter. When I do the dishes, I can see trees in the backyard instead of the Bennington's.

The living room is big but not too big. It has a fireplace. Pa said it will help heat the house in the winter. My bedroom is upstairs. It really freaks me out. Ma ordered a new blue shag carpet for it because all the floors are made of wood and squeak a lot when I walk around up there.

It is bigger than my old bedroom and has a window with a desk under it. I climb out the window and sit on the roof of the back porch and look all over the yard and down the driveway which is just plain old dirt and gravel!!! Can you believe that??? Also the dirt up here is reddish-brown because there is so much iron in the ground.

I like the yard. It is huge and has lots of trees. I haven't counted all of them yet but so far I did count twenty-three. They go all the way around the yard and into the woods. Those I do not like so much. Pa took me back there and I got freaked out so he had to bring me back home. I just know there is a bear in there, maybe even two, possibly three.

The garage is big. It is full of our stuff right now but as soon as it is cleared out, I'm going to make my own apartment in it. How cool is that? We do not have any neighbors but there are a few houses and a couple of old shacks a mile or so down the road on the way to town. I have not seen anyone come out of them so I do not know if anyone lives in them. Pa said some are just summer homes and some are not. Next time I ride my bike to town I will try to find out.

Ma does not like me riding my bike on the highway because of the semi-trucks. But if I beg her long enough she'll give in and let me. Pa told her he does not care if I ride my bike to town as long as I do not get killed.

Ma got mad at him. I think it is because she is pragnent (pregnant).

The air here smells good like Pa said it would, but I definitely miss the smell of the tar and diesel mix down by the train tracks.

It is very quiet here, especially at night. It is very dark so I keep a night-light on in my room so I can see. I can hear frogs, crickets, and things like that when I go to sleep and sometimes during the day too.

We also have a yard light that looks and works like a street light. I haven't gone outside at night too much, unless Pa or Ma are out there because there are bears here and all kinds of wild animals. I think I would scream my head off if I saw a bear. Ma said if I ever did see a bear I should play dead instead.

Bayfield is small but the streets are farout!! They are at least fifty times bigger than Summit Street! On the way to town I have to go up one of the biggest hills in Bayfield. It's called Kill-Deer Hill because someone is always running over a deer on it.

I go to Lake Superior a lot and eat ice cream at Mr. Macki's Maki's. Ma knew him when she was a girl. She said he is nice but I don't think so. He only has 3 kinds of ice cream but I have an idea for him.

I cannot weight wait for you to see the lake. It is way better than Lake Michigan, except it is very cold and you cannot really swim in it until July. There is a lot I want to tell you but if I do, I will have to write this letter all day and into the night. Pa said the phone should be in at the end of next week so I will call you at that time. Man, I can't wait to hear your voice. I don't have a dog yet but Pa promised I can get one pretty soon. I wonder what kind it will be. I cannot wait.

By the way, if you see Val, tell him I miss him very much and I will write him about some protesting him and his friends can do in Tomahawk, Wisconsin.

Also, I have four plans for us so far and have all the information written in my notebook.

Here they are:

(1) Go see where Ma's granny visited her and where Ma put tobacco on the highway (it looked like witchcraft to me even though Pa said it wasn't!)

(2) Eat pastys from Pasty Joe's in Ironwood, Michigan

(3) Look at the huge statue of Hiawatha (Ayenwatha as Ma calls him) (Also in Ironwood Michigan)

(4) Go bug Mr. Maki and eat ice cream by Lake Superior

Well, I better go so I can put this in the mailbox. Here in Bayfield we put our letters in the mailbox at the end of the driveway and put the red metal flag up so the postman knows he has to pick up some letters to mail for us. Everyone does it here. Isn't that cool?

Write soon.
Sincerely,
Your best friend,
Mosie Bitmen

P.S. I haven't made any friends yet, so don't worry, you are still my best friend and always will be forever (even if I do make friends here).

P.S.S. If you see Judy Lard-you know what, tell her I DO NOT miss her ugly face AT ALL!!!!!!

"Miss Candy M. Nelson, 628 Prospect Street, Barrington Ill. 60010," Mosie said out loud as she made sure her penmanship on the front of the envelope was extra neat. She gave the backside a lick and looked up at Willowdean, who was squirting a stream of green Palmolive Dish Washing Liquid into the sink.

"Ma, does that really soften your hands while you do dishes? What about, Ajax? Does it really leave your dishes squeaky clean? Do the suds really last from the first glass to the last greasy casserole dish?"

Willowdean sighed and turned up the radio.

"This is Tom Major and you're listening to WATW, Ashland and Bayfield County' s number one country station. And now here' s a question from Mr. Charlie Pride for all you fellows out there: Have you kissed your angel good morning?"

"Boy, *Pa sure* did, didn't he?" Mosie giggled and pointed to Willowdean's stomach. "And he sure did, '*love her like the devil when he got back home," too*, hey Ma?

"Hey Ma, since we do practically live on the moon, can I use one of your special edition Space Rover stamps? Ma, when do you think Pa will get me a dog?"

Willowdean shuddered. "Mosie, *please*, that's enough. No, I don't know when your father plans on getting you a dog, and no, you may not use my Rover Space stamps. I'm saving those, just use a plain stamp.

"I'll tell you what," Willowdean hurried to get Mosie a dollar from her purse. "Your father forgot his lunch again. Why don't you bring it to him? I'll give you some money and you can get an ice cream cone. Just watch for those darn semi-drivers; for some reason, they don't seem to know what 'yield to pedestrians' means."

Mosie knew the baby sleeping inside her ma was doing more than making her cry a bit more than usual. It was also making her crabbier than usual.

"Sure, I can do that," Mosie said as she grabbed Candy's letter. Standing inside the porch, she looked at Willowdean's dream catcher (once again hanging from the ceiling). And once again, she curled her lip at it. "Like it or not, you kind of do make it feel a little more like home," she said while tugging its feathers "just in case."

She opened the porch screen door, jumped off the steps onto the ground, grabbed her bright yellow ten-speed, Schwinn Super Sport, and slid John's lunchbox onto the handlebars. "After all, like Pa says, 'If the air is clean, and the birds are singing, and you got two bits in your pocket, life is good.'"

Making her way down the driveway, the lunchbox clanking all the way, Mosie put Candy's letter into the mailbox. "Bet she's at the library this very minute, sitting in the back reading a book, eating something soft and quiet like Hostess Twinkies, and wondering what I'm doing. Probably, between all of them tears of course," she thought. "And Sister Vern Mary, I bet she's kneeling in church right now, praying for God to keep me safe." She turned onto Highway 13, and so did her logic for becoming a nun.

"For two reasons," she said. "So not to have to get married and get pregnant like Ma, and two, so as not to be called an old maid like Miss Quincy, the librarian. Except I'll be the girls' physical education teacher, otherwise I'd have to be quiet all day, what with all that praying and confessing.

"Until then," she zipped between the faded white lines dividing the highway and gave them a count, "I guess I'll just have to spend all my time down at Mr. Maki's Novelty & Gift Shop by the beach, eating ice cream on his bench, and watching the seagulls swoop in from the lake."

Mosie slipped the lunch pail off her handlebars, stuck the bike's kickstand in the ground, and studied the shop sign John had special made—a fleet of boats floating carefree through turbulent blue waves.

Except for the two rowboats displayed on each side of the office door, *Bitmen's Fish N' Boat* looked and smelled like any other manufacturing plant with its smell of glue and bitter resin seeping from its long concrete walls, and mysterious rumbles mingling with grinding saws. Mosie walked up to the door and opened it.

"Good morning, Miss Bitmen," Ms. Bartelo's perky voice chirped.

Mosie liked Ms. Bartelo (and her smile). She liked how her orange painted lips drew back to reveal the whitest teeth she had ever seen. Even more, she liked the way Ms. Bartelo's long blonde hair sat on top of her head, pinned with a thick stick slid through a big leather buckle. And she admired the black velvet choker she always wore. But best of all, she liked how Ms. Bartelo didn't stare at her the way her Pa's old secretaries did.

"Mosie, just call me Mosie, everyone else does," she smiled and peeked around the door into the main shop. She knew not to go by John, especially when he was busy showing new employees how to do their jobs. *Men get thinking about stuff other than what's in front of them,* he once explained.

Giving him a quick wave, Mosie held up his lunch box. His face wrung with annoyance.

"I can take that," Ms. Bartelo offered, getting up from her desk.

"Oh, it's okay; thanks though. Pa's coming now."

Ms. Bartelo quickly sat down, pulled out some files, and began marking the papers inside.

“Hey Pa, you forgot your lunch. Ma asked me to bring it to you.”

“Yeah, yeah,” he grumbled, took her arm, and shoved her out the door. He rubbed the back of his neck and pulled out a smoke.

Mosie, rolling her lips back like Ms. Bartelo, smiled at him. John gave her a queer look. “What’s wrong with you?” “Nothing Pa,” she tucked her lips back into place.

“Next time, just give my lunch to my secretary,” he told her.

Studying the black grease trapped in the creases of his worn face, Mosie tried picturing him squeaky clean like Mr. Larson and smelling crispy-spicy like the Hai Karate cologne he always wore.

“Big-shot pencil pusher that one is,” John would point out when people like Mr. Larson were mentioned or came around his shop. “He wouldn’t know how to get grease off a monkey’s ass if his life depended on it. Those soft hands of his hands are as useless as butterfly wings.”

Once Val explained, “That’s how our father describes anyone who has to wear a tie for a living instead of grease.”

“Pa,” Mosie asked, “how does a monkey go about getting grease on its, *you know what* . . . its behind? And if it did, how would a person go about getting it off?”

John rolled his eyes. “What the hell kind of question is that?”

“I don’t know,” Mosie said as she kicked the sandy dirt on the ground. “I miss you.”

A grin slipped from the corner of John’s mouth. “Well, I miss you, too,” he said. “But right now, I don’t have time for any of that mushy stuff. And I don’t have an answer for your question right now either. The main machine is giving us grief." He coughed and pulled out his hankie. "Your mother okay?" he asked, blowing his nose.

"I guess. She's the same. Sort of crabby." Mosie scrunched her nose at the sun. "Hey Pa, when do you think I can get a dog?"

"When I get some damn time to go look at some." He threw his smoke on the ground and smashed it with his resin-covered boot. "Here," he shoved his handkerchief back in his pocket and pulled out his wallet. "Here's a few bucks. Go get an ice cream or a burger or something. I have to get back in there."

Mosie watched him lumber back to the shop. "And let your mother know I should be home for supper tonight." "Pa?" she said, gripping the handlebars on her bike.

He turned to her with an impatient look.

"See you tonight," she smiled.

His face softened. He gave her a wink.

She smiled back, not with Ms. Bartelo lips this time, but her own.

"Chocolate, vanilla or one of those twist cones, it's like deciding between Coca-Cola or Pepsi Cola," Mosie thought as she coasted to Mr. Maki's next to the lake.

The beach's only inhabitants were a young boy running in front of an old man and an old woman hobbling beside the lakes lazy waves.

On Mr. Maki's bench, a skinny teenage girl sat and feverishly licked her cone. *Bet she don't have an ounce of brains in that head of hers*, Mosie thought sneaking her eyes over the lanky teenager.

The strap to her halter top rested half-way down her arm, revealing a feathery birthmark on her bony shoulder similar in size and shape of Val's *special mark*, as Ma called it.

Instead of pulling up her strap, the girl twirled a strand of her thin, mousey brown hair. Her green-hazel eyes, smothered with blue eye shadow, and outlined with thick black eye liner, gawked at Mosie's Super Sport propped next to the dilapidated boy's bike lying in the sand patch in front of the stairs leading up to Mr. Maki's deck.

"Hope she's gone by the time I get back out here," she thought as she ran up Mr. Maki's steps. She opened the door.

From over his gold, wire-rimmed eyeglasses resting on the tip of his nose Mr. Maki peered at her. "You again?" he continued to wipe the counter in front of him. "You come to harass me some more about my ice cream?"

"Well, not harass, exactly," Mosie replied while looking through the glass top of the ice cream freezer chest.

"One, two—Mr. Maki, you have only three different flavors of ice cream, chocolate, vanilla and twist, which really is not just one flavor, but two in one, and it's not really ice cream, not really. It's a soft-serve."

"Yes, and you expect more? Every time you expect more. Why you come in here, always asking for more? Is not three enough for anyone?"

"Well, I'm glad you asked," Mosie leaned on the cold glass panel attempting another, *Ms. Bartelo smile*. "I think I might have a business deal for you that you can't refuse."

Mr. Maki gave her a stiff look and kept mopping the counter. "What, you think because your papa owns the new boat factory you can come here and harass me about my ice cream? If you were my little girl, I would put you over my knee and give you a good lickin' for harassing old men and their ice cream."

Mosie giggled. "Mr. Maki, I bet if you ordered just two more flavors for one week, you would make enough profit to buy two more flavors the following week."

He shook his head with a growl.

"See, down in Barrington, we have a special establishment catering specifically to only ice cream. It's called Baskin-Robbins 31 Flavors, but it has a heck of a lot more than just thirty-one flavors.

"See, my best friend Candy Nelson and I, well, we tried each one at least three or four times last summer."

"Yah and where do you think I will put all these, *thirty-one flavors*? Hmm? You think these freezers are cheap, hmm? Let me tell you little girl, they are *not* cheap!

"Now, what flavor you want today? I am a busy man and do not have time for such nonsense. Thirty-one flavors of ice cream," he mumbled, reaching for a plain, white cone. Picking up his ice cream scoop, he held it in his large pudgy hand ready to take Mosie's order.

"I'll have one scoop of pistachio and one scoop walnut, please."

"But I *have no* pistachio and no walnut. *Please* little girl, what do you want? Some Chocolate, hmm? Some nice vanilla, or maybe one scoop each, or maybe I get you a nice twisty from the twisting machine."

"I'll give you two dollars, one dollar for each scoop of pistachio and one dollar each scoop of walnut instead of one dollar for two scoops of chocolate, or vanilla."

Mr. Maki scratched his round, bald-head. Keeping his tiny blue eyes on her, he took out the small spiral notebook and pencil tucked in the front pocket of his apron. He licked the pencil tip and wrote the numbers.

"I-yi-yi. If I had pistachio and walnut, I would give them to you for that price. But I do not. Now, what do you want? Chocolate or maybe some nice vanilla?"

"What if you sold ten people one scoop pistachio and one scoop walnut, and ten more people just one scoop each, how much would that be?"

Again, Mr. Maki put his pencil to his little pad of paper.

"Mmm, that equals . . . forty, forty dollars, yes?"

"Yes. And what if you sold those same people one scoop vanilla and one scoop chocolate? How much would that be?"

"That equal . . . twenty dollars."

Again, Mr. Maki scratched his head at the numbers. "Ahh, I see!"

"Now, during the tourist season, how many customers do you have that buy ice cream?"

"Ah, a lot, yes," he chuckled, his fat round belly bouncing under his apron. He leaned on the counter. "You know for a little girl you are not such a dum-dum. But ugh! Them freezers, ah, now that costs money. Money I no longer have." Straightening up he sighed, grabbing his ice cream scoop. "Now, what would you like? Some chocolate, hmm? Maybe some nice vanilla? A twisty cone?"

"What if you could rent your freezers until you were able to pay them off?"

"No, too much business risk."

"What if I made a contract with you, that if you cannot pay off your new freezers by the end of summer, you can have my ten-speed Schwinn Super Sport? It's worth lots of money, probably as much as one freezer."

"Hmph, and your papa, he would let you do such a thing? Why would you do this?"

"Because I want one scoop of pistachio, one scoop of walnut."

"I-yi-*yi*," Mr. Maki said, shaking his head, wiping the sweat from the fat lines in his brow with his apron.

"Then it is a deal, yes?" Mosie said.

"Yes, it is a deal."

Mosie took Mr. Maki's plump hand into hers, giving it a shake.

As she headed down the steps, she licked her triple scoop of each flavored ice cream and plunked on the bench next to the lean girl with too long of legs. The girl reached inside her halter top, yanked out a packet of chewing gum, and shoved a piece into her mouth.

"It's funny," Mosie said, licking her cone.

"What, what's funny, my gum? Or getting three scoops of icecream; *that's* funny?" the girl rolled her eyes and stretched her skinny legs out in-front of herself.

"No, not your gum or these three scoops of ice-cream. I mean it's funny how something simple like an ice cream cone can change a person's whole life. Not just for an afternoon or even a week or just a summer but a *whole* life."

The girl gave Mosie a blank look. "You're not from around here, are ya?" she asked.

"No, I wasn't, but I am now I guess," Mosie held out her free hand for a shake. "I'm Katherine Rose Bitmen, but everybody calls me Mosie. I'm glad to meet you."

The girl stared at Mosie's dark fingers. "Well, I ain't no Margaret or Marjorie," she said, giving Mosie's hand a weak bounce. "I'm Peggy. And no, I don't have a middle name, and I ain't got a nickname either."

CHAPTER THIRTEEN

"Do we have any Hostess Ding-Dongs?" Mosie asked as she shoved a box of Crunch 'n Munch inside Willowdean's red-plaid, Green-Stamp picnic basket.

"In the next cupboard over," Willowdean said with a yawn and pushed her morning toast to the side. "What did you say this girl's name was?"

"Ma, I told you and Pa last night, it's Peggy, just plain old Peggy, remember? And Pa said she can't be Catholic with a name like that; and then he said, no saints are named Peggy, so that proves she isn't Catholic. You laughed and told him to stop being a clod, remember?"

"Did she say who her parents are?" Willowdean watched Mosie put on her shoes.

"Ma, kids do not go asking other kids that stuff. Geez, that is sooo not cool."

"Oh yes, how foolish of me to forget such a thing," Willowdean pulled herself out of her chair. "Maybe I should drive you and—" "Ma, geez, you're treating me like a baby, again. We're just going to the beach then a bike ride, so don't worry, okay? Are you going to be okay while I'm gone?"

"Yes, fine," Willowdean sat down. "Just be careful and watch out for those trucks, and cars. And don't try swimming--that water is too cold yet. You might get hypothermia, and . . ."

Willowdean's warnings were fresh as the early sultry air that rose from Lake Superior to the top of Kill-Deer Hill. Mosie perched on her bike and looked down at the tiny village with its cottages scattered in the hills that sprawled before the lake.

Pulling her feet from her bike pedals she launched off Kill-Deer Hill, and began sailing down Highway 13. Holding her speed all the way to Wing Avenue, she turned safely onto Washington and waved to Mr. Maki who was sweeping the sand and dirt from the deck of his shop.

"You want ice cream today?" he lifted his tiny blue eyes to her as she coasted to the bench. He put down his broom and wiped his hands on his apron.

"No, not today, Mr. Maki. Thank you though," Mosie said and pulled the picnic basket from her handlebars. She cussed as she stepped over the same scrappy (half-blue, half-red) boy's bike that was still lying in the identical spot from yesterday.

"Mmph, you got a mouth like a sailor boy," Mr. Maki said as he shoved his fists into his spongy sides.

"Well, for Pete's sake," Mosie tugged the back of her shorts. "Why would anyone leave their bike lying right where people walk?" She gave the bike a kick with the tip of her Keds. "At least the thing has good tires," she said with a grumble. "No fenders, but good tires."

"Yes, I know," said Mr. Maki. "I tell them kiddos, but they don't listen to old men."

"Were you able to find the freezers?" Mosie asked.

"I'll find out about the freezers when my distributor comes this week. Then I let you know, okay?"

"Okay. Hey, did you see that Peggy girl around here this morning? She's about half a foot taller than me, wears lots of makeup, skinny as a beanpole?"

Picking up his broom Mr. Maki started sweeping again. "Yes, I know this Peggy girl," he said, narrowing his eyes. "Why you want that girl, hmm?"

Mosie dangled the basket at him. "We're going to have a picnic and maybe go for a bike ride."

Mr. Maki snorted. "Ha! If you were my little girl . . ." he said, nodding toward the beach. "But I no stick my nose in other people's business."

Mosie scanned the shoreline and spotted Peggy stretched out on the beach. After hurrying down she plunked the basket next to her and unrolled her beach towel with a flick. She sat down. Peggy immediately started chattering about boys and how they swarm to her like bees to a honey-stick.

"Well, my pa is getting me a dog," Mosie butted in.

"Big deal," Peggy snipped. "Boys are way better than some stupid dog."

That's when Mosie realized three things about this Peggy girl:

1. *She definitely is not nothing like Candy Nelson*
2. *It isn't Peggy those boys are necessarily interested in*
3. *Maybe Pa's right; being fourteen, Peggy might be too old for me*

Peggy picked up her half-used bottle of QT tanning lotion and started greasing herself all the while rattling on about, "Clint Burgman and Kent, Kent Pankow—"

Mosie faked a choke. "Must have swallowed a bug," she rasped, sat up, and clenched her knees. She wanted to tell Peggy her mascara was melting under her eyes, and that she looked more orange than tan, and how the birthmark on her shoulder looked almost just like Val's, but she didn't.

"Lake Michigan is big, too," she said to change the subject. She picked up a handful of sand and rubbed the warm grit against her shins. "Everyone knows it's polluted, though. It's pretty mucky and smells like rotten fish, and you can't swim in it too long otherwise you break out in a rash and get sick. My brother, Val, and his friends are protesting to get it cleaned up. I bet they do it, too. He protests lots of stuff. Boy, I sure do miss him and my friend Candy. It's so different up here. You have any brothers or sisters?"

Peggy lay there; she responded with a few slothful snores and smacked her lips like a baby seagull begging for more fish.

"Yep," Mosie said, grabbing a Twinkie. "It sure is different up here."

She looked out at the lake and counted the silver waves rolling onto the shoreline. "Twenty," she yawned, licking creamy white-fluff from her fingers. She looked at sleeping Peggy. Mosie got up, walked to the edge of the sand, and gazed into the hazy horizon. The chill of the Great Lake swallowed her ankles. *I bet Ma dug her feet in this very spot*, she thought and scrunched her feet past the small smooth rocks.

Her toes found their way into the layer of sand and sunk inside the warmth underneath.

"I bet she had long hair like Val's, but with two braids, not one," she said to the sky, envisioning her ma as a young Indian princess. "And I bet she wore a beaded headband with a feather in it too, even prettier than her medicine bag. And a dog. I bet she had a dog. No, a wolf, Ma had a wolf!" She looked at Peggy napping contently in the sun and then turned back to the water to focus on the mound of pine trees looming out from the water, two miles from where she stood. It was an island.

"Madeline Island, home of the Golden Woodpecker," she whispered into the balmy breeze. "The first of the Twenty-two Apostle Islands. Twenty-three really, counting Dog Island."

She knew the islands were sacred to her mother's people and how to her father's, they meant money. For her, they were a mystery. That's when she got the idea. A notion even Val and his friends would think twice about. She raced back to Peggy. "You got any wood lying around your house?" she asked eagerly, jabbing Peggy with her toe. Peggy groaned.

"What you want with wood?"

"How much do you have?" Peggy didn't answer.

"Come on let's go," Mosie barked as she put on her Keds. Peggy didn't move. "I mean it, I'm leaving." Still nothing. "Okay, that's it. I'm taking off, with or without you." Mosie put on her shoes and tied them.

Peggy rolled over on her stomach. "Where, where you going?" she asked, lazily. "There ain't no place to go, this is it."

Bending down, Mosie ran her fingers through the sand. She squinted at the lake. "You ever been out there, out to Dog Island?" she asked, licking the sweat from her lips. The screech of seagulls and water lapping the shore filled the air.

"Have I ever been out *there*?" Peggy laughed. "Course I've been out there. Most guys around here do have boats, you know. And no, I haven't been to Dog Island. No one has. It's just a stupid story. It don't exist."

Mosie stared at the lake. It was almost the same azure-blue as the sky. "You don't suppose any of those boys you know would take me out there, do you?"

This time Peggy sat up. "Hey, what are ya', a boy moocher?" she snarled, brushing sand from her thin arms. Struggling to her feet, she clenched her towel and took a step toward Mosie. "Just 'cause your one of those rich, spoiled brats from Chicago and your dad owns the boat factory, don't think you're gonna get those city meat hooks of yours into any of *my* boyfriends!"

"What are you, nuts?" Mosie said, springing to her feet. "I don't care about boys—any boys—especially ones that go around doing things they oughtn't be doing. And we are *not* rich."

Peggy took a step closer. "What's all that supposed to mean?"

"Well, for your information, even if I *were* interested in boys and all that kissing crap, which I am *not*, it'll be the day I become someone's Katherine Rose, and he'll love me for me, not because I let him kiss on me, like *you* do."

Mosie bent down and shoved the Crunch N' Munch and

Twinkies back inside the picnic basket. "Well, you just stay here and wait for those stupid old boys. I'll figure out how to get to Dog Island all by myself, and when I do you'll be sorry. *I'm* the one who's going to find it, and *I'm* the one who everyone will be calling Bayfield's greatest hero explorer, *not you*!" She snatched her towel, headed up the beach to Mr. Maki's, and kicked up sprays of sand with her feet.

"Wait," Peggy yelled, running behind her. "I'll get you all the wood you need." Picking up the old ratty boy's bike laying in the sand, she swung her long legs over its duct-taped seat. Mosie looked up at Mr. Maki standing behind the door.

"You want a Ding Dong for the road?" she asked Peggy and dove her hand into the picnic basket. Peggy grinned as she grabbed the little brown cylinder wrapped in cellophane.

"I-yi-yi . . ." Mr. Maki frowned, watching them ride off.

"What ya' want to go out to Dog Island for anyway?" Peggy asked as they pedaled past Wing Avenue.

Mosie slowed down waiting for her to catch up. "To get a dog, what else?"

Peggy rolled her eyes. "You really are from the city, ain't ya'? I'm tellen' ya, there ain't no Dog Island. Even if there was, that ain't how you go about getting a dog."

"Aren't you, not 'ain't ya,'" Mosie corrected. "Man, what kind of school do you go to? Car!" She flagged Peggy to the side of the road.

"If you want a dog so bad, why don't ya' just go over to Mrs. Morgan's place? That's where everyone goes when they want a dog. She always has a batch of poodles running around her place. Beagles, too, if you're looking for a hound. She'll give ya' one for twenty-five bucks, no questions asked."

"No, no thanks, no poodles for this chick. Pothole! See, the way I figure it, since this is my first dog, it has to be special, really special, so I'm going right to the source, right to Dog Island itself."

"Yeah?" Peggy laughed. "Well, how do all those *special* dogs get from there to here, huh?"

Mosie cleared her throat. "Where do you live anyway?" she asked. "We're already half way to my house."

Peggy sped up. "Turn right at the next mailbox."

"Right? There's nothing down there," Mosie yelled over her shoulder.

"Just do it." Peggy huffed, trying to keep up.

Rounding past an old beat-up mailbox, Mosie turned onto a pitted lane strangled with swamp pine, and wild shrubs. Peggy's tires crunched behind her. Mosie's stomach tightened. She stopped, catching her breath. In front of her stood a small, two-story shack. Patches of brown shingles were stapled to its sides, hung in slapdash fashion. Mounds of trash lay burrowed beneath the weed-infested yard.

Peggy dropped her bike and headed to a sagging clothesline strung from one dead tree to the next. Plucking off a stiff, weathered dried shirt, she slipped it on. She looked at Mosie and frowned, her voice rasping with disappointment. "After everything you said, I thought you were different. But you ain't," she said as she pulled her blouse shut. "I can see it on your face."

She stomped to the house and climbed a stack of bricks that led to a door made from a fresh sheet of plywood. "That's okay," she spat as she tugged the wood-block door handle. "You just go find yourself another spoiled rich kid to hang with."

"Oh yeah?" Mosie snipped as she yanked up her shorts. "Well, you're snotty, and at least I'm not a snob who looks like a, sweet potato."

"Agh! A *sweet potato*?" Peggy spun around to face Mosie.

"Yes, an undercooked, practically raw, sweet potato that acts like all tuffy-assed!"

Peggy gave the door a hard kick. This time it sprang open with a wobble. Turning, she stuck her tongue out at Mosie.

"Wait," Mosie yelled, watching her disappear into the house. "I'm not spoiled; I've never had any friends either, except Candy. And she's really pudgy 'cause of her low blood-sugar', and she cries *all* the time, and nobody likes her, except me, and nobody likes me except Candy!"

"Oh yeah?" Peggy sniveled as she peeked out from the shadows of the house. "I bet you're just saying that," she hid her runny nose in her shirtsleeve.

"No, really, go ask my ma, she'll tell you. And you know why my hair's so short? She keeps cutting it. She thinks it'll make the kids at school stop teasing me for being . . . well, you know. But it don't. My brother Val had to show me how to wet it down with my ma's Dippity-Do until it grows back a little. Do spoiled rich kids have to do *that*?"

Peggy folded her arms. "Well, I don't know. You are kind of a bossy-big-mouth. And I don't really care for bossy-big-mouths. And you swear a lot, too."

"Oh yeah? Well, you know what your problem is? You're not very good at making friends when you have the chance, being the snob that *you* are. Matter of fact, your sort of ego-tistical, you know that?"

"Ego, ego, egolist . . . ?" Peggy tapped her foot against the bricks. "Oh yeah? Well, you're, well, I don't know what *you* are, Katherine Rose—*Mosie*—Bitmen. I ain't never met anyone like you and I hope I never ever have to ever-again, either. Do I really look like a sweet potato?"

Mosie furrowed her eyes at Peggy and nodded. "I think it's because of that QT tanning lotion. Candy tried it last summer, and boy did she turn out all goofy. Sort of like a cross between butterscotch and almonds."

Peggy looked at her arms. "Oh no, how long does it last?"

"Just a week or two, three tops."

"Great," she jumped off the brick-stairs. "Just great. Come on, I'll show you where the wood's at. Hey, how come if your dad owns a boat factory, you can't just get a boat from him? How come you've gotta make one?"

Well," Mosie said, "you might say this one is going to be a surprise."

Jingle-jingle-clank-clank, went the bikes as they rambled up the Bitmens' driveway. Attached to each of them were worn toboggans laden with planks of tired, old wood.

"Maybe it'd be better if you didn't say too much," Mosie said as she checked Peggy's orange and anxious face. "Especially about boats, Dog Island, or those boyfriends of yours." They spotted Willowdean inside the porch digging through a stack of unpacked boxes.

"You didn't say she was, PG," Peggy said. "You sure she won't mind me eating over?"

"Man, you don't know my ma. Just remember, shake her hand; she likes that. She says it's good manners, and my ma likes good manners, got it?"

The closer Willowdean got, the more enormous of a Ms. Bartelo smile Mosie flashed her.

"Why are you making that face?" Peggy asked.

Mosie dropped her lips. "Ma," she said, nudging her elbow into Peggy's ribs, reminding her to lift her hand, "this is Peggy."

"Well, hello Peggy," Willowdean said, taking her hand. It was limp with no power behind it, like her hazel-green eyes. "I'm Mosie's mother, Willowdean, Willowdean Bitmen."

"Peggy's normally not this color," Mosie said as she tugged Willowdean's arm away. "She used that QT Tanning stuff Candy used last year."

"Oh, I'm sorry," Willowdean said. "It's not that; no, I mean . . . say I bet you girls could use some lemonade and sandwiches.

Why don't you two go ahead, and do whatever it is you were going to do, and I'll be out in just awhile."

"Boy, your mom sure is nice," Peggy said as she grabbed her bike.

"Yes, she's something all right." Mosie watched her go up the porch stairs. "We better get this wood behind the garage before she gets back out here. She's decent about most stuff, but if she finds out what we're up to, she won't be."

"*We*?" Peggy said, over the clumping toboggans and timber. "This ain't no *we* thing, it's a *you* thing. I'm just here to watch and have some grub. Besides, like I told ya', you're just wasting your time, there just ain't no real place called Dog Island, and besides, I just know Mrs. Morgan would give you a poodle, two, or three even, if you got the money."

"Poodles," Mosie grumbled as she untied her sled. "I want a dog that's made just for me.

"What are you talking about? One made just for you?" Peggy asked with a grunt, yanking her sled next to Mosie's.

"Well, see, Ma said, The Great Spirit—"

"The great what?" Peggy's face lit up before Mosie could explain how animal spirits live in the clouds, coming and going from the life bridges from whence they came.

Willowdean headed for the picnic table carrying a platter of sandwiches balanced on top a pitcher of red Kool-Aid in one hand, and a bowl of potato chips in the other.

"Never mind," Mosie trotted behind Peggy.

Willowdean sat the pitcher on the picnic table, "Sorry girls. I'm out of lemon juice. I hope Kool-Aid will do." Peggy grabbed a sandwich. Mosie jabbed her in the ribs.

"Oh," she said, mouth full of tuna and celery bits. "I mean, excuse me. Thank you, Mrs. Bitmen, but you shouldn't have gone through so much trouble." She sat down and swung her long legs gracefully over the seat-bench; her shirt slipped past her shoulder. Willowdean spotted the birthmark and her face went white as the paper plates in front of her.

"Ma, are you okay?" Mosie asked.

"Yes, yes, I am," Willowdean said, forcing a smile. A crow cawed in the trees above their heads. Willowdean grabbed a handful of chips. "Peggy, may I ask who your parents are?" she asked. The crow cawed again.

"Um, they're the, um-um . . ." she stammered, her face turning red as the Kool-Aid in her glass. Dropping her napkin, she bent over to pick it up.

"Ma," Mosie quickly whispered, "you're embarrassing her; she's *underprivileged*."

Willowdean looked at the stack of sandwiches and took a deep breath. She closed her eyes.

"Are you sure you're okay?" Mosie asked again.

"Yes," Willowdean answered with moist eyes.

Peggy sat up and straightened her shirt to cover the mark.

"Here," Willowdean placed two more sandwich halves on Peggy's plate. "If we don't eat them, they'll go bad. And chips, they tend to get stale, especially in this humidity."

"Thank you, Mrs. Bitmen," she said. "These sure are good." Nearly squealing, she took a bite of her tuna sandwich, the biggest Mosie had ever seen (even bigger than Candy). Peggy lifted her head and her chewing slowed to a halt.

Beyond the rows of pink, honeysuckle bushes, and pine trees, hiding the house from the highway, a muffler-less car turned and started climbing the driveway. Then from the cloud of dust, an old rusty Ford appeared. The car stopped; the engine kept running.

"Are those your parents?" Willowdean's voice sounded unsteady over the rattle.

Peggy nodded and leaned downward to scratch her ankle.

A woman, tall and lanky, like Peggy herself, stepped from the car. Her purple paisley headscarf couldn't hide the Peggy-brown roots sprouting from her head of dyed blonde hair.

"Peggy honey, we were looking all over for ya'," the woman hollered over the roar of the Ford. "Mr. Maki said we might find ya' here. And sure enough, that little old sweetheart was right, wasn't he, honey?"

Peggy's dad sat behind the steering wheel and stared straight ahead. Mosie shuddered at the sight. She couldn't help it. His red bristle-short hair blazed like a miniature forest fire in the sunlight; his porcelain skin (frightening her most) was punctuated with, *Freckles, hundreds of hideous freckles!* She thought.

The woman made her way across the yard to the picnic table and her overly flared silky-slacks fluttered with every step. Willowdean glanced at the woman's taut stomach framed behind her tight, midriff blouse. The stomach jested at her with each hip-swaying step. "Gichimanidoo, help us," Willowdean prayed holding the edge of the picnic table, rubbing her bulging belly.

"Well lookie at you," the woman blathered, her hands on her slender hips. "Looks like your old man's been pretty busy. Ain't that just the sweetest thing? And at your ages."

She reached to touch Willowdean's stomach. Willowdean stepped away.

The woman looked down and ran her eyes over Mosie. "Hi hon," she said with a twisted-up smile.

Mosie held her hands behind her back, not offering one to her.

"This your momma?" she asked, snapping her gum. "Kinda cute, ain't ya', kid? On the short side like your daddy but cute."

"Mrs. Bitmen," Peggy said, cringing, "this—this is Corrine, my mother, Corrine Anderson."

Neither woman said a word standing face to face. The only sound was the crow crying in their silence and the snap of Corrine's gum.

She grinned and darted her eyes over at the car idling like an old army tank.

"Bet you can guess who that adorable hunk of man over there is," she said with a gummy snap-snap-snap. "And he's mine, *all* mine." She raised her skinny, bangle armored arm and waved to him. "Still just as cute as a button, ain't he? And let me tell ya', he sure knows how to keep a woman happy, if you catch my meaning." Willowdean hung onto the picnic table and slowly sat down.

Corrine snickered and blew Lenny a kiss.

"Well, talking about us girls being busy, whew! Peggy here has got some line-up like you would not believe.

"I keep tellin' her, *honey, one day all this hard work is gonna pay off, you just watch and see*; don't I baby?

"Course, I know our Peggy would rather stay here with you nice folks, enjoying these nice, elaborate surroundings, what with all this fine food and all, but see, the thing is, Peggy here has to be all the way over in Hurley this evening; and if we don't get a move on, she won't have enough time to get her *groove* on." Corrine giggled.

"Say thank ya' honey," she said, her voice turning to a stab. She grabbed Peggy's arm, and headed across the yard.

Peggy tried to pull herself from Corrine's clutch to look back at Mosie as she stood beside Willowdean.

"Thanks Mosie," she said, as her eyes filled with tears. "I sure had a great time."

"Sure," Mosie said. "Maybe we can get together again real soon.

Go for a bike ride or something."

Peggy sniffled. "Yea, that'd be cool."

"Oh, say," Corrine hollered to Willowdean as she shoved Peggy into the car next to Lenny, "if you folks are gonna be in town this weekend, you come on down to Lands Port tavern. It's right over there on Rittenhouse Avenue. You remember.

"Our little Peggy here has a gig there this Saturday night, and I know she'd be happy to see a friendly face out in the crowd. Wouldn't ya', honey?

"Tootle-bootles," she said over the rev of the car engine and pulled her long legs inside the Ford.

Lenny turned his head and stared at Willowdean. Without a word, without a flinch, he pulled away.

The thick puff of gray dust that had settled just moments before, rose again, following them back down the driveway and out onto the highway.

"Man, the Anderson's sure aren't anything like Candy and her parents, are they?" Mosie said as she picked up Peggy's empty KoolAid glass and placed it on the tray.

"No, no they aren't," Willowdean said, weakly. "No they are not."

CHAPTER FOURTEEN

Jingle-jingle-clank-clank, went the bikes as they rambled up the Bitmens' driveway. Attached to each of them were worn toboggans laden with planks of tired, old wood.

"Maybe it'd be better if you didn't say too much," Mosie said as she checked Peggy's orange and anxious face. "Especially about boats, Dog Island, or those boyfriends of yours." They spotted Willowdean inside the porch digging through a stack of unpacked boxes.

"You didn't say she was, PG," Peggy said. "You sure she won't mind me eating over?"

"Man, you don't know my ma. Just remember, shake her hand; she likes that. She says it's good manners, and my ma likes good manners, got it?"

The closer Willowdean got, the more enormous of a Ms. Bartelo smile Mosie flashed her.

"Why are you making that face?" Peggy asked.

Mosie dropped her lips. "Ma," she said, nudging her elbow into Peggy's ribs, reminding her to lift her hand, "this is Peggy."

"Well, hello Peggy," Willowdean said, taking her hand. It was limp with no power behind it, like her hazel-green eyes. "I'm Mosie's mother, Willowdean, Willowdean Bitmen."

"Peggy's normally not this color," Mosie said as she tugged Willowdean's arm away. "She used that QT Tanning stuff Candy used last year."

"Oh, I'm sorry," Willowdean said. "It's not that; no, I mean . . . say I bet you girls could use some lemonade and sandwiches. Why don't you two go ahead, and do whatever it is you were going to do, and I'll be out in just awhile."

"Boy, your mom sure is nice," Peggy said as she grabbed her bike.

"Yes, she's something all right." Mosie watched her go up the porch stairs. "We better get this wood behind the garage before she gets back out here. She's decent about most stuff, but if she finds out what we're up to, she won't be."

"*We*?" Peggy said, over the clumping toboggans and timber. "This ain't no *we* thing, it's a *you* thing. I'm just here to watch and have some grub. Besides, like I told ya', you're just wasting your time, there just ain't no real place called Dog Island, and besides, I just know Mrs. Morgan would give you a poodle, two, or three even, if you got the money."

"Poodles," Mosie grumbled as she untied her sled. "I want a dog that's made just for me.

"What are you talking about? One made just for you?" Peggy asked with a grunt, yanking her sled next to Mosie's.

"Well, see, Ma said, The Great Spirit—"

"The great what?" Peggy's face lit up before Mosie could explain how animal spirits live in the clouds, coming and going from the life bridges from whence they came.

Willowdean headed for the picnic table carrying a platter of sandwiches balanced on top a pitcher of red Kool-Aid in one hand, and a bowl of potato chips in the other.

"Never mind," Mosie trotted behind Peggy.

Willowdean sat the pitcher on the picnic table, "Sorry girls. I'm out of lemon juice. I hope Kool-Aid will do." Peggy grabbed a sandwich. Mosie jabbed her in the ribs.

"Oh," she said, mouth full of tuna and celery bits. "I mean, excuse me. Thank you, Mrs. Bitmen, but you shouldn't have gone through so much trouble." She sat down and swung her long legs gracefully over the seat-bench; her shirt slipped past her shoulder. Willowdean spotted the birthmark and her face went white as the paper plates in front of her.

"Ma, are you okay?" Mosie asked.

"Yes, yes, I am," Willowdean said, forcing a smile. A crow cawed in the trees above their heads. Willowdean grabbed a handful of chips. "Peggy, may I ask who your parents are?" she asked. The crow cawed again.

"Um, they're the, um-um . . ." she stammered, her face turning red as the Kool-Aid in her glass. Dropping her napkin, she bent over to pick it up.

"Ma," Mosie quickly whispered, "you're embarrassing her; she's *underprivileged*."

Willowdean looked at the stack of sandwiches and took a deep breath. She closed her eyes.

"Are you sure you're okay?" Mosie asked again.

"Yes," Willowdean answered with moist eyes.

Peggy sat up and straightened her shirt to cover the mark.

"Here," Willowdean placed two more sandwich halves on Peggy's plate. "If we don't eat them, they'll go bad. And chips, they tend to get stale, especially in this humidity."

"Thank you, Mrs. Bitmen," she said. "These sure are good." Nearly squealing, she took a bite of her tuna sandwich, the biggest Mosie had ever seen (even bigger than Candy). Peggy lifted her head and her chewing slowed to a halt.

Beyond the rows of pink, honeysuckle bushes, and pine trees, hiding the house from the highway, a muffler-less car turned and started climbing the driveway. Then from the cloud of dust, an old rusty Ford appeared. The car stopped; the engine kept running.

"Are those your parents?" Willowdean's voice sounded unsteady over the rattle.

Peggy nodded and leaned downward to scratch her ankle.

A woman, tall and lanky, like Peggy herself, stepped from the car. Her purple paisley headscarf couldn't hide the Peggy-brown roots sprouting from her head of dyed blonde hair.

"Peggy honey, we were looking all over for ya'," the woman hollered over the roar of the Ford. "Mr. Maki said we might find ya' here. And sure enough, that little old sweetheart was right, wasn't he, honey?"

Peggy's dad sat behind the steering wheel and stared straight ahead. Mosie shuddered at the sight. She couldn't help it. His red bristle-short hair blazed like a miniature forest fire in the sun light; his porcelain skin (frightening her most) was punctuated with, *Freckles, hundreds of hideous freckles!* She thought.

The woman made her way across the yard to the picnic table and her overly flared silky-slacks fluttered with every step. Willowdean glanced at the woman's taut stomach framed behind her tight, midriff blouse. The stomach jested at her with each hip-swaying step. "Gichimanidoo, help us," Willowdean prayed holding the edge of the picnic table, rubbing her bulging belly.

"Well lookie at you," the woman blathered, her hands on her slender hips. "Looks like your old man's been pretty busy. Ain't that just the sweetest thing? And at your ages."

She reached to touch Willowdean's stomach. Willowdean stepped away.

The woman looked down and ran her eyes over Mosie. "Hi hon," she said with a twisted-up smile.

Mosie held her hands behind her back, not offering one to her.

"This your momma?" she asked, snapping her gum. "Kinda cute, ain't ya', kid? On the short side like your daddy but cute."

"Mrs. Bitmen," Peggy said, cringing, "this—this is Corrine, my mother, Corrine Anderson."

Neither woman said a word standing face to face. The only sound was the crow crying in their silence and the snap of Corrine's gum.

She grinned and darted her eyes over at the car idling like an old army tank.

"Bet you can guess who that adorable hunk of man over there is," she said with a gummy snap-snap-snap. "And he's mine, *all* mine." She raised her skinny, bangle armored arm and waved to him. "Still just as cute as a button, ain't he? And let me tell ya', he sure knows how to keep a woman happy, if you catch my meaning." Willowdean hung onto the picnic table and slowly sat down.

Corrine snickered and blew Lenny a kiss.

"Well, talking about us girls being busy, whew! Peggy here has got some line-up like you would not believe.

"I keep tellin' her, *honey, one day all this hard work is gonna pay off, you just watch and see*; don't I baby?

"Course, I know our Peggy would rather stay here with you nice folks, enjoying these nice, elaborate surroundings, what with all this fine food and all, but see, the thing is, Peggy here has to be all the way over in Hurley this evening; and if we don't get a move on, she won't have enough time to get her *groove* on." Corrine giggled.

"Say thank ya' honey," she said, her voice turning to a stab. She grabbed Peggy's arm, and headed across the yard.

Peggy tried to pull herself from Corrine's clutch to look back at Mosie as she stood beside Willowdean.

"Thanks Mosie," she said, as her eyes filled with tears. "I sure had a great time."

"Sure," Mosie said. "Maybe we can get together again real soon.

Go for a bike ride or something."

Peggy sniffled. "Yea, that'd be cool."

"Oh, say," Corrine hollered to Willowdean as she shoved Peggy into the car next to Lenny, "if you folks are gonna be in town this weekend, you come on down to Lands Port tavern. It's right over there on Rittenhouse Avenue. You remember.

"Our little Peggy here has a gig there this Saturday night, and I know she'd be happy to see a friendly face out in the crowd. Wouldn't ya', honey?

"Tootle-bootles," she said over the rev of the car engine and pulled her long legs inside the Ford.

Lenny turned his head and stared at Willowdean. Without a word, without a flinch, he pulled away.

The thick puff of gray dust that had settled just moments before, rose again, following them back down the driveway and out onto the highway.

"Man, the Anderson's sure aren't anything like Candy and her parents, are they?" Mosie said as she picked up Peggy's empty KoolAid glass and placed it on the tray.

"No, no they aren't," Willowdean said, weakly. "No they are not."

CHAPTER FIFTEEN

JUNE 8, 1972

Dear Val, How are you? Fine I hope. How is your new job at Papa Joe's Pizza? Lake Superior is way cleaner then Lake Michigan so I hope your protests work.

How are Mr. and Mrs. Bennington? If you talk to them, tell them I say hi. Pa said you better be keeping the grass cut so you and Mrs. Bennington don't fight.

I made a new friend. Her name is Peggy Anderson. I think her parents are those people I heard Pa and Ma talk about and that I'm not supposed to know about. They came to pick up Peggy, and Ma was awfully nervous. When Pa got home I snuck down stairs and heard him tell Ma how sorry he was and that he did not know they were here. I don't think Ma believes him because she don't talk to him very much except when I'm around.

Pa said he did not want me hanging around Peggy, but I heard Ma telling him that was not fair and as long as no one say's anything it will be okay. She told him Corrine is so selfish, she would rather keep everything as it is.

Every time I ask them about Corrine or Lenny, they change the subject. I asked Peggy, too, but she didn't know anything about anything because that's how Peggy is. She never knows anything. Do you know what is going on?

Lenny and Corrine are pretty creepy, especially Lenny. They make Peggy call them by their first names. Isn't that far-out? And they don't go to church ether, not even a Lutheran church.

Peggy doesn't care about dogs or fishing or anything like that. All she talks about is boys, boys, boys and she sings in taverns even though she is only 14!

She's awfully skinny. Ma said it's because she probably didn't have the right nutrition growing up and that I need to be a little more understanding because of it and not be so mean to her like I am. I think she likes Peggy even more than Candy even if she does not like her mom or her dad.

When you come up for my birthday, will you please bring me a Papa Joe's pizza? Sammo's dosn't (doesn't have any grease floating on the top of theirs so they taste like cardboard. Also, there are only three kinds of ice cream up here: Vanilla and Chocolate and one called a twist. They think it's a whole other kind of flavor but it's really just Vanilla and Chocolate twisted together. Isn't that weird? It really sucks so I got Mr. Maki to get some more freezers so he can have a verity (variety) like at Baskin Robbins Thirty-One Flavors (but not as many).

Mr. Maki owns the Novelty and Gift shop down by the lake. It's the only ice cream shop around here. Ma said she knew him when she was a girl but she told me not to say nothing anything to him about it so I haven't. (She sure is strange like that sometimes.)

Well I think that's about all for now. Ma's making Butterscotch cookies for me and boy, do they smell good!

Love,

Your sister,

Moe Bitmen

P.S. I still don't have a dog yet but I will soon. Don't tell Ma or Pa but me and Peggy are building a boat behind the garage. Peggy got the wood and I stole some plans and other stuff for boat making from the shop.

P.S.S. If you see Candy tell her, I say hi. If you see Judy Lard-Ass don't tell her anything.

M*osie reached into the drawer and fumbled for the* Rover Space stamp booklet. "Ma, why do the Andersons make Peggy call them by their first names?"

Willowdean put the tray of fresh Butterscotch Toll House cookies on the counter and peered over the nook. "No way, young lady," she said. "I see what you're doing; use the other ones like I told you before."

"But Ma, what good are they just sitting there, huh?"

"Keep it up and you'll be hanging up the clothes all by yourself."

Mosie looked at the wet mound sitting in the clothes basket in the corner and shoved the Rovers back into the drawer. Taking out a plain eight-cent stamp, she gave it a lick and stuck it on Val's envelope.

"So why do the Andersons make Peggy call them by their first names?"

"Well, I'm not really sure," Willowdean poked her finger in a splotch of melted butterscotch. "Maybe some people just can't accept their age."

"What the hell is that supposed to mean?"

"Katherine Rose! The next time you swear I'm washing your mouth out with soap!"

"Well, I think it's creepy; and I think *they're* creepy; especially Lenny." Mosie got up and poured a glass of cold milk. She held it up to Willowdean. She shook her head.

"I don't know if it's that red hair of his, or all those *damn freckles* all over that ugly white face. Ew!" Mosie faked a shudder. "I bet Peggy's glad she don't look anything like him."

"Did I just not tell you I do not want you using that kind of language—and I certainly don't want you saying anything like that to Peggy, or anyone else. It's not right."

"Well, I don't think I have to. Peggy might not be the brightest shining star, but even she isn't *that* dumb not to see her and Lenny don't look anything alike." Taking a drink of her cold milk, she let a long rumbled burp of satisfaction erupt. Willowdean snatched away the empty glass.

"Katherine Rose, I don't know what's gotten into you, but it has got to stop. You're cussing, belching, sneaking stamps . . . God knows what else. It all has to stop. Do you understand me?"

She followed Willowdean into the living room and stood with her in front of the picture window. "You want me to hang the clothes out for you?" Mosie asked as she saw Willowdean wipe tears with her apron.

"No, no," Willowdean sniffled. "The fresh air will do me good, but thank you. Sometimes I wonder if moving back here was the right decision. Your father is having such trouble with the shop, and now with . . . oh look, here's Peggy now. Poor thing, look at her. I bet she's hungry."

"She always looks hungry even when she isn't," Mosie said, under her breath, watching her spindle her homemade boy's bike up the driveway; Peggy's long legs curled to her elbows. "Well, at least she has good tires on that thing."

Then came the knock at the kitchen door. It slowly opened and Peggy stuck her head through the door's entry. "Mrs. Bitmen," she said softly, "are you making cookies again, those towel house kind? I can smell 'em way outside; they sure smell good."

"Toll House," Mosie said. "They're called Toll House, not towel house." She read the sequin letters sewn across Peggy's blouse and asked, "What the heck you wearing? P. A.? What's that supposed to mean?"

Peggy clucked her tongue. "Ha! You know, you're not so smart after all, are you? For your information, P stands for Peggy, and the A is for Anderson."

"Would you like some cookies, Miss P. A.?" Willowdean asked.

"Oh, yes," Peggy beamed as she scooted herself onto the stool next to Mosie. Her mascara-smudged eyes gleamed as Willowdean slid a plate in front of her with a tumbler of ice cold milk. Mosie handed her a napkin.

"Here," she said, "you have stuff all over your face. Why do you have all that makeup on anyway? And what's with the shirt?"

"For your information, it's a country western blouse. It's from last night; remember I had another gig over in Hurley?"

Mosie gave the blouse another glance and bit her cookie.

"Afterwards, me and Kevin Dellmay, we went over to that big Indian statue in Ironwood and we . . . Owe!" Peggy screeched, grabbing her ankle. "What was that for?"

"Well, we better go; we have lots to do today," Mosie said, giving Peggy a scowl.

Willowdean tossed a handful of raw, butterscotch chips into her mouth. "What are you two making back there, behind the garage?" she asked.

"Well," Mosie said tugging the tips of her hair.

Peggy quickly flew off her stool and headed for the door. "I— I'm not making anything, Mrs. Bitmen," she said "I'm just watching."

Mosie stared at the stack of cookies. She grabbed one and held it up, counting the melted golden brown globs on top. "Ma, did you know there is an average of eight butterscotch chips in each of these?"

"We're not talking about chips in cookies," Willowdean kept her eyes tight on Mosie. She handed Peggy the platter. "These you may take home with you. Well?"

Mosie slid off her seat. "Ummm," she said, scampering next to Peggy.

"We're not really sure what we're making yet," she slowly pushed open the door and pressed Peggy out into the porch.

Sheepishly, Peggy looked at Willowdean. "Thank you, Mrs. Bitmen," she said, Mosie at her heels.

"Katherine, carry that bushel basket outside for me, please." Mosie turned to meet Willowdean's watchful eyes.

"Geez Ma, I'm not a criminal or anything."

"Yes, I know, you're a good girl," Willowdean followed her outside to the clothesline. "I just don't want you getting hurt, that's all."

"I know Ma," she put the basket down. She looked at the garage and the stack of wood behind it. "Sure you don't want any help?"

"Yes, I'm sure. Just mind what I'm telling you."

Mosie looked at her for a moment and then headed for the garage, Peggy close behind. "Geez, since Ma got pregnant she sure got goofy."

"Well, I don't think she's so goofy," Peggy said, gripping her platter of cookies. She glanced back at Willowdean who was pinning one of John's work shirts on the line. "I think she's one of the nicest moms I ever met. And why'd you go and kick me so hard for like that? What if I get a bruise?" She stopped and checked her shin. "Look, it's all red!"

"Well, I told you never to talk in front of my parents about all those damn boys you hang around with. Geez!"

"Well, I forgot, okay?" Peggy whined, rubbing her leg. "You didn't have to kick me so hard!"

"Well, I'm sorry," Mosie apologized and watched her suddenly limp across the grass.

"I don't think this is such a good idea, Mosie—you building a boat to go someplace that ain't real and lying about it; and with your ma being PG, and, well, it don't seem right, that's all. Can't you just go get yourself one of Mrs. Morgan's poodles? What's the dif anyway?"

"*Man*," Mosie grumbled, "Candy would never buckle under like this, *never*." She tugged the top of her shorts. "Besides, we've been over this eighteen times already; I know because I counted them, and this makes nineteen times; and that's why I'm not going to explain it to you again.

"Besides, I already have the blueprints stashed in the garage and all kinds of stuff. First, I'm going to show you where everything is for when you need it. I can just hear you now; 'Where's the nails? Where's the hammer?'"

Peggy clutched her plate of cookies. "I ain't Candy," she snapped. "And I ain't building no boat!"

Mosie kicked an old, nearly hollow stump of wood in front of the garage door.

"You'll need to remember to block the door otherwise she'll swing shut on you and you won't be able to see inside until you get the light on."

Peggy put her plate on the ground. "I told ya'," she folded her arms and refused to budge. "I ain't gonna help you build no boat. Ain't ya' scared of anything?"

"Hell no, why would I be? As long as I have my guardian angel and all those saints watching over me, I figure they'll take care of whatever will hurt me."

Looking closely at the shadows inside the garage, the hair on her arms shot up.

"I thought you just said you weren't afraid of nothing," said Peggy.

"Yeah, well, I ain't, er, I'm not."

"Sure don't look like it to me." Peggy took a bite of one of her cookies. "What about all those saints and that angel of yours, huh?"

Mosie sighed. "Peggy, I don't think even *they* can fight Mary Worth." She ran her hand along the inside of the wall "Anyone in their right mind is scared of Mary Worth. Even saints and angels." She flipped on the light. "You're going to have to remember, it takes four scotches across the right wall to find the light switch."

She looked over the clutter of boxes and hunks of broken metal gears from Bitmen's Fish N' Boats.

"Sorry about the mess," she said. "Ma's planning on having a rummage sale soon as she gets a chance to organize all this stuff."

Peggy looked at the hoard of boxes and knelt next to the one with a giant red tomato smiling up at her. She ran her hand over its lid. Her eyes lit up. "Albums," she said, flipping it open.

"Who's Mary Worth, and what's a *rummage sale*?" she asked, carefully placing the LPs in two stacks.

"A rummage sale is when you sell stuff you don't want any more, and Mary Worth . . . well you're better off not knowing about her."

"Okay. Hey, is your ma gonna be selling any of these, you think?" she asked, her eyes sparkling. She held up an album, tapping her finger on the cover. A drawing of a man in a suit sat on a log. Behind him, two Indians reaching for each other stood under a crescent moon hanging against an overly orange sunset.

"Running Bear. February 7th, 1960. John Preston Courville . . . Two minutes and thirty-seven seconds. I've been looking for this one for *years*."

"No, not that one, its Pa's favorite. It has his and Ma's special love song on it."

Ignoring her, Peggy headed for the record player that sat on John's workbench. Gently, she pulled the black vinyl from its sleeve as if undressing a baby, and placed it on the player. She picked up the hi-fi's long, metal arm, positioned it, and turned the machine on.

Mosie cringed. "Uh, I don't think that's such a good idea," she said, nervously.

Peggy smiled and turned up the sound. She waited. Then came her excitement.

She closed her eyes and slapped her hands against her slender thighs in perfect tempo to the beat of the drums. Deep, rich tones of men chanting, "Oonga-oonga-oonga-oonga," filled the garage.

Then, as if Peggy truly were Little White Dove and Johnny Preston Running Bear, they sang together, divulging the love between them; a love forbidden, a love that could never die.

It's true, Mosie thought. *Peggy Anderson really does know how to sing.*

"*On the bank of the river*," she bellowed strong and clear; "*stood Running Bear, young Indian brave; on the other, side of the river, stood his lovely, Indian maid; Little White Dove was her name.*"

Then, just as fast she had fallen in love with her own Johnny, Willowdean Blackbird ran across the yard, and stood next to her daughter. Peggy, throwing her kisses, called her to her side.

As if she too were still a young girl, Willowdean danced to Peggy's sultry voice rising above the grunge of boxes and grease (and too many loads of laundry).

Mosie swallowed hard to push down the lump in her throat. Her mother's hair, black and shiny, jostling with each beat, awakened a small spark of pride inside her. *She has to be an Indian princess, she just has to be,* she thought as she looked at her own brown sugar skin.

Willowdean caught her breath and stepped back while Peggy ended the song, bowing to Mosie's and Willowdean's applause, "*With a love that couldn't die. . .*"

"My lord!" Willowdean gasped, "where did you ever learn to sing like that?"

"From Corrine, I suppose," she removed John's record and placed it tenderly back in its jacket.

"Yes, I forgot." Willowdean stopped and held her breath, hoping to pull the words back inside her. "I mean, your parents must be very proud. You're so young to be able to sing like that."

"I guess," Peggy knelt before the red tomato box and thumbed through the rest of the records; she did not look up.

"Ma," Mosie whispered, "I think you're embarrassing her." Peggy glanced at her watch and put the albums back in the box. "I have to go," she said. "Lenny's probably up. Thanks for the cookies, Mrs. Bitmen." She hurried to the door. "Maybe I'll be back tomorrow," she said and slipped out the doorway. Mosie followed.

"Wait," she called. "I'll go with you."

Peggy picked up her bike and watched Willowdean head for the clothesline. "Tell your ma thanks for everything," she pressed the duct tape down on her seat, watched Willowdean pull Mosie's shorts out from the laundry basket, and then pin them to the fresh, taunt clothesline. She straddled her legs over the boys-bar, painted red. "I gotta go."

"Wait," Mosie repeated.

It was too late. Peggy, and her mousy brown hair fluttered limply in the wind down the driveway. She didn't look back.

CHAPTER SIXTEEN

The moon snuck glimpses of Mosie through the glass of her bedroom window. She pressed her thumb on its milky halo and thought of Peggy and how she might not be so bad after all. "Who knows," she told herself, "maybe when I get my dog I'll share him with her, even if she doesn't help me go get him."

The headlights from John's pick-up flashed across her bedroom ceiling.

"Katherine, are you asleep?" Willowdean called up the stairs over the revving of the truck engine.

Mosie heard the clutch grinding to a stop, and then the opening squeak and slam of John's truck door.

His call for, "Willowdeanie—Willowdeeenie," echoed` across the yard.

"Your father's been at Benny's again," Willowdean muttered more to herself than to Mosie. Willowdean sauntered into the kitchen to wait for John to stumble up the porch stairs and into the kitchen.

Mosie spied her way down the staircase, hid between the thick logs of the banister, and watched John waver. He looked at his chair as if trying to decide if the few steps to its wooden support would be his last steps ever. He took a deep breath and stared it down.

"What a night, Willowdeanie, what a night," he slurred, closing his eyes then shaking them open.

He focused on the path in front of him, shuffled forward, and gave the chair a few clumsy pats. Its legs toddling against the floor assured him he indeed had made contact.

"Yep," he grinned. "Me and this here chair, we been together all these years; haven't we, Chair?" He beamed proudly and gave it a shake.

He listened for an answer only he could hear then turned and concentrated on Willowdean.

"Just like you and me, Willy, just like you and me. I wouldn't trade either one of ya' for the world, either one!"

Willowdean tucked in her lips as she tried not to laugh.

"Well, thank you, John; I wouldn't trade you *or* your chair for the world either. But I bet I know what you would really like besides that old chair."

John's eyes gleamed. "Well, I know what I would like, but I don't think you would like. Hell Willy, let's find out!" he yipped playfully, wrapping his arms around her. Mosie flattened herself against the railing, not fluttering an inch.

"Careful Mr. Bitmen," Willowdean said as she walked him to the living room. "That's not what I meant."

Mosie sighed with relief. John moaned with disappointment.

"I have something even better," Willowdean said, as they caught their balance. She, slowly steered him down the hallway. "Something you *really* need."

John stopped and rubbed his cheek on top of Willowdean's head. "Dang woman, you sure smell good," he sniffed her hair. "What a night, what a night." He tottered a few feet then rested, his voice turning heavy.

"Ya know Willy, I gotta tell ya somethin', and it ain't very nice. It's about Corrine—" Willowdean pulled away.

"Aw, come on now baby," he said, pulling her to his chest. "I told ya', there just ain't no one for me any more 'cept you. Ya' want me to prove it? 'Cause I can, you know." Willowdean pushed him away. He wobbled. "Aw, come on, Willie, don't go getting all sensitive on me now. Hell, if I ain't learned my lesson by now I never will. Besides, I gotta' tell ya' this."

He tried steadying himself without Willowdean's help. She sighed and put her arm around his waist.

"Well, why don't we go in here, and then you can tell me," she led him to the spare bedroom.

Hearing him plunk on the bed, Mosie toe'd her way further down the hall and listened to John's muddled-up words. "Ya' know, I sat down with ole' Lenny after all these years. Turns out Corrine don't know a thing about nothin'."

"Foot up," Willowdean said. His work boots *thunked* on the floor. Mosie froze.

"Seems Lenny wanted to keep his business, *his* business after all. So I offered that jackal a job to show our appreciation. He turned me down! Used to be the best damn machinist I knew until he took up with Corrine.

"Hell Willie, she ain't changed one bit; let me tell ya' . . . those long legs of hers, still lookin' for some rich fella to wrap themselves around . . ." The bed springs squeaked. He tried getting up and then lay back down with a belch.

"You know what really gets me about those two? That kid of theirs. Willy, why, I seen them parade that young girl around those bars, singing and dancing; why, the way they got her getting money from folks . . . It ain't right, it just ain't right.

That's no way for a man to earn a living for his family, off his own kid like that; it ain't right, it just ain't right."

"You're right, John," Willowdean reassured him in hopes of calming him down. "Well take care of it in the morning, won't we?"

The springs rattled as he tried rolling off the bed. Mosie stepped away from the door.

"Why, I have a good mind ta' go back down to Benny's right now and pop that sorry S.O.B. right in the kisser; that's what I oughta' do, pop him right in the bloody kisser . . ."

"Yes John, we will do it together, you and I. But first, you lay here for a while and get some rest."

The light switch clicked on the wall and spread darkness under the door. The knob turned. Mosie sprang like a frightened deer and leapt down the hall and up the stairs to her room. She sat on her bed and looked out at the Moon.

"Dear Mother Mary," she whispered. "This is me, Mosie Bitmen, and I got a confession for you. I didn't know Peggy had it so rough. Even if she can sing and dance better than anyone I know it sure can't be any fun having to do it in order to support her folks.

"So Mother Mary, I promise from now on, I will take care of her, and I promise, when I get that dog of mine, I'll let her have half of him, no strings attached, I promise.

"And Mother Mary, please look after Peggy when I'm not there to do it for her. Oh yeah, just one more thing; Pa's been spending an awful lot of time down at Benny's in case you haven't noticed, so that's why I haven't been going to church as much, just so you know it isn't my fault.

"In the name of the Father, and in the Son, and in the Holy Ghost, Amen."

She looked at the alarm clock on her dresser: 3 a.m. It was now Sunday morning.

"Poor Peggy," she said as she drifted off to sleep and into the dream she would never forget, a dream that would change her life more than a move to a different town, more than a hundred flavored ice cream cones, even more than the reality of one day owning a dog.

She was carried home to Barrington and sent drifting upward into the vast darkness were dreams are made, away from Candy and Val, away from Mr. Bennington and all his prized roses.

She fought the pull and tried calling to them from beyond the rooftops and the town's steeples, but her voice was not heard. In the distance, a wondrous speck of light tugged her to its opening.

Then, within a twinkle of time (allowed only in dreams of such sort) she was safely inside and stood on a small wooden bridge at the edge of a swamp. Its creaking planks led her through thick foliage that swelled its sides. It brushed her legs.

A crow crossing the sky escorted her to the end of the bridge and to the place where all bogs and meadows, heavy with flowers, eventually merge and find rest.

There, another bridge, more golden then a hundred suns, arched across a bay of bogs and marshlands. To its left and to its right, a grove of evergreen and weeping willow trees stood, guarding its entrances; past that lay an endless body of blue water.

"This is sacred ground, Katherine Rose, fashioned by the Creator," a man said with a voice that tinkled like clear glass. "These are the very grounds your Earth Mother told you about."

Crows launched a happy cry of welcome that filled her ears as a man, tall and lean, garbed in a long blue robe came strolling on his golden bridge. Close to his side stood a dog, pure white as the man's hair.

"To your right, is Cat Island," he said raising his arms to point to the islets set about. "To your left, Bear Island and so forth," he said pointing to each, his long sleeves flowing though no wind blew.

"And before you is—"

"Dog Island!" Mosie said.

"Correct," the man chuckled deep and booming. "Now, notice the heavens."

Mosie lifted her eyes at the Caribbean blue sky. "You mean this isn't Heaven?" she asked.

"No, not quite. Do you see the clouds and the many creature shapes forming as they pass over this bridge?"

"Yes, I see them."

"Those are animal souls, the ones your Earth Mother speaks about. It is *here* that all animals come from when their human beings need them, and it is *here* they pass when their humans have learned their lessons taught by them.

"The bridge on which you stand is the very one that connects your world with these Hinterlands. But my Bridge, the one on which I stand, is where human soul and animal spirit meet again. But until that time, *no* human may pass on my Bridge.

"Take heed Katherine Rose, not all reunions are happy ones; an animal's heart is pure while a human's is not."

He held his hands to the sky and golden-orange kisses of every shape and size flew from his billowy sleeves and turned every which color as they scattered from islet to islet.

“Those, Katherine Rose are for a lesson of a different time, a time that will come all too soon. And speaking of time, ours has come to an end. Remember what you have learned here.”

His voice trailed off and Mosie woke to the smell of bacon and Willowdean’s Sunday buttered eggs.

CHAPTER SEVENTEEN

Mosie's legs stiffened as she pedaled up Kill-Deer Hill. She rested at its top and looked down the rugged red cliff. She watched a small group of crow's dash in and out of the base of the quagmire below and practiced what she would say to Peggy:

"*Peggy Anderson, you come out of that house. I have to tell you something, something really big.* That's how I'll start off.

"Then I'll look her square in the eyes and say, *Peggy Anderson, I promised Mother Mary that from now on I was going to look after you.* That's when she'll thank me and start crying and telling me what a good friend I am; then we'll hug."

Taking a deep breath, she whisked down Kill-Deer; another mile and she was peering down the pitted lane leading to Peggy's backyard. She cringed.

In front of the shack, like a guard dog, sat the rusted old Ford. Shirts and pants strung across the clothesline hung stiff and forgotten as the shingles dangled from the hovel Peggy was forced to call home. Determined not to be afraid, but to stand tall and strong like Val, Mosie headed down the driveway.

The yellowed bed sheet hanging in the upstairs window swayed to the side. Peggy's slight shadow peeked out.

"Peggy Anderson," Mosie shouted, hands cupped around her mouth to direct her words straight up. "This is me, Mosie, Mosie Bitmen. Is that you up there?" The sheet dropped to the side. The front door creaked open. Mosie's stomach flopped.

Standing in the doorway was Lenny, his red hair flaming at her. Mosie stared at the freckles smeared across his pasty skin. *Damn things look like a bad batch of liver paste*, she thought. She avoided his sour green eyes prodding her from head to toe and watched him bite the corner of his fingernail. She heard him suck something thick into his mouth. She gagged.

"Peggy ain't goin' nowhere," he chewed a hunk of his skin with his front tooth. "Her day's already planned. So you're the Bitmen kid." He spat the flesh on the ground and grinned. Mosie looked away.

"Yep, just as I thought. You're your pa's kid all right. No denying that."

"What's that supposed to mean?"

"Nothin, nothin at all, kid. I ain't sayin a word. That way no one can say I was the one stirring up problems. Not this time.

"Now, why don't you be a good little papoose and get on that fancy bike of yours and head on back home. Like I said, Peggy's got some things she's gotta do around here."

Mosie glared at him. She couldn't help what came out her mouth; all she knew is that it did, and that's when the problem between her and Lenny Anderson really began.

Picking up her bright yellow ten-speed Schwinn Super Sport, her voice rose to a near-scream. "I'm not a Papoose! I'm an Indian princess. And . . . and . . . I *hate you*! *Everyone* hates you, even *my pa* hates you!"

"A what? An Indian princess?" he cackled, his soft pouchy stomach quivering. "Kid, that's some imagination ya got there.

"Hey Corrine," he yelled inside the house, "you oughta hear what the Bitmen girl claims . . . claims she's a . . . *Indian princess,* and that she *hates* me, and so does everyone else here in Bayfield, including her very own pa, the *great* Mr. John Bitmen himself!" He turned to Mosie, his eyes narrowing into slits. Then came the sound telling her she was in trouble; the very same sound Tommy Peterson made when Sister Vern Mary wasn't around. Except, being a hundred times older and bigger, Lenny had more to work with than Tommy.

Sucking his sinuses halfway into his head, Lenny rolled the thick goo around the back of his throat. He sneered at Mosie, and then her shoes.

"My Keds," she shrieked, grappling her feet around her bike. "*Not* my new Keds!"

Grinning, he took aim; splattering a thick, brown jelly-ball an inch from her shoes. "I'm telling my pa on you!" Mosie yelled over his laughter.

"Ya, you do that. But I'm warning you, this ain't the city, and around here we don't let our injuns talk to us like that, especially little patty-pooses. Now get before I have to come after ya."

Brave like Val, brave like Val, Mosie repeated in her head as she bolted down the driveway.

She stopped and looked back at Lenny. She knew he wasn't afraid of her pa, or anyone else, especially her.

"Leo-*Nerd* Anderson!" she yelled, "I'll get you one day, I promise!"

Lenny broke into a fit of laughter (until Mosie waved at Peggy's bedroom window). Peggy pressed her hand against the glass and let the yellowed sheet fall between them. Lenny raced into the house.

"Don't you worry, 'Peggy No-Middle-Name' Anderson. I'll get you out of there, one way or another." The tires on her bike kicked up small puffs of dust and dirt as she sped down the dirt driveway.

Nearing the base of Kill-Deer, Lenny and his slime-blob clouded her mind. She looked at her shoes and veered to the side of the road.

"Another scuff." She sat down in the gravel. "*Injuns, papoose*— He's such a jerk." She sniffed up her tears, rubbed a black smudge from the side of her sneaker, and held her shirt to her nose. The air wasn't sweet anymore; it had turned rotten like Lenny.

"What the *hell* is that smell?" she said, looking over her shoulder. She spotted one of the desolate hunting trails John had warned about; the ones tucked between groves of hardwood trees and wild brush along the roadsides.

"Those paths," he had explained, "lead down into Kill-Deer's swamps. They're made by bears. Hunters use them to track their kill. Don't ever try venturing down one; you're likely to get lost. Those swamps go on for miles, and plenty of good hunters never made it out. Besides, you might come across a bear or some hunter thinking you're a bear and get yourself shot."

The moldy smell in the air grew stronger, and so did the snaps of twigs and the crunching of dead leaves. Studying the ground beneath the low laying branches, she thought of Willowdean and her warnings about strange animals, especially wild ones.

"Some are diseased and can make a person go mad in the head if they get bit. If you stare an animal in the eyes, you are calling it to a challenge."

Mosie froze. Her shirt slipped from her fingers.

A dark mound standing in the path lowered its head and swung it back and forth, inspecting her. It took a step forward and made its way up the narrow hunters' path. Mosie looked away just as Willowdean had instructed. She scooped up a handful of gravel, slowly stood up, and grabbed her bike. She put herself on it and gave the pedals a heavy push. The beast slowly passing her sat in the middle of the highway, yawned, and gave itself a good scratch about its floppy ears.

A dog, it's a dog! Mosie thought. *It must have been hunting for some time, maybe even lost.*

It was thin, pathetically thin; its skin ran tight between its ribs like dried-up dark molasses. Clusters of wood ticks, *Hundreds of them buggers,* Mosie thought, stuck to it like overgrown green gooseberries.

Under a black crust of swamp-muck, she could see a distinct dribble of white running from the top of the dog's head to the tip of its nose; the same splattering ran its underside, chest, legs and the tip of its tail.

If that thing lunges at me, I'll end up down in the ravine, and it'll get me for sure, Mosie thought, eying the distance between it and the side of the highway. She squeezed the rocks in her hand and looked up at Kill-Deer Hill, hoping her pa's truck would somehow miraculously appear.

"Go home!" she tried calling out to it, "go home." The words slipped down her throat. She tried again, this time mustering all the courage she had.

"Go home, get!"

With half-sleeping eyes, the dog panted and ignored her.

"Please, just go," Mosie tried cooing.

It flicked its head and growled a low *rooooo.*

"Please, Mother Mary, please let a car or truck, a bike, anything, anything at all come to my rescue, *please*." The dog looked up at the hill with her and whined.

In the distance, the sound of Marty Robbins and the roof of a semi-truck rose above Kill-Deer's summit.

"Thank you, Mother," Mosie whispered, "thank you."

The semi made the mount and began racing downward toward Mosie and the dog. "Marty's" blonde hair was slicked down nice and neat and his fluffy sideburns ruffled down his cheeks; she could see him through the windshield. "Wild as the Texas wind . . ." he bellowed, "Wild as the Texas wind . . ."

"Too fast," Mosie said, "too fast." She dared not wave, letting "Marty" know she was there.

Sudden movements will cause animals to attack, Willowdean warned in her head. *Running in the opposite direction means a chase for sure.*

The dog tilted its head, looked at her, and licked its lips. "Oh you damn thing!" Mosie, said. The animal, groaning a *roo*, scratched itself.

Mosie started counting the seconds it would take the truck to reach them. "Thirty-three, thirty-two, thirty-one. We're both going to get hit because of you, you idiot!" she screeched as she stared at the dog. She looked at the semi. She knew she had no choice (even if it meant being mad-capped forever because of a dog bite). She let go of the rocks and tossed her bike to the ground.

Racing toward the dog, she tackled it. It yipped.

The roar of the truck switched to a piercing explosion of wind, tumbling her and the dog, downward, rolling them over prickle bushes and jagged rocks. Crashing to the bottom of the ditch, they slammed against a boulder with a thud. The dog lay still and quiet. Mosie looked up the embankment. The ridge seemed a mile away. She winced from the sting pitting her arms and legs; she choked on the stale exhaust trapped in the ditch. Somewhere next to her the crickets began to chirp. "Sweet Mother Mary," she prayed, "what have I done?"

To climb to the top of the mound would take time. *Impossible with a wild animal at my heels,* she thought, looking back at the hound.

Rising to its legs, the dog pointed its tail stiffly downward. *Oh God, please, walk the other way*, she pleaded, watching it head toward her, one gimpy step after the next. Her body tightened. She closed her eyes and waited.

A warm, hiss of air rushing from the hound's moist nostrils pressed against her forehead; it carried with it the rotten stench of the swamps. Its muzzle nudged the front of her neck; its tongue, thick with saliva, began brushing her face as if tasting her. Mosie shuddered.

Without warning, the dog stooped down and lay next to her, forcing its head in the folds of her arm. It whimpered as if its momma had finally returned to it.

Mosie opening her eyes looked into the sky. A set of crows circling above let out a chant of mischievous *caw-caw-caws* then fluttered away. She peered at the dog. It avoided her gaze.

"For crying out loud," she said as she sat up and rested on her elbows. "That thing's as scared as I am." Gently, she placed her hand on its soiled coat. Lifting its brows, the dog sighed and let Mosie know that it too was relieved.

She pulled herself up from the ground. "Well dog," she said, trying not to let her words get unsteady. "I have to go now, so don't bite me or anything, okay?" Its tongue jigged from its mouth as it stood next to her. Its back came up to the middle of her thighs.

"I suggest you stay away from that highway up there," Mosie said as she headed for the embankment. She looked up the hill.

"And the Anderson house; stay away from *that* place. That Lenny sure is a mean son of a-you-know-what." Grabbing a clump of thick weeds she tugged them like a rope, yanking herself up. She looked at her sneakers as they sunk into the moist dark ground.

"Oh well, I have to wash them anyway," she sighed, reaching for more shrubbery. At the top of the cliff, she looked down at the dog. It watched her from its trough. *Ra-roo—Rra-roooo,* it bayed, wagging its tail. *Ra-roo.*

Mosie ran her hand over the scratches on her legs and arms. The scent of the wild dog and its swamp clung to her. She gave the hound one last look, and then picked up her bike. The hound let out a long *raa-roo-rooo-roooo* as Mosie lugged her legs over her bike.

She held in her tears as she looked up Kill-Deer Hill. She would be home soon enough and would need them.

CHAPTER EIGHTEEN

The kitchen door opened. Mosie had to think fast. She knew getting nearly killed by a crazed Marty Robbins driving a semi-truck would send Willowdean into a fit, especially if it was on account of saving a wild dog roaming the highway. And she knew she couldn't snitch on Lenny for calling her a papoose then spitting at her. Such a snitch might risk her loosing Peggy.

She knelt, pretending to fix the chains on her bike while Willowdean hurried down the porch steps.

"Guess Pa's going to have to look at it," she said with deliberate disgust, pretending she didn't know Willowdean was standing behind her. She stood up and squeezed the brake handles, then tugged the cables.

Willowdean pinched her nose with her apron. "What in the world happened to you?" she asked; the rotten smell sent panic flashing in her eyes.

"Look at your clothes, your legs, your arms. You smell worse than a skunk! *Katherine*, what did you get into?"

Mosie sniffled and wiped her nose with her arm in hopes her pitch would be successful.

"Well, you know how you're always telling me to be careful?" she said with the most modest tone she could muster.

"Yes, yes I do," Willowdean choked and backed away.

"Well Ma . . ." Mosie whimpered as she wrestled with the bike chains again, "I should have listened to you . . . I just should have listened. But no, I thought I knew better than you, and well, I didn't."

Turning to Willowdean, she sniffled again letting the tears saved since Kill-Deer trickle down her cheeks.

"Well, see, I went into tenth gear, just like your always telling me not to, and . . . oh Ma, I'm sorry. As you can see, I sure learned my lesson," she sniveled again, this time adding a few extra sobs.

"Oh my poor baby," Willowdean fussed, rushing to put her arms around Mosie. She backed away with a gag.

Confident her plan was working, Mosie gave Willowdean an expression of veneration she thought even God Himself would believe.

"Don't you worry, honey," Willowdean cooed, "as long as you learned your lesson, and promise you won't do that again that's all that matters. "Now, why don't you hose yourself off, and then come inside and take a nice hot shower."

Mosie rubbed her arms. "But Ma," she said with a moan, "the hose water is *sooo* cold, and I might catch a chill and get sick."

"I'm sorry, sweetheart, but I don't think I can take the whole house smelling like whatever it is you smell like. Just try to rinse off enough to get rid of some of that smell, and then come inside and shower."

Mosie puckered. "Okay, Momma."

"You're a good girl, Mosie," Willowdean mewed, heading for the house.

Mosie knew not to let go of her pitiful demeanor, not yet. And she was right. Just as expected, Willowdean stopped and looked at the bike. She furrowed her eyes.

Quickly, Mosie picked up the hose and turned it on. "Big stupid dummy, I am," she scuffed, running the frigid water up and down her legs. She gave a good shiver.

"Your father's still sleeping," Willowdean said. "When he gets up, he can look at your bike for you."

Mosie nodded. "Good."

"Where's Peggy? Wasn't she supposed to come back with you?"

Mosie watched the mud balls bouncing in the water jump on and off her Keds. "Um, she's still sleeping."

Willowdean bit her bottom lip. "Well, maybe after while she'll take a ride over."

"Okay Momma." Mosie watched her go up the stairs and into the house. She stared at the puddle and tapped her soggy shoes in the muck-water. "Marty Robbins," she snapped, her thoughts turning to the wild dog, and Lenny. "I wish I could tell Ma," she said as she turned off the hose. She walked to the porch and peeked through the kitchen door-window. Willowdean sat at the table, sipping her coffee. In front of her lay Granny's birch bark medicine book.

"Papoose, injun," Mosie repeated, watching Willowdean turn the pages. She covered her arm with her hand and went inside. "I don't need anything special," she said, picking up a cookie from the platter sitting on the counter. "I'm just scratched up a bit, that's all."

Willowdean closed the book. "Well," she ran her fingers over the white bumpy, birch bark cover, "maybe we should put some store salve on any way."

She got up from the table; under her thin blue robe, her hips swayed to the counter. She opened the medicine drawer, and pulled out a tube of store bought antiseptic and cotton gauze.

"I think you better shower before we put this on, and before your father gets up," she scrunched her face.

Mosie bit her cookie. "Ma, when we make a promise, we're supposed to keep it, aren't we? I mean, if it's a good promise, not a bad one?"

"Yes, yes we are."

"What if we break our promises, not on purpose, but say, if the promise was too big, and you really didn't know it at the time you made it?"

Willowdean cupped her hands around Mosie's face. "Katherine," she said, searching Mosie's 'Bitmen blue' eyes. "Sometimes, sometimes we all make promises we just can't keep, no matter how hard we try." She wiped the crumbs from Mosie's lips.

"But the most important thing is, keep trying, no matter how difficult it seems. You would be surprised what good can come from such a difficult promise. Now, go get in the shower. You're making me sick." She pecked Mosie's forehead with a kiss.

"Ma, I sure love you."

"I love you, too, and that's a promise I will always keep."

Hurrying down the hall, Mosie knew her promise to Mother Mary concerning Peggy truly was important.

Willowdean flashed her finger, motioning Mosie to her side by the counter.

"Your father has a headache," she said extra softly, scowling at John sitting at the table. "We need to be quiet." She twisted open the tube of ointment and spread some across Mosie's arm. "Maybe next Sunday you two can go to church."

John grunted and ran his fingers through his hair. "Flu," he mumbled. "Must have a flu bug."

"Yeah, The Benny Flu Bug," Mosie giggled. "You can only get it on Saturday nights."

"*Bullshit*," John spat and mashed his lips tightly together.

Willowdean tugged Mosie's arm. "That's enough," she scolded.

John rubbed his neck and glanced at Mosie. "What happened to you anyway?"

"Well, um," Mosie stammered as she counted Willowdean's swift and gentle movements as she taped the gauze onto her arm.

"Got yourself in trouble again, didn't you?" John said, giving his pants a tug. Mosie swallowed.

"No, I, um . . . I just had an accident is all. Kids can have accidents, can't they?"

"Accident? What kind of accident?"

Willowdean rubbed her belly. She sighed, shooting a glare at John. "She's fine, John, just fine. Mosie, after your father fixes your bike, why don't take a run over to Peggy's and see if she's up yet?"

"For the love of Pete," John moaned. "What did you do to your bike?"

Mosie jetted to the refrigerator. John rolled his eyes. "For crying out loud! Would you answer me?" Mosie stuck her head inside the fridge and took a deep breath. "I," she made sure her voice wasn't shaking. "I . . . fixed it . . . after Ma came back into the house, I fixed it."

"What was wrong with it?"

"The brake cable, the brake cable was stuck. That's all."

"Oh yeah?" John rubbed his neck. "Front or back?"

Mosie poked John's Sunday night steak wrapped in wax paper sitting next to the milk. "Um . . . um . . . the back, the back brakes. Ma, how long can an animal, oh, say maybe a dog or something like that, live in the wild on its own?"

"A long time, if it knows how to hunt well."

"Oh. Do they get hungry a lot? I mean, more than a dog that lives with people?"

"Yes, yes they do."

"Oh," Mosie said, peeking over her shoulder at Willowdean and John.

He was nursing his head while she put away the bandages and ointment. Mosie slipped the steak into her hand.

"Ma, what if—"

"That's enough!" John said, massaging his temples. "Dogs! For the love of Pete! Is that all you ever think about, dogs? I told you, I would get you one when I can; that should be good enough."

Quickly, Mosie stuffed his dinner down her pants. "Sorry Pa," she shut the refrigerator and smiled sweetly at Willowdean.

"I'll be back," she raced out the door before they could spot the lump of meat in her trousers. She jumped down the porch steps and looked up at the spackle of clouds coming in from the lake. "Two dogs and half a cat."

I wonder which ones are the animals, she thought about the man in her dream; the one who called himself Animal Spirit.

She grabbed her bike and looked up at the clouds again. *I wonder if one of them is for me.* She pedaled down the highway and kept an extra eye out for any vehicles traveling to the base of Kill-Deer. From the top of the ravine, the ditch didn't appear as treacherous as she had set in her mind, not since she was able to see where the rocks and picker bushes sprouted up.

"Wild or not, that dog has got to be hungry," she patted John's meal in her pants. She called down the gully. Only the *clicks* and *cleeks* of the bugs in the ditch answered back. She called out again.

"Oh dog, here dog . . . I have some food for you. Don't make me come down there." She studied the gully. Still, not a stir. She grasped a young sapling, set her feet in the moist, rocky soil, and then sat down. An avalanche of dirt slid down the knoll. She followed her footprints from her upward climb and slowly guided herself safely back down into the depths below.

After wiping the dirt from her pants, she looked over the ditch.

It was amazingly green with vegetation, and surprisingly quiet. At its edge, a line of thick brush hid the scanty trail leading to the swamps, the one she had spotted just a few, short hours ago; the one the dog had traveled, the one leading to the end of the Hunters Trail. She pulled the steak out from her pants unwrapped it, and held it in the air.

"Hey dog!" she hollered. "It's okay. You can come out now; it's just me, Mosie, Mosie Bitmen! I brought you something!" She flapped the meat and hoped the dog was near enough to catch its scent. A rustle came up behind her. She turned and held out the slab of raw meat.

Amber-brown eyes peered at her from the brush. Slowly, she knelt on one knee. Sniffing the air with its long hound dog snout and with its drip of white, the dog emerged. It took a few steps forward as its black, velvety ears swept and flopped against its sleek neck. It stopped as if on command, and cowered, tucking its white tipped tail between its long white legs.

"It's okay. I won't hurt you," Mosie said nervously as she got ready to toss the hunk of meat. "Just as long as you don't hurt me."

It took a few more strides forward, then, as if it too tired to move any further, it paused, layed down, and rested its head on its paws.

"Ah, you poor thing," Mosie cooed and squatted down with it. "Look at how damn thin you are."

Staying low, she wobbled toward it. It got up and pranced uneasily back and forth.

"Guess we're not sure of each other, are we? Well, I have to go anyway so I'll just give you this. I have other business to take care of you know. Besides, if my pa or ma drove by and caught me down here, there's going to be you know what to pay, that's for sure."

The hound raised its nose to the highway and sniffed the wind.

"What's the matter?" Mosie asked, looking up at the hill. The dog whined, lowering its head and trotted into the woods. That's when Mosie spotted Peggy standing at the top of the ditch, rock in hand.

"Peggy, no!" she shouted.

"Get away from that thing!" Peggy yelled back. "That's a wild dog; it'll bite you for sure!" She flung the stone, nearly hitting Mosie. "You'll get the rabies. It belonged to Lenny. It got away from him before he could shoot it. It's crazy!"

"Agh, *you're* crazy," Mosie yelled back as she looked at the dog. It hid in the bushes, shuddering. She held out the meat.

"It's alright. That's just Peggy," she called to it. "She ain't, err, isn't nothing, err, I mean, anything,"

The dog crept from the bushes and stood next to her. Mosie placed her hand on top of its head; the dog opened its mouth lavishing her hand with its tongue.

Peggy shrieked. "What are you doing?" she screamed.

Seizing the steak, the dog ran back into the woods.

"I'll be back, don't you worry," Mosie hollered to it. "*Don't you worry.*

"Peggy Anderson, you have the biggest mouth in all of Bayfield, you know that?" she huffed and climbed onto the road.

"And you're the *dumbest* city kid I ever did meet. Everyone knows Lenny got that dog from one of those animal shelters, and it turned on him. He wanted a hunting dog, but every time he brought *that thing* out, the stupid thing would shake and turn tail. Lenny did everything he knew to break it.

"He tried beating it. He tried starving it. He tried *everything* he could, but it still turned on him. That dog was just born bad, Mosie, can't you see that? It's got bad blood in it, and nothing you do can cure it.

Besides, if Lenny ever sees it, he'll shoot it and put it out of its misery; that's all a person can do, put it out of its misery. Now come on, let's get out of here before it comes after us."

"For crying out loud," Mosie spat, tugged her pants, and headed for her bike. "I might not know much about dogs, or any other animals for that matter, but I do know, that dog living in those woods isn't a killer no more then you're a—"

"A what, a *whore*? Is that what you were going to say?"

"No," Mosie lied. "A . . . a . . . killer like Lenny, that's what I was going to say; a killer, just like Lenny."

"*Well*," Peggy huffed with pride. "I am mean, if you haven't noticed, and I do have nasty mean blood running through me like Lenny."

With hands on skinny hips, she spat a small spittle of saliva onto the ground. Mosie pulled her giggle down into her stomach.

Peggy snarled and stuck her flimsy fists up to Mosie's face. "If you don't believe me, you can go ahead and give me a try."

Mosie could see the fear in Peggy's dull, hazel eyes. "Stop it," she ordered and backed away, pushing Peggy's hands from her.

"You're right. You *are* mean and nasty, a *real* killer, just like Lenny and that-that-that-that, *wild* animal down there in those woods."

"Yeah, well, you just remember that, Mosie Bitmen," Peggy gloated as she put down her shaking fists.

"Oh, I will, Peggy. I will!" Mosie grabbed her bike. "Just tell me one thing, okay?"

"Yeah, what is it?" Peggy snapped as she wrestled her home-made boy's bike from the ground.

"Is it a boy dog or a girl dog? What's its name?"

"Its name is Scarlet, and she's a bitch."

"That isn't right, Peggy. You shouldn't call an animal names like that even if it is mean and nasty and wild. It doesn't know any better."

Peggy laughed. "Tsk, no, you dumb city slicker, a female. That's what a girl dog is called, a bitch, and her name is Scarlet."

"Oh. How long has she been out there anyway?"

"'Bout a year. Hey, you ain't thinking of trying to tame that thing, are ya'?"

Mosie leered at the wooded swampland. "Heck no," she pictured Lenny going after the hound with a gun. "I don't want to get the rabies. Hey, Ma wants to know if you want to have Sunday supper with us tonight. I think she's going to be making chicken instead of steak."

"Sure," Peggy raced Mosie to the top of Kill-Deer. She stopped.

"Geez, now what's wrong?"

"Mosie, are you really an Indian princess?" Mosie grinned.

June 16, 1972

Dear Val,

I think I found myself a dog. But don't tell anyone.

Love, Your sister,

Moe

CHAPTER NINETEEN

"Gizhe-manidoo|g ayami`etaw anami`etaw zhawenim
baaba maandan
biisaojichaagomaa|g, ojichaag|wag aaniish naa . . ."
'Creator bless this little soul'

Peggy looked goofy as she crouched behind John's stack of firewood behind the garage. "*Like a crazy clown*," Mosie whispered.

It wasn't so much that Mosie's black and white polka-dotted rain slicker was three sizes too small for Peggy and that her elbows stuck out the cuffs; it was the way the streaks of black mascara ran down her blotchy pink powdered cheeks.

"Waterproof, my ass," Mosie said, watching Peggy rub the stinging dye from her eyes. "Told you, you were dumb for putting all that makeup crap on your face." The early morning plan was to secretly watch Willowdean say her prayers, rain, or no rain.

"Well at least I ain't sniffing these stupid old logs like I'm about to eat them," Peggy whispered back.

Mosie giggled. She was right. The smell of mushrooms and wet nuts fused with dirt on damp oak and maple logs replaced her previously favorite summer city odor: hot tar mixed with diesel.

"Oh, just be quiet," she said, fixing her nose on a piece of rough, smelly bark.

Peggy rolled her eyes. "Yea, well, you look like a nut, so there," she said, wiping her blackened cheeks against her wet arm. Mosie gave the log an extra-long hard sniff.

"Oh, and you don't?" she said, adding, "sixteen," to her count of the deep crackling echoes of thunder rolling from one side of the light-gray sky to the next. It seemed the rumblings were coming and going just to gather up Willowdean's prayers. It gave Peggy the jitters.

"What's she saying, what's she saying?" Peggy asked, as she tried to rub away the chain of goose bumps on her arms.

"How am I supposed to know?" Mosie pulled herself off the logs, thanking God the rain had stopped, leaving behind microscopic beads of moisture in the air and creating a veil of silvery haze.

"Is that an eagle feather she's flagging around? Cause I heard they use eagle feathers a lot."

"Oh brother, and I suppose you think they lived in teepees, too, huh?" Peggy blinked.

"First off, dodo brain, that isn't an eagle's feather. Eagle feathers look like they've been dipped in cocoa. The one Ma's got in her hands is just plain old black, so I'm guessing it's a crow's feather. Besides, Eagle feathers were used for medals to show how strong and courageous a Brave was for killing one of their enemies. And no, my mom's people did not sleep in teepees like out West. They lived in huts made out of birch bark, called wigwams."

"Oh," Peggy said, squinting through the mist, stroking her arms, the tiny nubs swelling up again. She watched the whitish gray smoke rising from the abalone shell in Willowdean's hands.

"Now what is she doing?"

"She's sending prayers up to the Great Spirit, to God.

See, my ancestors, they used tobacco to scare away any evil spirits that were trying to cling to their prayers. But this time Ma's using red willow leaves and sticks 'cause she don't have any real tobacco. That's what her people did when they couldn't get a hold of real tobacco leaves; they used red willow leaves and sticks."

"Oh." Peggy watched Willowdean sway the crow feather back and forth through the rising smoke.

"Val says since tobacco is used for just prayers and nothing else, it works better than the frankincense and myrrh in church.

"See, he found out years ago that priests used incense to mostly cover up everybody's B.O. He said people couldn't take so many baths back then, and that they really stunk because of it."

Peggy shivered so bad Mosie thought for sure she was going to run home. But she didn't. Instead, she bit her painted red lips like she was waiting for her thoughts to catch up with her. Then she said, "Mosie, I ain't ever been to church before. What's it like? Is it like witchcraft or something?"

"Naw," Mosie replied. "During the Mass, the priest comes in wearing a long colorful robe holding a bible up to his head. And then young boys, called altar boys, come walking in behind him, carrying lit candles. Then there's what's called, communion and confessions."

"It sure sounds like witchcraft to me," Peggy said, her eyes nearly twenty times larger than normal.

"Well, it ain't, er isn't! It's how God wants us to worship Him." Peggy started bawling. "Sure as heck," she said, staring at Willowdean, "me and your ma's going to hell."

"Oh, you and my ma are *not* going to hell; you're both going to purgatory. But don't you worry, Peggy; I can pray the two of you out of there. It might take an awful lot of Hail Mary's, but I can do it.

"See, me and Candy, we prayed her aunt Margaret out of there, and she was *twice* as bad as you. Besides, the Lord knows it isn't your fault you're the way you are; it's Lenny's. He's the one going to hell."

Peggy sniffled. "I sure am glad you made that promise to that Mary lady."

"It's okay, No-Name," Mosie said, patting Peggy's boney back. "Friends do things like that for each other."

"Friends? So, we're friends, really friends?"

"Tsk, of course we're friends. What did you think?"

"Friends," Peggy said under her breath. "Hey, if I go to the confessions and then the communions and start worshiping God, like He wants, *then* will He let me go to Heaven with you and your pa? What about Lenny, and Corinne?"

Before Mosie could answer, a flock of crows flew overhead and perched in the pines above them.

"Oh-oh," Mosie gulped, pulling herself and Peggy down behind the stack of wood. But it was too late. Willowdean stopped praying and headed right toward the racket, (and them). That's when she noticed the project they'd been working on, and that's when the birds started making a real hullabaloo. Mosie knew what it meant. Willowdean was taking it as an omen.

"Ma's funny hormones aren't going to get us out of this one," Mosie said in a near whisper.

"*Us?*"

Mosie grimaced. "Be quiet," she peered over the logs.

With hands on plumpy hips, Willowdean looked at the boat, then the crows. "Girls," she said, "what exactly are you two building back here?" Her voice was calm, too calm. "And Peggy, don't you try sneaking off." Peggy stopped in her tracks and her eyes widened with fear. Mosie stared at the lumber, and swallowed.

"Well Ma," she began, stepping slowly out from the wall of logs. "That there is just an experiment." She swallowed again and tried to wet her gullet. "You see, me and Peggy here, well, we figured since you and Pa are always talking about making your own boat one day, you know, after the baby comes, well, we figured maybe we could build you and Pa one, as a surprise."

She looked down at her shoes and scuffed them through the dirt, avoiding Willowdean's skin-tight stare. She knew her ma's silence meant they were in trouble. Holding her breath, she waited, hoping the act of kindness (and Willowdean's mixed up hormones) would make her cry from happiness instead of doling out a punishment.

Peggy's mouth stuck, unable to mutter a word. She bent down and anxiously scratched her ankle.

Willowdean crossed her arms.

"Well Katherine, the only problem is . . . we never talked about wanting a boat.' She pointed her finger at the house. "March! Both of you."

Peggy tried not to cry, just like Candy did the day Willowdean caught her and Mosie playing at East Park.

"It's filled with bums and perverts," John constantly warned.

"They knew they did wrong on purpose," Mosie recalled Willowdean telling Candy's mom, "since they both were crying about getting caught."

Mosie glanced at Peggy. "Don't you start blubbering," she whispered as she remembered the two lonely weeks without Candy. "It'll just make things worse." They climbed the porch stairs and stepped into the kitchen. "You two, sit and don't move."

Mosie leaned over the table and clutched Peggy's arm. "No matter what," she said, watching Willowdean make her way to the wash-room, "do not shed a tear about anything, not a *thing*!" Willowdean shuffled from the bathroom, plunked in her chair, and sighed.

"Girls," she said as her eyes teared up, "I'm having a hard time right now, and I just couldn't take it if something bad happened to either one of you. So please, don't try anything foolish. Promise me."

"Oh, don't cry, Mrs. Bitmen, please," Peggy jumped out of her chair. She put her arms around her. "We promise, don't we, Mosie? Mosie's pretty smart for a city kid. She knew how to get away from that wild dog when that big semi almost ran them over, and she knew how to get out of that ravine, didn't she?"

Mosie's head swam. "Doggone it, Peggy!"

"And we weren't really going to use that dumb old boat she's making to go look for Dog Island like she thinks we are. Heck, I would've stopped her."

Willowdean grabbed the edge of the table.

"Katherine Rose Bitmen!" she gasped and turned whiter than the bleached rocks along the shores of Lake Superior.

"Ma, no!" Mosie leapt from the table and shook her hands as if they were on fire. "Don't listen to her. It isn't like that, er, wasn't, not *that* bad . . . No-no . . . I-I mean, I was going to tell you; really I was, when the time was right. I mean, I wanted to, but—I'm going to kill you, Peggy, I'm going to kill you—"

"Fine, go ahead and kill me," she said, pulling Mosie's fist up to her nose. "I ain't lying to your mom. She's . . . she's an angel, that's what she is, an angel, and you don't even care; you're terrible, Mosie Bitmen, you're terrible, and I'll prove it." Peggy forced Mosie's fist to her nose. "Go ahead, hit me."

"Enough!" Willowdean shouted. "Mosie, sit down and be quiet; you too, Peggy."

Slinking into their chairs, the girls stared at Willowdean, their eyes glazed wide.

Willowdean wavered and headed for the sink. She turned on the faucet, filled a glass with water, and listened to the thunder clapping in the distance.

She took a long, hard drink. "Animal Spirit . . ." she said under her breath.

"Mother, you—you've never yelled at me like that before," Mosie said softly.

"And you have never lied to me like this before; except when you and Candy ran off to East Park."

"May I go home now?" Peggy asked, rising from her chair.

"No, no you may not," Willowdean made her way to the table. "You two are going to tell me what happened, and Mosie, don't you dare try telling me any more stories."

The more Willowdean listened to the explanations of worn planks of lumber, and how they were going to make their way to Dog Island with Mosie, and the encounter with Lenny, and how a wild hound dog named Scarlet came to her after the Animal Spirit dream, the more weak and ashen she became.

They sat silently together and listened to the last slaps of thunder rolling off to its next destination.

Nervously, Peggy wrung her hands. "Now may I go home?" she asked.

Willowdean looked at the girls and sighed.

"Well . . ." she cleared her throat and brushed her hands across her lap, "I wish you two would have just come and told me about all this in the first place."

"I wanted to, really I did," Mosie said. "But I figured you would get mad and ground me all summer, and I wouldn't get to see Peggy until school started."

"And I didn't hardly know any of this, until now, Mrs. Bitmen, really I didn't," Peggy said. "I tried telling Mosie how crazy mean that dog is and how it's gone wild out in the swamps and how Lenny's been trying to shoot it for a year now . . . and I tried telling her there just ain't no real place called Dog Island . . ."

Mosie sank in her seat. *Sure shit*, she thought, listening to Peggy rattle on. *She's going to run right to Lenny and tell him all about this.*

First, she's going to tell how Ma was in back of the garage burning strange plants in a sea shell in the middle of a rainstorm while singing and talking in that Indian language of hers.

Then, she'll tell on Scarlet, and show him where I found her. Then creepy Lenny will sneak out, find poor old Scarlet, and put a bullet in that pitiful hound head of hers before she even has a chance to scrounge up her next meal.

"Excuse me," Mosie said, "I don't mean to interrupt, but Ma, you're not going to tell Pa, are you?"

"No, no I am not. *You* are."

"But Ma—"

"Well, I'm not the one who lied now, am I?"

"No," Mosie looked out the window. She crossed her toes. "You're right and so is Peggy, and I apologize. I promise I'll never lie to either one of you again."

"And I'm sorry, too," Peggy offered and got up to give Willowdean a hug.

"Good," Willowdean said. "Now, I think I have an idea both of you will like. I think it's going to be extra hot today with high humidity. Matter of fact, by the time we pack up a picnic lunch and head down to the beach, it'll be so warm you girls will be able to swim."

Peggy put her hand up to the cool stormy air wafting through the kitchen door. "Uhuh," she said, smiling. "No way."

"Oh yeah?" Mosie challenged. "I'll bet you your last dollar it will, too. Can we do that, Ma? And maybe we can even make your special tuna fish sandwiches, the ones with celery bits in them."

Grabbing Mosie's hands, Peggy squealed with delight. "And strawberry pie for dessert? We can call it our Making-up Beach Lunch Party."

Willowdean laughed. "Okay, okay, let's get going then."

Peggy grinned as if she had just won her first beauty pageant and said, "I better get cleaned up," as she hurried to the bathroom.

Mosie watched Willowdean get out the tuna fish sandwich makings.

"I'll help you," she pulled a knife from the drawer. Seeing her plan of distraction was working and started chopping the stalks of celery.

"Ma, I didn't want to say anything, not in front of Peggy," she said softly, "but that dog Scarlet, she's in trouble, bad.

She's in terrible shape. Fact is, she's not even wild, not really; she's just scared is all, and Lenny's going to shoot her because of it just as soon as he can catch her."

"I don't want you getting between Peggy and Lenny, especially over a dog; it will bring nothing but trouble."

"I know, Ma. You're not mad at me, are you?" She handed Willowdean the bowl of diced celery.

"No, I'm not mad at you Katherine. I'm disappointed."

"I think I'd rather have you mad at me."

"White bread or wheat?"

"White."

"Don't ever trick me like that again."

"I'm sorry."

"Mosie, do you understand I don't ever want you being afraid to come to me or your father about *anything*. A lot happens to a person when they're growing up, even afterward's, too."

"Yeah," Mosie hugged Willowdean extra tight. "I won't. I promise.

"Ma, when did you get your first dog?"

Willowdean scooted the sandwiches over to Mosie.

"Here, cut these," she said. "Then wrap them in wax paper.

Some things are best left in the past."

"Ma, is there really such a person as Animal Spirit, or is he, you know, like Mary Worth?"

"We can talk about that at a later time."

Peggy waltzed into the kitchen just as Willowdean was placing the pie and sandwiches into the plaid Green-Stamp picnic basket.

Mosie reached to wipe the makeup off Peggy's face. "You look like a third-rate Prima Donna," she said.

"Jealous?"

Mosie laughed. "No way."

"Girls," Willowdean handed Peggy the picnic basket. "Go to the car while I grab some blankets. I'll be right there in a few minutes."

Willowdean hurried to her bedroom and slid open the closet door. She grabbed the blankets folded neatly on top of her willowreed trunk. Granny whispered in her head. "*The Bridge has opened. You heard her yourself.*" Willowdean stepped away from the trunk. "No, not my Katherine, not now."

"*It's too late.*"

"But it's such a hard lesson."

"*Yes, and also one that teaches so much.*"

Turning back to the trunk, Willowdean turned back to the trunk and opened it with trembling hands.

Carefully, she dug to its very bottom and pulled out a dark-brown wool blanket, the very one Granny herself used when she was a child. Putting it to her nose, she took a deep sniff. His smell was gone.

"Bagwaji- Ode`imaa|ns, Wild Heart," she said.

"So it is for all bagwadasim|oog (wild dog), who no longer have ojichaag|wags (spirits of the living)," Granny said, reminding her how *"They take their Earthly scents with them when they cross back over The Bridge. You know that."*

"I will not allow it," Willowdean held back her tears and put the blanket back in its chest. "I will *not* allow it." She closed the lid.

CHAPTER TWENTY

As predicted, the day was growing hotter by the minute, and so was Bayfield Harbor (and so was Peggy). She grunted as another young, swimsuit-clad male tourist walked past the edges of her towels and blankets.

"Ugh, he's such a hunk!"

"Ah geez, for crying out loud," Mosie looked at Peggy's glazed eyes.

The Glaze of Passion. That's what Val called it, even though Mother Prudence said it was just plain *Filthy Lust*. Well, whatever it was, Mosie knew she didn't want any part of it.

"That's what's going to send you to hell," she picked through the mound of tiny pebbles in her hand.

Peggy snorted. "For what?"

"For looking at boys like you do. I counted six of um' so far, and six times you said, 'Ugggg! What a huuunk.'" She put her hand up in the air and swirled it.

"Tsk, I did not go and put my hand up in the air and twist it like that," Peggy coiled her fist around like a dancing air snake. "And I did not make my eyes and tongue pop out like that either."

"Oh, just be quiet and pull your bikini straps up like a young lady before Ma comes back and sees you."

"I can't help it," Peggy tried not to notice the firm backside of another beach-walker. "I just get stirred up down there. That's all."

"Peggy-No Middle-Name-Anderson, what the hell are you talking about?"

"Well," she turned over on her stomach to face Mosie, "You know, that feeling, that *special* feeling you get just thinking about kissing? Well, it's *that* special feeling."

"No, I don't know, nor do I care. Hey, why don't you try thinking of something else next time, like pumpkins at Halloween or something like that?"

"Tsk, pumpkins at Halloween; that's gotta' be the stupidest thing I ever heard. Pumpkins."

Peggy snatched a peek at a boy sitting a few yards in front of her and Mosie. She smiled, but her grin faded as his lips twisted at her with an uninterested smirk. He reached up and grabbed hold of another girl's hand.

"Besides," Peggy said, "I don't know if it'll work. That feeling gets pretty strong sometimes."

"Well, if that don't take care of it, ask Mother Mary to help you, and then say some Hail Marys, and a few Our Fathers until your fires are put out."

"But I don't know those prayers, or any prayers, Mosie, not a one."

Mosie sighed. "Oh boy. I'll write them out for you so you can learn them, okay?"

"Okay, but what if that don't work either?"

"Well, Sister Vern Mary said it works nearly every time, and she should know since she's a virgin, being married to Jesus, you know. But whatever you do, don't touch yourself down there. According to my friend, Candy, it'll just make it worse. "Peggy watched the boy give his girlfriend a kiss and took a bite out of her sandwich.

"Mosie," she said, "do you think your pa will let me go to church with you guys this Sunday?"

"Sure, but it's called Mass, not church. Hey, Ma's over there at Mr. Maki's. Let's wave."

Willowdean waved back from Mr. Maki's deck. She gazed over the Great Lake and then stepped inside the novelty shop. Time, like a seafaring mirage, seemed to be fading backwards. The same old smell of aged dust and stale, black licorice greeted her like old friends.

Mr. Maki looked up from his cash register and closed the drawer. Its tiny bell had the same tinny-clang, and he, the same nod.

"Good day," he said, his voice a bit deeper, a tad rougher than she remembered.

With a smile and a bashful nod back, she picked up a hand-basket sitting at the door's entrance. Its yellow and red-striped cloth was a bit torn and faded and its brown wooden handle, worn smooth from years of use, seemed much smaller in her hand but still familiar. So were the clinks and clanks of some-one picking up items and placing them back on the wooden shelves.

Tourist, she thought, slipping between the aisles (and mem-ories) of a much younger Mr. Maki.

She knew how he had wanted a child all his own and how Mrs. Maki had forbade it. It was common knowledge, now lost with those many years gone by.

Mrs. Maki's concern about going belly-up emphasized how raising a child would get them there all the quicker. Mr. Maki was reminded of this every time Mrs. Maki caught him indulging *his youngsters* with a few pieces of penny candies when they'd come into the store.

Come Christmas, Mrs. Maki found no shame expressing her thoughts of her husband's *foolishness, and squandering of profits* every time he'd dress up in his Santa outfit and sneak presents of *questionable damage* to children all around the Bayfield area. However, to him, both the Red Cliff and Bad River Indian Reservations, were the most special.

One by one, the children grew and left Mr. Maki behind with his empty pockets.

"Oh, these are nice." The woman's voice was familiar (too familiar).

The rounded mirror attached to the wall and ceiling gave Willowdean full view of Mr. Maki and his store (and the woman).

And she was right. The woman's voice belonged to Corrine.

"Yah," Mr. Maki said, "I get them from that catalog the ice-cream man bring me." He bent under the counter, pulled it out, and wet his thumb to rifle through the already worn pages; all twenty-two of them.

"I suppose he make a little something on the few orders I give him. He says to me, 'Mr. Maki, these are fine items and the ladies do like them.' So he is right?"

Corrine snapped her gum and held up a pair of long, dangling plastic earrings next to her ear. "Well, I do like the assortment of these."

"Yah, that little Bitmen girl, she not so dum-dum. Her big-city ideas not so bad." Mr. Maki chuckled as he pulled out his hankie. He blew his nose, looked up at the mirror, and quickly shoved the handkerchief back inside his pocket.

"I get the new freezers tomorrow, then, ice cream, lots of ice cream."

"Oh please," Corrine said. "Ugh! You simply have no idea how rough it's been on me and Lenny since John and Willowdean moved here with that little twerp of theirs."

Looking up into the mirror, Mr. Maki coughed. He watched Willowdean pick up a bottle of maple syrup. Pretending to read the label, she then placed it inside her basket and moved to the next shelf.

"Why, they're stealing our precious little girl right out from our very arms of love," Corrine said.

"Everyone in Ashland County knows how me and Lenny take an overpowering sense of pride when it comes to grooming our little Peggy; and all for those bright lights and that big stage of Nashville. Lord knows, it ain't easy."

Mr. Maki squirmed as he and Willowdean listened to her babble on.

"Only a mother's true love can see a part of her own flesh go through such a process," Corrine said in a most painful way.

"After all, what does anyone know about having to spend all those long hours in smoke-filled bar rooms, having to protect their only child from the yearnings and desires filling nearly every man in there? Why, passing through those tavern doors every Friday and Saturday night, you can see it right in their eyes.

"No, I'm sorry Mr. Maki, but no one knows the agonies that me and Lenny endure just for our little Peggy. And then to see all our hard work being lost to people like the Bitmens . . .

"No, I'm sorry, but it just ain't right. Besides that, that little girl of theirs just ain't right in the head. Why, she went and told my Lenny, she's a Indian princess. *A Indian princess*, why, can you imagine?"

"An Indian princess?" Mr. Maki said. "Mmph, now that not be such a bad thing. I know a real Indian princess. I not see her for a long time. But her sister, yes. Her sister, she not such a princess."

Corrine rolled her eyes and giggled. "Now Mr. Maki," she said, tapping the top of his hand. "Wasn't it you who always said, not everyone needs to be a princess? And half-sisters, Mr. Maki, half-sisters, not full sisters, remember?"

Having her fill of both tales and trinkets, Willowdean strolled up to the counter and sat down her basket.

Corrine jumped back and turned a strange hue of alabaster white.

With each unleashing mound of hodgepodge, and every zealous punch of the register, Mr. Maki's face lit up while Corrine's sank.

"That will be $105.69, please," he sweated with eagerness.

Digging deep inside her purse, Willowdean shot a glance at Corrine and yanked out two $100 bills and then placed them in Mr. Maki's chubby hand.

"I am so sorry Mrs.," he said, turning red, "but I cannot break that."

She knew Mr. Maki didn't recognize her. The years between them left her as different to him as he was to her. Though no wrinkles crested her brown sugar skin, she was no longer the young, pretty girl with long black hair brushing against the swell of her waist. Life had dimmed the fire in her midnight eyes, the fire that once lit up the store when she'd come with another order of Granny's fine maple syrup. The young girl inside her screamed: *It's me, Mr. Maki, your Little Pocahontas.* She put her hand inside her purse. "Oh, I'm sorry," she said. "Will this be all right?"

"Yah, now that I can do." Wiping his brow with his shirt-sleeve, he gave back a hundred dollar bill and took Willowdean's twenty dollar bill. Carefully he counted out her change.

"Thank you," she said, taking her bags.

"Yah, you come back again, yes?"

"Yes, yes I will," she said, walking away. Glancing at Corrine one last time, she quietly shut the door.

"You know that lady?" Mr. Maki asked.

Corrine nervously fondled her pocketbook. "Well, I thought I did, from a long time ago." Willowdean walked to the car and waved to Mosie and Peggy.

Peggy, waved back. Her summertime tanned fingers tugged up the straps of her swimsuit, and then poked Mosie's arm. Mosie poked her back and sprinted to the car, nearly flipping over the picnic basket in her hand. Peggy followed.

Willowdean rested her head on the steering wheel and closed her eyes as she listened to the delighted laughter of the tourists and the cries of seagulls that mingled with the crashing waves of the lake. *After all these years, everything has remained the same*, she thought, *It is I and Corrine who are different*.

"What's wrong, Ma?" Mosie asked

"Oh I'm fine. I think I just need a nap. Guess I'm just plain worn out again, that's all."

"Don't worry about supper," Mosie said. "I'll make it."

"Well thank you, sweetheart. I sure would appreciate it." Willowdean started the car. "Peggy, are you coming home with us or are you going to your house?"

"I think I better go to my house. I have to rehearse for this weekend. Lenny and Corinne have some new material they told me to go over."

Willowdean cringed.

"So, what songs are you practicing?" Mosie asked to make sure Peggy had forgotten about Willowdean's prayers and the fact Scarlet was still alive and on the run.

"Well, I'm not sure. But I hope there ain't gonna be any ones about kissing or making love in the moonlight." She giggled and jabbed Mosie with her elbow.

"Well, if there is, just remember: think pumpkins." "Pumpkins?" Willowdean asked.

"Um, yes pumpkins," Mosie said quickly before Peggy could say a word. "You know, to concentrate on when she sings."

"Why pumpkins?"

"So I don't think about—"

"So she don't think about other stuff, that's why, just her songs. Hey, what did you get at Mr. Maki's? I'm going to go see him tomorrow, you know, on business. Want to come, Peggy?"

Peggy shrugged and grabbed a left over tuna fish sandwich. "Sure, maybe." Willowdean pulled the car to the side of the road next to the dilapidated mailbox.

"Well, thank you Mrs. Bitmen, for the ride home, and for such a good day."

"You're welcome. Why don't you take the other sandwiches too? Unless you want me to save them for tomorrow, but I was hoping we could have something else."

Peggy glimpsed through the trees up the driveway. No Ford.

"Sure. I bet they're not home yet," she said as she stuffed the sandwiches down her front.

"Are you sure you don't want to come home with us?" Willowdean asked.

"Thanks, Mrs. Bitmen, but I had better not. Thanks again."

They watched Peggy jog up the driveway, holding her chest full of sandwiches. Willowdean rubbed her belly. "You didn't say any more about that dog to her, did you?"

"No. What's wrong, Ma?"

"Nothing, nothing's wrong as long as you stay away from that wild dog."

"But Ma, you don't understand. Scarlet needs me, really she does. She isn't a bad dog like Peggy says. It was Lenny who was bad. Don't you understand that?"

"Yes Katherine, I do; more than you know. That's why I don't want you near it.

"I didn't want to tell you this and ruin the surprise, but your father bought a pup from Mrs. Morgan the other day. They'll be ready to go right around your birthday. Now, doesn't that sound better than trying to tame some wild hound dog?"

"No Ma, it doesn't! Mrs. Morgan breeds those poodles of hers just for the money; it isn't right, not when there's dogs out there like Scarlet that need a home, dogs that need love and extra help . . . it just isn't right Ma, and you know it. I don't want one of Mrs. Morgan's poodles. I want Scarlet!"

"No Mosie. You cannot have Scarlet. You have no idea what comes along with dogs like her and what they do to a person and, well, you're better off not knowing. The subject's closed."

Mosie stared out the car window and searched the shadows between the trees for any signs of the great, smelly hound. Something even deeper than all the tall grass blurring along

Highway 13 told her no matter what anyone said, Scarlet belonged to her, and she belonged to Scarlet.

"Don't worry girl," Mosie said. "I'm coming for you. Just hold on."

And the crows were hovering above Kill-Deer.

"Yes indeed; I'm coming."

CHAPTER TWENTY~ONE

"Tom Major here for WATW, Ashland County's number one country station. Now for a little tune to help us say good-bye to another great day here in Ashland: 'Indian Lake,' by Freddy Weller; but first, this message for Super H Foods, serving all of Ashland and its surrounding communities from its location at 5111 East Main Street since 1926—"

"I hope your father's in a good mood," Willowdean got up from the sofa. "He just pulled in."

"So do I," Mosie straightened the silverware on the table. Through the porch windows, she could see his hands glued to the truck steering wheel. He took an enormous breath and his shoulders heaved up to his ears then dropped back as the air let out his lungs. He reached for his brief-case and opened the truck door; his feet hit the ground like heavy weights, lagged slowly to the house.

"Hope he likes his frosties," Mosie poured a Hamm's into a tall, freezer frosted glass. She sat it next to his dinner plate and forced a sweet-steady smile as he entered the kitchen. She turned up the radio. Freddy Weller began singing:

"*Indian Lake is a scene you should make with your little one . . .*"

Sucking on his lower lip, John handed Mosie his attaché-case and narrowed his eyes at the special table setting and the frosted glass of beer.

"Okay," he said, rubbing his neck, "what the hell did you get into this time?"

While Freddy told how they'd *swim in the cove,* and, *have a snack in the grove,* and maybe even, *rent a canoe,* Mosie hurried to the stove. "Pa," she said, "have a beer; dinner is just about ready."

"Must be something big," he plopped into his chair. He pulled off his work boots and took a draw from his beer. "Where's your mother?"

"In the bathroom, I think," Mosie pulled the broiler pan out of the oven. "She was extra tired today, so I offered to make supper. I hope it's okay. I made you steak and salad and . . ."

John chugged his Hamm's and belched. "Mmph. Can't wait to hear what you did. It must be a real doozy."

Mosie rushed to the freezer for another glass. She placed it, and a new bottle, in front of him. He rolled his eyes.

"Look, you can hand me frosties all night long, but it won't—"

He looked up, his words dropping with his jaw. Willowdean stood in the kitchen doorway. She cleared her throat.

"And that's it for me tonight," Tom Major announced. "Stay tuned, here at WATW—"

Mosie gasped. "Ma . . ." Willowdean sauntered to her chair and sat across from John. His eyes popped.

Her lavender dress and soft make-up accentuated her sweet brown skin and dark eyes.

John slugged his beer straight from the bottle. "All right," he said, wiping his lips. "What the *hell* went on today?"

"Here Pa," Mosie placed a hunk of juicy red meat on his plate. "Here's your steak, medium rare just how you like it.

"And Ma, here's yours; thoroughly cooked, no blood." She hurried to the counter and grabbed a large bowl of freshly cut greens. "And there's baked potatoes, too," she served Willowdean her salad and then served John his. She placed two fine red tomatoes on top.

"What would you like on your spuds, Ole, Borden's sour cream or Land O' Lakes butter?"

Willowdean gave John a shy look. "Sour cream, please."

John glanced at her and shoved a forkful of salad into his mouth. "Butter," he said. "All right, what did you two get into?"

Willowdean ran her hand lightly across her lap and gave him a girlish grin. "Well . . ." she said, her voice sweet as sorghum on warm biscuits in the morning, "there *are* different kinds of trouble a person can get into, you know."

John swallowed. "Yeah?" Willowdean flashed her black eyes at him while he forked in a mouthful of greens.

"Yes. Some big, and some, well, small. Katherine, maybe you would like to help me."

Mosie nearly sank inside her salad. The tangy smell of the Catalina dressing tapped her nose. "Don't you and Pa want to eat alone tonight?"

"We're a family," Willowdean pulled out Mosie's chair at the table. Mosie picked up her plate. "How's the steak?"

"Perfect," John said. "Now, what the *hell* did you do?"

Mosie took a stiff drink of milk. "Umm . . ." she took another.

"I umm . . . talked Peggy into helping me build a boat, so I can find Dog Island, and I got into a fight with Lenny Anderson, and almost got hit by a semi-truck because I found a wild dog alongside the road that Lenny wants to shoot in the worst way. Isn't that just *thee* most *terrible* thing you *ever heard*, Pa? Someone wanting to shoot a poor, *defenseless* animal? Tsk!

"*Geez* Pa, why would someone want to go and do something like *that,* even if it did belong to Lenny at one time?

"Oh yeah, and Peggy asked if she can go to Mass with us this Sunday, and I told her yes, *if* that's okay with you, of course."

"And," Willowdean crept in, "I went ahead and told Mosie you bought her a puppy from Mrs. Morgan, and that it will be ready by her birthday next month." She quickly squeezed John's hand. "You're wonderful, John, just wonderful."

John stopped chewing and his lips disappeared with the meat inside his mouth. Mosie got up from the table. "Want another frosted Hamm's, Pa?"

"Yeah, I'll take another one. And when you're done eating, you can get your ass to your room. You're grounded.

"And you," he said, pointing his fork at Willowdean, "the next time I tell you something, I don't want you opening that yap of yours. You got it?"

Mosie looked at the pink alarm clock on her nightstand: 10:06. She sat on the edge of her bed and stared at the window, now a whole fourteen tiptoes away (since 'Norstrom's' moved her bed to the other side of the room when they came to install the new mod blue shag carpet that Willowdean ordered).

Nevertheless, it didn't matter what was under Mosie's stocking feet: old, dull wood floors, or the glossy kind at Miss Marino's Dance Studio, or carpeting. The window was still fourteen creaks, squeaks, and snaps of worn joists, and subflooring away.

"Twenty-eight total, there and back," Mosie told herself. "Twenty-eight steps there and back. She sighed and thought about the sleek, well-manicured dance instructor.

"She had the patience of a saint. After all, it wasn't *her* fault Ma insisted I continue with those dumb old ballet classes."

Even after four years of Plies, Fouettes and Battements Degages, Mosie still couldn't help but struggle with the dance floor.

And each week during those long years, Miss Marino would watch Mosie come up behind the other students like an oversized toddler just learning to walk. *"My dear,"* she'd sigh empathetically, *"I am truly sorry."*

And once a year Miss Marino would inform Willowdean how,

"It is very fortunate we humans have different fortes in life." And each year Willowdean reminded her how it was, *"Mr. Bitmen is paying the dance studio, and quite handsomely at that."*

Nevertheless, it was Mosie and Miss Marino who knew that no matter how many dollar bills Mr. John Bitmen passed on, Mosie's hands would never land gracefully on the dance room barres; and tonight was no different (except this time Mosie would alight onto the sill of her bedroom window), "a whole fourteen tiptoes away."

She stood up and boosted herself high on her toes, forcing her weight upward in hopes her feet would somehow become light enough to trick the floorboards. She took a step, wavered, and then again, and again; each time thanking Miss Marino for what little she was able to accomplish.

But, alas, the floor did groan, stopping her in her tracks. The clock seeming to tick louder realized her *forte* truly did not lie in lovely, swooping moves, but just plain old ordinary ones. "Hurry, just run and get it over with," it seemed to be telling her. Mosie listened, and did; she ran tip-toey to the new, white dotted Swiss curtains covering her window, and her hand touched the sill, and then pulled the curtains aside. The brightness of the pale-blue moon flooded the yard and showed her the dirt driveway below. She looked at her desk and picked up the last gift Val had given her: a green army surplus backpack and matching girl's army hiking boots. She looked at the clock. 10:15. It was time to go.

From the top of the staircase, she listened to John's muddled snores and the hum of Willowdean's fan. The sounds meant she was secure; however, if caught, she was armed with plenty of excuses for any and all interrogations.

If found snaking around the kitchen she would plead, *I needed a little midnight snack.*

Once outside, she would explain, *I needed fresh air.*

However, if found riding her bike in the blackness of the night down Highway 13, she would sound the ultimate retort:

Thank god you found me! I was sleepwalking and found myself way out here. Geez, I don't know what I was going to do. I'm so scared!

There would be no need to muster up phony tears of fear. Those would come easy enough. She slunk down the banister, then across the living room and made her way into the kitchen. Sidling next to the refrigerator, she opened it and cringed. Its usual smooth, daytime squeak sounded extraordinarily loud in the quiet of the night. She opened the freezer door, pulled out a good-sized roast, placed it inside her backpack, then slithered to the door, and took one last listen.

John's snores continued as did the whirl of Willowdean's fan. "Clear," she put her hand on the doorknob. Slowly, she twisted it and stepped into the night. She wasn't alone.

Night crickets and nocturnal bugs filled the darkness with unremitting discussions of bullfrogs in love down in the swamps.

The frogs echoed back with their deep, groggy *eerr-rruup-eerrrruup* of, *mind your own business.*

Mosie flailed her arms at the bloodthirsty mosquitoes, thick as the evening air. "Ma and those damn 'Chocks' vitamins with extra iron of hers!" she swatted away the parasites that were seeking fresh nourishment from her iron-rich blood. She sat on the steps, reached into her backpack, pulled out a can of Off mosquito repellant, and covered herself with its wet bitter spray. Relief.

Standing under the glow of the moon, she tugged up her new cotton, Puma athletic socks. She knew she was breaking Commandment number five.

"I know I should honor my Mother and Father, but what about the animals? What would Saint Francis do or Saint Blaise?" She guided her bike down the driveway and pedaled into the muggy night, praying to Saint Christopher for traveling protection.

Her bike tires spun faster and faster along the roadside and flared up chinks of tiny grains of sand and grit under her fenders; the *tingting-tang's* spat out an ode all their own. She grinned and made it one of the things she would boast about to Candy. After all, if such a sound did exist in the city, it was muted by traffic and the need to pay attention.

"It's strictly a country thing, not city," she practiced pointing it out. "Just like the sky." Now her sky. Her northern Wisconsin sky with its twinkling stars, blinking and dancing from one endless horizon to the next. And she sparkled with them.

It now seemed impossible how she and Candy hadn't been brave enough to stray from their own backyards at night, let alone venture out to hunt down some wild dog in the woods, a dog Lenny Anderson claimed to be insane.

"I won't let him shoot you," Mosie pumped the bike pedals with determination.

She looked into the blackness over Kill-Deer that hung like a massive stage curtain, thick and heavy. Spotlights emerging over its crest stopped her in place. "Car beams," she reasoned. "Just teenagers." The lights faded down some abandoned road to the left then stopped.

Pedaling on, her thoughts turned back to Scarlet and Candy. "You see," she resumed the heroic speech she would give once the old hound dog was found and tamed.

"What it really takes to be brave is doing what you know is right, even if it means being scared, or even if other people think you're wrong, or even strange, for that matter." She found herself on top of Kill-Deer and looked down its sleek neck.

"I'm coming, girl. I'm coming!" she shouted. Taking in the night and its air, she coasted downward and drifted thirty yards past the bottom. She stopped. Any trace of the hunting trail leading to the swamps was nowhere to be found. She slid the backpack off her shoulders, dug inside, and pulled out a flashlight. She turned it on. Its thin beam shined across a thicket of trees. Determined to find the trail, she headed down the side of the highway with John's warnings following.

CHAPTER TWENTY~TWO

Mosie took a deep breath. The shine of the flashlight pitched the side of the highway. Before her in the gravel was the scrambled patch of bikes and shoes she and Peggy made earlier that day.

"Saint Christopher, I sure hope you're still with me," she took in the scent of the cinnamon-ragweed and the quagmire now dampened from the night. She climbed down the trench.

Rocks tumbled ahead of her grunts and groans and announced her arrival to the furrow creatures hidden in the darkness of the gully's belly. Their stammering *t-t-t-'s* and *tsk's* fell silent for a moment then roused again. Images of Scarlet desperately searching for food and comfort in the summer heat, and the bitter winds of winter chasing her along rows of weeds, both alive and lifeless, conjured in Mosie's mind. *How many times has that poor old thing been through here*? She thought.

She now understood why the dog's survival could not depend on the need to seek out human companionship no matter how much she wanted it. She listened for signs of her. None.

"Dog, hey dog, I'm here," she yelled. "It's me, Mosie, remember?

Please don't be scared." Nothing.

She turned to face Kill-Deer and the swamp. "The hunters' trail has to be here somewhere," she studied the tall trees barricading the marshlands in the distance. Again, she called out. "Scarlet . . . Scarlet."

She flipped the beam of light ahead of herself and walked on. That's when she caught sight of it, the path, laying almost invisible. "Scarlet . . . Scarlet." Neither yowl, nor yip was heard. As she worked her way down, she searched the mangled clusters of limbs, hardwood, and tangled brush that ran alongside the edge of the swamp. "There has to be a way in, there just has to be."

She looked back at Kill Deer, that monstrous cliff that held up the road leading to town; its silhouette devoured the night sky. It was here, at the very edge of its bottom, that the marshlands began. She turned and gave the flashlight a flick and continued walking. That's when she saw the opening of the swamp, sized not for a large animal to pass through, but medium. She got on her belly and stuck her head through the arch of briers and thorns.

It was there, under the blush of the moon that she laid her eyes on the world her pa warned about; the secret kingdom held back in time, and refused to be touched by man.

Lavender-blue fog danced among the swollen quagmire. Muted bull frogs heard from her backyard now pierced her ears.

"Scarlet!" she yelled. The words sank through the swamp bottoms like the lost hunters trying to invade this private world. With them, her heart was trapped somewhere beneath the endless islandbogs. For any animal or man, it would be impossible to find their way among the tamaracks standing tall and strong with their tree limbs reaching upward and spilling into the night sky.

"I don't want one of Mrs. Morgan's stinking little poodles," she opened her backpack and pulled out the hunk of now half-frozen meat. "Those dogs will have homes . . . and get to be spoiled and die old and happy but not Scarlet." She looked up at the moon. "It's worse than being . . . blue forever. Well, girl, wherever you are, this is for you."

She took one last look at the magic inside the swamps and placed the meat on the ground. "I hope we can meet up again someday. And if we do, I won't let you be blue any more. I promise."

As she rose to her feet, a patch of rustling weeds caught her attention. "Scarlet, is that you, girl?" she asked. "If it is you, I sure wish you'd show yourself." She held her breath and waited for the snapping and crackling of the foliage to stop. Without warning, her arms flailed up protecting her from the strong odor of seared rubber filling the air.

"Ah geez, for the love of . . ." she said, watching a critter wobble back into the woods, leaving its overwhelming stench behind. "Skunk!" she yelled, running to the hill. A thudding rumble followed behind her, knocking her and the air in her lungs to the floor of the gully. Her stomach went cold as she rolled herself into a ball. *Bear,* her mind snapped, *bear . . .* It grunted with excitement and turned her over as it flared its nostrils. Turning its head toward the tree line, it sniffed the rustling swamp brushes and drew the frogs into a quietness.

A mound, dark and thin was making its way toward the hill. Smelling the bear, it stopped. The bear protected its claim by lifting its paw from Mosie's body and swaggered to the small, waiting beast.

Mosie sobbed and listened to the wild screams coming from the two animals, struggling to hold their ground. She opened her eyes and watched the bear's massive paw give the smaller animal a final grapple. It bit back hard, twisting the meat inside the bear's leg. Beaten, the bear vanished into the night swamps. Mosie raised her arm.

"Scarlet, my Scarlet-Blue . . ." she cried. Torn and bloodied, the dog whined and headed toward her. Mosie clung to her. Scarlet's throat rumbled deep and low. A rustling, strong and heavy, was breaking through the ravine.

"No! No!" Mosie cried.

The night cracked with an explosion. Blue fell beside her with a thud and jerked. Then came the silence.

Mosie looked up. Lenny stood over her and the hound with his gun.

CHAPTER TWENTY~THREE

Willowdean's balsam-fir resin wrap was working like a charm as it drew out most of the throbbing and stinging burn from the bear claw mark on Mosie's thigh, but it did nothing for the ache of losing Scarlet). She stared at the charcoal-gray tree shadows dancing on her bedroom walls. The clanks of Willowdean's pans and running water in the kitchen gave no comfort to being home instead of lying dead, half-eaten somewhere in the woods. Bear attack or no bear attack, she was in trouble.

"If that bear had wanted to do worse, it would have," Willowdean had said. "*You're* lucky it was only curious. And *we're* lucky Lenny was out hunting it."

It was almost 8:30 in the evening, and the sun was getting ready to dip under the horizon. John's truck rumbled up the driveway and grated to a stop. He was late, but not late enough.

"Scarlet was still alive this time last night," Mosie cried, and lay back down, covering herself with her bed sheet; the echoing cracks of Lenny's rifle and Scarlet's last whimpers crawled under with her. And so did the memory of Lenny bringing her home to face John and Willowdean. She brushed away the tears trickling down her cheeks and hoped last night's nightmare would go with them. It didn't. The grief inside her was spreading like the gravel crunching under John's work boots.

"Wha-wha-whatever you have to do to me, you have to do to me," she rehearsed and fought the pinch in her throat that cut her words short.

"After all, whatever punishment you and Ma give me can never take away me getting Scarlet killed like I did."

The rattling pans in the kitchen stopped. For the first time in her life, Mosie heard her mother swear. She poked her head out from the sheets.

"Damn you, John Anthony Bitmen; you were at Benny's again," Willowdean said, her eyes flaring with rage. "You are one of the most selfish men I know."

John stood in the doorway. Willowdean slammed a pan inside the sink.

"Your daughter, your *only* daughter, is lying upstairs scared to death, and heartbroken, and what do you do? We both know the answer to that, don't we?

"What, John, what are you going to do when this one comes?"

She held her belly and cradled it. "I'll tell you: The same thing you did when I had Valerie and Katherine. That's what you're going to do."

John headed for the refrigerator; the smell of stale beer and musty perfume spoiled the air.

"You're . . . you're doing it right now, aren't you?" Willowdean's voice softened to a mere whisper. "It's her. This was all a lie. You knew she was here all along. Oh John."

Grabbing a Hamm's, he opened it and took a hearty slug. He straightened himself. This time there were no playful,

Willowdeanies, no sparkles of love dust blinding his eyes. He ran his fingers through his hair. "*Me*, I'm the selfish one? I'm the one busting his ass trying to give you the best! Besides, I told you, I'm too old, and too tired to raise another kid." He leaned on the refrigerator and buried his face in the crook of his arm. "How many times did I tell you to go get your mistake taken care of? If you would have just done like I told you . . ." He peered out at her; his eyes cold as the beer in his hand. "Hell, I am a man after all," he drawled and took another slug of beer.

Willowdean turned to the sink. She stared out the window into the falling night. She fought back her tears and choked on her own words. "For eighteen years, I have put up with your affairs, your drinking, and broken promises. I didn't do those things, John. You did. And I didn't make this baby on my own, and you will not blame me or this child for your shamefulness."

She turned the faucet on and reached for the Palmolive. Giving the bottle a hard squirt, she watched the colored bubbles fill the sink. "You go to your Catholic hell," she spat. "Both of you."

John cleared his throat. "Well," he placed his empty beer bottle on the table. "Guess there's no reason for us to pretend anymore, now is there?" He passed behind her; the scent of beer and stale perfume trailing after him. Willowdean clutched the sink.

"That's right, go on and pack your stuff, Mr. *Big Man* John Bitmen." She wept.

Mosie yanked off her sheet and scooted out of bed. "What's Ma talking about?" she said, heading for the staircase. "Affairs, drinking, pack your stuff?"

She looked over the banister and down into the living room, where the light from John's room shone in the hallway; his drawers slid open and closed with a bang. His light went out.

Mosie watched him walk into the living room, broken as one of the hobos along the railroad tracks at East Park. Carrying nothing but his suitcase and with his heart tucked somewhere between the few shirts and pairs of pants inside, he headed to the front door; the very door he had walked his little family through, and into this far away place, this Bayfield they had come to know as home.

"Pa!" Mosie hollered. "No!"

For the first time since last night, her mind wasn't filled with Lenny, bears or Scarlet. She flew down the staircase and grabbed John's hands, hoping her touch would give him a reason to stay.

"Please Pa," she begged as she yanked his hands from the luggage. "You don't have to go. We can fix this. We can fix anything me, and Ma did wrong. I promise."

"Katherine," he said. "Stop."

Looking into her Bitmen navy blue eyes, he said, "We need to talk." He nodded for her to open the door. Under the paleness of the yard light, she followed him into the garage. He turned on the light and helped her up onto his workbench.

"Does it hurt?" he ran his fingers gently across the markings on her arms and legs. Mosie looked down at the tomato box, the one that held Pa's *Running Bear*. She shook her head.

John cleared his throat. "Yeah, your Ma sure has a way with those medicines of hers, just like her granny; better than any doctor." He tried to grin. "Bet you were scared shitless."

Mosie didn't answer.

He grabbed her, surrounding her, and her purple-black bruises with his arms. “What the *hell* were you thinking, girl? You could have been killed. Don’t you ever try pulling another stunt like that again, you hear me?”

“Yes, Pa,” Mosie buried herself deep inside his arms and hoped he would never let go.

He waited for the lump in his throat to go down. “I guess you heard everything me and your mother said.”

Mosie looked at the record box and recalled the looks of the man sitting on the log, the one with the two Indians kissing under that orange sky with its bright moon. “Pa,” she said, “you don’t drink, not that much. And I never saw you with another . . .” John nervously patted his shirt pocket and pulled out a crushed pack of Tareytons. “Maybe if I . . .” John stopped her.

“Katherine, none of this happened because of you, so I want you to get that out of your head right now, do you hear me? This whole move has been hard on all of us.”

He lit his cigarette with his Zippo and held the flame to Mosie. She blew it out.

“I know you miss your friend Candy, and your brother Val. I guess the joke’s on me because I miss your brother, too. He’s a good brother, Mosie, and a fine young man. A better man than I am.” Mosie couldn’t ever remember John talking like this, especially about Val. Nor could she recall her pa having tears. *Maybe he’s cried before, maybe even a hundred times before,* she thought as they leaked from his eyes as if he had done it a thousand times before.

He took a puff of his cigarette. Mosie could hardly breathe as she sat listening to him.

“I’m sorry,” he coughed. “You heard me and your Ma saying things you shouldn’t have. Here, all this time I was trying my damndest to make sure you and Val would grow up good and proper, and here I am, the one who didn’t do the growing.” He rubbed his neck, as smoke drifted from his nostrils.

“Guess that mother of yours is right about me. I am a devil of a man to live with, and I should go to hell. I don’t know how your mother put up with me all these years. It seems I just can’t grow up enough to do right by her. But that’s between her and me.”

He closed his eyes. Then came the words Mosie feared more than anything. They shot through her like one of Lenny’s bullets.

“Katherine I’m not leaving you. I want you to know that. I’ll never leave you. I’m going to stay down at the shop until things get worked out around here.”

Mosie’s heart was breaking, and he knew it. He forced a little laugh.

“Like it or not I am your pa, and will be forever, and there’s not a thing you or anyone else can do about it.

Now, I have a couple of rules for you,” he tugged his pants halfheartedly and tried to make his voice firm.

“I don’t want you riding that damn bike of yours on that highway anymore, do you hear me? If you or your Ma need me, all you have to do is call, and I’ll be here lickety split.

“And stay the hell away from the Andersons! Even though Lenny saved your life, he’s a mean kind of crazy, and I don’t trust him, do you hear me?”

“But Pa,” Mosie jumped in, “you don’t understand; Scarlet’s the one who saved me, not Lenny; I tried telling ma but she wouldn’t listen and . . .”

John smacked his cigarette onto the ground.

"Damn it Katherine," he said, "don't you understand? That dog was as dangerous as that bear. If the bear wouldn't have killed you, that dog would have, if Lenny hadn't come along like he did . . . now I don't want to hear any more about it, do you hear me?"

Mosie jumped off the bench and broke into tears. She ran for the door. John grabbed her.

"I'm sorry, kid. I'm sorry," he pulled her to his chest. "But you have to stop your lies. Why, they'll turn on you and swallow you up if you don't; and before you know it, a time will come when I and your Ma won't be able to help you because of them."

"But Pa, I'm not lying," Mosie cried and pushed him away. "I loved Scarlet, and she loved me. If she didn't, she never would have done what she did."

John sighed and ran his fingers in his hair. "Girl, you don't know the first thing about dogs; you can't tell a good one from a bad one. I asked around about that hound, and there's not a single person in Bayfield who would have stuck their neck out for it. It's been nothing but a nuisance since it got away from Lenny. Agh, what does it matter anyway. It's too late now." He lit another smoke and took a heavy drag from it.

"Pa, do you really have to go? Ma won't be mad for long, I just know it; it's those hormones of hers; Sister Vern Mary said . . ."

John stared at the floor, his eye-skin crinkling. "I think the best thing I can do for her, and all of us, is give your mother a little space and time; to think things over, you know; try to figure out how to make things better." He took a deep breath.

"Well kiddo', guess it's time."

Mosie put her hand on his shoulder. “Pa, if you need to talk, I’m here for you,” she took his hand and squeezed it full of last hopes of him staying.

He squeezed back. It was empty.

“That’s my girl. Now, remember what I told you.” He grinned and gave his pants a gentle tug. Mosie looked away.

“Pa, would you mind if I didn’t see you leave?” John nodded and looked down.

Without a word, without a glance, Mosie ran to the house. The porch door banged shut, echoing John’s freedom. He turned off the garage light, picked up his suitcase, and walked to his truck. He tossed his luggage in its haul, opened his door, and slid inside. He stared at the house. The one people like the Benningtons would give their firstborn for.

“Goodnight Willie,” he turned the key to his truck. “Good-night."

CHAPTER TWENTY~FOUR

Peggy looked over the makeup spread across Mosie's dresser. She picked up the eyeliner and lit the end of its tip. "Okay," she blew on it, cooling. "Now close your eyes." Peggy pulled Mosie's eyelid taut and ran the softened pencil tip across the roots of her eyelashes. "Now the other one."

"Geez, you mean you go through this every day?"

"Yep, sometimes two or three."

"Why?"

"Mat Larson, Brian Andrews, Eddie Mason . . ."

"Aren't the prayers working?" Mosie tried not to move.

Peggy giggled. "It depends on which fellow I'm with. Keep your eye still." She swept a wisp of mascara over Mosie's lashes. "Mosie, I sure am sorry about your mom and dad."

"Thanks Peggy."

"Corinne left Lenny once."

"She did?"

"Sure, a couple of times. The first time was the worst. I was plenty scared. Lenny didn't know nothin' about being alone. Heck, I was making meals by the time I was nine years old. Powder please."

A soft cotton puff danced across Mosie's face; Peggy's gentle fingers followed.

"So the second time she left, I already knew how to take care of me and Lenny so it wasn't so bad, not like the first time. By the third time, it was actually pretty nice." She put her hand over Mosie's forehead, shook the can of Aqua Net, and sprayed her hair.

"Geez," Mosie said. "Well then, close your eyes and mouth." Peggy put her out her hand. "Comb please."

"No, I don't mean the hair spray. I mean you, Lenny and well, you know."

"Oh. Naw, it's not so bad, not really. At least when Corrine's gone, I don't have to listen to her and Lenny fight and argue, and when Corrine does comes back, which she eventually always does, she always has presents for me and sometimes even for Lenny. Okay, look up." She plucked Mosie's hair and smiled.

"Besides, when she's gone, Lenny don't drink half as much as when she's there. Not after he sobers up anyway." Pulling strands of Mosie's hair to the front to frame her face, she said, "I sure am glad you don't like boys yet." She carefully covered Mosie's eyes and took her hand. "No fair peeking," she took her to the closet. "Not until we get you dressed."

She flung open the closet door, put her hands on her slight hips, and looked over the selection. "Mmm," she hummed. "Don't you have anything, well, sexy? How about a good tight skirt, something nice and short?" She pulled one out and held it to Mosie's waist. "*Way* too long," she frowned.

"Well, they're all that length. At Saint Anne's, we weren't allowed to wear anything above the knees."

"Fine. We'll just have to make do then, that's all." She yanked out Mosie's best summer floral Sunday skirt. "Here, this one. Yes, and this blouse, white chiffon."

She motioned for Mosie to step inside the skirt. Rolling the waistband, Peggy cleared most of Mosie's thigh.

"No way," Mosie protested as she looked down at her knees that weren't so baby soft round any more. "Pa would kill me if he seen me dressed like this."

"Well, he ain't gonna, so be quiet," Peggy unbuttoned the first two buttons on Mosie's blouse. She pinned it back and showed that Mosie was "wearing a bra".

"Peggy, I ain't, I mean, I am not . . . I refuse to . . . Peggy-No Middle Name-Anderson, I will not go out looking like a . . . like a two bit you know what!"

Peggy grinned and shoved her in front of the mirror.

"Now, before I let you look, just remember; you're still Mosie Bitmen, okay?"

She spun her around. Mosie gasped. "That don't look like me, not at all! I . . . I look . . ."

"*Sexy*!" Peggy shrieked with delight. "Just plain outright, sexy! Don't you *love* it?"

"*Yeah!* I mean, *no*, no I don't. I look like one of those girls Val brings home; the ones who . . ." She put her hand to her face and felt it. "Is that *really* me?"

"Yep, that's really you. But just stay away from my boyfriends or else!"

"Or else *what?*"

"Or else they'll want to kiss ya'," Peggy laughed and ran to the bed to grab a pillow. "Like this." She gave it a big hard smooch.

"Peggy!" Mosie giggled and tackled her.

"Well, I had better get dressed before Ma calls us to go," she smacked Peggy with the bolster one more time.

"Yeah, guess so. But just so you know, I really am glad you don't like the boys yet 'cause you sure are a knockout."

"Yeah well, I'll knock *you* out if you ever dress me up like this again," Mosie laughed, slipped out of the skirt, and into her jeans. "Hey Peggy, I don't mean to sound like a snob-ass or anything but, you know that birthmark of yours on your shoulder? It looks almost like Ma and Val's."

Peggy pulled her sleeve down and took a look. "Yeah, it looks like Corrine's too. Ain't that weird?"

"Yes, yes it is," Mosie answered. "Strange."

They headed downstairs. "War paint feels like crap," Mosie mumbled. "How can you wear this stuff anyway?"

"War paint," Willowdean repeated as she watched them pass her bedroom. Looking in her mirror, she said, "war paint," again, and opened her vanity drawer to grab a tube of lipstick.

"Some wars are worth fighting," she spread the red wax across her lips. She rubbed her belly and stared at herself. She looked at John's picture. "And some are not." Wiping off the lipstick, she put away the tube.

"Are you girls ready?" she yelled.

Mosie scrubbed the makeup from her face while Peggy touched hers up.

"Ma, I have to see Mr. Maki today," Mosie opened the door to the station wagon. "He got another cooler, and we have to pick out some flavors for him, so can you drop us off and then pick us up when you're done shopping?"

Peggy clucked her tongue. "Can't we just sit on the beach and watch—"

Mosie pinched her arm.

"That hurt," Peggy whined and rubbed the red mark.

Willowdean squeezed behind the steering wheel. "Stop fighting, you two."

"She started it, Mrs. Bitmen." "*You* did," Mosie countered.

"Enough, both of you, or you'll both stay home."

They settled back in their seats and ignored each other while Willowdean headed down the driveway. "That's better," she turned onto the highway. Mosie watched the side of the road. "Ma, how long does it take a dog to decompose?" "Gross!" Peggy cackled.

"A year, about a year," Willowdean answered. "But sometimes Mother Earth will call on her children to help her in special cases." She turned on the windshield wipers. "No beach today, girls."

"Doggone it," Peggy huffed as she looked out at the gray sheet spreading across the sky. Mosie shut her eyes. They were nearing Kill-Deer.

"Look, Mrs. Bitmen," Peggy leaned over the front seat. She pointed to a semi-truck parked at the bottom of the hill; its taillights were blinking off and on. Willowdean slowed down.

"That looks like Kenny Johnson's truck. He is such a hunk."

Mosie opened her eyes. "Hey, that's the bozo that almost ran me over," she sat up. "He's an idiot."

"No . . ." Peggy countered fluffing-up her hair. "He's all right, really he is. Maybe we should see if he needs some help."

"Just keep going, Ma," Mosie said. "He doesn't need our help."

The windshield wipers flipped across the windshield like an arm trying to hide what lay ahead. Still, Willowdean watched him take his coat off and place it over a large bulge inside the back of the semi. He shut the doors and turned to Willowdean and flagged his arms for her to go around. His young face filled with alarm. She slowed down.

"Oh my," she said, "that looks like blood all over his shirt."

"See!" Mosie screamed. "He *did* hit someone!" She rolled down her window. "Idiot!"

"Mosie!" Willowdean snapped, "Roll up your window and sit back."

"Oh stop, Mrs. Bitmen, please stop. Kenny wouldn't hurt a fly. If he did hit someone, he would need our help wouldn't he?"

Willowdean could see the panic on his paled face as he ran to the front of his cab. She slammed on her brakes. Peggy jumped out of the car. "Kenny," she called and ran to the side of the truck door. "It's me, Peggy."

Kenny wiped the rain from his piercing blue eyes and looked down at her. "Peggy? Peggy Anderson?"

"I must look a mess," she dabbed the mascara running down her cheeks. "Are you okay?"

"Yeah, yeah, I'm all right, but I found a half-dead dog lying along the road here. Looks like someone shot it and just left it. I gotta' get it over to Doc Ruden's ASAP. Who's that you're riding with?"

"Oh, them, that's just my friend Mosie and her mom, Mrs. Bitmen. Did you say a dog? A shot dog?"

"Yeah, yeah. Hey, I gotta get rollin'. Thanks for stopping," Kenny grabbed his door handle.

"Hey, um, what kind of dog did you say it is?"

"Why? You know someone missing their hound?"

"Ah, well, I might; I'll find out and let Doc Ruden know, or *you*," Peggy answered with a flirty smile and shut Ken's door.

Through the rain, she watched the tail end of the semi-truck lights disappear in the distance.

"What happened?" Willowdean rolled the car up to Peggy.

She looked at Mosie. "He didn't hit anyone," she quietly got back into the car. She opened her purse and pulled out her hairbrush.

"Boy, I must look like a drowned rat," she said anxiously and turned to the window to run the brush through her hair.

"Well, what *did* he hit?" Mosie asked. "A deer? What?"

Peggy didn't budge. "Nothing, he didn't hit anything. Here," she uneasily handed Mosie the brush. "Fix that stuff on top of your head you call hair."

"So what was he doing?" Willowdean asked. "Why did he have all that blood on his shirt?" Peggy hesitated.

Fondling her purse, she looked at Willowdean. "He, he," she stuttered. "Well, I don't know if I should tell you this 'cause I don't' think you're going to like it, and I sure don't want to have to be the one to tell ya."

"Ah geez, for crying out loud," Mosie said, "just tell us."

Peggy took a deep breath. "You ain't going to like it, Mrs. Bitmen. You ain't going to like it one bit."

"Well, why don't you let me be the judge of that."

"Okay. Don't say I didn't warn ya. Kenny found . . . well . . . he found Scarlet."

Mosie screamed.

"Oh lord!" Willowdean gasped.

"Is she, is she—" Mosie's eyes filled with tears. She jumped into the front seat. "Ma, follow him, please, please." "Peggy, is the dog . . ." Willowdean said.

"Yeah, she's still alive, but barely. Kenny is on his way to Doc Ruden's with her, over in Ashland. But we ain't never gonna catch him, Mrs. Bitmen, not when he's in a hurry." "*Ma*," Mosie choked.

"Mosie, can you handle it if she—if she, doesn't survive?"

"Ma," Mosie gulped, "I owe her my life, and if she doesn't make it, at least she'll know I'm with her."

Willowdean turned on the headlights and switched the wipers to high as she pressed her foot down on the gas pedal.

Please God, please don't let Scarlet die, Mosie prayed as they sped through Bayfield, along Highway Two into Ashland.

CHAPTER TWENTY~FIVE

Mosie barely read the sign: Ashland Animal Hospital. She jetted from the station wagon and raced ahead, leaving Willowdean and Peggy behind. She flung open the entrance door, hurried inside, and stood at the counter. "Hey, anyone, hey!" she yelled, frantically ringing the little bell sitting on the counter. Peggy was Right; Kenny and his Truck weren't anywhere to be seen. Except for the three of them, the parking lot and waiting room was deserted.

"Calm down," Willowdean said holding the door open for Peggy.

"For crying out loud," Mosie hollered, "This is supposed to be a hospital, where *is* everyone?"

A young receptionist walked out from the shelves behind the counter with her arms full of bandages and medications, and a surgeon's mask covering her mouth.

"I'm sorry," she apologetically checked her supply card. "I'll be with you as soon as I can. We have an emergency that just arrived."

She grabbed a package of syringes and headed for the swinging doors marked Private.

"No wait," Mosie yelled. "Is it a hound, a smelly, old hound girl, brought in by a truck driver that looks like Marty Robbins?"

"Slender?" the young woman asked, "With blonde hair and ruffled sideburns?"

"Yes," Mosie said, nodding.

"Yes, that was him," the girl replied with relief. "Are you her owner?"

"Yes, no, I, I mean, she doesn't have one, not really, just sort of."

"I'm sorry, but unless you're her owner, we cannot permit you to see her. It would be a good idea if you called her owner. It isn't looking good, and Doctor Ruden isn't expecting her to make it."

"But-but-I-she's . . ." Mosie started crying. Willowdean held her shoulders and looked at Peggy. Peggy scratched her ankle and looked at the floor.

"If the owner were here, then would we be able to see her, if the owner gave permission, is that correct?" Willowdean asked.

"Yes, if the owner gave consent. But if you'll excuse me, I really need to get back in there," the girl dashed to the private doors.

Peggy looked up at Willowdean. "Oh boy, Mrs. Bitmen," she said stepping up to the counter. "Lenny ain't going to like this. He ain't going to like it, not one bit. Lady," she blurted. "Err nurse, hey you, come back; *I'm* the owner. *I'm* the owner!" she yelled. "Mosie can go back with you."

The girl kicked the doors open with her foot and stuck her head out. "We need to hurry."

The doors were at the end of a hall that seemed as long as the field leading to the woods in Mosie's backyard. Behind them lay Scarlet, *her* Scarlet.

"Since she is so weak, the doctor didn't want to risk putting her completely under, so please be quiet and try not to cause the dog any distractions; no sudden movements, no outbursts. We need her to keep calm as possible. She's heavily sedated which causes a sense of confusion and will cause a migraine headache that might make her nauseated. If she vomits, she'll aspirate."

The nurse pushed open a heavy metal door with her shoulder. Mosie's legs weakened. A tall man clothed in white, stood stiff and rigid over Scarlet.

Above the doctors' head hung several plastic bags mounted to skinny metal racks. Their clear tubes carried liquids into Scarlet. The rhythm of her heart beeped weak and unsteady across a monitor. "May I, may I touch her?" Mosie whispered with eyes full of tears.

Dr. Ruden glanced from his mask. "Owner?" he asked in a hushed tone as he nodded at a small box mounted to the beige colored walls.

"No," his assistant lifted out a mask and handed it to Mosie.

Ruden rolled his eyes and shook his head toward the door.

"But she has permission from the owner," the girl placed the load of supplies on the table-tray next to him.

He flagged his gloved hand red and wet with Scarlet's blood at the lamp next to the bags hanging above his head. The nurse yanked it downward closer to Scarlet's leg.

"Don't look good," he mumbled as he patted the gaping wound with a handful of gauze. "She's in bad shape to start with; owners like this ought to be shot themselves." For a quick moment, his dark brown eyes glared at Mosie.

"Scarlet," she whispered and held back the tears inside her eyes. "Her name's Scarlet, Scarlet-Blue, 'cause that's all she's known since the day she was born, being blue." Scarlet flinched at the sound of Mosie's voice.

"Good name," Dr. Ruden motioned with his head for Mosie to step forward.

She rushed to Scarlet's side, bent down, and put her head on top of Scarlet's. Tenderly, she fondled Scarlet's long, black velvety ears. The monitor beeped with strength.

"It's okay," Mosie cried, "it's okay; we're together now. That's all that matters. No one will ever make us ever leave each other again, you hear me? From now on, you're going to be mine, and you're going to run and play and have as much to eat as you want and . . . and no one is ever going to lay another hand on you except to love you. You hear me, girl?"

Dr. Ruden glanced at his assistant, then Mosie. "How did this dog get in this condition?" he asked.

"She, she went wild in the woods. Please Dr. Ruden, don't let her die. She's a good dog; nobody knows it, but she is." The sound of metal spat against metal.

"Got it," Dr. Ruden sighed with relief staring at Lenny's bullet. "Let's sew her up."

Mosie watched the nurse hand him a long needle and spool of thick, glossy thread. His dark brown eyes darted at Mosie.

"I'm going to be honest," he looked back at Scarlet-Blue's leg. He shoved the needle and thread through her flesh, gave it a yank and then shoved it in again. A hollow sound filled the room as he pulled the thread through. Mosie looked away.

"She's sick," Dr. Ruden said. "Really sick. It's going to take a miracle for her to make a comeback."

Mosie smiled and stroked old Scarlet-Blue's thick, fur. "I'm a Catholic, Dr. Ruden, and if there's one thing we Catholics know how to do, it's pray for miracles." Dr. Ruden grinned.

He removed his gloves, threw them in the trash can, and walked over to Mosie. He put his hand on her shoulder. "Stay as long as you want," he said. "If she really isn't your dog, she ought to be." His assistant's eyes smiled out at him as he turned to leave the room.

"He's a good doctor," she placed the long-handled steel scissors and knives into a cleaning bucket. She smiled at Scarlet. "Seems he cares more about his animals than most human doctors care about their patients. Dr. Ruden will do everything he can," she turned off the over head light.

"Oh-oh," Peggy groaned in her chair. Through the small windows of the private swinging doors, she watched Doctor Ruden's, surgical skull-cap bobbing toward her. She picked up the *Gun Dog* magazine laying on the end table next her and slumped down in her chair to hide behind it.

Dr. Ruden grunted and led his assistant to the front desk. He sighed long and hard while he leafed through the paperwork attached to his clipboard.

Willowdean rose from her chair and ran her hands down her dress to chase away any wrinkles.

"You're Bitmen, Willowdean Bitmen?" Dr. Ruden asked dryly as he removed his cap. His long, wavy brown hair splashed across his shoulders.

"Yes, yes I am," she walked to the desk.

"I'm Dr. Ruden, Dr. Travis Ruden. Whose dog is that in there?" Peggy buried herself further behind the magazine.

"That, Dr. Ruden is not the biggest concern right at this moment," Willowdean said. "The dog is; and so is the girl at its side, not who the dog belongs to."

The corners of Dr. Ruden's lips lifted upward into a grin. "Umph," he rumbled and lifted his eyes to Willowdean. They sparkled with amusement. Willowdean softened her voice. "Is she going to make it?"

"The girl looks good and healthy, so I would say yes," Ruden chuckled. "But the dog, well, I wouldn't put my nickel down on her, and not due to the wound, but because of her health in general. Under normal conditions, a dog could make it through something like this pretty good, and with very little complications. Is that the owner?" he asked nodding at Peggy. Peggy pulled the magazine closer to her face.

"Well," Willowdean smiled with a girlish giggle. "It's a little complicated." Peggy pulled down the magazine just enough to see Willowdean dangling her shoe from her toes.

"Oh-oh," she gulped and shoved her face back behind the magazine.

"Actually Doctor—"

"Travis," Ruden said. "Call me, Travis."

"Well, alrighty then, Travis." Willowdean leaned her top half almost on the counter. "That little girl sitting there is Peggy Anderson; Lenny Anderson's her father. He's the one who owned Scarlet, not Peggy. She ran off on him, Scarlet that is, not Peggy, and no one has been able to catch her; until Mosie, I mean Katherine, my daughter, came across her.

"See, John, Mosie's father, wanted to get her a birthday puppy from Mrs. Morgan, but Mosie, well, she has it in her head that this Scarlet is meant to be her dog."

"Seems to me, the dog has the same notion in her head too," said Dr. Ruden, his tone turning serious. "I'm going to be honest. There's only so much I can do. But if she does make it, who's going to be responsible for her? It'd be a shame to put her through all this and have her placed in a shelter. A place like that would kill a dog like her."

"Oh boy," Peggy peeked out from the magazine. "Lenny ain't gonna like this. He ain't gonna like it not one bit!"

CHAPTER TWENTY~SIX

John crouched in front of Blue's cage. "Lenny has everyone in Bayfield convinced she's some kind of mad dog gone wild in the swamps." Dr. Ruden's mouth tightened. "This dog hasn't shown any signs of aggression, not even when I cleared out her stitches. If you ask me, that gun should have been turned on Anderson."

John stuck his hand between the wire mesh of Blue's cage. She sniffed him and then gently licked him and settled her snout back under her long white stocking-socked legs.

"I'm sure if Mosie could have gotten a hold of that rifle that night, she might have done just that," John stroked the top of Blue's head. "The way they protected each other; guess I should have believed her. Blue. Good name for a dog like this."

Dr. Ruden sat on his stool and looked over the paperwork. "Unfortunately I have to agree. After cleaning her up, I recognized her. She came into the shelter as a runaway before Anderson got a hold of her. According to Peggy, Scarlet's *co-owner*, that was approximately three years ago. She claims Anderson got her for hunting purposes. I guessed her at two years old back then, so that would put ole' Scarlet-Blue here at about five or so." He took the pen from his pocket, clicked it open and started marking something on the papers on his clipboard.

"Going back in her records, I see at that time I had made a guess about her background. Someone had dumped her off in the woods." Dr. Ruden looked down at her. "Normally abandoned animals are timid at this point and have a hard time learning to re-trust us humans. And in Blue's case, well . . ." He glanced at her again. "Frankly, there's some pretty hard decisions that are going to have to be made."

John stood, running his fingers through his hair. "What do you mean?" he offered Doctor Ruden a Tareyton. Doctor Ruden flagged his hand and leaned against the counter. Holding the clipboard against his white smock, he clicked his pen, looked at Blue, and then John.

"Well," he said with a sigh and rubbed the back of his neck, "we can't explain it, but it's a known fact that sometimes an animal will somehow actually pick their human instead of the human picking the animal. They come around at the strangest times.

"And Scarlet, or Blue here, is one of those cases. I know because of the way she responds to Mosie; it's unusual, to say the least. If anything, this dog should either be dead, or filled with such hate for people that she should be wild as a wolf. However, she isn't." He handed John a paper cup filled with water. John threw his cigarette inside it.

"Yeah, I heard that before, but I thought it was just a bunch of bull shit," he said. "I wanted to get Mosie one of those little white poodle pups from the Morgan farm, even paid for the damn thing in advance, but Mosie; she didn't want anything to do with any of that. But after what her and this hound have been through, maybe she's right."

Dr. Ruden nodded. “Well, I don’t know who picked who,” he clicked his pen and went back to his scribbling, “but I think it’s a good match.”

John knelt back down next to her. She peered at him with her golden-brown eyes. She began to shake. “She’s awfully skittish.”

“Yep, I know,” Dr. Ruden kneeled next to them. “It’s a shame. And from what Peggy described, I have to conclude Anderson had no right taking her from the shelter in the first place, not for what he was expecting from her, anyway.”

“What do ya mean?” John asked.

“Well, to start with, he trained her all wrong, made her gun-shy even worse than what she already was; and then expected her to perform like a champion field and gun dog. When she didn’t, he abused her and tried to get her to do what she couldn’t. Guess I would have run off too. She can hunt though, that’s for sure; otherwise, she wouldn’t have been able to survive like she has.”

“Asshole,” John said, reaching through the bars and patted her. His calloused hands turned as soft as Blue’s black velvet ears.

Doctor Ruden smiled. “You know,” he said, “I’ve dealt quite a bit with those pups of Mrs. Morgan’s, and ailing or not, I’ll put my money on this hound over one of those dogs any day.” He gave Blue a good scratch around her ears. “Yep, you’re a good girl, aren’t you,” he said. “Mosie’s right. You just need some time to prove it.” He stood and opened the cupboard. After pulling out a shoe box filled with small clear bottles of liquid, he took one out and held it to his eyes.

“Those Morgan dogs,” he said, reading the label on the bottle, “are bred until there isn’t anything left to them. And the pups . . ." he opened a drawer and lifted out a long needle-syringe. ". . . have to bare genetic defects. Bad hearts, hip problems . . . sure wish there was a way of stopping people like Mrs. Morgan, and Lenny Anderson." He gave John a hard look.

"Just between us," he said softly, "Scarlet-Blue here had a couple of litters herself. My guess, wolf pups. It's not unheard of. The wolf population is just beginning to rise in this part of Wisconsin. A few years back, wolves were unheard of in these parts due to what's cruelly labeled as Mandatory Hunting. Now they're just beginning to be seen again. And I think maybe this little girl here has recently seen one or two herself."

"You mean, she's . . . are you saying what I think you're saying?"

"There's a possibility. This Anderson, you sure he isn't going to be trouble, especially with her possibly being, well, shall we say, in the family way? Course I won't know for a few more weeks when I can test her again. Being on so many medications it's hard to get a correct read. But if she is, she may not even carry them due to her condition." John stood up, straightened himself, and rubbed the back of his neck.

"Put it this way John," Dr. Ruden swabbed the syringe with a cotton-ball soaked with alcohol, "I would be more worried about Anderson and the people of Bayfield than her giving birth to a batch of wolf pups."

John lit another smoke and took a deep inhale. "Well, Doc, you've met my daughter. Who'd you rather go up against?"

Dr. Ruden perked a grin. "I see your point." He looked down at Blue. "Well old girl, I hope this is the last one of these for a long time." He drew up a dose of liquid medicine into the needle. Blue twitched her nose. She could smell it.

"This is Acepromazine; it's going to relax her for the trip home. Home," he repeated, tapping out the tiny bubbles of air inside the shot. "Now that has a really nice ring to it, doesn't it? *Home.*"

Gently, he took hold of the flabby skin behind Blues neck and slid the needle in.

"You're still pretty sick, but I can't do any more for you here," he rubbed the nape of her neck while she fell asleep. "Now, when you wake up, you'll be a little confused over your surroundings, but I have a feeling that won't be a problem for long."

He motioned for John to help lift her onto the gurney.

"My assistant has all her medications and some bandages ready for you. She'll meet us out front in the parking lot," he released the brake on the gurney.

Guiding Blue to the end of the hall, Dr. Ruden pushed the silver disk on the wall.

"You have something to carry her in?" he waited for the doors to swing open.

"Willowdean had one of the fellows down at the shop put a cage together," John pushed Blue past the door, and into the parking lot. They rolled her to his pick-up. Dr. Ruden took the bag from his assistant and handed it to John. He gave Blue one last stroke down her slim body. "If she needs anything, I want someone to call me right away, night or day."

"We're going to miss you," the young girl rubbed Blue's slumbering belly. The three lifted her into the giant cage that sat in the hull of John's pick-up.

"I got a couple of guys from the shop to help me unload her," he wiped the sweat from his brow. He flipped a heavy sheet of canvas over the huge, wire crate, leaving left plenty of space for fresh air. He shut the tailgate.

"I want to thank you, both of you," John offered his hand to Dr. Ruden and his assistant.

"She *does* look better than when she came in," Dr. Ruden said with satisfaction and accepted John's handshake. "Mosie deserves a good pat on the back, too," he said. "If it wasn't for her coming in for the last couple of weeks like she did, I don't think this dog would have had a reason to pull through. Tell her congratulations from us; she got herself a dog."

Dr. Ruden and the girl stepped away from the truck. They waved to John and Blue. They were heading home.

CHAPTER TWENTY~SEVEN

The air could not have smelled sweeter, the sky look any bluer. "Why were Pa's workers here?" Mosie frowned as they pulled into the driveway and passed through the dust cloud kicked up from Stubby Murphy's truck.

Willowdean bit the grin from her lips. "To help him with something I suppose."

"Probably to take some more of Pa's stuff down to the shop," Mosie whined and slumped down in her seat. "I can't see why we couldn't go and see Blue today. I was going to take her out and walk her around to build up her leg some more. I even got her a maple sugar candy and one of those cans of little weenies from Mr. Maki's. Doc Ruden said it's okay to give her a special treat now and then. Geez!"

"Well, maybe we can go see her tomorrow, how about that?" Willowdean parked the station wagon. "But for now I think we should go talk to your father to see if he needs anything else before he leaves." She stepped out of the car and concealed her giggle with her purse. Mosie reluctantly followed her to the garage.

"Hi Pa," she eyed the inside of the garage for any missing articles.

John gave his trousers a tug. "While you and your mother here were lounging down at that beach all day, your old man was pretty busy," he said gruffly. "It seems if things need to be done around here, I have to do that, too." He flashed his eyes at Willowdean. "I started cleaning some of this out of here, and you're going to finish it."

"But Pa," Mosie protested, "I don't know what you and Ma want done with this stuff."

"Well, for starters," he growled, "you can go over there to the back, behind that wall of boxes I made. It's a job and a half, but I think you can manage it. Besides, it'll keep you busy and out of trouble for a change." Willowdean squeezed out a slight snicker and she watched Mosie hiss out a sigh as she followed John to the back of garage.

"Pa, I ain't, I mean, I haven't been in any trouble for a good two weeks now," she argued. "Geez."

"Yeah-yeah, well," John argued back as he took her behind the boxes. "We'll just make sure it stays that way, now won't we?" He stepped to the side. The creases in his face cracking into a hundred tiny smile-lines. Mosie stared at the cage. She focused on the mound sleeping inside and blinked at it again, and then again. Then came her gasp.

She staggered backwards and barely eked out, "I'm-I'm going to freak. *I am* freaking! Blue . . . Pa, it's Blue . . . oh Pa!" she screamed, held down the top of her head, and stepped in every direction. She found her father's arms.

"It was your mother, too," he laughed and beamed at Willowdean.

"She's pretty foxy, that mother of yours; telling me to stop at Doc Ruden's to pay the bill, and then having him suggest I have a look at *your* dog, and all the while having Stubby Murphy make a cage for her behind my back, at the shop, *just in case*."

"Ma!" Mosie bleated and threw her arms around her.

"She's going to need a lot of care," Willowdean said. "Do you think you can handle it?"

"Oh *yes*!" Mosie choked. "Thank you . . . thank you . . . *thank* you!"

Willowdean closed her eyes and took a deep breath. "Ganawenim idash gikinoowizhiwe niin odaanisimaa+g (protect and guide my daughter)," she whispered.

"Ah, geez Ma, don't worry," Mosie whispered. "It'll be okay, I promise."

Mosie knelt beside Blue and watched her skin, taut as a drum, heave up and down against her ribs.

"Hey girl," she stretched her fingers through the cage. She gently swept them across the top of her head. "It's me, your friend, Mosie Bitmen."

Blue caught Mosie's scent, twitched her nose, and opened her eyes. Her tail, flapped against the cage. Then it stopped. She closed her eyes.

"Is she going to be okay?" Mosie kept her hand on Blue.

"The Doc gave her a shot to relax her for the drive over," John explained as he lit a smoke. "She's still in tough shape, kiddo, and has a bit of tick fever left in her, but the Doc thinks she might make it.

"He can't do any more for her at his place, so he thought maybe between you and your mother . . ." He looked at Willowdean. "He gave me these meds," he handed her the bag.

Willowdean took it and quickly withdrew her hand from his deliberate touch.

"I'll bring them in the house and organize them," she said, stiffly. John watched her strut past the boxes and out the door. He took a puff from his cigarette and smothered his disappointment. He turned to Mosie.

"I was thinking you might want to hang out here, so me and Stubby and a couple of the other guys from the shop fixed it up the best we could."

Mosie looked at the cot not more than ten feet away from Blue's cage. On it sat a set of clean sheets, a couple of army blankets, and a pillow. Under the window stood the worn green bookshelf John liked so well.

Instead of his collection of mismatched wrenches, screwdrivers, drill bits, and used oil rags, a large quantity of dog supplies was stacked on the freshly washed and news-papered shelves.

To its side, an old card table was covered with one of Willowdean's orange floral oilcloths; its edges dangled and rested on two brown metal chairs. "One for you, and one for Peggy," John said.

"Thank you, Pa." Mosie wiped the tears from her eyes. She gave him a hug.

"You're welcome," he ruffled her hair and kissed the top of her head. "I suppose I ought to get back to work. You going to be okay?"

Mosie looked at Blue, who was sleeping contently. "Pa," she said, "I don't suppose you'll answer just one more prayer, will you?"

"Well now I don't know. What is it?"

"Well, um," she said staring at the floor. "It'd be awfully nice if you came home. I'm sure Ma wouldn't mind."

John cleared his throat and peered in the doorway, hoping to see Willowdean standing there, her black eyes sparkling with the same question. Nothing.

"Katherine," he sighed. "That isn't a prayer I can answer. Not now. But if you have any troubles with the dog, give me a call. Doc Ruden said you have to walk her every four to six hours, so don't forget."

John looked at his watch. "I got to go, kiddo. Want to walk your old man to the truck?"

Mosie stuck her hand in Blue's cage. "No, I think I want to stay here with her, if that's okay." "Sure," John replied.

Mosie kept her eyes on Blue. "Thanks for everything."

John reached out his hand to pat her head. He stopped "You're welcome," he watched her count the mesh wires on the cage with her fingers.

"Four-five-six . . . Ma is right," she said. "Dogs are like babies; they do come to you when you need them the most."

John turned away. Mosie listened to his boots cross the floor.

"One, two . . . my pa is gone. Three, four . . . he slammed the door. Five, six . . . I wish him and Ma could get themselves fixed." The truck rolled down the driveway.

"Seven, eight . . . I think it's too late."

CHAPTER TWENTY~EIGHT

Blue had one heck of a limp as she hobbled around the yard and sniffed the ground on nothing but three legs and a prayer. "That's right," Mosie said, "this is your yard now, our yard, yours and mine." The white tip of Blue's tail beat the air faster than hummingbird wings. Her *aw-roo* wasn't strong and powerful like out in the woods, but Mosie could tell she still meant it.

Aw-roo, aw-roo-oo, she said again; this time she kicked her head backwards and bounced on her good front leg. After licking the bandage wrapped around her bad leg, she went back to smelling the ground and dropper her girl part.

"That's how Peggy goes outside, too," Mosie laughed. Blue looked up at her and whined.

"Oh come on now, she's not that bad. Matter of fact she's even okay. Here, I'll show you." They slowly made their way behind the garage; Blue hopped faithfully alongside Mosie.

"See?" she, said, patting the lumber. "Peggy's been helping me with this. Do you know what it is?" Blue fluttered her eyebrows.

"It's a boat, or will be I should say, once we get her done. Blue, have you ever heard of, Dog Island?" Blue perked her ears and whined.

“Well that’s where I was heading; to come and find you,” Mosie said putting her arms around Blue’s neck. She gave her a hug. “Ma was right after all. She knew you would get here sooner or later.” Mosie sunk her face into Blue’s black velvety fur and kissed her. “Thanks for coming, Blue.” Blue put her bad leg on Mosie’s knee and licked her forehead.

“Well thanks girl, you’re welcome. You know,” she looked back at the boat, “I bet ma won’t mind us finishing her up, not now anyway. And I bet Pa would even help us, when we need it, that is. We could use it to go fishing and—”Blue stretched her neck, sniffed the boards, and backed away with a growl.

“What’s wrong?” Mosie asked giving the boards a whiff. “Oh, I bet you smell Lenny, don’t you girl? Guess the smell of stinky old Lenny Anderson is something nether one of us will ever forget, huh?” Shuddering, Blue nudged closer to her.

“Well, don’t you worry,” Mosie coddled her. “There’s no way he can hurt you anymore. I won’t let him.” She helped Blue back inside the garage, closed the door, and lifted her on to the cot; the metal legs rattled under Blue’s tremors.

“You know,” Mosie sat next to her and steadied the cot, “you are the bravest dog in all of Bayfield; and the prettiest too.” Mosie unfolded a blanket, covered her up, and tucked it over Blue’s head like a giant bonnet. “You shouldn’t let stinky old, Leo-Nerd get to you like this.

“You know, Blue; I knew a girl back in Barrington that used to get me rattled up just as bad as what Lenny gets you rattled up. Her name is Judy Larson, but Candy and I call her Judy Lard-Ass. She doesn’t have any fat on her, but we just call her that to be mean.

“Well one day, Lard-Ass and her gang were being super mean to me and Candy. So, I whapped her a good one right in the nose. Matter of fact I broke it. That's what Sister Vern Mary told me anyway, and Sister never lies."

Blue lapped Mosie with her tongue and laid her head across her lap; her shakes receded as Mosie went on.

"After that, Lard-Ass still tried to pick on us; but I think it was more for show than anything because whenever she started anything, I would look at her straight in the eye, and then she'd come up with some cockamamie story; like remembering how Father Dressler or Sister Prudence asked her to help burn palms or some damn thing.

"None of it was true, of course. No one is allowed to touch anything Holy and Sacred except the priests and maybe a nun if it's an emergency." Mosie narrowed her eyes. "We know you can't give Lenny a good bop or anything, but I sure can."

Blue yawned. She licked Mosie's hand, and then fell peacefully asleep. Slowly, Mosie rose from the cot and looked over Blue's supplies.

John thought of everything from the old wind-up clock sitting on the table to the fifty-pound bag and fifty cans of high quality dog food that were faced meticulously on the shelves.

Even a good assortment of better quality treats sat next to the row of prescription bottles Willowdean had arranged neatly on the shelves. Picking up the pill bottles, Mosie read the labels. *Blue Bitmen*, they said.

She sat on a metal folding chair and went through Dr. Ruden's instructions:

1. Walk canine: Every four hours for fifteen minutes excluding nighttime sleeping hours.
2. Triamcinolone Acetonide Ointment: Clean wound daily-Replace bandage.

3. Rimadyl: Every six hours given with food for pain and inflammation.
4. Panolog: Two drops per ear three times daily.
5. Chloramphenicol: One capsule every six hours for infections.
6. Buspirone Hydrochloride: One tablet to be given for anxiety when needed.

"Pa is right," she put down the list. "Blue is going to be a lot of work, but work I won't mind." She checked the time on the clock. "Almost 2:30."

That's when she noticed the book sitting on the table, the manual with a picture of a young boy holding his finger over a sitting dog. She picked it up and read the title, *How to raise your puppy into a dog*. She flipped open the cover:

To my sister, Moe

Happy thirteenth birthday

Love and peace,

Your big brother,

Val

"Val!" She smiled.

The door creaked open. She looked up. It was Peggy. "I'm running away, and no one's gonna stop me!" she cried, breaking the stillness of the garage.

"Shhh," Mosie hushed, quickly leaning over to put her hands over Blue's ears. Blue jerked. "She's sleeping," Mosie covered her up. "She smelled your dad on the boat boards and got herself sick. "Shhh, shhh," she shushed. "It's okay."

Peggy stood in the doorway, sniffling. She wiped the tears from her eyes and gawked past the wall of boxes. "So it *is* true.

Your pa *did* go get her," she burst into sobs. "This ain't good. This ain't good at all, Mosie, not at all."

Blue twitched and lifted her head at Peggy; her tail slid between her legs. "*Damn* it, Peggy," Mosie kept her voice calm and steady. She followed Blue under the table and stuck her hand under Blue's nose. "What the hell's the matter with you? Not you Blue, Peggy."

"Oh Mosie," Peggy gasped and cupped her hands around her mouth. "Corrine, she . . . she left. She left me for . . . she left me for . . . for . . . for your *pa!*" Mosie froze.

"And she snitched too, Mosie. Corrine snitched. Your pa told her about Scarlet; So when her and Lenny started fighting, she went and told him all about Doc Ruden, and how your pa brought Scarlet here, for you. She did it to get back at your ma; now Lenny's going to fix it so Scarlet is taken away and put down."

Mosie grabbed Blue's collar and squeezed it; she squeezed it hard, not letting go.

"Then, Lenny said we *all* can go to . . . to . . . to hell . . . including . . . *me!*"

She buried her face in her hands. "I hate them . . . I hate them, and I ain't never going back there as long as I live! Did you hear what I said?" she sobbed.

"Yes," Mosie said as her guts turned sour. "I heard you." She swabbed the sweat and tears running down her cheeks. "But it isn't true. My pa would never leave my ma for someone like . . ."

Peggy's sandals shuffled next to the chair. She pulled it out and its feet grated on the cement floor. Blue shuddered and panted as if the blood inside her was starting to boil. "Calm down," Mosie crawled closer to her.

"Calm down?" Peggy sobbed. "How can I calm down? Corrine and your . . . *your pa* . . . What are we going to do, Mosie? What are we going to do?"

"Hand me that green bottle there on the table. Not the red one, the green one."

"That's no answer!" Peggy shrieked.

"Not for us, you knot head, for Blue here; she's going to have a heartache if I don't calm her down; now give it to me, and hurry up."

Corrine slipped the bottle under the table and Mosie grabbed it and read its label. "Buspirone Hydrochloride. Here girl," she shook one large white tablet into her hand. "You have to open your mouth and swallow this, okay? It won't hurt you; it'll make you feel better, I promise."

Blue's eyes narrowed into slits and roamed side to side as she searched for a way out; her tongue kept slinking frantically in and out and oozed drool to the corners of her mouth. Carefully, Mosie slipped in the pill. It fell to the floor with the movement of Blue's tongue. Mosie picked it up and tried again, this time shoving it further down Blue's throat and clamping her mouth shut. Blue balked and then swallowed.

"Good job, good job," Mosie repeated over and over, stroking Blue's throat. "One, two, three . . ." she counted as she watched Blue's noggin nod its way to her paws. ". . . twenty-one, twenty-two, twenty-three." Blue closed her eyes.

"Why would she do that?" Mosie finally asked while petting Blue as she slept.

"Cause your ma was flagging her money around in Mr. Maki's store one day when we were at the beach. She went and shoved a $2,000 bill under Corrine's nose and told her to sniff it good and hard 'cause it was the only $2,000 she was ever going to see."

Mosie stopped petting Blue. " Peggy," she laughed, "they don't make $2,000 bills.

"Well, that's what Corrine told Lenny when they were fighting; I heard it myself. That's when she slipped up and said how she thought your pa should have given *her* that money instead of your ma. That's when Lenny really let her have it. He kicked her out and made her leave right then and there. He wouldn't even let her get her clothes or nothin', not even her makeup or curlers. He said, 'Mr. Big-shot John Bitmen can pay for all that since he's the one that's been keeping her busy down at Benny's." Peggy sniffled.

"That's when Corrine told him about Scarlet; she said: 'I ain't afraid of you, Lenny. You can't even shoot that miserable ole' hound dog ya' hate so much. For your information, ya' missed her head and got her in the leg. The damn thing's sittin' at Willowdean's house right now, and she's laughn' ta' folks all over town; tellin' them how you're so worthless ya can't even shoot an old hound dog the proper way.'

"That's when Lenny said he's going to kill Scarlet; even if it he kills him; he said it'll upset you, and then your pa will leave Corrine.

"Then he said your ma is the one that started the whole thing by getting herself pregnant again. He said that's what she gets for not doing what her man tells her to do, and for showing off his money like she does.

"Oh Mosie, he was *so* mad! He was going to come down here tonight and shoot Scarlet himself. I tried to stop him, really I did.

"When he grabbed his rifle, I didn't know what to do; so I bit him in the arm as hard as I could. He yelled something dirty filthy, and then smacked me a good one, see?"

Mosie climbed out from under the table. She looked up at Peggy and gasped. Her swollen lip was a puffy purple from top to bottom.

"I'm sorry Mosie, really I am," Peggy cried again. "I tried. I tried so hard . . . He . . . he was so drunk, and so was Corrine." Mosie scampered to her feet.

"It's okay. You're here now, and you're safe as old Blue." She put her arms around Peggy and pressed her bones against the girl. "You did good, No Name. You really did."

"Thanks Mosie," Peggy let her nose skid across her sleeve. "You don't think your ma knows your dad is with Corrine, do you?"

"Yes, I think she might."

"She must hate me, just hate me."

"No, no she does not. Ma doesn't blame someone for something another person does. She knows you had nothing to do with any of this."

"Are ya sure, really sure?" Peggy sniffled. "She won't make me go home, will she? Lenny's drunker than News Year's Eve, and meaner than I ever saw him. We had to miss my gig tonight because of it all, and that means no breakfast." Peggy sobbed and laid her head in Mosie's arms. "It ain't fair, Mosie. It just ain't fair."

"No, no it isn't," she rocked her back and forth. "It isn't fair, and no, you can't go home. Ma should take a look at that lip of yours and put some balm or something on it."

Peggy placed her finger on her mouth. She winced. "Ouch. He's going to come after us, Lenny is, after me and Scarlet, err, I mean Blue, soon as he sobers up."

"I was thinking about that," Mosie said.

"What are we going to do, Mosie, what are we going to do? He's awfully strong for his size, and Willowdean can't fight him off, not being PG anyway; and we're just kids. Heck, one blow from his fist and . . ." She squeezed her eyes and shuddered from the thought.

"And if I call Pa, he'll make me give up Blue so there's no more trouble between them other than what already is. When do you think Lenny will be sober enough to come after you, and Blue?"

"Tomorrow, maybe the next day. He's pretty lit and has a square of beer at home, so chances are he'll just keep on drinking till it's gone. When I ran out, I took his car keys and flung them in the woods."

Mosie laughed. "You took the keys?"

Peggy gave a little chuckle. "Yeah."

"Geez, No Name, I didn't think you were that smart! But if Ma finds out about any of this, she'll get upset, and get all worried, and then she'll call the cops, or worse yet, she'll call Pa; and then all hell *will* break loose . . . I got it," Mosie squealed. "I know what we can do; it's so simple I should have thought of it sooner. I think I know just the place to hide you, but you're going to have to be extra quiet, promise?"

Peggy tried to smile.

CHAPTER TWENTY~NINE

"Well no name, this is it. Are you ready?" They stared at the heavy wooden doors at the top of the concrete steps. Peggy pulled Willowdean's herb compress from her lips and read the sign out loud with Mosie: *Holy Family Catholic Church.*

"I never thought I'd ever set foot in such a building as this one," Peggy fumbled with the buttons on the special Sunday sweater Mosie gave her. "They sound like angels in there." She looked down at the ground and took a deep breath.

"Mosie, I gotta' tell ya' something," she put the compress on her lips. She took it off. "I do have a nickname, but I'm afraid you ain't gonna like it. It's *Peg-Her*. '*Peg-Her* when she's drunk, *Peg-Her* when she ain't.' That's what most folks in this church know me as . . . *Peg-Her*, just so you know."

"Well, you know what?" Mosie gave the back of her skirt a tug. "It don't matter. Just about everyone I know has another name people call them by. Take Stubby Murphy for instance; Pa said his real name is Melvin. And then there's Mrs. Bartelo, Pa's secretary, but you don't want to know what they call her when she's not around.

"Matter of fact, some of Pa's workers down in Barrington used to call Val something, too, that wasn't so nice when Pa wasn't there to hear them. So see, it don't matter if they got a name for you, everyone has one."

Peggy held the herbs to her lips and smiled. "Really?"

"I just said so, didn't I?" Mosie pinned their scarfs to their heads. "Well, let's do it," she took Peggy by the arm. "One, two, buckle our shoes." She put her foot on the first step. So did Peggy.

"Three, four . . ."

They climbed the stairs and Mosie opened the door. "This is it," she whispered entering the foyer. "Holy Family Catholic Church." Sticking her fingers in the small basin protruding from the wall, she turned to Peggy and made the sign of the cross.

"I'm good," Peggy showed Mosie her hands. "See, clean as a whistle."

"No Peggy, this is Holy water. It cleans you up *inside*. Come on, I'll show you where I and Pa like to sit."

They walked arm in arm down the aisle through the stone-cold silence and slid into the very first pew. Peggy stared at the man standing in front of the altar. His belly that protruded under his black robe was just right for a man well fed (not too much and not too little).

"That's Father Perkins," Mosie whispered extra soft into Peggy's ear. "Since you're not Catholic, you don't have to do anything but sit and listen. That's the rules."

Mosie pulled down the leather-covered kneeler at their feet, knelt down, and again made the sign of the cross, this time folding her hands. She closed her eyes and prayed without a sound while Father Perkins turned from the altar. The stubble of hair on the sides of his head matched his light-gray eyes. As he made his way to the podium, he grinned cheerfully at Peggy.

"Well now, this *is* a very fine Sunday morning at that, isn't it?" he asked. A chain of stiff coughs answered back. Mosie glanced at Peggy.

"She's beautiful," Peggy gulped and pointed to the marble statue that stood in the corner in front of them. "Is she a goddess?"

"Don't point, it's rude," Mosie whispered. "No, that's Mother Mary. Now pay attention. Tsk, goddess!" Mosie chuckled. "Geez."

"*Oooo* Mosie, who are *they*?" Peggy pointed to another sculpture standing at the other side of the altar. "I ain't *ever* seen such a fine family." Mosie snatched Peggy's hand from the air.

"That's the Holy Family, Joseph, Mary and Jesus as a young boy. Now sit still and listen to Father Perkins, and *stop* pointing."

"I wish we could of seen them coming in with their candles and—" Mosie hissed a shush.

Peggy sat quietly and stared at the statues. They stared back while Mosie and the others rose and knelt, repeating complicated rhymes and pledges.

Then, Father Perkins did a little cooking. Mixing a little of this, and a little of that, he closed his eyes and bowed to his guests, chewing what he had made.

"It must be good whatever it is," Peggy watched him savor every bite before serving it.

"What kind of snack was that?" she asked, while Father Perkins washed his tiny dishes after everyone was fed.

Mosie giggled. "That wasn't a snack. That's a communion wafer, the Holy Eucharist. *Snack!*" she repeated and stood up again with the others.

Father Perkins lifted his arms in the air and smiled. "Mass has ended, go in peace," he boomed and blessed them all with a giant sign of the cross.

"I can tell he means it, too," Peggy held her finger to her lip and her eyes welled up as Father Perkins turned from them. He genuflected before the huge crucifix suspended in the air behind the altar. That's when congregation sang out:

"*Morning has broken like the first morning. Blackbirds have spoken like the first dawn . . .*"

"You got a tissue?" Peggy asked.

Mosie dug in the pocket of her sweater.

"Where's the one I gave you? What's the matter with you?" She handed Peggy a pink floral hankie. "*Now* why are you crying?"

"I can't help it, Mosie. I just can't help it. It is magic, just like I thought it would be," she blew her nose and watched the two altar boys sway gracefully down the aisle behind Father Perkins; the cuffs of their black pants kept perfect timing with their white, lacy smocks.

Mosie stepped out from the pew and gave Mr. Maki a wave as they followed the crowd down the aisle. He gave her the okay sign.

"You didn't get bored?"

"No, not at all. Well, maybe a little when everyone was lining up to get a piece of whatever that Father Perkins was putting on their tongues. Come-moon-in wafer? Is that what you called it?"

"Communion Wafer. It represents Jesus' body."

Peggy's eyes got big. "You mean you people eat other people?" she asked as her voice almost disappeared.

Mosie laughed. "I think Father Perkins should explain things to you."

"You think he would? You don't think he would mind?"

"He's right there, why don't we ask him? But remember, we have to stick together like glue."

Father Perkins' greetings and well wishes fluttered above their heads in the warm morning breeze; his affectionate laughter gushed as a handful of the Peterson children ran around the bottom of his long, black cassock and tapped the tops of his shiny black shoes as they completed their circles.

Peggy smiled and pressed the hankie close to her lips. "That's Mr. and Mrs. Reo, with Mr. Pell, and his wife," she said. "Oh they're awfully nice people. They come into Lands Port tavern just about every Saturday night.

"Hi Mr. and Mrs.—" she called, with a huge wave.

Mosie watched them quickly look away and continue their conversation with Father Perkins. "Asses," she grumbled under her breath as she saw the smile on Peggy's face disappear. She grabbed the sleeve of Peggy's sweater and pulled her through the crowd.

"Come on," she squirmed past the group. "Father Perkins, this is my friend, my *best* friend, Peggy, Peggy Anderson. She's a singer, and a real good one, too. She sings at the Lands Port tavern most Saturdays and over in Hurley, too." She squared her eyes at the group. They fidgeted nervously as they stood to the side.

"Most folks here already know her on account of that, since *they* go and see her there, but I figured since you didn't, I thought maybe I should introduce her to you, myself."

Mr. Reo looked at his wristwatch and cleared his throat. "Boy, look at the time, Father. We really must be going. Great Mass," he stepped away with the others.

Father Perkins looked at Mosie; his eyes held an extra sparkle and his grin was especially broad.

"Katherine, Katherine," he stretched his hands to her. "Now, this is your friend you say? Peggy Anderson? How nice to meet you, Miss Peggy Anderson." Brightly, he took her hands in his. She beamed.

"Sorry," she grabbed Willowdean's little bundle of brown herbs from her pocket. She held it to the trickle of blood escaping from the crack in her lips.

In the twinkling of an eye, Father Perkins' dug in the cuff of his sleeve and flicked open his handkerchief. "Saints in Heaven!" he declared and held it firmly to Peggy's mouth. "We best have Mother take a look at that."

Tagging close behind, Mosie followed his thumping heels as he ushered them quickly back inside the church and down the aisle toward the altar.

Peggy looked up at the dangling crucifix and into the bloodshot eyes of Jesus that looked down at her with pity. "Thank you," she whispered up to Him.

The clopping of Father Perkins's shoes against the marble floor headed for the far wall of the Sacristy behind the altar; an open door led them to his rectory and to the smell of pot roast and apple pie snuggling the crooks and crannies inside.

"Mother, we have two little visitors," Father Perkins yelled over the squeak of tennis shoes on a basketball court, screeching from the television set in font of two recliners, inside the living room. "One is in need of medical attention."

He turned over the handkerchief dangling from Peggy's lips and waited for the kitchen door to swing open.

Within a moment, a miniature woman, grandmotherly and plump, raced into the living room and snapped off the TV. Gingerly, she entered the foyer as she wiped her pudgy little hands on her brown gravy and cranberry sauce splattered apron.

"I see, I see, Papa," she said in a thick Polish accent. "The little Bitmen girl an' her little friend. Come in, come in."

"Katherine, you remember Mother Magdalene, our Mother Superior, and music teacher."

"Yes, hello, Mother," Mosie bowed her head slightly.

"Auck, Sister Maggie, you call me Sister Maggie; and hello to you, Katherine Rose. Oh, now, dis' poor little lamb," Sister Maggie took Peggy's face into her hands and the smell of garlic and sage filled her nose. "Papa did not box you for falling asleep during his Mass, now did he?"

"N-n-no, Mother," Peggy stammered. Despite the ruddiness of the little nun's hands, they were warm and soft, like her dancing blue eyes.

"Mother, why do you say such things, huh?" Father Perkins laughed and showed them into the dining room. "Now, to make up for Mother's mocking, you two must stay for dinner."

Mosie looked at Peggy, and then Sister Maggie. Even though Sister Maggie was shorter, much rounder, and a hundred times older than Peggy, Mosie now understood what Val meant about, *soul mates*:

"Soul mates are two people meeting for the first time but deep down, they both already know everything about the other one; they just need to be reminded."

"Soul mates," that's what Val would call them, Mosie thought. *Long, lost soul mates.*

"Maybe next time, Father. Blue needs her medication, and Pa's coming today, and . . ." she stopped. She had said too much. "But, maybe Peggy could stay, if she wants to that is."

Father Perkins took Mosie by the hand and led her to the foyer.

"God works in strange ways, Katherine Rose," he looked straight into her dark navy blue eyes. "Sometimes He grants us ways to . . . perceive things so there is no need to ask questions that might embarrass His children."

"You know about Pa and Corrine and . . . Peggy, don't you Father?" She bowed her head, unable to look him in the eyes.

"You're a good girl, Katherine. A good friend. We will take good care of Peggy. That is why you brought her here, yes?

"Now, keep your head bowed so that I may bless you."

Mosie looked down and stared at that place between best Sunday shoes and overly waxed gray speckled floors. The warmth of Father Perkin's huge hand warmed the top of her head and made her want to cry in a good way. But she didn't.

The wind whistled in her ears, and carried her down Highway Thirteen on her bright yellow, ten-speed, Schwinn Super Sport, pushing her home to Blue and John's truck.

"He's early," she joggled up the driveway as she checked her watch. She put her bike against the house and raced up the porch steps.

"Blue . . ." she heard John say, his words dropping to a mumble. Willowdean inserted a troubled, "I expected this. I didn't need Doctor Ruden to confirm it." Mosie backed away from the door. She ran to the garage.

Awe-roo, awe-rooo, Blue welcomed her home. *Awe-roo, awe-rooo.*

"Blue," Mosie hurried behind the wall of boxes. Blue's white tipped tail thumped hard against the cage. Kneeling beside her, Mosie unlocked the door. She turned to the doorway. The smell of John's cigarette wafted through the garage. His face pinched in worry.

"Hey Pa," she saw he was thinner than when he had left last time. "What are you doing here? I didn't think you were coming until later."

John squeezed his cigarette with his lips. "Where's Peggy?" he asked, a trail of smoke escaping from his nostrils.

"Um, at Father Perkins'; she's going to have dinner with him, and Sister Maggie."

John pulled out a brown metal chair and ran his fingers threw his hair. "I got a call from Doc Ruden yesterday," he sat down and watched Blue eagerly licking Mosie's hands. He took a draw from his cigarette. Mosie lifted Blue's leg.

"He took her cast off," she said. "See?" Blue made her eyes nice and sleepy like she always did when Mosie paid her leg extra attention. Kneading it gently, Mosie thought back on how Doc Ruden had acted when she and Blue walked into the exam room.

She recalled the way his eyebrows mashed together, and how he had shaken his head of long wavy hair. She could almost hear the snap of his rubber gloves as he took them off and tossed them extra hard into the trashcan beside the examination table.

You can take her down now, he had sounded disappointed. *Your dad down at the shop?* he had asked. Mosie looked at her pa, then at Blue.

"There's nothing wrong with her," she said firmly, letting her out of her cage. Blue jumped on the cot and buried her head in Mosie's lap. Mosie pressed her face against Blue's, giving her kiss after kiss. John rubbed his neck.

"Mosie, how much do you know about, well . . . shit . . . how pups are made?"

Sitting on a little brown metal chair in the middle of a garage, John Bitmen found out his little Katherine Rose knew a bit more about such delicate subject matters then he did. He clenched his lips. "Val!" he snapped under his breath. "I'm going to kill that kid!"

Unwilling to admit Peggy was the one who had given her such detailed instructions concerning the birds and the bees, Mosie counted the tar spots on Blue's legs and chest.

Twenty-two, she finished up and thought how she could blame Judy Larson instead but not for at least twenty-four hours seeing she had just received Holy Communion (forty-eight hours counting Father Perkins' double blessing).

"Mosie," John said, "Blue . . . Blue's going to have pups, but we can't . . ."

"Pups, puppies? Little furry bundles of joy? Oh Pa," Mosie screamed as she hugged Blue. "When, *when* is she going to have them? How many? How—"

"Mosie," John snapped, "these pups aren't . . . they're not . . .they aren't . . ." He watched Blue kiss Mosie as if she knew she understood her condition.

"Ah damn it," he cussed under his breath and rubbed his neck again. "Doggone it, Doc Ruden believes these pups are fathered by a wolf, not a dog. Do you understand what I'm trying to tell you? Blue's pups are wild pups."

"But Pa, their still puppies, Blue's puppies, *her* babies."

"Yes, half hers, and half wolf. The wolf part of them is going to take over the Blue part of them. There's no way any one will take any of her pups, and your mother . . . well. We just can't have a pack of wolves hanging around here, especially with our own baby on the way." Mosie's eyes began to fill with tears.

"It's downright dangerous. No matter how much you think you might be able to tame them, they're still wild and always will be."

"No Pa, you're wrong, and so is Doc Ruden. Blue could never have mean babies; her babies will be just as good as she is, even better than Mrs. Morgan's! And if they're not, I could tame them, Pa, I know I could . . ." Mosie glared at the huge cage not even ten feet away. "Ma was right. I should have taken one of Mrs. Morgan's stupid white poodles and that way Blue could have at least kept her babies.

"Oh Pa . . ." She started sobbing. ". . . not Blue's pups . . ."

John got up from his chair. "Now, now," he sat next to her on the cot and covered her with his arms. "It's not your fault. It isn't Doc Ruden's fault. It isn't anyone's fault, not even Blue's. It's just the way nature is.

"Look," he put his hand on top of Blue's head, "look how happy she is."

Blue turned her snout up, lavishing John's hand with her kisses. He smiled and playfully grabbed at her tongue.

"She hasn't had it so good, not ever," he said. "Why, I bet if she could talk, she'd be yapping at you all the time, thanking you, telling you how much she loves you." Mosie sniffled.

"You think so, Pa? You don't think her having to sleep in a cage some nights makes her sad?"

John gave a light laugh. "What do you mean *some nights*?"

"Promise you won't tell Ma?"

"Promise."

"Well, after Ma goes to bed, I sort of sneak Blue upstairs with me, and when Ma's in the bathroom in the morning, I get her out before she even knows Blue's been there." John chuckled.

"See? How much better can she have it, huh? Hot meals, room to run, the best snacks a dog could possibly want, plus, one of the softest beds in town."

Blue turned her golden-brown eyes up at Mosie and lapped the tears from her cheeks. Mosie kissed her.

"True love," John chuckled. "True love. Now make me a promise, okay?" Mosie nodded and wiped her nose on her sleeve.

"Just don't go kissing any boys like that until you're at least thirty-six."

"Oh Pa," Mosie cried and buried her head in his chest.

"There is one thing though I do have to ask you," he softly rocked Mosie in his arms. "You can't tell anyone about Blue, not even Peggy. Word gets out old Blue girl here is going to whelp, and the whole damn town will be after her for sure—not just Lenny."

It was awfully quiet as the three of them sat, holding each other; Mosie did not dare to ask what they were planning for Blue's pups and John was not able, nor willing to tell her.

Dear Val,

In case you don't know, Blue is going to be a momma. Pa said Doc Ruden told him we can't tell anyone, not even Peggy. He said it's because Blue's pups are going to be wild since their daddy is a wolf (a real wolf!) and everyone will try to hurt her if they find out, especially Lenny Anderson.

Pa has a plan for the puppies and I have a feeling I know what is. Promise you won't say nothing, but I have a plan too!

Love always,

Your sister,

Moe

P.S. Just so you know, Pa thinks you told me about sex. Boy was he mad. But as soon I can, I will tell him Judy Lard-Ass did it (even if she didn't).

CHAPTER THIRTY

Laying behind the garage, Mosie rested her head on Blue. Blue stretched and groaned with contentment as the warmth of the early afternoon sun snuggled beneath her fur. Mosie reached under Blue's belly and rubbed it. It had grown fat and lengthy like her nipples.

"It isn't a half-bad day," Mosie plucked a blade of knee-high grass. Nibbling it, she squinted up at Peggy; her frilly yellow blouse and matching shorts looking out of place next to the half built boat. Sister Maggie snooping in the church thrift cellar and hoarding first picks for her *Sweet Peggy Girl* popped into Mosie's mind.

Peggy bent over and picked a nail from the rusty can sitting at her feet; her newly shagged hairdo dripped off her shoulders like layers of brown honey. "So, Lenny's okay with you staying with Father Perkins and Sister Maggie?" Mosie asked.

"He doesn't know," Peggy answered. "He's been drunk since Corrine's been gone, and she's been seeing to it that he stays that way. She buys him beer and leaves it for him in the car. She said he's so stupid, he probably thinks he's been going to town all this time and getting it himself." She placed her hammer against the nail, and started tapping it into the board.

"He keeps threatening on his dead mother's grave if he catches me anywhere, especially here, he's gonna kill me, so

I figure as long Corrine keeps him drunk, and I keep him fed, I'm pretty safe, at least until he sobers up anyway.

"It's funny," she turned to Mosie, "But the more I'm away from him and Corrine and that shack, the more I realize, I mean . . . Mosie, not that *you* would, but do you ever feel embarrassed about your folks?"

Mosie pulled up a fresh piece of grass. Closing her eyes against the sun, she concentrated on the kaleidoscope of reds, orange and yellows swirling against the black canvas of her eyelids. "Yes Peggy I do," she answered.

Peggy picked out another nail and gave it a whack. "I suppose it don't help with Corinne being with your pa. You know Mosie, I've been thinking. Wouldn't them getting together make us related someway? Kinda like sisters of sorts? I always wanted a sister, even a brother. That sure would be something, wouldn't it, if they got married? Willowdean would be kind of like my mom, a stepmother, and then we really would be sisters. Wouldn't that be something?"

Mosie rolled over on her stomach and watched Peggy from between Blue's ears. Peggy pounded the nail perfectly into the board. "It sure would. And think of how much trouble we could *really* get into."

"I don't know," Peggy wrinkled her brow. "If Willowdean was my mother, I don't think I'd ever want to get into trouble. Hey, guess who came in the Landing this weekend?"

"Who?"

"Big Bertha Brown." Peggy giggled and grabbed another nail. "That's not her real name. No one knows her real name. That's just what everyone calls her: Big Bertha Brown.

"And she is *big*! You know, I bet she's as tall as this boat, and just as wide. Wanna hear something even *more* strange?"

She giggled. "Some people think *she's* really a *he*. Ain't that too weird?"

"Naw, not really," Mosie said watching a patch of small puffy clouds pass overhead. "There's chicks like that down in the city. Val said they're called transvestites. He said they're just guys who like dressing up in women's clothing, that's all.

"He brought one home once. You should have seen Pa. I'll never forget the look on his face when he realized he'd been sitting there smiling all flirty-like, visiting with a guy all that time. Pa hauled him out of the house so quick no one had time to say goodbye.

"Val got mad. He said the poor guy was just trying to make a living selling Avon beauty products and thought maybe Ma would like to try some out.

"Ma said, *He was one of the prettiest women I ever saw and your father, too, apparently*. Boy, was pa really mad then."

She squinted at the clouds, pursed her lips like a cannon, and shot a cud of wet grass up at them. "Damn it," she cussed and rolled out of its way as she saw it heading back down. Peggy stopped hammering.

"Mosie," she put her hands on her hips, "you really need to do something about that mouth of yours, you know. It's gotten really bad. And you're just making that up; Val did not bring home a,Transistor-Type!"

Mosie picked a fresh blade of grass and flicked the tips of Blue's ears with it. "It's pronounced, trance-vest-tight," she chuckled as she watched Blue's ears twitch. "How do you know he didn't?"

"Well, I don't, okay? Heck, half the time I don't know if you're lying or telling the truth. But not this time; this time I can tell you're telling a tale." She stepped away from the boat and looked it over. "She sure is coming along, don't ya' think?"

"She sure is," Mosie snuggled against Blue. She smelled wonderful for a hound dog. The lilac shampoo mix Willowdean concocted was lingering just as she promised it would.

"Can we paint her pink?" Peggy ran her hands over the boat boards.

Mosie sat up and kissed Blue on her snout. "Pink?"

Peggy nodded. "Yes, pink. It looks, well, *pink*."

"Um, sure, but just the inside. The outside has to look really natural in order to fool the fish so it doesn't scare them away. What about a name? How about we call her Big Bertha Brown?"

"Big Bertha Brown," Peggy repeated as she looked the boat over. "A pink boat named Big Bertha Brown."

"Sure, why not?"

"Okay then," Peggy said. "Big Bertha Brown, it is. I sure am glad you decided we should keep working on her. Aren't you?"

"More than you know," Mosie rubbed Blue's belly. "More than you know." She brushed herself off, got up, and ambled over to Peggy. She inspected the boards and gave them a solid slap. "Five more planks, then we have to seal her.

"Pa gave us some good high-quality marine polysulfide sealant. He said we need to make sure we take extra time to caulk her properly with it because it'll keep us from sinking." They looked at each other, then at Big Bertha Brown.

"Do you think she'll really float?" Peggy asked. "Do you think we'll really be able to use her, for real?"

"I'm betting my life on it," Mosie gave Blue's head a scratch.

"What do ya mean by that?"

"Nothing. Pa said we're doing everything right, so, I'll bet my life on the fact that she'll float, that's all. I bet we can get three people in her. You, me, and Blue."

"*Blue*?"

"Well yeah, Blue, who else?" Mosie roughed her hands in the nape of Blue's neck. Blue licked her hands, and then pointed her nose to the air.

"Yes, you Blue."

Peggy rolled her eyes. "Oh brother. Something just ain't right about that."

Blue took off for the grove of pine trees lining the driveway. *Awroo, aw-roo-rooo*, she bayed and sniffed under the bushes. Pawing the ground, she worked up a spray of dirt.

"Look at her go," Mosie gloated. "I bet she's digging for that soup bone Ma gave her last night."

Peggy slapped a stray mosquito from her arm. "Hey, want to hear a new song Sister Maggie taught me this week?" she flicked the tiny brown splat from her arm.

Mosie shrugged her shoulders. "What song?"

"The one we sang at church a few of weeks ago, remember, the first time I went to church, err, Mass?"

"Nope, I don't remember; but go on and sing it if you really have to," Mosie kept her eyes on Blue.

Staring past Mosie's shoulders, Peggy took a deep breath and stood quiet as the wind in the pine trees. Mosie gawked at them with her. "What are you looking at?" she asked.

"Well, Sister Maggie told me when I'm about to sing, I need to clear my mind; so that's what I'm doing. I'm clearing my mind." She took another breath and continued gazing.

Blue nabbed the soup bone, tossed it in the air, and tackled it. She ran to Mosie and dropped it, panted anxiously, and brushed against her legs waiting for her to pick it up and throw it.

Mosie tossed it. She cheered as Blue caught it and sailed across the field. Peggy stomped her foot. "Doggone it!" she snapped. "Now I have to start all over."

"Sorry," Mosie stared back up at the trees.

Taking a soft breath, Peggy gently cleared her throat. Then, sweet and fine as if an angel were touching her, she began to sing: "*Morning has broken, like the first morning; Blackbird has spoken, like the first bird . . .*"

Her stare floated from the top of the trees to Mosie's eyes. Mosie stared back.

"Is it really that bad?" she asked, her face wilting.

Mosie took a deep breath. "No Name, I hate to say it, but you sound better than Debbie Reynolds in *The Singing Nun.*"

"*Really*? You *really* think so?"

"Hell yes. I said so, didn't I?"

Peggy bounced up and down. "Well, that does it . . . See, Corrine, she don't want me singing like that in the bars. She said people don't want to hear that sort of stuff when their sucken' down their beers.

"So I told her how Cat Stevens sings that very same song, and then she said I could sing it but not like a church girl.

"Mosie, I'm gonna do it! I'm gonna sing just like how Sister Maggie said I can sing, like how God meant me too." She beamed, swinging back and forth and hugging herself.

"Peggy Anderson, what the hell are you doing?"

"I can't help it. I just can't. Sister Maggie said I should give myself a hug every time I do what God wants. She said if He could, that's what He would do to every single one of us every time we do what's right because He loves us. She said they're called *God's little Love Hugs*. And it works too, go on, try it!"

Mosie scrunched her nose. "Well, I never heard of anything like that."

"Well now you have. And you want to know something else Sister Maggie told me? She said we are who God wants us to be, so it's best not to fight being ourselves even when other people don't want us to.

"She said that's when we get frustrated and get into trouble; trying to be what we're not on account of other people. And you know what else? I haven't been with no boys, Mosie, not a one!

"Sister Maggie has me so busy with learning how to cook, and learning how to clean, and sing." She grabbed Mosie's hands and started swinging them from side to side. Her hazel eyes sparkled. "You were right, Mosie," she said. "Someday *I will* become someone's Peggy, and he'll love me for me, and not because I let him kiss on me.

"Boy, the sky sure is blue today, ain't it?" Peggy flopped down in the grass and pulled Mosie with her. She reached over and patted Blue. Mosie smiled.

"Boy Mosie, she sure is getting fat. You know, one day I'm gonna leave this rotten old place, and when I do, I'm gonna touch the sky and I'm gonna grab me a handful of them stars up there. Even if I can't see them right now, just knowing they're up there waiting for me is good enough for me." She put her hand in Mosie's, raising it with hers. "Right there," she pointed a little left from the sun. "Right up there . . . that's where I'll be, right—up—there . . ."

Mosie's stomach fluttered. "That's a long ways away, No Name, with a whole bunch of nothing in between."

Blue sat up and turned her nose to the air. She nudged herself under Mosie's arm and started to shake. "What's the matter, girl?" Mosie stroked her up and down.

Blue smelled the air, poked her head out, and growled powerfully enough to make the fur on her back stand stiff-straight like the hair on a dead man's arm. Peggy's eyes grew large as craters. Mosie stood up; her heart was racing with the strain of her eyes as she searched through the trees at the edge of the yard; in the distance there was a roaring sound, a hundred times worse than Val's van.

"What the hell is he doing here?" she said as she watched Lenny's Ford heading up the driveway. She grabbed hold of Blue's collar and pulled her down between her and Peggy. She knew if Blue got away, they'd have trouble for sure. And if Lenny got a good look at Blue's underside, he'd have the sheriff and all of Bayfield coming after poor old Blue just like Pa and Dr. Ruden said he would.

"Oooo, he must of sobered up!" Peggy gasped as her hands shook like someone had stepped on them. "And he must a found the extra set of keys." She started to cry.

"I told you . . . I told you he swore on his dead momma's grave if he caught me over here he'd make sure it'd be the last time." He revved the engine and let it idle.

Through scrub-weeds and tall grass, they watched him open the car door. Blue rolled back her lips, exposed her teeth like daggers, and prepared for war as he placed one foot on the ground, then the other. Mosie knew Blue would destroy Lenny before he could destroy her.

"What do we do? What do we do?" Peggy flattened herself against the ground.

"Why'd you have to wear all that yellow for?" Mosie whispered. "He's going to see you sure as shit."

"I—I felt yellowy today. That's all, oh Mosie, help!"

"Of all days for you to feel *yellowy*. Help me hold Blue down; if he sees her, he'll kill her."

"Her?" Peggy sobbed. "What about *me*?"

Lenny rested his undersized arms on the car roof and studied the house. Blue shuddered as she smelled the brown arm-pit stains in his T-shirt.

"Three,"' Mosie counted as Lenny pulled his face back and sucked the snot out of his sinuses to the back of his throat. For three seconds, he rolled that thick glob of mucus on the back of his tongue before spitting it out. Then, he yawned like a snake getting ready to spring. Peggy shut her eyes tight.

"It's okay," Mosie whispered. "I got a plan.

CHAPTER THIRTY~ONE

A row of boxes crashed to the floor. Lenny snapped his head toward the garage. “Red squirrels,” Mosie whispered through the high weeds and tall blades of grass that hid her and Peggy.

“Uh-oh,” Peggy countered, “guardian angels . . . flapping their giant wings.”

Like an oily snake, Lenny slithered over the graveled driveway toward the garage, his boots did not even stir a pebble. Hands on hips, he gawked at the door as if figuring how to get inside. Crash. More boxes.

“Listen,” Mosie said, pinning Blue underneath her, “soon as he sticks his head in there, you take my bike, not yours, and get yourself over to Sister Maggie and Father Perkins as quick as you can. You’ll have to hurry; I don’t know how much longer I can hold Blue down like this.”

Blue growled and pushed her head through Mosie’s arm. Peggy looked at Lenny and hesitated.

“It’s okay,” Mosie said, shoving Blue back down. “Nothing will happen to him. I promise.”

“Mosie, I know you don’t like Lenny, and you have good cause not to; heck, most of the time I don’t like him much ether, but he is well, *my* pa.” Peggy eye’s softened. “Try to remember that, okay? And Blue, I know neither one of us was kind to you, but if I make it out of this, I'll make it up to you for sure." She smiled at Mosie. "*I* promise."

Mosie smiled back. "Okay," she rasped. "Get ready."

Lenny stretched his scrawny arm toward the door, turned the knob, and opened it. "There's your chance," Mosie watched him peer inside. Slowly, carefully, he slid into the darkness. "Now go," she yelled in a loud whisper, pushing Blue's head down again. "And have them get Pa."

She crouched low and watched Peggy twist her way through the pine trees along the driveway. "She'll make it Blue, don't you worry. If anyone can give old Lenny the slip, it's Peggy . . . and you," she said, watching Peggy slink between the Ford and the edge of the porch. Still no Lenny. "She's making it . . . Get ready."

Peggy held her breath and leaned toward the bike. As she grabbed it, it slipped from her hand and crashed to the ground. The garage door flew open. "Sweet Mother Mary," Mosie said wrapping her arms around Blue. She dove into the grass; Peggy rolled under the Ford, her yellow outfit baring itself like a beacon in a storm.

"Trapped like rats," Lenny said as he headed toward the house. He laughed as he climbed the porch steps. "Come out, come out, wherever you are," he said, sticking his face against the screen, looking inside. "Olly-olly oxen free." Peggy didn't move. She watched Lenny lite a cigarette and then turn to look over the field.

Crows flew from the side of the garage.

"A-ha! Now I gottch-ya's," he sneered and rushed back to the garage. Peggy rolled out from under the old Ford.

Yanking up the bike, she saddled it and flew down the driveway in near silence. "Angel's wings," Mosie said, crushing

Blue's collar in her hand, "Angel's wings. Now's our chance." Blue twitched her snout and drew back her lips, ready to rip apart the very air between her and Lenny.

"Wait . . ." Mosie hustled herself and Blue across the yard. "We have to get inside the house before he does."

She hurried up the steps, and set foot inside the porch. Spotting one of John's old tire irons tucked next to the kitchen doorway, she grabbed it, and shoved it down the back of her pants—"just in case"—and barged into the kitchen, bolting the door shut.

"Katherine Rose, what are you doing?" Willowdean yanked the iron from her backside. "What did you get into this time? You're white as a sheet."

"Nothing Ma, nothing," she pulled the kitchen door curtains together tight as she could. "Quick, call Pa; it's Lenny, Lenny Anderson. He's right outside, and he's heading this way!"

"Yes, I know," Willowdean said, setting the tire iron next to the door. "I asked him to come over. Look at you, you're shaking like a leaf. You have to settle down. And where's Peggy?"

Mosie backed away. "What? Why'd you go do that for? You know he's going to take Peggy away and have Blue killed! How, *how* could you do that, Ma, *how*?" With Blue at her side, she turned and ran from the kitchen.

"Mosie," Willowdean shouted and chased after her. "Running away like this won't solve anything; that's why I called him *and* you're dad. It's time we sat down and talk this mess out. Please, be reasonable!" Mosie's bedroom door slammed shut. There was a sound of muffled dragging on carpeting.

"Don't you move that bed," Willowdean yelled. "You'll rip that new carpeting." She waited. Nothing. "Well then, I and

Lenny will just have to eat the extra gooey batch of butterscotch cookies I made all by ourselves."

"Good! I hope he chokes on them and dies!" Mosie yelled.

"Katherine! That's a terrible thing to say. And where is Peggy?"

"I'm not telling, so don't bother asking again!"

"Mosie, please, be sensible."

Nothing but the sound of Willowdean's fan in the living room window hummed through the house. "Well then, you just wait until your father gets here." Still silence. And then it came: the three feeble knocks of Lenny Anderson.

Willowdean sighed. She looked at the top of the staircase. "Coming," she patted the wrinkles from her dress and headed to the kitchen. She flipped over the curtain on the door and peered out at Lenny. He was muttering to himself as he stared at the floor, impatiently rubbing the back of his neck.

"You haven't been drinking, have you?" Willowdean asked.

"No, I ain't been drinking," his tone was filled with irritation as if being interrupted from one of the best conversations he ever had.

"Do you promise you won't try any monkey business?"

"Do you want me to come in or not?"

"Do you want to come in?"

Lenny leaned in the doorway and bit a flab of skin on his thumb.

"Look it Willie, either you want me to come in, or you don't. I ain't got time to play these little games of yours. I got too much to do besides stand outside your damn kitchen door begging ya to come in. This ain't 1954."

"Leonard Arthur Anderson, you know better than anyone else, you do not have a single thing to do. Even if you did, you wouldn't do it any way." Willowdean turned over the lock.

"Yeah, well, I guess everyone has the right to their own opinion as to what's important and what's just a waste of time," he stepped inside and glanced over Willowdean. He nodded at her belly. "Looks like John ain't the only one who hasn't been sitten' around."

Willowdean blushed. "You haven't changed one bit, have you Lenny?"

"Yeah, well," he flopped down in John's chair at the kitchen table, "I tried that once, and it was more of a pain in the ass then what it was worth." He took in the house. "Either that old man of yours did good by you after all, or he couldn't stand being with ya. What'd he do? Fix this old place up as an excuse to get away from ya?"

"You know as well as I do that John has never been the type to sit around," Willowdean picked up the coffee pot from the stove. She filled their mugs and grabbed the platter of cookies. "I made these just this morning; why don't you try one?"

With his hand shaking, Lenny took a draw from his cigarette. Willowdean put a cup next to him on the table and placed a cookie on his plate.

"I made them for Peggy and Mosie, err, Katherine, but she decided to wait until John, and Corrine get here." She turned to the window. "They should be here any time."

"Who you kidding?" Lenny shoved half the cookie in his mouth. He chewed it and winced. "Mosie, or whatever you call her, didn't want to sit in the same room as ol' Lenny. Can't say I don't blame her. Me and that kid of yours don't seem to hit it off too good, if you know what I mean." He dug his tongue inside his back tooth and nibbled a chunk of wet butterscotch then swallowed it. "She's wild, that girl. Just like her momma used to be."

"Lenny, please," Willowdean said quietly. "This is neither the time nor the place for that. Besides, that's all in the past; we were all young and stupid. You know the reason I called you and you agreed to sit down and talk this through. It's very painful what we're all going through, and making threats to split up the girls and to take away Mosie's dog is just adding to their fear and pain, and ours too."

Lenny brushed the crumbs from his jeans and bit the other half of his Toll House. "Yeah, guess you're right. You always did have a sense about you. But ya have to admit, the four of us sure had some mighty high times together.

"Remember that one night over at Rainbow Falls? That crazy sister of yours!" He chuckled, clasping his hands behind his head.

"And John! Boy-o' boy . . . now those were the days, weren't they Willie? Not a care in the world, thinking those days would never end . . ." He laughed and rocked back and forth on the hind legs of his chair. Willowdean got up from the table.

"Now, where in the world did I put that sugar bowl," she opened a cupboard. "John has to have his sugar with his coffee."

Lenny nodded at the table. "It's sittin' right here in front of ya," he said, running his finger tip over its delicate rim. Willowdean wrung her hands. "I can remember the day my momma gave you this sugar bowl as if it were yesterday. Yep, my momma, she sure was mighty fond of you, Willie." He picked up the china and looked over its rim at Willowdean. The tobacco stains on his fingers matched the floral brown painted on the side of the bowl.

"Lenny, please," Willowdean held onto the counter. "Katherine doesn't know."

"Remember what she said to ya when she gave it to you? Ya don't? Well, I sure do. She said: 'No matter how much sugar this here bowl will hold throughout the years, it will never be as sweet as you.' Ain't that what she said to ya, Willie, the day ya went and married big old city boy, John Anthony Bitmen?"

He held the bowl up to the light and watched the dark shadows of his fingers dance through its delicate ware. Willowdean bit her lip.

"That's enough Lenny," she snapped as she glared at him. "I'm sorry I even asked you here. I thought maybe after all these years you had come to your senses. But I see your still—"

"Now how long would you say you had this thing? Let's see . . . Valerie is what, eighteen; ain't that right?" He shifted his squinty-green eyes at her and watched her wipe the tears rolling down her cheeks with the back of her hand.

"Aw, hell," he spat. Running his fingers through his hair, he snapped forward in the chair. He placed the sugar bowl back down on the table. "Listen to me . . . coming in here talkin' like a fool after all this time . . . acting just as bad . . . hoping to get you flared up before John gets here.

"I sure do apologize, Willow. Guess it's still got me riled, worse than I thought. The way I figured it, it should of been you and me sharing this here sugar bowl, not you and John."

"Maybe you're right," Willowdean replied, as her voice cracked. "John . . . my sister . . . Corrine. Nothing has changed between them, and nothing ever will." She peered out the window.

"Deep down, I knew nothing would change the way they felt about each other, no matter how many miles or years were put between them. I knew she was the real reason John wanted to move back here. I've tried, Lenny, lord I've tried, and I suppose you have too, in your own way." She straightened the edge of the curtain hanging above the sink.

"I knew he was tricking me. I guess I just wanted it done and over with, and that's why I really agreed to move back here. I knew she was here; I could feel her. It wasn't for Mosie or Val, not really. It was for myself. I just couldn't stand living a lie any longer. Pretty selfish of me, isn't it?"

Lenny took a drink from his cup. "Yeah, yeah it was, Willie. But you're right. Hell, Corrine, she ain't never been faithful to me either. But you know what the worse part of this whole deal is?" he asked, giving a little cackle. "Momma. Momma never could stand Corrine. I think she's what put her in her grave."

"Lenny," Willowdean laughed and dried her tears. She sat down at the table and held his hand.

"I missed you, Lenny. I really did. But, Katherine, she doesn't know anything about Corrine and you or Val. I wanted to keep it that way forever; especially after I and John made the mistake by telling Val everything. Look what happened."

Lenny leaned forward in his chair. The silence between them was thick as the maple syrup that had drawn them all together twenty-one years ago.

"You told Valerie?" Lenny asked. "That's why he didn't come?"

"Yes," Willowdean nodded. "Yes Len. That's why I wanted you to come here before John and Corrine, so I could tell you myself. He turned out good, Len, real good. You'd be proud of him, I know you would."

Lenny turned away and buried his face in his arm. A heavy rasp rolled from his chest. His shoulders shook. Willowdean reached over and touched him.

"I've been trying to forgive you and John for eighteen years," he said, his voice tight with sobs. "And I have to admit, the day Corrine brought little Peggy home, I thought maybe it would of made us even-steven, but it didn't, did it? I mean, Peggy, she's a good a kid and all, and I love her like I ain't never loved nothing before besides you. But she ain't blood Willow, she ain't *my* blood. She's John's and Corrine's, just like Val is yours and mine.

"It broke me, Willie. It broke me so's I couldn't make it back."

"Well, you're here now," Willowdean said gently, holding onto his arm. "And that's a start, a *big* start."

He wiped his face with the sleeve of his shirt. "Damn if I can figure out how all this got so messed up. Guess I made it even worse, trying to scare poor little Mosie, hoping I'd keep them two girls away from one another, and you and John. I was downright scared, Willow; scared of losing Peggy and Corinne to you and John, just like I did Val."

"Len," Willowdean said, "John doesn't know about Peggy, not unless Corrine told him; he never mentioned it to me. You know he isn't one for children, so even if she did tell him I don't think it would matter to him. I don't want the girls to find out about any of this, not like this. It'd be too hard on them."

"We've all been fools," Lenny sniffled. "Wastin' all these years on the wrong ones."

"Yes, yes we have, Len. But who's to say what will happen in the future? Len, would you like to see a picture of Valerie?"

Lenny shrugged. "Don't see what good it'd do, but I can't see what harm it would do either." His eyes filled with excitement.

"Good," Willowdean got up. "There's a picture of him on the fireplace; come on, I'll show you."

She took him by the hand and led him to the living room. "It was taken last year, for graduation." Lenny pulled his hand away. He nodded at the staircase.

"Ah, Willie, I hate to tell ya, he said, "like it or not, I think that little Mosie of yours got herself a good earful."

The color drained from Willowdean's face. "Katherine!" she gasped. Mosie stood up.

"I hate you!" she spat, "and I *hate* you," she sobbed and gave Lenny a venomous glare. He froze. Blue was gazing down at him; her fur rose like short black barbs. She snarled as her lips curled back in a sneer.

"Stand still, Lenny, stand still!" Willowdean tried to sound calm. But he didn't listen and ran to the porch.

It didn't take long, just a matter of seconds (but those seconds did come).

It was as if the devil himself had gotten into that house, that day in June, the day Blue let loose and Lenny let out a scream. Then came the quiet. Willowdean raced into the kitchen and grabbed the tire iron, long and black. Mosie tried to pull it from her hands. She couldn't. Her mother's fear clung to it.

"No Ma, you'll kill her, you'll kill her!"

"I have to!" Willowdean shouted, pushing Mosie out of the way.

Mosie shrieked and threw herself between Blue and Willowdean.

She looked up at the mighty piece of iron.

"Kill *me*, not her!" she shouted.

Then it came. The dull thud.

"My God, what have I done?" Willowdean screamed, "My God, what have I done . . ."

There was no humming of Willowdean's fan, no Charlie Pride singing about, *loven* and *turtle doven*, and certainly no *Running Bear*. There wasn't even the sound of the sudden winds coming in from off the lake.

The only sounds were the chokes coming from Lenny. Blue had got her way.

"I want my girl and her momma," he gurgled, slapping his hands in the pool of red surrounding him. Blue whined and backed away as if the blood and Lenny were poison. Willowdean grabbed the phone.

"The ambulance, it's coming," she sobbed, pushing Mosie out of the way. "It's on its way . . . it's on its way, Len." She placed a stack of towels next to him and began daubing up the dark red, almost black liquid.

Trembling, Mosie slowly opened the kitchen door. The shrill sound of sirens cried in the distance.

"They'll be here anytime, anytime," Willowdean cried, mopping up Lenny.

"Blue, come," Mosie whispered. They stepped onto the porch.

"Hold on, just hold on Leonard," Mosie heard Willowdean begging over and over again. She sat on the porch steps and put her arms around her Blue.

"Hear that, girl?" she rubbed her head against Blue's chest.

Old Blue didn't smell of lilacs any longer, and her coat wasn't glistening clean. She stank of Lenny Anderson's blood.

"You know I love you, don't you?" Mosie ignored the warm, sticky wet against her cheeks that smelled of oily fish. Blue's tongue lapped in and out of her mouth. Mosie touched it and tried to smile. She couldn't.

"You look almost as bad as the day we met, you know that?" she said as warm tears rolled down her face. Blue whined and tried to kiss the tears away.

"I know you were just doing what you thought best, Blue. That's why I'm doing do what I think is best." Mosie hugged her. Without a word, she gently unbuckled Blue's collar.

"If you ever need me girl, you'll know where to find me. Now get." She slapped the old hound's rump. "And don't you *ever* stop running ether." Through her tears, Mosie watched her Blue fly across the field.

The winds sweeping off Lake Superior carry lots of sounds: some good, and some bad. But the worst are those of young girls in June crying in the midst of sirens and the cracks of rifles.

CHAPTER THIRTY~TWO

"Ya, it's hard seeing a papa in this shape," Sister Maggie cupped her chubby little hand around the crucifix hanging from the strip of brown suede leather around her neck. "Especially when it's your own papa." She kissed Jesus' tiny bare feet and pushed the up arrow on the elevator's control panel. If there was one thing she knew all too well (besides praying and how to make the best pierogies in all of Bayfield) it was how to get around a hospital, especially to an ICU ward.

Willowdean put her hand on Peggy's shoulder. As they waited for the ding of the elevator announcing its arrival, they read the plaque on the wall:

Memorial Medical Center— Ashland Wisconsin—1972.

The steel gray doors opened and they stepped inside. The receptionist looked up from her desk, and sadly shook her head as the doors slid shut and sealed the three of them inside. With a jerk, the elevator slowly lifted them to floor number two. Peggy took a deep breath.

Willowdean snapped open her pocketbook, and passed Peggy a handkerchief and a few extra tissues (pink, her favorite color in the whole wide world). Peggy didn't say, "Thank you, Mrs. Bitmen." She didn't have to, just as Willowdean did not have to say, "Here honey, you'll need these."

"Now Peggy," Sister Maggie began, "your papa, he will not look like your papa. But you no worry, he still your papa. When you see him, you must remember that, hear," she tapped a stout finger to her head. "Keep it in your mind, okay?" Peggy nodded.

"Now, your papa, he will have tubes in him, but that is good. They give him food and water so he does not go hungry or grow thirsty. So those tubes are a good thing, yes?"

Again, Peggy nodded. She tried swallowing. Her throat wouldn't let her.

"The bandages, Peggy girl, the bandages are also good. They cover wounds, so they stay nice and clean, free of germs. And them bruises . . ." Muttering something holy in Polish, Sister crossed herself.

"Bruises are God's way of healing our human bodys," she said. "So you do not be afraid of them bruises. Just remember, My Sweet Peggy Girl, what you are about to see, is still your papa, and *you must not be afraid*! *Mph*!"

Peggy looked down at her yellow dress, Lenny's favorite color. She thought how only the two of them knew it and gave it a quick pressing with her hands just like Willowdean had taught her. She clutched her tissues and thought of other things she knew about Lenny that no one else did (like his drunken admittance to nearly killing a man for looking at Corrine and her long legs).

"*That's how come I never fought a man over her again*," he admitted to Peggy one night in a drunken slur before passing out on their ratty old sofa.

"*When they found that city fellow half dead up at Rainbow falls, I swore I'd never would do that again. They could of hauled my ass off to jail and thrown away the key if they woulda caught me; and I couldn't stand never holding you, or my Corrine in my arms again.*"

Come morning when Lenny had sobered up Peggy asked him about it. He told her to, 'shut her damn mouth or he would do it for her'.

But she knew it wasn't one of those made-up stories that drunks sometimes tell. She knew it was true because she remembered hearing about it down at Mr. Maki's Novelty and Gift shop back in 68' when she was ten years old.

She recalled that day, and how she had gone into Mr. Maki's to get an ice cream cone and how the sheriff had come in. Truth told, everyone in Bayfield suspected Lenny Anderson of hurting that man, but no one could find any real proof.

"*I'm sorry,*" the sheriff had said, "*but there just isn't enough evidence to prove anything. You know as well as I do I can't convict a man for such a deed on account of who he is.*"

The man Lenny nearly killed (she had learned) was none other than Mr. Maki's very own brother.

The elevator clanked to a stop. She tucked the hankie and tissues (along with her memories) in her pocket and took a step backward, bumping up against Willowdean's bulging momma belly.

"It's okay," Willowdean squeezed Peggy's shoulders. "We're here with you."

Peggy grabbed the hankie and put it to her eyes to push the tears back inside.

"Sometimes," Willowdean said, "the best things can come out of the worst things."

Sister Maggie gave Willowdean gave a pleased smile. "Yes," she took Peggy's hand. "This is very true. Now we go see your papa."

They marched down the hall and ignored the water-colored paintings that hung between the rooms and gave only quick glances to those lying in beds beyond their open doors.

The sound of mechanical whooshes and pulsating beeps grew louder. Sister Maggie's hand tightened around Peggy's.

Then, in that strange time caught between too fast and too slow, they stood in the last doorway at the end of the hall. Tucked in the arms of the little Felician nun, Peggy wept. And for a moment, for just one quick moment, the machines seemed to stop.

She was right, Sister Maggie was. Under all those bruises and bandages, tubes and stitches was Peggy's papa: Lenny Arthur Anderson.

"Oh Peggy," Willowdean said softly and helped her to the tan, vinyl chair pushed against the wall. "Lean on me, it's going to be okay, just lean on me." She took Peggy into her lap and gently brushed her hair from her face.

"Shh, shh, shh now, it's all right," she cooed, cuddling her in her arms.

"Th-th-that's my daddy," Peggy sobbed. "Th-that's my daddy . . ."

"Yes, yes, that is your daddy," Willowdean rocked Peggy back and forth. As she held back her own tears, Willowdean bit her lip. "And he always will be, no matter what." Peggy rested against Willowdean, and wept uncontrollably.

"We know it's scary seeing him like this, but did you know that you can be scared and *still* be strong at the same time?

I bet you didn't know that, did you?" Willowdean stroked Peggy's hair.

Sister Maggie sat in the chair next to Lenny's bed and reached into the pocket of her black habit. She tugged out a rosary and kissed its cross. She closed her eyes. Her lips moved silently in prayer.

"I don't want to be strong," Peggy whimpered. "It's too hard."

"Yes, we know that, and believe it or not, so does Lenny," Willowdean stared at him.

"You know, Peggy, he wasn't always so mean and ornery. There was a time when he was one of the bravest men in all of Bayfield. And he was scared a lot of times, too," she whispered.

"Lenny?" Peggy sniffled.

"Yes, Lenny," Willowdean chuckled. "Let me tell you a little story about, well, your Lenny. Would that be okay?" Peggy nodded.

"I bet you didn't know that Mr. Bitmen and I were friends with him a long, long time ago, did you?"

Peggy shook her head. "No."

"I didn't think so. Well, we were. Matter of fact we were pretty darn good friends at that; even with Corrine."

"You were?" Peggy sniffed.

"Yes, yes we were. We were very young, just about your age. Back then, Mr. Bitmen and his parents and brother, Andy, used to come to Bayfield every summer to stay. That's how we met, me and Mr. Bitmen." Peggy heaved a relaxing sigh. Willowdean went on.

"Do you know what frogging is?" she looked down at Peggy's head.

"Yes," she nodded. Willowdean laughed. "I had a feeling you would.

"Well, your mother and I didn't. Not until one very hot summer night, back in 1949. That's the night your daddy and Mr. Bitmen assured me and Corrine they knew everything there was to know about frogging and they'd be more than happy to show us."

Peggy giggled. "You mean Lenny and Mr. Bitmen?" she asked, now wide-eyed.

"Yes, Lenny and Mr. Bitmen. I know it's hard to believe, but they were once young, too. We all were, at one time." Willowdean sighed.

"Well, that night they promised it would be the best time either one of us girls ever had. They said, *Black River Harbor is the best frogging spot around.* However, the problem was none of us knew how to drive yet, so of course nobody had a car. So your momma, Corrine, suggested that we take, well, *her* parents car.

"At the time it sounded like a good idea so that's what we did. We waited until her momma and daddy were tucked tight in their beds before we snuck into the garage and pushed the car down the driveway.

"Once your daddy figured out how to move the stick on the steering wheel and the clutch at the same time, we were on our way to Black River Harbor. But by the time we got there, all the frogs were gone.

"Lenny said it was because we took too long to get there and that they were tired of waiting on us; but, if we sat real quiet and real close to each other down on the beach, he was sure we would be able to find one.

"Well, Corrine and I wanted to be able to see at least one of those things, so we followed those boys in the moonlight over the long swinging bridge and down to the beach and did just what they told us to do.

"We sat as close to them as we could, and were quiet as church mice; we watched the waves glistening toward the shore like blue diamond's sparkling in the moonlight. The sound of the waves crashing along the beach was so relaxing . . . Wave after wave of sparkly blue diamonds . . . the coolness from the lake washing over us in the sultry night air . . .

"Anyway, after a while I suggested that maybe we were just wasting our time and that we should go back home.

"*No, no,* your daddy said. *I thought I just saw one coming in right over there.* He pointed his arm in front of Corrine but we girls couldn't see anything. So Lenny pointed again. This time he got so close to your momma. He grabbed her really tight and kissed her, right smack dab on her lips. *Frogging!* He shouted. Then he tried to get another kiss from her.

"Corrine was so mad that the boys had tricked us like they did; she pulled me up from that beach and hauled us back over that swinging bridge to the car and jumped in behind the wheel determined to leave the boys behind.

"However, instead of putting the car into reverse, she put it into drive, and we ended up in the harbor. And so did the car! We were yelling and screaming, trying to get out of that ice-cold water. But we couldn't! That's when Lenny came running. I can still see him as if it were just last night. He looked so scared crossing that bridge . . . with it swaying this way and that. We were scared, too! For him *and* for us.

"He made it, though. And scared or not, he jumped in that harbor without even thinking twice about it, and pulled us both out.

"Boy, did we get it when we finally got home. It took us until nearly noon the next day! Our parents were so worried about us—I would have been too! We deserved every lick from that paddle stick. But if it wouldn't have been for Lenny, me and Corrine wouldn't be here.

"He's a very brave man, Peggy. He's done a lot of things like that for people. They've just forgotten. That's all."

"Lenny?" Peggy picked up her head from Willowdean's chest. "Oh, you're just making that up, Mrs. Bitmen," she said wiping her nose in her hankie.

"No really, he really did. Maybe one day he can tell you about it, and some other things."

Peggy looked over at him. "Can he hear us?"

Willowdean cleared her throat. She looked at Sister Maggie,

"Some say yes, some no," Sister said. "I say if his ears no hear, his heart inside surely does. So yes, I say yes, he can hear."

Peggy slid from Willowdean's lap and walked closer to his bed. "What made him so mean?" she asked in a soft voice, peeking at his bandages and sleeping face.

"Oh, life," Willowdean answered. She looked down at her dress and it a pat. "Sometimes life does that to people."

Peggy looked at him intently and dabbed her tears. "Is he in pain?"

"No, no pain," Willowdean answered.

Sister Maggie put her rosary back into her pocket. She shifted her weight in her chair and lifted her hand to Willowdean. She grunted as Willowdean yanked her up.

"Yeah, we go now and wait. This is time for Papa and Daughter."

Peggy sniffled. "Sister Maggie, Mrs. Bitmen, thank you, thank you both, for everything."

"You are welcome, My Sweet Peggy girl," Sister Maggie nudged Willowdean toward the door. "Now, you tell your papa what it is that is inside you. He will hear, do not worry that pretty, pretty head of yours; he will hear. Mph!"

Peggy sat down in the warmth of the chair left behind from Sister Maggie. She stared at the tubes and bandages, trying to think of them as being good things, not bad.

"Lenny," she said, "can you hear me?"

Nothing on him moved, not even an eyelash on his swollen purple-yellow eyelids. "You look pretty tough, Lenny," she got up to study the white lines spiking up and down on the monitors. She poked his hand. "But like Mrs. Bitmen said, at least you ain't feeling nothing. So that's good.

"Sister Maggie told me I should talk to you. I guess this is a good time since you can't tell me to shut my yapper. Well . . ." she let out a long, heavy sigh.

"First off, I'm wearing a really pretty dress, yellow, your favorite color. It's practically brand new. Sister Maggie got it for me from the thrift cellar in the church basement."

She rubbed her finger on his hand and stared at him, hoping to see a flinch. "It has small white dots on it called Swiss-Dots." She cleared her throat and took a deep breath. "I'm sorry for not being home with you as much as what I used to be. It ain't . . . I mean . . . it isn't . . . that I don't care about you, 'cause I do. I want you to know that."

She listened to the beeps from the monitors. "I promise, when you get home, I'll be there, okay? And I'll be good, too. I promise. I'll try so hard. You'll never have to chase me all the way down to Lake Superior to try and drown me ever again.

"In the meantime, I'll be staying at Father Perkins and Sister Maggie's house . . . if it's okay with you. It feels good there. It's clean, and I don't mind helping with chores.

"Sister Maggie is always telling me what a good job I'm doing, and she's teaching me how to cook real meals.

"And Father Perkins, he's been teaching me about God, and His son Jesus, and all those buddies of His that He hung around with . . . The Apostles, that's what they called them. Did you know that not many people liked *any* of them?" She walked to the window and rested her elbows on its cool, gray marble ledge.

"I like it there Lenny. I do," she spotted Willowdean's station wagon in the parking lot. "And I haven't been with a boy for . . . well . . . an awful long time now it seems.

"Willowdean said you and her, and Corrine, and John, were all friends when you were all young. She said you were brave. I wonder why you guys aren't friends anymore?" She squinted at the blue water tower across the parking lot. "Ashland," she read under her breath.

"She said you're a good man, deep down. Maybe you're one of those that Father Perkins talks about. He says, *'just because a person goes to church every Sunday and gives a bunch of money doesn't mean it's a ticket into heaven.'*

"He said, if a man is good and decent inside and don't go to church, he just might stand a better chance of getting into heaven than a man who goes every Sunday and does all kinds of bad things on the side.

"And, he said a man shouldn't judge another man, that judging is God's job 'cause we might think someone is good when they're not, and think someone is bad when they ain't, err, isn't.

"You know what *Sister Maggie* told me?" she giggled and checked behind her shoulder. "Well, I'll tell ya', but you can't say nothing to anyone."

She leaned down next to his ear and snickered. "Sister said . . . Sister Maggie says," she repeated, trying not to laugh. "She says: *'My Sweet Peggy Girl, any ass can slide itself in a pew. And I've seen many of them rascals taking up space! Mph!'*

"Isn't that something Lenny? Whoever heard of a nun saying swear words about people? Not that Sister Maggie swears or anything, well, not very often, but it is funny how she put that, don't you think?"

Peggy bent down and looked so close at him she could see the fleapits in his face. She gulped. As quick as his lips curled a smile, they drooped back down.

"You *can* hear me, oh Lenny," she cried and her eyes filled with tears.

"Nothing matters as long as you get better," she rubbed his arm between the clear plastic tubing and white cotton gauze.

"I ain't never held your hand before, Lenny, but I'm gonna right now." Hoping his grin would rise again, she slid her hand cautiously over his. "Geez, Len, your hand ain't that big after all. And it sure is soft. I think we need to pray now, together. I'll go first." She sniffed up her tears.

"This is the best prayer there is. Since you don't know it, you can just listen. Besides, I don't say it like other people do, not when I'm saying by myself, anyway."

Peggy shut her eyes and lowered her voice.

"Our Papa," she began. "Who lives up in Heaven. Your name is holy. Please Papa, please help us to do your will here on Earth just like in Heaven, instead of us doing our own will.

"And please forgive me and Lenny for our sins, just like how we forgive every single person who has sinned against us. And please, God, don't let us get anymore more temptations than what we already got, and please help keep us away from the bad stuff, and bad stuff away from us. Love, Peggy and Lenny Anderson. Amen."

Before her tears could drip onto Lenny's clean white bandages, she pressed her handkerchief against her cheeks.

"Well, I suppose, I should go now," she sighed. "You're probably tired of all my blabbing.

"There's just one more thing." She stroked the top of his head. "Sister Maggie taught me a song. I've been practicing it every morning down at the lake. Would you mind if I sang it to you before I go?" she asked, taking a deep breath, looking down at him.

The sweetness of her voice sang out, and over her Lenny: "*Morning has broken, like the first morning, Blackbird has spoken,*

like the first bird . . ."

When she finished, she stared at him and bent down to kiss him softly on his forehead. She took his hand in hers. "Promise me you'll find a way to come home, Daddy, please?"

He tried squeezing her hand. He wanted to tell her something was coming; something his momma had always talked about. Angels. And a ladder belonging to Jacob. But he couldn't. It was too late.

Peggy was already turning and walking away from her Lenny and his machines.

CHAPTER THIRTY~THREE

Willowdean placed another "Thank You" on the neatly stacked pile next to her arm. "If this keeps up," she marked off another name on the list in front of her, "we'll have to hire Peggy a secretary."

Mosie stabbed her tuna fish sandwich with a potato chip. Willowdean mashed her eyebrows. "Well, it don't have any taste," Mosie pushed it away.

"That's just in your head, it does, too. I used real Hellmann's, not salad dressing." Willowdean picked up the next, 'card of mercy' (as Sister Maggie called them). "It's almost a shame to open this one," she flipped the spectacular red, white, and blue Fourth of July stationery back and forth.

Mosie put her head on the table and rested her chin on her fist as she watched Willowdean guide the gold letter opener across the envelope. She pulled out the contents and her eyes darted across the first few lines. "Oh my, now this is something," Willowdean mumbled. "Listen to this:

"Dear Miss Peggy Anderson,

"It is with great honor that we, the 4th of July committee of our wonderful town of Bayfield, request your presence as Grand-Marshal for this year's 4th of July parade. We have once again engaged the 'Country Squire's Band' for this year's street dance. They have agreed it would be a privilege having you perform for a special segment of their show. In return, they ask that ten percent of this year's proceeds be donated to help cover medical expenses for your father, Leonard Anderson.

"Please contact us ASAP with your decision.

"We look forward . . .

"Well, that sure would help pay for the medical expense that our home owner's insurance doesn't cover; plus it will give Peggy some extra, too. Isn't that just wonderful?"

"Yeah, T-riff," Mosie rolled her eyeballs.

Willowdean skimmed over the letter one more time. "That means Peggy will need a whole new outfit," she headed for the phone. "Something Fourth of July-ish, but not too cool; the winds coming off the lake still have a chill on it at night. I had better call Sister and see what she thinks; we only have a few days."

Mosie got up from the table. "Don't you think you ought to be calling Corrine instead? After all, she still is her mother, isn't she? I'll be upstairs," she added with a bite and skirted past Willowdean.

"Katherine, please wait."

"Why? So you can tell me for the millionth time how, '*Nobody could have guessed how such good can come out of such bad?'* Ma, they would of found out about Leo-Nerd and his bad liver eventually, what with all that drinking he does."

She squinted her eyes with disapproval and rubbed the railing leading up the staircase. "You know, Mother, I may not have heard everything you and Leo-Nerd were talking about, but I heard enough and saw enough—the way you were holding onto him . . . and Blue, she didn't deserve being killed, not for what you did: you missed Blue's head and broke Lenny's legs. It's Lenny's fault, all of it; if he hadn't been so cruel to her, she never would have . . . oh forget it. Nobody cares, so what's the dif? After all, she is *just* a dog. A dog nobody wanted in the first place."

Willowdean took a deep breath. "No, no she wasn't, she wasn't just a dog," she rubbed her stomach and hung the phone back on its cradle. "I think it's time I show you something."

"What, something for Peggy or something for *Lenny*?"

"Neither." Reluctantly, Mosie followed Willowdean down the hall to her bedroom.

Willowdean sat on the bed. Ignoring the squeaks from the springs sinking under her weight, she nodded for Mosie to sit next to her.

Mosie shook her head. "Nope."

"Okay," Willowdean ran her hands across the oversized pink flowers on her dress.

"First," I need to apologize to you. I was hoping somehow everything would magically disappear on its own, but it hasn't, has it? If anything it's gotten worse."

Mosie fiddled with the pockets on her shorts. "I didn't know anything was wrong until we moved here. Now everything's wrong more than ever, and I don't know who to blame—you, Pa, Lenny, Corrine; Val for not moving with us so he could stop all of this."

She ran her fingers across Willowdean's fancy Chenille bedspread and counted its corded white humps. '*One row, two rows . . .*'

"Well," Willowdean finally said, "I have a confession to make, and I'm so very ashamed. I was trying to protect myself more than you, or anyone else."

"Protect yourself? From what? *Three rows, four—*"

"Oh, a lot of things; things that open old wounds and turn them into new ones all over again. But mostly the embarrassment of you finding out . . . The shame." The bed squeaked as she shifted her fanny.

"You know Katherine, sometimes when we're young we do things without thinking about the consequences. Like when you and Candy ran off to East Park, or how you were planning on building that boat to find Dog Island."

"Me and Candy running off to play in a park when we were eight years old isn't *anything* compared to what *you* did," she jabbed the puffy lines on the bedspread.

"You're right. I'm sorry," Willowdean looked down at her lap and pricked one of the printed flowers with her finger. The silence in the room grew strong enough for the walls to hear Mosie count. *Eight rows, nine—*"

"How much of what Lenny said did you hear?" Willowdean found the courage to ask.

"Enough to know something happened between you and him." Her stomach dropped as the words came out. "And that Val isn't . . . isn't really Pa's son on account of it. Eleven, twelve!" she said out loud.

Willowdean's head swam. "I and your father wanted to tell you, together, when the time was right."

"Is that why he didn't move up here with us? 'Cause he knows he's not really Pa's, not really?"

"Yes," Willowdean nodded. "But Val will always be your father's son even if he isn't from his own blood."

"Did you love Lenny?"

"No, not in that way, not then."

"Did you love Pa in *that way*?"

Willowdean prodded her flowers. "I thought I did. We've been together for so long now—Katherine, I want to show you something." She got up from the bed and slid open the closet door.

Mosie craned her head around Willowdean's backside in hopes of getting a glimpse past the hanging row of neat colored dresses, slacks, blouses, and sweaters. She couldn't tell if it was relief or regret on her mother's face as she pulled out the willow reed trunk. She shuffled it to the bedside, plunked on the bed, and leaned back on her elbows.

"You're not too disappointed with me, are you?" she rubbed her stomach and tried to catch her breath. "I know all this is very hard on you." She reached up to stroke Mosie's face. Mosie pulled away. "You are my daughter. Try to remember, no matter what, your father and I will always love you *and* Val."

Willowdean sighed and ran her fingers across the four birch bark pictures sewn with strips of leather on top of the trunk. "Jiimaan," she said as she touched the first etching.

Mosie looked curiously at the drawing. "That means canoe, boat: Jiimaan." "Gee-men?" Mosie repeated.

Willowdean smiled. "Close; gee-m-on, gee-m-on."

"Gee-mm-on. Oh! Gee-mmon," Mosie repeated. "Like government men with a cold: Jiimaan."

Willowdean laughed. "Well, that's a long way around it, but yes, Gee-mmon. Misaabeag ininiwag . . ." she said as she touched the next one, "the giant man; misaabeag ininiwag." She looked at Mosie and grinned. "We can practice. And this one, this is, Nanabozho." She touched the white rabbit, chuckled, and shook her head.

"Nana-boo-zhoo," Mosie repeated.

"Good, very good. There are as many stories about Nanabozho as there are Nations," she tapped the picture with the tip of her finger. "He's the teaching trickster Spirit. He teaches through pranks and mischief, some good, some not so good. Nanabozho. I think maybe my nookomis was filled with Nanabozho's spirit."

The last and final word came out quiet and somber. "Animosh." Willowdean stroked the sketch of the dog, her eyes dancing as if fire was set inside them. "Animosh."

Mosie shifted on the bed and broke the spell of the word.

"I had bezhig animosh, one dog, too," Willowdean's said, her voice soft and wispy. "I named her Bagwaji Ode`imaa|n. It means, Wild Heart. However, I called her Odie for short. She too was an abagwadasim|oog, a wild dog, like Blue.

"And like you, I too didn't understand why my mother fought me having her. It was as if she feared Odie before she even came; like how I feared Blue before she came. It meant the Bridge would open. And it has."

Mosie cleared her throat. "Like the bridge in my dream?"

"Yes, like the bridge in your dream; the one I also had at your age. You are growing up, and I can't stop that from happening no matter how hard I try." Willowdean wrapped her hands around Mosie's face.

"Thunder across the Water, most Spiritual beliefs are foolish to those who don't understand them, and The Bridge is a part of that. So was Blue. She had done her job, and she had done it well. After all, if it wasn't for her, it would have been many years before you would have learned about Val and Lenny.

"Katherine, does it really matter how Valerie got here as long as he did get here? Isn't that what's important?" Mosie leaned against Willowdean's shoulder. She stared at the picture of the Animosh, blurry in her tears.

"Blue was a gift," Willowdean put her arms around Mosie. "Just like my Odie was a gift; they came to us with lessons; the greatest and hardest being given when they left us. They taught us we *have* to live on, even after losing something we love so deeply. It's our job.

"Would you like to see something I've been saving for a very long time?"

Mosie nodded. She focused through her tears as she watched Willowdean open the lid of the trunk. Before her lay the items she had never seen before: photo albums, a few old dolls and a stack of letters tied together with once white ribbons that were now yellowed and browned from age. And a dried and crackled flower that had not yet bloomed.

Willowdean picked up a dark-brown wool blanket on the bottom of the trunk, and held it close to Mosie's nose.

"See, the scent is gone now," she said. "Granny taught me about the ojichaag|wags, the Spirits of the Living, and how they take their Earthly Scents with them when they cross into the next world, across The Bridge. But like memories, they always leave a little for us until they make their final walk.

"My Granny had used this very blanket when she was a young girl for her first animosh, and so had my mother. How I miss them," Willowdean put it to her own nose.

"I found Odie in the woods; like Blue she too was terribly hurt and my mother had a fit when she saw me and Granny carrying her home in this blanket. She knew what it meant. Just like how I knew what it meant when Blue came to you in that ditch, and saved you from that bear. And just like my mother, I was enraged with the Creator and wanted to ignore it, hoping Blue, and Lenny, and everything would just go away. But it didn't. With Blue, it all came.

"Katherine, I don't want what happened between me and my mother to happen to us. Here," she said placing the blanket in Mosie's lap. "You take this, for next time, for your next animosh." Willowdean touched the blanket, knowing it was the last time she would hold it as her own. "It is now for you, and your child; when the time comes. I just wish I hadn't been so foolish. It could have been filled with Blue's scent, at least for a while."

Willowdean closed her eyes and welcomed Granny's voice: *Lessons are hard, no matter how old we get. And the hardest ones are those that teach us the most.*

"Odie will be at Dog Island for me when I get there, just like

Blue will be for you." She sighed. "Well, I guess that's it for now." She got up from the bed. "I think we're going to be just fine, don't you?"

She shut the trunk, and slid it across the floor and back into the closet.

"I think I had better call Corrine and let her know what's going on." She smiled at Mosie.

"Ma, what if Blue doesn't want to be there, what if she doesn't want to be at Dog Island? What if Blue wasn't meant to go there yet, what if . . . what if I go get her and bring her back? Maybe I can . . ."

"You put those thoughts right out of your mind. She was on a mission, and she fulfilled that mission. If it wasn't for her, I never would have told these things, and Lenny wouldn't be getting the help he needs. And Peggy, she would never have come to see that all, anooj awesiiyag's, animals, have a purpose and must be respected. Now, don't you think Blue did enough for one dog?

"Besides, she's probably having the best time of her life, playing right along with Odie and all the other dogs there on Dog Island. Would you really want her to miss out on that? Mm?"

"No, I guess not," Mosie answered. "I . . . I just miss her so much, Ma. It-it hurts so much." She started to sob. "You don't think it hurt her when they . . . shot her, do you?"

"No, she didn't feel a thing. Those men are trained hunters, not murderers. I know they were compassionate. Now, I have an idea for you.

"I think maybe after a while you should give Candy a call. Maybe you want to invite her up for your birthday. She can ride up with Val, stay a week, and then ride back with him. I'm sure Candy's mother would agree to it."

CHAPTER THIRTY~FOUR

Mosie haden't written or called Candy as much as she would have liked, so when Candy answered the phone Mosie found out just how quick a person can change unless they're keeping up with them.

She didn't care if Candy had sprouted size thirty-six B boobies almost overnight, and didn't care if she was invited to every single one of Judy Larson's swim parties. And she sure didn't care if Candy and Tommy Peterson were going steady and had discovered those pangs of passion Mother Prudence always lectured about. *After all, he was the one who put that horrible old toad in my galoshes in the second grade and made us both scream. She must have forgotten about that,* Mosie thought, listening to Candy blather on.

Besides, Peggy was up to a size *thirty-eight* B, and could sing and dance better than Judy Lard-Ass any day (and she hadn't let a boy touch her for over a month). She didn't tell Candy any of that. She couldn't even if she wanted to.

Candy was talking so loud and so fast, Mosie didn't know what she was saying (until she heard Candy saying something about Val).

"Oh-my-god!" Candy gushed. "He is way *too hot*! If I didn't have Tommy, I would have Val.

"Judy-L, that's what we all call her now, Judy-L—Judy-L has been trying to get him over to her place *all* summer."

Mosie couldn't take it no more. She just couldn't.

"Yeah, well, he doesn't go out with school girls, just women," she said. "Besides, Val and my friend Peggy have a date all set up for when he comes up for my birthday."

Candy screamed. "You don't mean that slutty hick-chick with greasy brown hair and duct-taped shoes you were telling about, do you? Oh-my-god! *Nooo* way!"

Mosie's face was red hot angry. She had wanted to tell Candy about Pa and Corrine, and Lenny and Val, and how, deep down, she really missed Peggy, but was too afraid to go see her on account of Blue attacking Lenny after she promised she wouldn't let her do that. Mostly she wanted to tell her about Blue, and how she missed her more than anyone, or anything in this whole wide world.

And, she wanted to tell her she was no longer her best friend and never could be again, size thirty-six B boobies and Judy-L swim parties or not.

"Well, I better go," Mosie snipped. "Ma said I could talk for ten minutes, and *you've* talked for twenty."

Candy cackled and ignored what Mosie had just said.

"Oh, my-god! *You're* actually hanging with a country chick! Wait until I tell Judy-L! She's going to die. She's just going to *die*!"

Candy squealed. That's when Mosie knew for sure Candy wasn't Candy any more.

"Judy-L, Judy-L," she mocked as she hung up the phone leaving *fancy pants* Candy Nelson laughing all by herself.

But what was making her sadder than mad was the fact that she knew Candy was never going to hear the rocks clicking under the fenders of their bikes, or all those bugs sing to one another especially at night.

Nor was she going to see the sun explode over Lake Superior at dusk with so many colors it was hard to count them all.

But worse than anything, though, was Peggy and Candy weren't going to fall asleep next to her and Blue on her birthday as they would try counting the stars.

She doubted Candy remembered Ma's little seed purse she made for her. The one with the pretty little rose floating on the water with the black bird flying over it. Or even wanted to.

Mosie pulled hers out from inside her shirt. "Medicine," she said letting her tears drop inside.

Mosie opened her eyes and looked out the window. *There's at least thirty of them buggers if not more*, she thought.

"We are going to have a wonderful picnic," Willowdean prattled on. "Sister Maggie is bringing strawberry pie and—"

That's when the notion hit Mosie like a bullet. And she had to think fast.

"I think maybe after we eat . . ."

"Ma, did they find Blue's body?"

Willowdean's tone dropped. "Blue's body?"

"Yes, did they find her?"

"Well, yes, I'm sure they did. But maybe we should talk about something else today. After all, it is the Fourth of July. I'll bet after today Father Perkins will prefer Grey Poupon on his ham sandwiches in place of ordinary French's yellow. A little Grey Poupon perks up just about anything, don't you think?" Willowdean fiddled with the radio dial.

"Hellman's, Ma, you know I only like Hellman's."

As they reached the peak of Kill-Deer, she peered over the top of the trees and watched the black-winged patch swoop in and out of the marsh.

"Ma, I can't go!" she yowled.

"Can't go?" Willowdean glanced over the rim of her sunglasses.

"What do you mean you can't go? Are you sick? You don't look sick."

"I just don't want to go. That's all," Mosie whined and poked the stars on Willowdean's dress hoping to distract her from the crows circling and diving in and out of the quagmire.

"Are you down about Candy?"

"Naw, I just don't want to go, that's all. Please, just stop the car and let me out."

Willowdean turned down the radio. Her Fourth of July excitement wilted.

"I'm sorry Ma. I'm just not . . . in the mood for celebrating, that's all."

"It's me and your father, isn't it? And you're uncomfortable seeing Peggy. Peggy doesn't know anything, Katherine. Your father doesn't even know that you know, not yet. I think too much has happened to all us and it might be better to wait and just sit down as a family and talk when things settle down. But until then, we should carry on the best we can, and enjoy . . ."

Mosie sighed. "No Ma, it's not you, it's not Pa, and it's not Peggy, or Candy."

"It's Blue then."

Mosie stared at Willowdean's stars and turned away from the truth for which they stood. She squeezed her eyes shut and held her belly.

"It's my stomach Ma; I don't feel so good. I didn't tell you but while you were getting ready this morning, I sort of ate all the cookies."

Willowdean gasped. "Mosie! That's crazy; there were over a dozen of them." She leaned her forehead on the steering wheel.

"Katherine, sometimes I could . . . well, never mind what I could do. I'll turn around and drive you home. Eating a dozen cookies!"

"Can I keep my sandwiches?"

"Yes, you can keep your sandwiches. But I don't want you eating them or anything else for a while. Do you understand?"

"Yes," Mosie answered and watched the side of the road turn to a blur.

"I'm sorry, Ma. Will you please tell Peggy I'm sorry, really sorry, about everything?" she asked as they pulled into the driveway. "And just so you know, I think Pa's dumb for giving you up for Corrine. You're the best ma anyone can have, just so you know; and you're even prettier than Lori Mavis' ma, even if you are a little chunky and don't wear war paint on your face all the time like she does."

"Well, thank you sweetheart," Willowdean patted Mosie's hand through the car window. "When I get back, we'll have another girl talk, how about that? If you're up to it that is."

"Sure Ma, sure we will." She bent inside the car and kissed Willowdean on the cheek. "I love you, Ma," she said.

Mosie waited until Willowdean left the driveway before stepped into the house. She knew she didn't have much time. She grabbed a notebook from the counter, sat at the table, and wrote on its cover: *Dog Island*

Opening it, she printed on top of the first page: *Things to bring,* and underlined it.

"Where do I start?" she clanked the pen against her front teeth. "Of course."

She began the list:

(1): Food

(2): Can opener

(3): Lighter—lots of matches

(4): Toilet Paper . . .

(25): Blue's special high-quality protein dog food (plus snacks)

After putting the pen down, she opened the drawer and stared at the lunar rover space stamps next to Willowdean's special personal floral stationery lying alongside the gold, "Luxury writing instrument; Sheaffer Legacy Heritage pen, used only for the finest of occasions," she mocked in a smooth, deep manly voice.

"Well, I hope this counts." She began writing:

Tuesday, July 4, 1972

Dear Val,

I hope everything is going good and that you are in good health. I heard Ma telling you what happened here on Thursday, June 29th. Today when Ma and I were going to town for the big 4th of July celebration I saw a bunch of crows, at least thirty of them flying over that marsh I told you about. I just know those birds were telling me Blue is down there waiting for me.

So by the time you get this letter, her and I will be at Dog Island. Don't worry about us. We will be just fine. I am packing enough food and supplies to last us at least a week.

I will try to be back by my birthday next month. If not, tell Ma I'm sorry she went through so much trouble making my birthday cake. If I get anything good, you can keep it. Tell Pa I said that so he doesn't try taking it away from you like he let those men take Blue away from me and how he let Corrine take him away from Ma.

I'll be back as soon as I can (I hope.)

Love,

Your sister,

Moe

P.S. I will bring one of Blue's pups back so you can see it when you come up.

P.S.S. It's okay Lenny is your real dad but just don't call him that.

She folded the letter perfectly just like Sister Vern Mary had taught, and slid it into one of the exclusive envelopes that came with the paper and pen set. Using her best penmanship, she wrote on its front:

Valerie Alexander Bitemen

130 Wool Street

Barrington Illinois 60010

She gave the beautifully flowered seal a lick, hallmarking it with a kiss.

"Please God, protect me and guide me on my journey," she prayed as she tore off an eight-cent lunar rover space stamp. "Sorry Ma; but if you're going to do something wrong, do it right. Besides, I can't think of anything more special than this."

She placed the stamp in the left top corner of the envelope and set her left hand on top of it. "I hereby pledge," she said, raising her right hand, "either way, dead or alive, I am going to get Blue to Dog Island!"

She looked at the list, headed for the cupboard, and grabbed her first jar of Willowdean's homemade gooseberry preserves. That's when it struck her: saying and doing would be two different things. Getting Big Bertha Brown down to the lake wasn't going to be any easy task, especially with everyone running around.

She placed the jars of jam and other food items neatly inside the spare boxes on the porch and marked them off the list, and then read the next item. "Batteries." She headed back inside. She stuck her hand in the junk drawer and picked up a wad of string.

"Eureka!" she declared, dangling the string in front of her face. She hurried down the porch the steps and headed for the garage. There, by the back door, under the Army blankets sat Blue's cage, and next to it, a box filled with her half-gnawed chew toys. Mosie picked up Blue's favorite, Ma's old soup bone.

"Independence Day it is!" she proclaimed as she stashed it on top of Blue's supplies.

Kicking the empty boxes out of the way, she looked underneath John's abandoned workbench. They were still there: John's creepers; the same ones she and Candy used as skateboarding go-carts, just last summer.

"Three of them," she pulled them out and rolled them to the back door.

She grabbed a bunch of ropes that were hanging above Blue's cage and headed for Big Bertha Brown.

"This should work," she placed the creepers in three single rows next to Bertha. Feeding the ropes under the creepers, she pulled Bertha down on top of them. After wrapping the ropes around Bertha, she tied them and gave the boat a good shake. It didn't move. Big Bertha Brown was strapped down good and tight and just about ready to go.

With one rope left (not too long and not too short) Mosie ran back to the house. She looked down at Peggy's half-blue, half-red boy's bike laying in the mud. That's when it hit her.

"Ah, damn it to hell!" she cussed. Her bright yellow ten-speed Schwinn Super Sport was still at Sister Maggie's and Father Perkins'.

"Well, at least this one has good tires," she picked up the bike and wiped the dried muck from its seat.

Mosie walked it over to Bertha and tied one end of the rope underneath its seat; the other end went for the middle creepers. She gave the makeshift boat trailer a firm pull and laughed. "It works," she gave it a harder tug and watched the creepers move Bertha forward. "It actually works!"

Slowly, she pulled the bike and the boat up to the porch. After loading the provisions into Bertha's belly, she checked each item off the list.

Five very important items were missing, though:

"Two life jackets, one for me, one for Blue, two oars and . . ." She raced back inside the house and went to her room.

"Animosh," she took the wool blanket from her bed, and put it to her nose. "Blue, you *are* more than an animosh."

Digging in her pants pocket, she pulled out her coin purse. She counted the green bills Willowdean had stashed inside. "$20.00, that should be enough."

She hurried down the stairs and made her way to the bathroom.

"I'll get the oares and life jackets at Mr. Maki's," she said as she finished her business.

"If he asks why I'm buying them, I'll say they're a present for . . . for, oh heck I'll think of someone," she opened the linen closet.

She grabbed the large pink flowered box of Modess and the little white garter Willowdean insisted she use instead of safety pins. "Why don't they just put glue or tape on the bottom of these things?" she asked as she dangled the sanitary belt in the air. "Just in case."

She looked in the mirror and announced: "Time to go."

CHAPTER THIRTY~SIX

Mosie shut the kitchen door and flicked on the porch light because it would be dark before Willowdean got home. She stood on the steps and looked up at the fleet of clouds heading toward Bayfield from The Great Lake. "Animal spirits," she said, "coming and going."

Checking the supplies one last time, she covered them with a sheet of canvas and stared at Big Bertha and then Peggy's bike. She thew her legs around it. "It's going to be some ride." She steadied herself and turned the pedal-rods with one mighty grunt.

The front lifted and dropped back onto the ground. She tried again, this time forcing her weight toward the handlebars. She pressed forward.

"Come on . . . just . . . one . . . more . . . good . . ."

She rattled down the driveway and hooted, "Watch out Highway Two, I'm coming through!"

The creepers shimmied under the rough terrain and shifted. Mosie jerked the handle bars to the left to swing Big Bertha back into place.

She bungled past the last row of cedar trees and honeysuckle bushes along the property line. "Kill-Deer is one mile. That should give me enough time to get a good feel for her."

Mosie churned the pedals, picked up speed, and wondered what Willowdean was going to do when she realized she was gone.

Would Willowdean call Pa right away or wait in hopes she'd come home soon? What about the police and Val, would she call them? What about Peggy, would she start crying because she knew where Mosie was going?

She wondered if the fireworks of the star-spangled-banner in all its glory would remain visible once she got past Madeline Island, possibly Basswood (maybe even Hermit).

"And what's the night sky going to look like out on the Lake in the middle of the night? Did I bring enough kerosene for the lanterns?" She huffed and made her way toward Kill-Deer.

She stopped to take in its girth as it rose in the distance like an obstinate wall determined to divide her and Blue. Getting to its top was hard enough and with Bertha, it was going to be even tougher. She caught her breath and launched in to a slow roll; little by little it gathered speed to make the mount of Kill-Deer.

"Whoo-boy," she puffed as she hit its base.

While forging on, she fought the weight of Bertha pulling her backwards. She pushed down on the metal-rods under her feet and rotated them with already straining muscles. It was no use. Bertha was just too heavy.

She got off the bike, rubbed her legs, and studied the distance between her and Bertha and the crest of the hill. A handful of crows looped in and out of the trees that crowned its peak.

"There has to be a way," she walked around the boat.

She sighed, bent down, grabbed the ropes, and studied them. "Knots are too tight," she stood back up. "Well, there's more than one way to skin a cat."

Picking up the bike, she pitched it in the boat on top of the sheet of canvas and supplies and then walked to the stern. She placed her butt against it, grit her teeth, and gave Bertha a good shove.

"Again!" she repeated. "One . . . two . . . three . . . whooo!"

She turned to look up Kill-Deer. "Only about fifty more shoves to go," she said with another determined push.

The smell of the swamp grew stronger along with the cries of the crows that urged her on.

"Thirty-eight," she huffed and stopped to rest.

Sweat ran from her brow; she counted the birds veering for the marsh. Each return trip brought more. After taking in a deep breath, she started shoving Bertha again, and her knees bent in exhaustion. The crows perched on the tree limbs flicked their mighty black wings and exploded with excitement as she gave one last thrust. Together, she and Big Bertha Brown conquered Kill-Deer Hill.

She looked down the sides of the cliff and its outcrops. Jagged stone plummeted downward and ran almost perpendicular to the tamaracks and black spruce below. The swamp sprawled before her (further than her eyes could see) and the only way in was through the secret opening.

Mosie stationed herself on the cliff's edge and lifted her arms high in the air. "Blue!" she yelled; her voice dropped somewhere in the quagmire below. She tried again in hopes that one of the crows would catch the words and carry them through the bogs.

"I'm coming Blue . . . I'm coming." She turned to Bertha.

She leaned her backside against the bow of the boat and pushed her weight against it, this time deliberately holding back its speed in order to guide it safely downward. When she reached bottom she knew her mission was just beginning.

"The blanket," she took the bike out of Bertha. She tossed back the canvas, grabbed the wool blanket, walked to the bank of the gully, and dug her heels in the dirt. She sat down and slid to the bottom.

The scent of warm cinnamon and anise bonded with the July heat and fungus seeped into her nostrils; a trifle assortment of scanty weeds fought their way out of their dirt-parched graves and stood exhausted. She glanced over at the site of the bear attack and took a deep breath then began making her way to the small hidden path (and Blue).

She followed the wall of Brier Rose, Winter Thorn, and Teasel Burr that twined their way along tree trunks and scrub brush like barbed fencing. Finally she found the entrance.

Flattening herself close to the ground she squirmed under the spiny needles that poked from the arched opening that led into the swamps of Kill-Deer Hill. Mosie rose to her feet and stood at the edge of a small clearing. The magic that danced under the violet haze of the night was gone.

The majestic trees she witnessed floating about the quagmire were now anchored tightly deep inside miles of white and green sphagnum moss islands.

And somewhere, beyond the sixty feet of solid ground in front of her, was Blue. Somehow she would find her.

"Blue! Blue! Blue!" she yelled, letting the crows guide her through thigh-high grass to the islands of trees.

Tiny black bugs and hungry ticks clambered up her legs. She brushed them away and continued making her way to the end of the rim of solid ground. Her next step was the first moss island.

Its coolness surprised her as her shoes settled into its spongy padding. The ground sprang back up as if she had stepped on a giant marshmallow.

"Blue!" she called again as she passed through clumps of tall and low brush.

She plucked a simple round leaf and checked its bottom. She recognized its furry brown backside and bit it. She spit it out.

"Swamp tea! Tastes better as a tea, too! Bitter." The slight pause brought water seeping across her feet. Stepping too hard or standing too still would cause her to drop through the moss and would trap her in the rusty-orange liquid below. She thought of the missing hunters and vigilantly walked on calling for Blue.

"Blue, Blue!" she shouted again and again, stopping only long enough to listen and watch for signs that would bring the two of them closer.

Flies zipped and buzzed, mosquitoes snipped and whizzed past her ears. A splash sounded on her left. "Blue?" she yelled.

A beaver launched into a patch of open water and swam toward the bottom of the red clay bluff that formed Kill-Deer, a safe distance away.

She looked up at the highway and narrowed her eyes. A semitruck decked out in a dazzling display of red, white and blue, was shooting like a rocket across the hill. The beaver popped its head above the surface of the water then retreated nervously back into the murky protection of its bog.

"Marty!" Mosie yelled. "You freak, slow down!"

The shrillness of her voice dropped to the nethermost point of the marsh. And so did the rumble of Ken Johnson's truck. Under its girth, an avalanche of gravel and red clay let loose. The crows gave an angry caw as tiny air bubbles floated to the top of the water that surrounded Mosie's tennis shoes.

"Jerk!" she spat and watched a waterfall of earth and rock plummet downward; it splashed an overhang just above the base where Kill-Deer and the quagmire connected.

Through the sparse branches of pine trees she spotted a grotto beneath the cliff. She pressed on in its direction.

Tiny cotton balls attached to tips of slinky blades of grass wisped past her legs. The last purple blooms of fading Bog Laurel, turning pink to white, crushed beneath her feet. Brazen red Pitcher Plants stood erect and ignored her as they continued capturing their small preys of insects.

She stooped and squinted at the small earthen cave, her heart racing, and watched a black form move about the inside. It nudged its head against the ground. It lay down, not moving, not making a sound.

In the stillness, the buzzing of deer flies surrounded her with their weightless bodies and nested in her glossy black hair. Their stinging bites penetrated her from top to bottom. Swishing her head, she slapped them away, and cried from the heinous attack. The form raised its head and stumbled to its feet. Mosie tried to catch her breath. But none was to be had. The black mass was charging.

The screeching of the crows forced her onto her feet and charged her forward as she ran faster than she ever thought possible. Through brushwood and tears, she saw it was Blue—*her Blue*.

With a mighty lunge, Blue knocked Mosie down and pinned her. Her tongue frantically washed over her. Mosie hung on desperately and kissed Blue's muzzle over and over again. They clung to each other, shaking wildly as they cried in the coolness and horrors of the swamps of Kill-Deer.

Gently, Blue took Mosie's hand in her mouth and led her to the solid ground of her cave and a bed of stubble grass clumped within a stretch of thick, black fur. Mosie's eyes swelled. Blue licked the lumps hidden inside and gently nudged them toward Mosie.

"Damn, they're beautiful girl," Mosie said proudly as she picked up each and every one of the six pups, "just beautiful."

She put them to her nose to draw in the musky smell of puppy breath. She kissed each one, set them back in their bed, and looked around the cave.

"So this is your home away from home," Mosie picked up a leg bone from some unfortunate deer.

"Those gun shots must of scared you half to death so you ran to the only place you knew was truly safe." She kissed Blue on top of her head. "It sure does stink in here, though, like something's half rotten." She looked over her shoulder toward the back of the cave. A skull leered at her.

"You old dog, you," she chuckled and got up to take a better look at the mound of fur and bones. "He sure got his, didn't he?" She bent down and picked up a piece of bristly hide. "That old bear sure isn't going to cause anymore grief to any one, is he?"

Aw-roo, roo, Blue answered firmly.

Mosie looked down at the squirming pups under Blue's belly. Their high-pitched squeals quieted as they began nursing. Mosie looked Blue in the eyes.

"I'm not going to lie to you girl," she sounded as serious as John. "But we got to get you and your babies out of here, out of Bayfield.

"They wanted you dead before and then what happened between you and Lenny . . . if they find you and your pups, they'll . . . well. They'll kill them too."

Blue perked her ears. She growled.

"There's only one way I can protect you and them, but you'll have to leave here with your babies."

Blue looked around the cave panting nervously. She stared at her litter. Trustingly, she sat her paw on Mosie's thigh and nudged her head against Mosies arm with approval.

"It's settled then," Mosie untied Granny's blanket from her neck. "We're leaving for Dog Island—today, right now. I brought this; it belonged to my mother for *her*, animosh." She laid the brown wool down on the ground. Blue sniffed it. "Your pups will be safe in here," she helped Blue tuck them inside.

Blue limped over to a freshly killed muskrat and dragged it across the cave floor to the entrance.

"Naw, you can leave that here. I brought you your special high quality protein dog food, plus snacks." Blue wagged her tail.

"We'll have to fix this leg of yours once we're in Big Bertha," Mosie gently lifted Blue's paw into her hand. "Right now, we don't have time. The sooner we leave the better." She gave Blue a hug and stood up with the blanket of pups.

"Well, guess this it, huh?"

Blue looked around her cave. *Aw-roo,-aw-roo,* she flipped her tail from side to side.

Together they walked to the mouth of the hollow and looked out at the swamp. Mosie reached down inside her shirt.

"Here girl," she handed Blue her soup bone. "Happy Fourth of July."

Blue snapped it into her mouth; trotted forward, and left the cave behind for the last time.

Cautiously, they walked to the edge of the bog. Mosie, bent down and ripped hunks of moss from the ground. "This will come in handy," she told Blue and shoved it into the blanket around the pups who wiggled safely in her arms. "It's a natural antibiotic, good for infections; besides, your babies will need a place to pee once we get on Bertha, and so will we."

Blue lowered her head.

"Hey, if it was good enough for my people and their babies, it's good enough for you and yours," Mosie said and pointed to the arched entrance. Blue looked up at her and softly growled.

"I know you can fit through there. Because I know this is where you came from when we first met." Ruffling her jowls, Blue got down on her belly and shimmied through.

Mosie passed the pups through and sat them next to Blue's long legs. She looked back at the quagmire, shivered, and crawled through the hole.

"Once we get back to Bertha, you and your babies are going to have to hide under the tarp," she explained as they hiked toward the ditch. "It's for your own protection, okay? So, under *no* circumstances can you let anyone, not even Pa, see or hear you." When they reached the bottom of the hill, she tied the blanket of pups around her neck. "You better let me go first. If any anyone comes, I can flag you back down."

Mosie climbed to the top and surveyed the road. Except for Big Bertha Brown standing patiently waiting for them, not a car was in sight.

She hurried to the boat, pulled back the tarp, put the pups on the floor of the hull, and then raced back to the gully. Again checking the highway, she motioned for Blue to come up.

Blue lumbered up the embankment and held up her bad leg. She *rooed* as she ran to Mosie and the boat, and her pups.

"Okay girl, I'm going to have to lift you up to get you inside," she put her arms under Blue's belly. Her doggie boobies were warm and full of milk. *"Eww,"* Mosie puttered. "I love you Blue, but damn, those are gross, girl. Now, as soon as you get in, I'll get you some food and water."

She grunted and boosted Blue up. Blue clawed Big Bertha's side with her good paw and climbed inside. She sniffed the blanket and gave it a nudge. The pups squealed and poked their half-wolf, half-canine heads out at their momma. Mosie put her hand by their tender little mouths. They twitched their noses eagerly against her fingertips. They backed away, ruffing out teeny growls and squeaky little barks.

A-wo, a-wo, one dared. Mosie laughed. Its miniature white legs barely supported its round white belly as it lunged forward and tripped over on its paws. Mosie ran her finger down its dark back.

Ever so gently, she pulled the white tip on its tail.

Ro-ro, it peeped out in protest and turned to nimble Mosie's fingers.

"You know Blue, I just don't understand grownups. Why they would want to hurt little ones like these is beyond me."

She poured water from a jug into Blue's bowl and then dished up her food. "There you go, girl," she gave Blue another hug and kiss and then pulled the tarp over Blue's head. "I'll leave enough of a gap so you'll have plenty of fresh air. And remember, stay down. Here we go."

Mosie looked up at the sky and said, "Please God, please let me get them to Dog Island safely." The clouds were taking shape. She took a deep breath and looked down the highway. That's when she saw it, the Jeep—a sea-foam green Willy's station wagon Jeep, and it was coming their way. The honking horn churned her stomach.

"Blue," she gulped, "*stay* the *hell* down, for the love of god. It's Father Perkins!" She knew there were only two things she could do:

1: Tell Father Perkins the truth and sign Blue and her pup's death warrants

2: Lie to Father Perkins and burn in Purgatory forever

Father Perkins pulled up and stuck his head out the window. "My, my, my, what do we have here?" he asked as he stepped out of the jeep and eyed up Big Bertha Brown. "What may I ask, Katherine, are you doing? Your mother informed me that you weren't feeling very well. I thought maybe I would come see if there was anything I could do to lift your spirits before the parade starts."

Seeing a twinkle of suspicion in his eyes, Mosie stared at the squished bugs on the bumper of the Jeep. She started counting them. *One, two, three . . .*

"Well, Father, you see . . ." she stammered, "me and Peggy . . .

we made this boat together, and we named it Big Bertha Brown."

"Yes Katherine, go on."

"Well, I thought due to the fact that I and Peggy haven't been able to see each other since . . . Lenny, because of the . . . well . . . you know . . . circumstances . . ." *Four, five, six* ". . . I thought maybe . . . I thought maybe, maybe I would take her down to the lake, the boat that is, not Peggy since she has to be in the parade all . . ." Mosie said turning whiter than the swamp cotton grass-balls stuck to her pants.

Seven, eight, nine, she counted faster than she ever counted before. Her stomach twisted tighter than the knots on Bertha's towropes.

"You suddenly don't look to well, Katherine," Father Perkins said. "Is there something you would like to tell me? I'm listening."

"Father, I . . . I." *Eighteen, twenty-one, nineteen . . .* the numbers jumbled in her head. Her lips parted. She gave them a lick. "Father, I wanted to get Bertha down to the lake to—"

She looked up at the clouds. They were moving, turning slowly, growing darker. A handful of crows soared to the top of the trees behind Father Perkins. She cringed and waited for them to scream. She couldn't take it, she just couldn't. She looked at the ground. And the crows shouted.

"Father Perkins, I was planning on . . . if I could that is . . . I wanted to surprise Peggy with the first ride inside old Bertha; you know, seeing how she helped make her and all."

Father Perkins stepped toward the boat. He tapped his lips with the tip of his finger. "Yes, I see," he picked up the ropes and held them in his hands. He looked at Mosie. Her head whirled as his gray eyes stared at her.

"You mustn't try something like this. It's very dangerous. I wish you had called me."

"You're right Father, I'm sorry, Father," she almost yelled with panic. "Do you think you can help me, Father?"

"Katherine," he let the ropes fall from his hands, "what kind of an example of our Heavenly Father would I be if I refused to help such a fine young girl as you?" He grabbed a tow chain from the back of his Jeep.

Mosie placed the bike on top of the canvas, making sure not to lay it on Blue and the pups. "Shhh, shhh," she hissed to warn Blue not to move.

"*Thank you*, Father," she grinned with relief as she watched Father Perkins feed the chain underneath the creepers. He clamped the hook to the back of his bumper. Slowly they headed into Bayfield.

"Father, may I ask you for just a couple more favors?" she asked pulling Val's letter from her pocket.

"Yes, I suppose so."

"Can you mail this for me?" She ran her finger across Val's name and address then handed him the letter. "And the other favor is since I want Big Bertha to be a surprise. Would you mind not mentioning any of this to anyone, especially, Peggy? It'd be fun to wait until the fireworks, don't you think?"

"Yes, I can see that," Father Perkins slipped the letter under the visor above his windshield. "You are a good girl Katherine; just as your parents and Peggy's say." He slowed down.

"That is our Peggy's house, is it not?" he looked down the potted lane. He stopped.

"Yes Father, it is," Mosie stared at the dangling flaps Peggy had known as home.

Her yellowed curtain-sheet bleached from the sun now hung forgotten out her bedroom window. Mosie could almost see a trace of Peggy's shadow standing behind it. She pushed the lump in her throat down and watched a skunk scamper through the front door.

"Father, no one, not even Lenny can return to that miserable shack, can they?"

Father Perkins cleared his throat. "No Katherine, they cannot, not even Lenny."

"Father, is Peggy going to be alright? I mean on account of what happened to her pa and well, you know, what's going on between Corinne and . . ." she looked down at her hands.

"Yes I am sure she will. Thanks to you."

"Me?"

"Yes, you Katherine. You did promise our Holy Mother of God to watch over and protect our Peggy, did you not? And wasn't it you who brought her to the doors of Our Lord?"

"Yeah, I mean yes Father, but how did you know about my promise?"

"Peggy. She told Sister Maggie and me everything. It seems you have played a hand in her, recovery, if you will. She is very fond of you, Katherine, and has been missing you a great deal these last few days. I believe she used the term, *I love Mosie as a sister,* if I'm not mistaken."

Mosie wanted to tell Father how she too had come to love Peggy as a sister and how on account of Willowdean and Lenny, maybe

Peggy *was* her sister after all.

She bit her lip and looked out at Lake Superior sprawling past the edge of Bayfield like an endless blue carpet. They drove on in silence to the boat launch down from Mr. Maki's.

"Thank you Father," she watched him unhook the boat. Together, they slid it into the water. "Thanks for the lift and everything," she said kept her eyes on Bertha as she bobbed up and down. She listened to the waves that clapped against her sides.

"Is there something wrong?" Father Perkins asked.

Mosie stared at the dead bugs on Father Perkins' Jeep. She figured they were God's way of showing her how, just like them, He was going to squish her for lying to His Father Perkins.

"No, no Father, nothing's wrong. I can take it from here. Boy, won't Peggy be surprised?" she forced a big grin. "Gee, the parade will be starting any time now."

She looked out at the lake and her stomach fluttered.

"Remember Father, don't tell *anyone* I'm here. It'll be our surprise, okay?"

"Well, just mind yourself now," he got into the Jeep.

"Father," Mosie yelled, "Father, take good care of Peggy, will you?"

Father nodded.

She watched him drive off and was regretful for praying Candy's Aunt Margaret out of Purgatory.

At least, I would of had someone to visit with, she thought and wondered if Father Perkin's would try to pray her out of purgatory, even if she did lie right to his face.

She crossed herself (three times for good measure) and then headed for Blue and the pups.

"Good job," she roughed up Blue's ears. "Good job! You doing okay in there?" Blue gave Mosie's hands a lick.

"Good. I just have to get a few things at Mr. Maki's, and then I'll get you and your little ones where you need to be."

The clouds hung heavily in the sky as she walked to Mr. Maki's and hoped nobody would notice her in the crowd. Especially Mr. Maki.

She grabbed two oars from the wall, two bright orange life jackets from the rack, handed him the items, and then her money keeping her face to the floor.

"Thank you, come again," he quickly snatched the $20 from her hand, eager to grab another bill from the woman next to her.

She banged her way through the crowd, not caring who she swatted and jabbed with the ores. *After all*, she thought, *I am on a bigger and better mission than first picks for ice cream.*

As she pushed through the crowd, she set her eyes on the clear path between the rows of bronzed beach loafers, crying toddlers, and already worn-out mothers. She dug her feet into the warm sand and charged forward, dragging the ores behind her.

John was right. Taking the extra time to caulk Bertha properly with a good high-quality marine polysulfide sealant did pay off. She was dry as a bone.

In the distance, the crowd cheered as the sweet voice of Grand Marshal Peggy Anderson floated in the warm summer breeze along the shores of the Great Lake.

Blue's golden-brown eyes looked trustingly into Mosie's.

"Are you ready?" she slid herself into Big Bertha Brown. "Love you too, Peggy," she launched off into that Great Lake called Superior.

"Love you, too."

CHAPTER THIRTY~SEVEN

Bayfront Park was beginning to swell with excitement. Father Perkins followed the parade down Mannypenny Lane and raised his black cassock garbed arm to cross the onlookers. He nodded politely at the shouts of invitations to picnic lunches and grill outs that drifted through the Jeep windows as he drove on, knowing the well-meaning generosities would soon be forgotten.

"Ahhh youth," he said as an extra-wide smile crossed his face as he watched a long-haired teenaged boy scamper in front of him. With extra zeal, he gave the lad an additional blessing. The boy waved back and produced two erected middle fingers.

"Forgive him. He is young," Father Perkins mumbled and skirted the Jeep past him to up to Peggy's float and *'Country Squire's Band'*.

Leaving Mannypenny Lane, they proceeded onto First Street. Peggy and *'Country Squire's Band'* were the first to pull into the end of the parade parking slot reserved just for them.

"Careful," Father Perkins chuckled to himself as he watched Peggy tumble backwards into the hay bales stacked on the flatbed trailer.

"I swear," Ken Johnson put his guitar down to Peggy a hand up. "Todd does that on purpose every time. You'll get used to it. By this time next year, you'll be a pro just like the rest of us." He grinned as he plucked straw out of Peggy's hair. Her eyes grew larger than the cymbals on Keith's drum set. "You mean, you boys want *me*? For *real*?"

"Yep. We'll talk business later but right now it looks like you've got yourself your first admirers," Ken gestured to the small mob coming up alongside the float.

Peggy looked down at Willowdean and Sister Maggie.

"Mosie, where's Mosie?" she asked excitedly and reached for John's hand to help guide her down.

"She's home. She's not feeling well," Willowdean answered.

Corrine pushed Willowdean to the side with her shoulder and grabbed John's free arm. "Johnny, did you hear that? Did you hear what Kenny said?" she shrieked and jumped up and down, her jewelry *tinging* with her.

"God have mercy!" Father Perkins declared as he watched her kiss John's cheek. "*A man who commits adultery lacks judgment; whoever does so destroys himself; Proverbs, 6:32.*

"But it's the innocent that truly gets hurt," he added as Willowdean and Sister Maggie disappear into the crowd.

He turned his Jeep onto First Street then on Rittenhouse Avenue and spotted Michael Peterson marching to the park with his wife and brood of little Petersons. He stuck his head out the window and called to him.

Peterson waved back. Turning to Mrs. Peterson, he gave her instructions to wait for him at the light post at the end of the block.

"Father," he chuckled as he jogged up to the Jeep, "I believe the park is the other way," he reached his hands out to Father Perkins. "Maybe you would like to follow us," he teased.

"No, no Michael that is a very generous offer that I cannot accept," Father Perkins laughed. He grabbed hold of Petersons' hands and gave them a tender squeeze. "But since you are in such a giving mood this fine day, may I ask a favor?"

"Yes Father of course, anything, anything at all."

"Will you be spending a portion of this afternoon with, Mother, err, Sister Maggie?"

Peterson looked nervously over his shoulder. His tribe was heading closer for the streetlight. "I can't think of any other way I *can* spend our afternoon. Half of Bayfield's population is right over there." He laughed, gesturing to his fine little collection. "Don't tell me the Good Lord has you out on a mission, today of all days?"

"Yes, I'm afraid His work has no holidays. There is a lamb I need to see. That is what I need you to let Mother know. I will be back when I can. Can you do that for me Michael?"

"That Father, is not a problem," Peterson answered. "Is there anything else I can help you with?" he asked anxiously as he watched Mrs. Peterson grab two of the youngest of the group darting into the street.

"No, that is all. You're a fine man, Michael, a fine man." He raised his hand to bless him.

"Oh, no need for any of that, Father," Peterson snickered and turned from the Jeep.

"I think you've done that one *too* many times to me and the Mrs. Our table won't hold even one more of those little blessings of yours," he laughed and headed to his small flock.

"God Bless you Michael Mathew Peterson, and the Mrs. too," Father Perkins shouted after him.

He took his foot off the clutch and headed out to Highway 13.

"What Lord, what do I say to such a man as Leonard Arthur Anderson?"

Except for half a dozen cars, Memorial Hospital's parking lot was almost deserted. Father Perkins' Jeep was the only one taking advantage of the spaces reserved for Clergy. He stared at the Sick-Call Kit sitting on the seat next to him.

"Why Lord," he ran his hands over its soft, gray suede case, "why must we wait until Saint Barbara comes to hold the hands of our sick and dying before we are allowed to give your children the hope found in these anointed instruments?"

He unzipped the case and took out its purple silk stole; kissing it, he placed it around his neck and straightened its golden fringes. He picked up a round, gold-plated container.

He held the pyx in the palm of his hand, unclasped it, and checked the fresh supply of Holy Eucharist Sister Maggie made that Saturday. Snapping it shut, he slid it into the pocket of his cassock.

The Goupillon was filled Holy Water and ready to sprinkle. Nestled next to the bottle of Holy Oil, his two finger cloths laid clean and white.

He stared at the crucifix between the two white candles, sighed, and zipped it shut. After tucking it under his arm, he made the sign of the cross, then opened the Jeep door and made his way across the parking lot.

The hospital's thick glass doors swung open. The coolness of the conditioned air swept across him. He grinned at the half-dozing receptionist across the waiting room. She snapped herself up and caught her head as it fell forward toward her desk. Her eyes sprung open at the site of Father Perkins.

"Happy Fourth of July," she strained not to let her voice come out droopy. "You must be here to see Mrs. Lockmeyer."

She looked over the patient roster and gave Father Perkins a bright grin.

"Happy Fourth of July to you . . ." he replied as he looked at her nameplate. It was pinned the wrong way round.

"What room is she in?" he asked with uncertainty.

"Room 213."

"And Len, err, Leonard Anderson, what room is he in?"

"Leonard Anderson," she repeated as she ran her finger down a list. "Leonard Anderson, mmm . . . I'm sorry Father, but I don't see a Leonard Anderson listed." She looked up, her face flushed with embarrassment.

Father Perkins smiled. "Sorry," he whispered and leaned close to her even though no one was around. "My mistake. I forgot to mention, he is in the, well, the *special unit*."

"Oh, okay," she responded with relief and pulled open the bottom drawer under the counter. She hauled out a black, unmarked binder and ran her finger down another list. "Room 1B," she whispered back. "Security code, 1469."

"Thank you, Miss . . . Miss. . . ." He nudged his head at her name-tag.

She flipped it over. "Nancy, Miss Nancy Hawthorn," she giggled girlishly.

"Well thanks, Miss Nancy Hawthorn. You have been a tremendous help." He raised his arm and gave her a blessing.

"Why, you're Father Perkins, aren't you! Thank you, thank you Father Perkins."

He turned and made his way to the elevator. He pressed *B*. The doors opened with a clank. Slowly, he sank downward. The elevator opened with another clank.

He stepped out and made his way down the long, half-lit hall to a set of thick metal doors. He punched in the special numbers *1469*, and the door opened to a day room that was bright, cool and clean, and decorated with red, white, and blue stars twirling from the ceiling on the ends of yarn. In the corner, a television blared, and so did a young man.

"Cool man!" he declared as he hopped over an armless orange metal chair. "*One Life to Live* is on."

After plunking himself down on the hard seat, he elbowed his viewing partner. "Sure beats sitting in the hole don't it?" he grabbed a handful of jellybeans from the end table. "Hell, I could stay in here all summer for all I care." He shoved the sugary beans into his mouth. "Man, I'm tellin' ya, that Tommy Lee Jones playing Dr. Mark Toland is going to go places. You watch and see."

A middle-aged nurse ran to greet Father Perkins. "What a wonderful surprise!" she gushed. "I'll gather everyone up."

"Thank you Nurse Atkins, but I'm here to see someone specifically." He looked over the mass of heads. "My man is right over there," he said, gesturing to the back of the room.

Lenny sat in the windowsill. His bandages were gone except for the ones wrapped around his hands.

"Perhaps when I'm through . . ."

"Of course, Father. I'm sorry."

"Oh no need for apologies. How is he doing?"

"Physically he's doing better than we ever expected. From what I heard from some of the men here, it's his orneriness that's brought him this far in such a short time." She chuckled, and then turned serious. "Some of the doctors are saying his recovery is nothing short of a miracle. I'm inclined to believe it, Father. Even where the dog did the majority of its damage is almost completely healed. And as you see, there's very little scarring.

"But what concerns me is his silence. He's very quiet, Father. One of the quietest men I have ever cared for. It's a blessing you came. He keeps mumbling something about a ladder belonging to someone named, Jacob. But when asked who this Jacob is, he clams right up and leaves the room; and always with such a strange look on his face; a look of confusion and remorse. Perhaps you might be able to get through to him."

"God willing, Nurse Atkins, God willing."

Father Perkins walked quietly across the room and stood silent while Lenny peered outside the window.

"I know you're there, Padre. I can smell ya'," Lenny finally said without turning his head.

"Yes, Leonard, I'm here. I can wait until you're ready."

"Well, knowing you, you'd stand there till hell freezes over if that's how long it'd take. Sooo," Lenny quipped as he grabbed his canes. "I might as well just get this over with."

He slid off the ledge and hobbled to room 1B. Father Perkins shut the door. Nurse Atkins smiled.

Lenny wrestled himself onto his bed, let out a long sigh, and closed his eyes with a cough. "Ain't supposed you got a cigarette on ya? No, I didn't think so," Lenny said dryly. He watched Father Perkins kiss the purple stole draped around his neck.

"How you feeling, Len?"

"How am I feeling . . . Mmph, let's think about that for a moment. How am I feeling . . ."

"Not physically Len, not physically. You know better than anyone in Bayfield that I understand what you are going through physically, and I don't mean the dog attack, so let's not play these little pity games. I want to know how you feel inside that noggin of yours."

"Now what in the blazes do you want to know that for? You think you can just go around, raising those holier-than-thou hands of yours and magically take away all the suffering a body's got locked up inside them? Well, this is one old boy that has more pain than those hands of yours can handle—Dang you, Ralph, you old sly son of a— " Lenny spat and turned to glare out the window.

Father Perkins rested his head against the cold concrete wall; the commotion in the day room filled the silence between them. Nurse Atkins' voice turned firm with reproach concerning the over use of certain words. Finally, Lenny spoke.

"You get me every time, don't ya, Ralph?"

Father Perkins shut his eyes. "Do you want to begin, Len?" he asked evenly.

Lenny wiped his gauzed hands across the tears that rolled down his cheeks. "Bless me Father, for I have sinned," he began. "As you know, my last confession was one year ago . . . today . . ."

The hum of the air conditioner was the only sound left by the time Father Perkins rose from his chair. Taking the pyx out from his pocket, he opened it and walked over to Lenny's beside.

"The body of Christ, Leonard," he whispered, "the body of Christ."

Lenny nodded an amen and opened his mouth.

Father Perkins placed the little white wafer on his tongue.

"God Bless you Len. I will let Katherine know what you said. Jacobs ladder . . . huh . . . I'll be. You know, they're claiming your recovery as a miracle, don't you?"

"Yeah, well, let them claim whatever they want. I heard them saying a lot more than that about me." He turned back to the window.

"You get some rest, Len," Father Perkins headed for the door. "By the way, I do agree we should talk with Corrine and Peggy together. I will be with you all the way, Leonard. You know that."

Father Perkins went quietly out the door. Somberly shaking his head, he flagged Nurse Atkins over to a secluded corner. "May I request Len be given an hour of self-time?" Nurse Atkins smiled.

He punched 1469 into the keyboard on the wall and slipped through the door.

Lake Superior looked wonderful as he rounded the last corner of Highway 13 and so did Bayfront Park, and all the people strewn about its midst.

"Lord," he said, "These are good people, your people. I ask that you bless each and every one of them; Catholics and Protestants, Lutherans alike; even the Baptists," he prayed.

He looked at his watch. "Seven o'clock. An hour and Peggy has her day," he spotted Val's letter stuck under his visor. "Just enough time to do a few more errands."

The sun hung over the lake and waited to end its day. Willowdean sat on the edge of the picnic table with Peterson No. 5 on her knee. She dug in her purse for a rubber band.

"This will help cool you down," she swept the little girl's sweaty blonde tufts into a stubby little ponytail. She blew the back of her tiny neck; her delicate shoulders lifted from the sudden chill.

"Better?" Willowdean asked.

The flaxen nub bobbed up and down. 'Number five' slid from Willowdean's lap. Like greased lightning, she ran across the grass.

"Spud!" Sister Maggie shouted.

"Me-me-me," 'Peterson Number Five' shrieked as Sister Maggie slugged the ball up in the air.

Willowdean sighed and weaved her own hair into a braid as she watched all the Petersons wait for the ball to come down.

"Okay Petersons, big and small," Sister Maggie boomed, "Now you know the game of Spud. You Petersons, you show Sister Maggie how good all you play together," she instructed them.

"Now-now," she chortled at the tolls of disappointed *Ahh's* and exaggerated *no's*, as she handed the ball to No. 5.

She waddled to Willowdean and poured herself a tall glass of cherry Kool-Aid. "The Good Lord, He must have things a little backward, yes?" she sat her hefty hips next to Willowdean. "Ya, He gives *them* all the energy and leaves *us* with leftovers."

"No," Willowdean gave a weak smile. "We just used all ours up."

"Mmph!" Sister Maggie grunted. "It's that man of yours, yes? Shame-shame-shame on him! And that Corrine, too." She slammed down her glass.

Willowdean tugged her locket watch-necklace up to her eyes: 7:05.

"Sister," she rubbed her belly, "it's not just John and Corrine; it's also Mosie and Val, and Blue.

"I hate to say it, but I was foolish to trust John's decision to move back here. He said it would *help* our family." She took in a breath. "The truth is, Sister, I knew better, deep down. After all, this isn't the first time John has done this. I guess I just wanted it done and over with.

"When the kids were small, I was able to keep it from them. I think sometimes they were the only reason I really stayed with him all these years." She looked down and patted the stars on her dress.

"Now being back here, I see he did marry the wrong girl. And I, I married the wrong man. But it's not us I worry about so much. It's Mosie, and Peggy. It's hard on them going through all this. And that dog, it was Mosie's only saving grace, but I found that out too late. Due to my own stubbornness.

"She always wanted a dog. That's the one thing that made this move easier for her. Losing Blue like she did only makes things worse."

"Willowdean," Sister Maggie said, "I think you are a woman of honor, yes?"

Willowdean nodded.

"Yes. I can tell. *By their fruits, you will know them.*

"You do not come to the thrift shop to haggle over gossip in the corners. You stay to yourself, do you not?"

Again, Willowdean nodded and kept her eyes on her stars.

"Mph, let me tell you a story," Sister Maggie stared at the lake.

"Being a woman of honor, I know you will not repeat such stories, yes?

"There was a young girl once, a long time ago. Not a little girl but not a woman. She was much like our Sweet Peggy.

"When the Great War came to her little village, she had to put away all childhood playing and help feed and protect her family. But this young girl, she had no special talents worthy of anyone's hard-earned money like the others in her village. She had spent too many days playing with her dollies and too many hours chasing after all the things little girls chase.

"One day, her papa, he got very sick and no longer could do anything but lay in his poor little bed, coughing and coughing till the blood of his lungs come out.

"Her momma, she try her best and could do no more.

"Well, this girl, her heart broke and her stomach, too, did what she must: Save her family.

"So, when the soldiers come, she told them of her sick papa and tired momma and how their bellies hurt from hunger day and night. She told them if they feed them and protect them, she would do for them things no girl should do. So, she do them even though it break her heart.

"Okay, a month go by and no womanly blessing come to her. Another month, still no womanly blessing. Agh! She know inside why they not come.

"So she go to the old woman who not live in the village but outside the village. The old woman, she did what she did to all young girls and then the young girl, she never got womanly blessings ever again.

"Now, her papa and momma, for long time they never go hungry and no soldiers come to hurt them. They did not know why but were thankful.

"Then one night, other soldiers come. Different soldiers.

"The young girl, she tell them what she can do for them but they not listen. They say, 'You have something we *do not want!*'

"So they come and beat her poor papa for having nothing for them except his dirty-dirty daughter.

"Her papa, he died not from beatings but from the pain in his heart over what his daughter had done.

"Willowdean, young girls sometimes they do things. Right or wrong, they do things.

"But Jesus, *mmph*! He did things too! *Good* things! It is His good things that take away *all* them wrong things.

"But that young girl, she would not learn of Jesus for some time.

"Still in her village, Niegowic, in Poland, she turn into a woman.

"One day her heart inside tell her: *Go to church*. She was scared of those in her church of her youth, Saint Florian, the one of her papa and her momma. But she go anyway.

"To her surprise, there was a new priest, a young priest, twenty-eight years old, two years younger than the woman.

"He was different, that priest. He played soccer with the children and grownups, too. And he go hiking, bringing others with him.

"But most he enjoyed writing his nice stories and poetry and would invite all the young ones to perform those plays he would write.

"His name was Father Wojtyla, Karol Wojtyla. He too lost his papa and his momma and his brother during the Great War.

"Soon the young woman come to call him just Karol. That is when she learned of this *new* Jesus. That is when she decided to become who Father Wojtyla called his, Little Sister Magdalene.

"That was 1948. And her Jesus, He still teach her things even today."

Willowdean looked at Sister Maggie. She was staring at the lake as if part of her were trapped in its bitter, cold bottom.

"This girl, she was like Mary Magdalene?"

"Ya . . . like Mary Magdalene."

"Maggie, what's your real name?"

"It was, Bodgana, Bodgana Kozlowski. In Polish it means *A gift from God.*"

"And that's why you have taken such an interest in Peggy."

"Ya, and other girls too."

Sister Maggie jumped as the *'Country Squire's Band'* made their announcement.

Willowdean checked her necklace: 7:50.

"Ten minutes early," she cleared her throat. "Maybe we should get in line. Bodgana, thank you for sharing your story with me."

"Ya ya, now, we get in line now. Up front, stage right," she chuckled and wiped a long lost tear from her eye. "Tsk, that Papa! He going to get an ear-lashing when I get a hold of him!" she said, as they headed toward the lake.

"Well, try not to be too hard on him," Willowdean laughed and gestured to the black shadow heading toward them.

Sister Maggie held her fist in the air and shook it. A relieved smile crossed her face. "You, you are a very naughty boy!" she yelled. "Very naughty."

Father Perkins picked up the bottom of his robe and darted across the grass. He looked at Sister Maggie as if he really had been a bad little boy.

"Ya! Mmp! You better run," she teased.

"Come Papa, our Sweet Peggy Girl is looking for us, see?" she pointed to the stage. They ran to the front of the crowd waving.

Peggy grinned and glowed as if she were a true bona fide beauty star.

"She is too beautiful!" Sister Maggie shouted over the people and wiped tears from her eyes. "Just beautiful! Mph and mmph!"

Peggy blew them a kiss. "Is Mosie still sick?" she yelled down at them over the roar of the crowd.

"What did she say?" Father Perkins asked.

"I think she asked about *roses on a stick*," Willowdean answered.

Shrugging, they looked at Peggy.

"We forgot to bring you roses," Sister Maggie shouted back.

"No, Mosie . . . *Where's* Mosie?"

"No, Peggy girl, don't sing that!" Sister Maggie hollered. "Oh Lord, I think she wants to sing, *Sing a Song of Posies*. That's one of our warming up songs."

Ken Johnson began his announcing. "Well folks, here she is, the one you've all have been waiting for, Little . . . Peggy . . . An . . . der . . . suuuuuun!" The crowd broke into applause.

"Why, if I didn't know better, I'd say that's Marty Robbins up there," Father Perkins shouted over the thunder of people.

Willowdean looked at the young man strumming his guitar, cueing Peggy.

"Yes, yes he does look like Marty Robbins, doesn't he?"

"Quiet now, the two of you," Sister Maggie snapped and gave them each a stern look. "She is going to start."

That's when Peggy gave her last bow and opened her mouth. "I would like to dedicate this song to two very special people in my life," her voice echoed through the speakers and across the lake.

She looked over at John and Corrine—Corrine flagged her arms, squealed, and stepped out from the line of people with John's hand in hers.

"Father Perkins, Sister Maggie, this one's for you. Thank you, thank you both." Corrine's face soured.

"Thank you for . . . making me the *Happiest Girl in the Whole USA*!"

Her voice rang clear and strong; the crowd roaring with delight, demanded another. She looked at Ken. He nodded yes, his eyes sparkling with hers.

"Well thank you, thank you all. Most folks don't know this," she said, "but Donna Fargo's real name is Yvonne Vaughn. I just thought you all would like to know that.

"Now, I'm gonna sing this next one on behalf of someone that I care a great deal for. And I ain't saying any names either; she'll know who she is."

The crowd laughed and hushed as Peggy put the microphone up to her lips. She threw Corrine a stinging look. "This here song is by, Miss Loretta Lynn."

Willowdean put her hands to her mouth and giggled. Peggy winked at her and belted out: "You ain't woman enough to take my man . . ."

Peggy clapped back and squealed with delight at the crowd. "Thank you, thank you folks; you've all been very good to me today, and I want to thank all of you for everything you're doing for me and Lenny, my dad.

"I know if he was here, well, never mind any of that. By the looks of things, we got a really exciting fireworks display this year, and it's about to start.

"Now after they're all done, we want you folks to come on back, and we'll have some more music for ya's.

"And don't forget, the *'Country Squire's Band'* is gonna be at Big Top Chautauqua this next Saturday coming up. I hope you all can make it." She took a deep bow.

She looked back at the bright lights and the crowd lying in its shadows and saw Kenny smiling at her, just as the first bang of the night echoed over the lake.

The white flash caught the angry glow on Corrine's face as John slipped from her grasp and turned to Willowdean.

"Willow," he called and ran to her under the sparks and pops of the blue and white light filling the park. "Willow." He peaked over his shoulder and into the shadows of the night. Corrine watched him, stood snapping her gum, and tapped her foot impatiently.

"Willow . . ." He kept his voice soft and tender as he took her hands in his. "Willow, honey, I know what I did was wrong," he looked deep into her midnight black eyes. She looked at the ground to hide the blush on her face.

"I know I can't ever take it back, no matter what. But I want to make it up to you somehow. I know we can still be a family, if you let me try. If it's alright by you . . . if it's okay . . . I mean . . . if you still love me, can I . . . can I . . . can I come home?"

Willowdean smiling tenderly and squeezed his hands. They were warm, and rough. "John . . ." she leaned her head against his chest. He kissed her. She listened to his heart beating fast, as if they had just made love. "No John, no you may not," she whispered and pulled away from him and the smell of Corrine set in his shirt.

She turned. She was heading home. Home to Mosie.

From the top of Kill-Deer's crown, Willowdean watched the balls of color bursting in the distance just as she and John had the night they left for Barrington. The eighteen years that passed between them seemed so far and long away, yet close, as if they were left over from yesterday. She rubbed her stomach; her tears came easy and ran down her cheeks like the trails of white sparkles collapsing over the lake. She knew her time with John had ended. And she was alone.

She drew herself back into the station wagon and wondered what the days ahead held.

She pulled into the driveway, grateful to see Mosie had left the porch light on and was already in bed. "Tonight is not the night to tell her about my decision; maybe when she's able to let go of Blue, after the baby's born," she made her way to the porch. She sighed at the boxes scattered about.

"What a mess," she said. "Ether those squirrels or Mosie got into them again. The baby gave a flutter.

She opened the kitchen door, flipped on the light, and sat down in her chair at the table. She held her hand tight to her belly. There was no mistake, the baby was rolling.

"Mosie!" she yelled and her belly, "the baby's moving, come feel. Katherine, Katherine Rose, the baby . . ."

There was no answer; no stirring, no radio, no TV, and no Simon nor Garfunkel singing upstairs with Mosie.

"Mosie?" she yelled through the silence, "are you okay?"

She rose from her chair and thudded up the stairs. "Mosie, why didn't you . . ." She snapped on the light. Mosie's bed, neatly made from the morning was empty. "The blanket—" She gasped. "It's— gone." Her head whirled. Nausea began filling her gut.

"Mosie, where are you?" she cried as she raced down the stairs.

"Answer me . . . answer me right now!" Dashing from room to room, she rushed to the porch, the fire of fear filling her. Her breath heavy, she struggled to call into the night.

"Please, Mosie, *answer* me, where are you? *Where are you?*"

She battled her way to the garage, panicked. She opened the door and turned on the light. It was still and vacant. John's green shelves stood empty.

"*Katherine*!" she cried as she made her way to the wall of boxes. "Oh God, *please, no* . . ." She opened the back door, her breath caught deep inside her. "*Naanoondaagoziwag-manidoo-nandaagosiwag aazhoogaam* . . ."

Terror carried Willowdean back to the house, the kind of terror that turns picking up the phone and dialing it into a nightmare. Her confused fingers dialed number after number. She hung up the phone and tried again, this time deliberately forcing her finger in the very last number, *O*. Trembling, she gave the tiny, silver finger-guard a whirl. She let go.

"Operator, emergency . . . emergency . . ." she choked. "*Oh God*, emergency . . . emergency . . ."

CHAPTER THIRTY~EIGHT

Waves slapped against Big Bertha; thick, oily night waves. Mosie and Blue watched the specks of colors from the fireworks jet into the dark sky; their fading glints of glory fizzled downward and seared the shores of Bayfield. A rapid round of firecracker booms echoed across the lake and launched the final claps of appreciation from the shores.

"Well, that's that," Mosie lit one of the kerosene lamps. She checked the oars inside their locks and yanked the rope off a rotted stump protruding from the rocky shoreline. She pulled up anchor and began rowing past the last cove of Basswood Island. "I'm glad we got further than I thought we would," she pointed her nose behind her shoulder. "Hermit Island is right there. See the trees?"

Blue turned her snout to the air and began sniffing. The smell of camp fires from Madeline Island mixed with those on Basswood and drifted away from them. "Hermit has a good sandy beach. We can sleep there for the night."

With calm, unworried eyes, Blue watched her as if she knew Mosie's determination was stronger than anything that may lie ahead.

The calm waters made rowing over to the tiny island peaceful and easy. Coming in along the shoreline, Mosie stuck her oar into the water to measure its depth. Knee high. She jumped eagerly out the boat and stretched her legs in the needle-cold water. She caught her breath in a shiver, grabbed the rope, and towed Big Bertha onto the strip of brown sandy beach. Blue whined impatiently as Mosie held the lantern in the air to cautiously search the beach and wooded tree line for any signs of life.

"Okay," she said in a hushed tone as she put the lamp down on a block of brownstone. "Let's get you and those pups out of there.

"We can only stay the night, so don't get too cozy," she pulled the boat further up onto the beach.

"And no fire tonight either, too risky. Someone's sure to see it."

Carefully, she picked up a pup and kissed it. It smelled of marsh moss and Blue. Its warm, plump body squirmed. She snuggled it against her. She picked up another one. Their paws tangled in her tee shirt. Blue gently rolled an extra whiny pup into her mouth. It quieted instantly. She followed Mosie to shore, and plopped her baby on the blanket next to the others.

"So that's how you do it," Mosie rubbed Blue's head. "And your teeth don't hurt them, huh?"

Blue sneezed, then nudged her babies tightly together. Quickly, she limped back to the boat. "I'll get the last two for you," Mosie offered and followed behind her.

Jumping into Bertha, Blue rutted her head in the moss and jawed another pup into her mouth. "They sure mean a lot to you, don't they, girl?" Mosie asked and reached for the last two. She followed Blue and put the pair next to hers.

Blue layed down close and licked each one. Instantly, they kneaded her full, white speckled underside and started to suckle. She nestled her head in Mosie's lap and her eyes softened with sleep. Mosie hugged her tight, her fur still soft, still warm and comforting.

"I love you," she cooed as she ran her finger down the dribble of white on her head down to her nose. Scratching her floppy ears, she kissed Blue and then lay down on the blanket, pillowing her head with her arm. She looked at her watch. A sick stirring was beginning to roll in her guts.

"Ma's been home for an hour now," she looked at the stars that were so close she tried to pluck one from the sky. "She's probably worried out of her mind. She's already called Pa . . . maybe even Val.

"But the way I figure it, when I get back they'll be so glad to see me they won't do nothing to me. Maybe they'll even give me a real *special* birthday party—seeing I'm still alive and not dead. Who knows? We'll see."

She yawned, blew out the lantern, and laid her head on Blue. It wasn't the waves slapping against the rocks or the tide rolling calmly into the inlet just beyond her feet lulling her to sleep; nor was it the soft mewing of the pups; it was Blue, and the cadence of her spirit. Together they drifted off to sleep.

The Great Lake took hold of daybreak, and crept its chill and fog over everything in its way. A pink blush washed the sky. Mosie looked out at the early silver morning water and reached for the blanket, snuggling even closer to Blue and the pups. Blue rose to her feet. The pups squealed and grunted as Blue's warmth left them.

Mosie rolled into a ball and pulled them next her, trying to ward off the cold. The waves patting the shore and a gull floating overhead squawked at Big Bertha, nestled contently in the sand. Blue hobbled back to her pups.

"We're not going to have much time," Mosie yawned. "See?" She pointed to a line of boats in the distance. "Search boats more than likely. They can't see us though. Too far." She stretched and headed to Bertha for a roll of toilet paper.

"That leg of yours doesn't look so good. I'll have to clean it up again before we go; we have a long day a head us," she said as she headed for the trees.

Blue looked up at the circling gull that was searching for food. She growled and lay down on top of her babies.

"Suit yourself," Mosie yelled from behind a maple tree as she watched the schooners zip below the horizon. She hurried to Bertha, pulled out the Apostle Island chart and a box of Pop-Tarts along with Blue's breakfast. "You want to eat now?" she held up a can of high quality protein dog food.

Raw-rooo, Blue wagged her tail.

Mosie opened the can of savory meat chunks and gravy, plopped them in Blue's bowl, and then ripped open the box of Pop-Tarts.

"This, this is our map from here on," she munched on the soft pastry square.

Licking the gravy from her chops, Blue looked up from her breakfast.

"If we lose this, were in big trouble. There's a total of 850 miles circling the twenty-two islands out here. Pa said it's called an Archipelago, and each one has its own story. Impressive isn't it?" Blue looked up and sneezed. "Most of the islands are only three miles long, some a little more. Right now, we're about nine miles out." She looked out at the lake and bit her Pop Tart.

"But the one island that's not on this chart is Dog Island. No one's really ever seen it, you know, well, except you since that's where you came from. I sure wish you knew how to get there." She opened another Tart. "What I have to figure out now is what channel we should take, the north, or the west. The south is way down here, and there isn't much down that way except Long Island, which isn't really an island anyway so we'll exclude that area; for now anyway.

"And don't worry about water, we have plenty of that," she said as bits of dry Tart sprayed from her mouth. She took a drink from her thermos.

"The lake water is so pure; all we have to do is boil it for two minutes so we don't get sick. We can do that at night and then pour it into our jugs and drag them in the water on the side of Bertha. That way it'll be cold when we want some.

"Did you know the lake is only around 40 degrees? That's about what a refrigerator is. That's what Pa told me anyway. But you don't care about any of that, do you?"

Ra-roo, Blue agreed and lapped the side of Mosie's face. Mosie cuddled her with an extra hug. "Well, what do you think?" she showed Blue the chart. Blue nudged it, making a spot with her nose. Mosie put her finger on the wet mark. "The west channel. Looks good to me."

Getting to her feet, she gathered up the supplies and put them in Bertha.

"Here girl," she pulled out the medical box. Blue hobbled over to Bertha.

"I'm going to put a new piece of moss on that leg of yours and wrap something very special around it to help keep it clean and covered. I just knew these would come in handy," she laughed, pulling out the floral box of Modess. "They should do the trick."

After putting a layer of moss around Blue's leg, she strapped on a pad, securing it with the sanitary belt. "Looks better on you than me," Mosie chuckled. She took out the life preservers.

"Now, depending on the chop of the water and which way the wind holds . . ." she slipped Blue's front legs through the straps, ". . . and how far Bertha carries, we should be able to pass through Oak Island . . . and . . . Stockton Island by mid-day, Manitou Island by early afternoon, *and* if we can, we'll camp out on Ironwood Island," she latched the buckles shut on their life preservers.

"All righty then; looks like we're all secured. Ready?" Mosie shoved Bertha into the water. Blue sat rigid as her babies sniffed the strangeness surrounding them. The lake had a bounce, *from the tide*, Mosie thought as she kept close to the shoreline.

Blue's tail tipped up and wagged at a Common Tern that dashed across the beach. *Roo*, she bayed playfully as it sprinted to the edge of the sandbar.

It stuck its black-tipped red bill into the water, and retrieved a tiny silver minnow. It quickly swallowed the fish before it had a chance to squiggle away from its fate. Blue growled and waved her tail as the bird's pale gray wings took flight.

"Hey look, Blue," Mosie pointed to a clearing between a gap of hardwood trees. "I wonder if that's the place where those millionaires lived back in the 1800s that Pa told me about; there were two of them, Fredrick Prentice and William Wilson. They say their money's still buried there somewhere because no one's ever found it.

"Now why would anyone go and do something like that?" She shook her head. "You know there's a lot of stories about these islands . . ."

They rounded *Look Out Point* on the tip of Herman as the sun was gaining in the sky. Mosie focused her eyes at their starting point and sighed. "Man, this is going to take longer than I thought!"

Blue put her head down and closed her eyes. Hermit Island was floating off in the distance. And so were they.

CHAPTER THIRTY~NINE

Holy Family Catholic Church's parking lot was full. Not a spot left. "God save me from what I have done," Father Perkins whispered from the vestibule as he looked out at the people. He wiped wine from his lips, slipped the decanter back on its shelf, and closed the cabinet; his hands shook as he raised them to bless himself. Straightening his cassock, he headed for the archway, steadied himself, and concentrated on the lectern. "Forgive me Father," he prayed, lowering his head.

With his head swirling he walked out and held the sides of the podium. And for a few moments he watched the assembly milling about as some searched for space in the already packed pews; others stood patiently in the back and along the isles and waited for him to turn on his microphone. And he did.

"People . . . people . . . please . . . may I have your attention," his voice blurted thickly over the heavy mumblings. "I want to thank everyone for coming." Daring to raise his eyes, he saw John sitting in his and Mosie's front pew.

"I apologize for the . . . I apologize—" He cleared his throat and repeated, "I . . . apologize . . ." He looked down. The church was growing quiet. *Somehow by the grace of God let me deliver this message*, he thought.

"As you know, Katherine Bitmen, known to most of us as Mosie, the daughter of John and Willowdean is . . . missing.

"We have every reason to believe she is . . . that she has . . ." As he forced the words from his mouth, Father Perkins voice cracked. "Sometime between noon yesterday and 9 p.m. last night she had taken a small handcrafted row boat out onto the lake.

"I . . . I . . ." he stammered. "John, I . . ." He hid his face in his arm, broke into sobs, and stepped down from the marble platform. He rushed to the vestibule. Murmurs rose from the crowd.

John walked up to the platform. "Folks, thank you for coming," he began, and his voice was thick and low. "I want to make this quick as possible. As you know, every minute, every second, counts so I won't go into anything other than the main facts.

"Most of you know my . . . my daughter," he choked. "She is resilient and young, but being young, and from the city, she is unaware of what the Great Lake is capable of.

"It's true, the boat she is in is, one she and her friend, Peggy Anderson, crafted themselves."

Above the muttering congregation, the sound of women's gasps and weeping rose. John's throat tightened.

"I inspected the boat myself but hadn't tested it." He sucked in his breath and went on. "From Father Perkins' report, the boat looked seaworthy from what he could tell.

"Mr. Maki has come forward to report he had indeed sold two oars and two life jackets yesterday. We believe he might have sold them to Mosie.

"I have taken the liberty of making copies of a chart of the islands and ask that each of you take one as they come around, even if you have one of your own. It is the same one

Mosie has, and I am hoping this will avoid any conflicts or confusion as far as navigation is concerned.

"Now, last night a small fleet from the Coast Guard began searching the lake and islands, but they haven't found any . . . any . . . any signs." John bowed his head. "I'm asking, I'm begging . . ." He raised his tears to the people.

"As a father, please somebody, anybody who has any knowledge of these waters, or has anything that might help, please . . ."

"I go," Mr. Maki shouted and jumped from his seat. "Ya', I go. I get my things and . . ."

"Count me in," Michael Peterson joined in. "If it were one of mine—"

Doc Ruden bounced up. "Count me in too, John."

"Ditto," Ken Johnson rang out, getting to his feet. Todd and Keith rose to stand beside him. "That goes for all of us," he added.

"You know you can count on us, John," Stubby Murphy shouted out as he stood with his line of co-workers and Mr. and Ms. Bartello.

A blue-haired thrift cellar lady stood up. "We might be too old to go out on the water," her voice crackled, "but we can still pray, can't we?" She turned to the group of women behind her. Their white heads nodded in agreement as they snapped open their pocketbooks to pull out tissues and rosaries.

Father Perkins stood in the shadows and took a slug from the now almost empty bottle of wine. He watched as nearly every man and every woman stood, one by one, and took their places alongside John Bitmen.

Sister Maggie patted Willowdean's hand. "Words give little comfort, I know," she got up from John's chair. "But your Mosie, she is strong, and she has good mind too," she poured them more coffee. Peggy sat next to them. Her eyes were swollen shut from the salt of her tears. "And we have something too, something much more powerful than in that lake."

"Thank you Maggie," Willowdean said; her voice was raw, drawn, and almost impossible to hear.

Sister Maggie turned and skittered to the window. "Ya I think they here now," she pulled the curtain open. "Ya, your son and his friends they are here."

Willowdean's weak legs got up from the table. She held tight to her chair as she waited for the porch door to open, then the kitchens. Exhausted, she fell into Val's strong arms. He held her close and rubbed his cheek against her head. He kissed her.

"Ma, its okay, I'm here now, I'm here."

Val helped her to the sofa and knelt next to her. She wept in his arms and didn't notice the string of long hairs tracking into the kitchen with Mr. and Mrs. Bennington that brought up the tail end.

Rocking his momma in his arms, Valerie cried with her. "We'll find her Mother . . . I promise, we'll find her."

Peggy stood up and offered him her coffee. He shook his head. "No, no thanks," he rose to his feet. "You're, you're Peggy," he said, taking her hand. His grin was slight. "I remember you. I'm . . . I'm your brother, Valerie." He took her into his arms. She melted inside the gentle strength within them.

"I and the guys are heading in. Mrs. Bennington and—" he paused looking at the little Felician nun.

"Maggie, I'm Sister Maggie," she whispered.

"Mother, Mrs. Bennington, and Sister Maggie . . . and . . . and Peggy are here. They're going to stay with you until we get back." He hugged his mother tight and nodded to Mrs. Bennington.

"Oh Willowdean," she cried and rushed to her side.

"Mavis, oh Mavis," Willowdean sobbed as they clung to one another.

"It's all my fault, *all* my fault."

Lenny sat on his window ledge, his eye on the TV.

"Shut up, all of you!" he yelled and hobbled over to turn it up. "*Shut the hell up*!"

"We have a report that a young, thirteen-and-a-half-year-old Bayfield girl has been reported missing.

"Katherine Rose Bitmen, also known as Mosie, was last seen by her mother, Willowdean Bitmen, at around 11 a.m. yesterday.

"The youth is suspected of taking a small, handcrafted rowboat out on Lake Superior.

"Her mother believes she has a dog with her, and is trying to rescue the animal by bringing it to the legendary Dog Island. The family is asking for any help—" Lenny grabbed his canes.

CHAPTER FORTY

Blue stood up and growled at the boats in the distance that formed a searching V; their engines roared faintly across the lake.

"No don't," Mosie scolded and clutched the sides of the boat, "you're rocking Bertha." Blue lay down next to her pups and covered them with her body.

"That a girl, you protect those babies of yours. They have a right to live just like you do; besides, the people on those boats can't see us, not yet anyway; we're too small."

The vessels split off and each raced to a different island; the mounds were dark and low in the distance, and some were lying out of sight beyond the vista.

"Oak is the one on our right. Stockton is on the left," Mosie watched one of the crafts as it veered off to the left. It was heading for the docks stationed on Stockton with its white beaches, and Singing Sands, (the ones that magically hum when touched the right way). The ones the tourists talk about. There the little schooner would block Mosie's passage. She would now have to pass to the left side of the island, the rugged side, the side heaving upward like Kill-Deer with its rough, cliff base line of brown, red, and sandstone.

"Man, if they catch us, you and your pups are not the only ones they're going to kill," she looked over her shoulder at the dark hillock of forest behind her. Blue poked her head up and whined. They were now fifteen miles from home.

"We're about half a mile away from land. I bet we can make it before they can," Mosie wiped the sweat from her face with her shoulder as she kept her pace steady.

The breeze gave a sudden turn and blew southeast instead of southwest. It was now working with them, instead of against; it cooled them and forced the waves to push Bertha along.

Mosie looked starboard and down into the lake. She took an oar out of its lock, stuck it straight down through the clear, waving water that was blue as glass, and tried to touch bottom. The rocks and halfsunken boulders looked huge under the magnification of the lake's frigid water.

"She's pretty deep," she pulled up the paddle. "I bet it is true . . . I bet Superior doesn't give up her dead." Putting the oar back into its lock, she began rowing.

Blue's nose stood straight up and sniffed the air. It twitched faster than a bug's butt. The waves picked up strength and slapped Bertha with more intensity. She waddled. Blue's legs shook. She whimpered and lay back down on her babies, then hid her snout under her legs. Mosie stopped rowing.

"You smell it, too, don't you, girl?" Mosie studied the line of thunderheads that were building over the horizon behind them. The sound of rumbles of thunder gathered in the distance. She cringed.

"Yep, there's definitely a storm coming in," she looked at the now graying water that would soon be black as the sky.

"Pa told me if a storm comes from the north, it's going to be a bad one." Another rumble rolled. Mosie kept her eyes glued to the shoreline and grabbed the sides of the boat. A deep, heavy wave rolled in, lifted Bertha's bow, brought her down, and tottered her from side to side. Mosie looked at the sky. It was darker. Dangerously darker.

Again, Bertha plunged up then down and this time tousled Mosie, Blue, and the pups back and forth. She thought of Willowdean and John, of Val and Peggy.

"We're heading to the left, to Stockton" Mosie checked behind and her voice sounded frail in the rising wind.

"We can't stay in Bertha, that's for sure," she huffed. She ignored the cramps that were taking hold of her arms and kept rowing. "We'll have to hide in one of the caverns until the storm passes." the screeching of gulls overhead grew louder. Again, Mosie looked stern side; this time she saw the trees on Stockton, trunks and all.

"We're doing it girl, were doing it. I told you we'd do it!"

Ra-roo, ra-roo-roo, Blue cheered her tail clumping happy relief against Bertha's sides. They rounded Stockton's first inlet. "There's got to be a cavern somewhere with some ground to it pretty soon, there just *has* to be."

The wind rushed past their ears and was turning cold, Northern cold. Blue shifted her eyes nervously from one side of the sky to the other and crouched even tighter against her babies. In the distance, muffled booms thundered across the lake and became clearer, calling out fingers of lightning. Heavy globs of cold rain spat down on them. The sky glowed a pale yellow hue.

Ra-roo-roo, Blue cried, got up, and stuck her head under Mosie's arm.

"We have to find shelter and fast," she watched the rocky outcrops along the shore slowly disappear under the cloak of rain.

A thunder-crack rifted the air. Its sister lightning bolt flared across the sky and shattered into copious bloodless white veins. The sound pulled Blue from Mosie and sunk her as far down over her babies as she could go.

Mosie stretched her foot toward Granny's wool blanket and flipped it over Blue and the pups. She missed. Blue looked up, shivered, and blinked the rain from her golden-brown eyes. Lowering her head, she burrowed her snout under her long legs and kissed her pups that squealed under her weight.

"There," Mosie yelled over the rain that was now pounding them like bits of stone. "Right there, girl, there's a spot."

She struggled to paddle, and made her way to the small clearing set below a wall of tall cliffs. She looked out at the lake and cursed. A whitecap was rolling a hundred feet in front of them to find its way to Bertha. Then came another, and another, shoving Bertha closer and closer to the wall of the tight rocky cove.

"Pa," Mosie cried. She tried not to lose control of the boat and feathered the oars like he had shown her. Bertha was defenseless against the Great Lake and slammed into the brownstone wall.

The impact jolted Mosie and flew her to the left, then the right. Blue rolled and hit Bertha's side hard. Banging the brownstone one last time, Bertha gave up the fight but held her ground. Blue pulled herself to her feet and sniffed the air wildly. *Aaa-rooo, rooo, rooo*, she yelped and staggered to the side of the boat.

A pup, a lone pup bobbed in the waves. It thudded against a group of rocks. A foaming white wave reaching up grabbed it; the Great Lake was having its way and pulled the puppy and its tiny yip under the water. With a bay ripping from her throat Blue followed her baby.

"No . . . no! Oh God . . . please . . . no!" Mosie screamed. "Blue!"

Aw-roo aw-roo-ooo, she called back, her eyes wild with fear in the maddening cold of the Lake. She struggled to keep herself above its wild depth. Her gimpy leg was sinking. Mosie grabbed a paddle, and stuck it into the sandy lake bottom to steady herself and the boat.

"I'm coming, Blue! Hold on girl, please, just . . . hold on!"

She placed her hand on the wall of rock; it slipped on the sleek wetness. She tried again. She pushed and swayed Bertha, catching her in a snag of rocks.

The thrust of the oar under the water hit sand. Mosie heaved a powerful push, broke free, and headed for Blue. But the lake remained determined to keep old Blue and her pup.

Another surge hit. Its undertow sucked Blue further away. Mosie ignored the needles of rain and bolts of lightning that shot across the sky and rowed over the crashing waves.

She found her Blue, now hanging motionless beneath the cold gray water. Mosie watched her sink further, further away.

Without a word, without a sound, Mosie latched her feet under the seat of the boat and leaned over its side. She gasped and forced the top half of her body downward into the biting cold of thick, murky grayness.

Her fingers numb, hit something hard. She strained to open her hand and grab it, then closed her fingers. The lake choked her with its iciness and slapped her back. Struggling with the weight at the end of her arm, Mosie fought back and pulled herself into the boat.

"Please . . . please God," she was breathless as she looked down at Blue's limp body. The lake was inside her now. Deep inside. Kissing her, Mosie wept.

"Bree—bree—breeeathe . . . just breathe . . . please, Blue . . . for me . . . your babies . . . Don't leave us . . . please don't leave us. We're so close . . . so close."

Mosie rocked her and wiped away dribbles of warm liquid that seeped from her lips and black leathery nose. A crack of searing thunder riveted across the lake as if it had no end. Mosie cried out. "Help . . . oh God! Please! Please . . . anyone . . ."

Blue's ribs bellowed slightly. "That's it, girl," Mosie choked as she felt a warmth in Blue's body. She looked up into the sky as if God truly did hear her.

From above the roar of the wind, she heard someone calling her name. She looked back at the alcove along the shore and heard the voice calling again. She looked up at the cliff and saw him standing on its edge.

"Moe," he called out again, waving his arms. "Moe!"

"Oh Val, please, *please* help us," she screamed, unable to control herself. "The oars, I—I lost the oars."

"There's no time to get them," Val yelled back. "There's another storm coming in any time. A whole line of them. Don't move, Moe. I'm coming down."

Val peered over the edge of the bluff, grabbed a handful of saplings, sat down, and dangled his legs over the side. He cautiously stretched his feet onto a shank of jetting rock and began working his way down onto the ground of a small slit of sand. Looking at the water line slashing against Bertha, he yelled out, "How deep is she?"

"Ten, fifteen feet," Mosie shouted back as she clung on to Blue, whose eyes were now open.

"Val's here," she cooed to her and lay her next to her pups.

Val staggered over the rocks and looked for a clearing in the water. The bite of the water took his breath as he dived in. "Give me the rope," he chattered as his body popped up and down with the waves. "If I pull myself in, I'll flip you. Quick, give me the rope." His face was turning pale.

"I'll have to tow you, but you're going to have to help me." His voice was weakening. "No time for me to use the dog's life jacket; dump your load, fast, all of it." His breathing quickened and was becoming shallow. His hands fumbled to tie the rope around his waist and moved slower and slower in the ice water.

"Hur-hurry Moe-Moe," he clung on the edge of Bertha.

"Ni-ni-nice paint job," he chattered softly as he tried to keep his eyes focused on Bertha's pink belly.

"Peggy . . . Peggy did it, Val, Peggy!" Mosie cried and shoved boxes of supplies overboard. She grabbed Granny's blanket and she held it to her face. "I'm sorry Momma," she wept and put it over Blue. "I'm sorry Val . . . Ma warned me, Ma warned me, and I didn't listen . . ." she sobbed, watching her brother turn gray against the black waves.

"I-it's okay, Moe; everyone n-n-n-needs an advent-t-t, adventure." She reached over the side and kissed him. His skin was cold, a different kind of cold she had felt only once. "Val, Candy made me touch her aunt Margaret when she was lying dead in her coffin when no one was looking," she confessed and rubbed the top of his head as he bobbed up and down. Val spat out a mouthful of water.

"C-c-creepy man, c-c-creepy," he mumbled and broke a smile.

"Yeah, creepy man," Mosie sniffled back and watched him swim off with the rope. Big Bertha started moving toward the shore.

Blue gave a feeble *roo*, stuck her nose under Mosie's hands, and gave them a weak kiss. "We're safe now," Mosie reassured her and stroked her head. "We're safe. Val's here." She watched him pull himself onto the shore and collapse. The rain and lightning broke to a dull pitch.

Mosie rolled Blue's pups inside Granny's blanket, jumped from the boat and onto land, and raced to Val's side. She placed the pup's warm bodies against his and covered them all with the wool blanket.

"No Val, you can't sleep-you . . . have to stay awake, really you do," she shook him as he tried to fall asleep.

"Just for a little while, man," he tried to open his eyes. He squeezed Mosie's hand and smiled. "You're safe now." His eyes shut and his smile faded with the grip of his fingers. Slowly, he let go.

"No Valerie, don't—don't do that!" Mosie sobbed and shook him again.

She stood and ran to Bertha. She picked up Blue, held her close, and buried her face in the dog's dark fur.

"Hey girl," she carried her to shore, "I don't have long. I got to help Val. He's my brother, the only one I have. And you, you're more than just a dog, you're my best friend, the best friend I ever-ever-ever had, besides Val."

She put Blue as close as she could to Val and the pups; Mosie sniffled the tears and rain that ran down her cheeks. "I have to go for a little while," she said and gave them both a kiss. "But I'll be back, okay?" She pulled Granny's blanket over them and stood up. Blue's golden-brown eyes held their glassy gaze out at the sea.

"I'll be back as soon as I can," she looked up at the ledge of the cliff. "I promise."

CHAPTER FORTY~ONE

The path that led Lenny and Mr. Bennington from the rain-soaked beach of Stockton Island up to the high forest-land leading to the cliffs on the other side of the island was longer and steeper than Lenny had remembered. He leaned against a maple tree at the top of the trail and shuffled the rifle strapped on his back. He looked down at the dock and watched Mr. Bennington securely tie the boat they and Val had used to make their way across the lake. Mr. Bennington made sure he had left enough room for John and his group of longhairs and headed up the path.

"You don't look so good, old man," he looked at Lenny's pale face. "Are you sure you want to go on?"

"Well, if that ain't calling the kettle black," Lenny snapped, as he grazed Mr. Bennington up and down. He hunkered up a ball of snot and shot it on the path in front of them.

"Sorry," Mr. Bennington murmured and bent down to wipe a splatter of muck from his red, white and blue tennis shoes.

Lenny laughed. "Well if that ain't the most sissified thing I ever saw." He bent over, grabbed a handful of mud, and pitched it at Mr. Bennington's shoes. Mr. Bennington's eyes flared.

"Look, *old man*," Lenny said stiffly as he grabbed his canes. "We ain't playing Navy out here. There's a kid out there, and I plan on finding her, and that dog. So either get rid of that yellow city backbone of yours or get your ass back to the boat."

Mr. Bennington watched Lenny pull himself off the tree and hobble down the long, twisting path. He looked down at the boat rocking in the pier. He hadn't forgotten Mosie's laugh, nor her sparkling, navy-blue eyes and the way they conveyed a secret approval of him as she studied his every move around his rose gardens or the hems of Mrs. Bennington's dresses.

He stared at the mud on his shoes. "Wait, Mr. Anderson, wait," he shouted racing down the trail. "Name's Lenny," he said, not bothering to take his eyes off the footpath. "Just plain ol' Lenny."

Mr. Bennington spat on the wet pine needles in front of him. "Royal," he said, "name's Royal but call me Roy. So ah, what do you have planned for that gun of yours?" he asked as he stepped up alongside Lenny.

Lenny kept walking.

The waves of thunder were leaving the sky. Mosie's hands and fingers sunk into the layers of spongy moss that swaddled the trunk of the tree at the top of the cliff. She clung to it and eased herself up into the forest canopy. It was as if she had climbed into the pages of Sister Vern Mary's storybooks. She rested in the silver mist hanging in the

emerald-green foliage surrounding her and caught her breath. The smell of damp mildew and mushrooms filled the air. She left the last rumbles of thunder and thrashing waves behind and stepped past the bright yellow fungus brackets that jutted from the trees and the toadstools that spilled before her.

"Seven miles long and three miles wide," Mosie took the compass from her pocket. "That's what lies between Val, and Blue, and her pups . . . and life. North East, gotta' go North East."

She pulled her medicine bag out from under her shirt and held it in her hands. "God . . . Creator," she stared at the little blackbird flying over the single rose floating in the Great Lake. "This is Naanoondaagoziwag-manidoo-nandaagosiwag aazhoogaam, Thunder across the Water," she said. "I know I've done lots of wrong things; that's why you have to let me do this, to make up for it all."

A black feather floated to the ground and landed at her feet. She looked up. Droplets of rain pinged on the leaves in the tree branches and spat down at her. A flicker of black caught her eye. A solitary crow was sitting and preening itself, and turned its attention to her, then gave a soft caw. Other crows came and fluttered silently to the treetops. She bent down and picked up the feather. It was still warm.

"Not for me Lord-Creator," she said, "for Val and Blue. Let me do this for them."She looked through the forest and could see a tiny pincushion of daylight breaking between the trees. If ever a song clung to Mosie's heart it was now; for it was a new day, *Fresh from the word.*

"Thank you Peggy," she kissed the medicine bag. When she slipped the feather inside, the crows flew.

"Morning *has* broken," she sang out her feet carrying her as they had through the tall weeds of her yard that hid her from Lenny, and as they had over the bogs in the quagmire leading her to Blue. Her legs lifted and jumped over fallen logs, rocks, and stones. The last of the rain rushed across her face and cooled her from the humid air; she welcomed it as the crows led her further and deeper into the woods.

Truly, it was a day she never would forget, the way that morning had broken. The way the black birds flew with her, mounting higher into the sky, leaving her, knowing she was on her way home, truly home.

Home. It was deeper in her than the woods before her, and the waters behind her. "Ma, I'm coming!" she shouted, "I'm coming home, please, please don't cry!"

In her mind, Willowdean smiled at her; her brown sugared skin shined just like how Pa told her it did when it touched that Great Lake called Superior.

"Momma, I'm here, I'm here!" she yelled and ran wild in the woods, hoping John would somehow be at the other end of the island.

She could almost smell Willowdean the same way the pups lying next to Val could smell their momma.

The last bits of rain dropped from the sky and washed the sand from Val's face. The sun was growing strong again and warmed his body. He opened his eyes.

A dozen eagles, carrying the currents of the wind, soared above a raft traveling on the waves. A man piloted the raft. Val raised his head. Tiny grains of sand stuck to face.

"Ahoy!" the man called and lifted his staff. "Ahoy, I say!"

His cargo was like none Val had ever seen. A strange lot, they were, the man and his cargo. Animals of every kind rode with him.

Blue rustled under the blanket and shoved her head out from it. She jumped to her feet, snapped her tail in the air, and yowled as if she knew the man. He was coming closer, close enough for Val to see his snow-white hair and long blue robe with its wide sleeves.

"You seem to have something of mine," the man called above the clash of the now crystal diamond waves.

"I'm sorry," he said, with a boom, "but I need to take her back with me now. I've journeyed very far for her; you can understand. I'm sure."

Val watched Blue bolt from Granny's blanket. She charged forward and leaped through the white sparkling froth of the water.

Roooooo, rooooo, she cried, and her pup was swimming next to her side.

"Who are you?" Val called out.

"Me?" the man laughed. "Why, my young man, I happen to be The Keeper of all Animal Spirits, that's who I am.

"Will you please tell Katherine Rose what a wonderful job she has done for me? Can you do that for me, young man? She will understand. She and I met before.

"And one last thing," he lifted his arms, "if you will, please give these to her." He raised his hands toward the sky and glints of golden-orange floated from his billowy sleeves and landed next to Val. "She'll know what they are."

"Wait," Val yelled. "I don't understand!"

"Oh, you'll be fine. You see, everyone and everything has a Keeper, a Keeper for their Spirit.

"You just need to find yours, that's all. Once you do that, you'll be just fine too, just like Naanoondaagoziwag-manidoo-nandaagosiwag aazhoogaam and Blue here," he shouted and turned the raft toward the horizon.

Val's eyes drooped. They were heavy tired. And so were Blue's. She lay next to him and her pups, but her eyes held their gaze on the waves before her. Val touched her. Her last breath was nowhere to be found.

Mosie saw them, Lenny and Mr. Bennington, as they hobbled and stumbled along the northeastern path leading to her.

"*Mr. Bennington?*" she gasped as her stomach nearly flopped to the bottom of the forest floor. Her heart sank as she caught a glimpse of Lenny's rifle and the worry on Mr. Bennington's face. The crows were nowhere to be seen (or heard).

She slipped behind a tree and waited for them to pass. She could almost smell Lenny and she could hear Mr. Bennington talking about their days gone by in Barrington.

"Then there was that time, she and Candy decided to venture over the rail road tracks to East Park, all on their own," he was saying as they rounded a bend in the path and his voice trailed off.

"He's going to shoot her," Mosie said under her breath. "He's going to shoot Blue; and Mr. Bennington, he won't be able to stop him."

She looked toward the other side of the island. She wasn't close enough to its end. If John was there, they would never make back it in time to stop Lenny. She promised God-Creator this was the last promise she would ever, ever keep.

"Leo-Nerd," she said, under her breath and stepped out from the tree. "I made a promise to you, and I'm keeping it. This is the day I'm finally going to get you."

Mr. Bennington's words garbled over the rustling of Lenny's feet shuffling on the forest floor. Both stopped.

They stood at the edge of the cliff. Lenny looked down. Mr. Bennington stood at his side, and was still and erect as an old soldier. Lenny pulled his rifle from his back and placed its butt on his shoulder. He looked down its stock and peered through the sights. A dribble of sweat dripped in his eyes. Mr. Bennington covered his ears and bent down. Lenny pulled the trigger. A shot rang out across the lake and echoed (perhaps forever).

"No!" Mosie shouted, running toward them. "No!"

Her foot caught a rotted branch. She hit the ground and lost the air inside her; a prickle of pain twisted up her leg. Mr. Bennington turned to her, his face white with fear.

"No!" she screamed again and pulled herself from the soaking wet ground. "Lenny, please *no*!" she sobbed and struggled to move her foot. She felt her senses swirling away from her. Then, as if she were falling into a dream, all was black.

Lenny's liver-spotted trembling hands turned her over. "Run!" he snapped and wiped the dirt from her face. "Quick, run and get John.

"Tell him to bring the schooner around to Kelly's Cove, and be fast about it. Tell him it's at the end of the North East Trail. He'll know."

Mosie slowly opened her eyes. She turned from Lenny's red hair and freckles and watched Mr. Bennington scurry down the path; he waved his arms about as if a hive of honeybees were attacking him.

"Settle down, little missy," Lenny stroked the top of her head. "I ain't gonna do you no harm."

"Papa!" Mosie cried out. "Papa!"

"Yeah, he'll be gettin' here soon enough," Lenny said and wiped more dirt and sweat from her face. "Everything's going to be just fine. You ain't hurt that bad . . ."

"I hate you, Lenny . . . I hate you," she tried to pull away. She fell back into the blackness.

"Yeah," Lenny chuckled, grinned, and watched her sleep, "you and a lot of people."

The putter of John's boat sat and hummed under the cliff. "Put your arm around my shoulder," Lenny demanded.

Mosie did as told. Together they tottered to the edge of the cliff. She watched her pa jump from the railing of that mighty boat with a leap she never knew he had inside him. Tears streaked down her cheeks as she watched him bend over a heaping mound of black lying next to Val and Blue. John looked up at them and nodded his head.

"Damn bear," Lenny cussed. "Ya' never know where you're gonna find them," he shifted his rifle to the other side of his back.

Mosie looked up at him. His eyes were red with tenderness as he looked down at John and Val.

"You never really meant to shoot Blue that night, did you?"

"She got in the way is all," Lenny rasped. "She got in the way."

CHAPTER FORTY~TWO

Bayfront Park Beach was now the empty beach Mr. Maki had dreaded all summer. "Ya," he shook his head and swept the last of the summer sands from his steps. "You kiddos better eat up them cones, or they go bad. Ol' Mr. Maki not order no more till next season."

He looked out at the low, white capping waves of the mighty lake. It was pushing against the shore as if trying to move it. "I-yi-yiyi," he put his hands on his hips and shook his head. "This winter, she be a bad one, watch and see." He looked over his deck and compared Mosie's bike to Peggy's brand new twelve-speed and laughed, his round belly jiggling with delight. "Whoever think an old man like me go flying to Florida to be with his brother for a whole winter because of bicycles and ice cream cones. Ha-ha-ha!

"Ya, you kiddos, you have a good winter," he rushed inside and slammed the door. He pulled the curtain and flipped the sign. It read: 'Gone Florida-Closed to next season'.

"What a darling, that Mr. Maki," Peggy licked her triple scoop. She yanked out a packet of chewing gum from her pocket and offered Mosie a stick. "It's funny." She laughed and shoved a piece in her cone.

"What, what's funny?" Mosie stretched her legs in front of herself and pushed her piece into her cone. "A cold, bad winter, *that's* funny?"

"No, how something simple like an ice cream cone really can change a person's whole life; not just for an afternoon or a week or just a summer, but a *whole* life. Remember, that's what you told me when we first met, and it's true, isn't it?"

The sun dipped behind another series of clouds. Mosie tucked her coal-black ponytail inside the hood of her sweater. "Yeah, yeah it is. You know what's even *more funny*?" She bent over and plucked an orange and red maple leaf from the top of Peggy's new school shoes.

"Thinking you're going to really hate someone and it turns out they're the best thing that ever came along." She picked up the pup sitting at her feet. Its stubby little white tipped tail beat the air faster than hummingbird wings.

"Who would ever expect Mrs. Morgan's Sir Lancelot of being Blue's lover?" she ran her finger through the pup's tight little curls, giving him a kiss. "It's a miracle how that little guy made it all the way to Kill-Deer and back home again without so much as a scratch. Almost as if it were meant to be.

"With the pups being so small, ol Blue was PG longer than what Doc Ruden knew. That's why it seemed she had the pups so quick." Mosie started counting the pup's twenty-two specks of tar splatted on its tiny white legs and chest.

Peggy pulled another pup up into her lap and gave it a taste of her cone. She looked at Mosie. "Talking about stuff like that, Kenny's younger brother is sort of cute in his own way, don't you think?" she flicked her eyebrows up and down. "He's going to be in your class, you know."

Mosie laughed. "Stop looking at me like that. I'm not interested in him or anyone, especially someone named Taddy. Gad! Who in the hell would name their kid something like that, anyway? Tad, here *Taddy* come to mother. That's worse than Milton."

Peggy crossed her long legs and sighed. "Okay, but just so you know, if I and Kenny do get married, we might name our first baby boy, Norbert, after his dad. Which reminds me," she said pulled an envelope out from her jacket. She handed it to Mosie.

"Our brother Val gave this to me. He asked me to give it to you after he left. It sure was nice having him around for the summer.

"Oh, and this—Val said not to open it until after you've read the letter."

Mosie took the small box from Peggy's hand. She put it next to her ear and shook it. "He'll be back when Ma has the baby," she placed it in her lap.

"Or when she and Lenny tie the knot, whichever comes first," Peggy charged the tip of her shoe at the pups to chase them under the bench. She shoved the last of her cone in her mouth and sat back. She then folded her arms and looked thoughtfully into the sand. "Now I know why he never wanted me calling him anything other than Lenny. Guess it's going to take a while for all this to sink in, isn't it?"

"Yeah, it sure will," Mosie answered. "Who would ever have thought things would end up this way?"

"Lenny said treatment wasn't so bad," said Peggy. "He thinks Father Perkins has a good chance of making it, and he's going to write the Diocese asking that they let him come back to marry him and Willowdean. I didn't know a nun could be a bridesmaid, did you?"

"No, no I didn't."

"Any way, Lenny really was a good father, in his own way, I guess."

"What?" Mosie asked.

"Well, think about it, Mosie. I wasn't even his own flesh and blood and since him and Corrine weren't even legally married, he could have put us out on the streets anytime he wanted, but he didn't."

"That's true. How did he put that now?"

"He said, *hanging on to me and Corrine was like hanging on to a piece of his Willowdean and Val, but after a while he got to loving me, just for me and no other reason.* It makes me feel good, Mosie." She gave herself a Love Hug.

"Oh brother," Mosie said and shook her head. She looked at the letter sitting in her lap.

"Well aren't you gonna read it?" Peggy asked. Mosie picked it up and took a deep breath.

"I suppose." She tucked the pup in her sweater. It padded a few turns then rolled into a ball and closed its eyes to nap.

September 7, 1972

Dear Moe,

By the time you read this, school will be almost starting. What will you write for your "What I did on summer vacation" essay (ha-ha)? Man. That was the best birthday party Ma ever gave you. Man, you raked it in this year, thanks for sharing!

Lenny and I are probably busy with our new business. He sure has a mind for it. Who ever thought the likes of us would ever pair up and start a car detailing service? I have a feeling the Bennington's will be one of our best customers beside

Lard-Ass and Candy. Wait until those two chicks see Peggy perform down here at the Catlow on Christmas break. She and the 'Country Squire's Band' are going to knock them dead. By the way, doesn't Ken Johnson look like Marty Robbins? Man!

I sure don't know how I feel about Ma not taking Pa back. I guess she has the right not to. She must have got tired of him tugging his pants at her too (ha-ha). Who ever thought the old man was the type to fool around. Let's just hope they don't have any more surprises up their sleeves. Man.

Moe, I'm really sorry about Blue. Lenny feels bad about it too. He really meant it when he told you Blue was only protecting her own from someone she knew was no good. I can honestly say as I'm getting to know him he isn't so bad to have as my blood father after all. I think he's finding that old part of himself that I met that year when Pa took me hunting and that Ma was in love with for all these years.

I know no body besides you, Ma and Lenny believes me about that man I saw that day out in the Apostle Islands. I guess it don't matter as long as you believe me. That guy said you'd know what's in the box.

I hope one day you can tell me.

Well I guess that's about all for now.

Tell our sister I send my love. I think she's a pretty groovy little chick.

Love,

Your brother,

Valerie

P.S. Take good care of those pups of yours. Blue would be happy knowing you had them. I know she would. And by the way, thanks for the adventure. It was the best one yet.

Mosie put the letter back in its envelope. She shook the box and loosened the white ribbons Val tied to it to keep it closed. She poured the insides out into the palm of her hand and smiled.

"What are those?" Peggy asked peeking inside her hand. "Seven blue Agates? I never saw blue agates before. Where would Val get those from?"

"Boy have I got a story for you," Mosie answered and looked up into the sky. The clouds were traveling out from the Islands and heading inland. "Man, they sure are forming something big," she nodded at them. She looked at Mr. Maki's sign. At the top of the maple tree, a crow called out. "Good luck on your journeys," she turned back to Peggy and the rocks in her hand.

"No, No-Name, I'll tell ya, these aren't just any old agates, you know." She squeezed them tight, held them against her cheek, and smiled.

"These are kisses, one-of-a-kind kisses, Blue's kisses. And they belong to a real, bona fide Indian princess."

The End

THE RAINBOW BRIDGE

(Inspired by a Norse legend)

By the edge of a woods, at the foot of a hill, is a lush, green meadow where time stands still. Where the friends of man and woman do run, when their time on earth is over and done.

For here, between this world and the next, is a place where each beloved creature finds rest. On this golden land, they wait and they play, Till the Rainbow Bridge they cross over one day.

No more do they suffer, in pain or in sadness, For here they are whole, their lives filled with gladness. They romp through the grass, without even a care, Until one day they start, and sniff at the air. All ears prick forward, eyes dart front and back, Then all of a sudden, one breaks from the pack. For just at that instant, their eyes have met; Together again, both person and pet.

So they run to each other, these friends from long past, The time of their parting is over at last. The sadness they felt while they were apart, has turned into joy once more in each heart. They embrace with a love that will last forever.

ABOUT THE AUTHOR

Ann was born in the Chicago area. She and her family moved to the Wisconsin Northwoods when she was thirteen. Living in both locations has given Ann a useful insight as a writer to both city life and country.

As years passed, Ann's dream of becoming an actress was not to be. In its place she took the advice of instructors from long past, and put the characters dancing in her head loose on paper.

Her knack for writing (along with an active imagination) gained Ann employment consisting of writing newsletters and advertising for several businesses.

Forever writing unshared stories, it wasn't until her twins were raised and with children of their own, did Ann finally find time to get truly serious about her stories. With the help of a very dear friend and a few family members, Ann found the courage to share her fictional writings which led to finishing her first novel, Dog Island.

Ann completed her second novel, Behind the Green Door-memoir of a time traveler, and is looking forward to writing its sequel.

Ann's own life, filled with happiness and joy, sorrow and hard times, blends the perfect combination used in her novels that readers carry with them long after the last page is turned.

You can follow Ann on social media at:

Amazon.com~amazon.com/Ann-M.-Andrashie
Facebook~facebook.com/AnnMAndrashie
LinkedIn~linkedin.com/in/annmandrashie
www.ann-m-andrashie.com/

Reviews Are Always Welcome

CPSIA information can be obtained
at www.ICGtesting.com
Printed in the USA
LVHW080634271222
735871LV00009B/418

9 781737 047902